CHANCE,
KINGS
AND
DESPERATE
MEN

CHANCE, KINGS
AND
DESPERATE MEN

A NOVEL

Shawn Frederick

Chance, Kings and Desperate Men
Copyright © 2015 by Shawn Frederick

This is a work of fiction. The names, characters, places, or events used in this book are the product of the author's imagination or used fictitiously. Any resemblance to actual people, alive or deceased, events or locales is completely coincidental.

Cover design by Michael Want

Book design by Maureen Cutajar
www.gopublished.com

ISBN: 978-4-9908360-0-9

CHAPTER 1

Becker watched more blood fall from the cut on his chin and explode into starbursts on the mat. He was leaning forward, elbows on his knees, head down, studying the looping pattern the drops had formed on the canvas with the slight swaying of his head. The pattern seemed important. The fight didn't. He tried to steady himself as he aimed the next drop.

"Hey, get your head in the game, Sport. You're bleedin' all over," Angie half-shouted in his ear as he stepped into the corner from the mass of humanity around the ring. Becker gave up on his artwork, sat back on the stool, and let Angie go to work on his face. His friend was in his element – working the crowd, finessing side bets, bargaining, charming, cajoling. He seemed pleased with how things were turning out. Maybe he has misjudged the situation, Becker thought. His chin had just been split open by an accidental head-butt while his opponent was methodically caving in his ribs with body punches. The pain had gone from dull ache to sharp, stabbing agony.

"This is good," Angie said, dabbing collodion on the small cut.

"What's good?" Becker said.

"Blood." Angie made it sound obvious. "It's show biz, Matt. The hero doesn't win in the first scene. You need to play it out for a while before you finish up."

"So now you're a drama critic?" Becker said. "Angie, that's one tough Mick,"

"Mick," Angie said. "If he's a Mick, then you're a Mick."

The club manager had come over to Becker's corner before the fight and asked his name.

"Matt Becker," he answered.

The man frowned and pulled on a bulbous, furry earlobe.

"What kind of name is that?" he asked.

"It's American," Becker said with an offhand shrug.

"Don't crack wise with me Sonny or you and this guinea midget will be walking out of here in your shorts."

"English, I guess," said Becker. He knew there was an English version of the name. He hoped the man didn't ask about his family, a polyglot mixture of French, German and Jewish.

"You guess? What is Mendy giving me here?" He looked right and left at nothing in particular, his upper lip starting to curl.

"Becker, Becker, Basher, Belter...," he said under his breath, digging in his ear with a stubby index finger. "That ain't gonna work". He turned and walked over to speak to the referee and ring announcer. He was back in less than a minute.

"Tonight you're Matt MacCready," he said.

"If you say so," Becker said.

"I just said so, Sonny," said the manager as he turned his back and walked away.

Angie had been watching, one eyebrow raised. "Some people just go through life looking for it," he said, shaking his head.

So Becker had been introduced as Matt "Manslaughter" MacCready and his opponent as Kevin "Crusher" Ryan as a bit of theater to please the hometown crowd, but ethnic origins were forgotten once the opening bell had sounded. Becker had come out using speed and reach to keep his stockier opponent at bay with jabs and crosses while he looked for weakness but Ryan had perfected a waist-level duck-and-weave to break up combinations and get inside to work the body. His hips and shoulders swung with savage grace as he put the full weight of his body behind each punch without losing his balance. Becker had no choice but to lock his opponent's upper arms to stop the attack and roll out and away, throwing fast head shots to keep the man off him. But the short, powerful blows to the ribs were taking a growing toll on Becker's longer torso and Ryan had been careful to keep his head low, his guard up and his chin tucked. Becker's head shots weren't slowing him down. Ryan had swelling around his eyes, a cut on one eyebrow and a minor nosebleed, but he kept coming. Well, Becker thought, like his father always said, there's no shame in taking a beating.

"Give it up and sit down. You look like a pencil," someone shouted from the crowd in the middle of a round. There was a brief eruption of laughter and back-slapping. Becker didn't take it personally. He had other things to worry about. I do look kind of skinny compared to this guy, he thought. He's built like a boxcar.

"So what is he?" asked Becker.

"He's that Polack kid, what's-his-name, his father used to have the garage on Atlantic Avenue," Angie said.

"Can't remember...starts with a J," Becker said. "Is that his father in the corner?" An older man was wiping sweat from Ryan's shoulders and neck. Angie glanced over.

"No, it ain't. Now, stop talking or I'll never get this cut closed. Oh, the hell with it. Better to just let it bleed. So listen – I'm just going to reel in a couple more live ones. Hold him up a little longer and then finish this. We'll have a nice piece of change."

With everything going on in the world, Becker thought this was a damn-fool way to spend a Friday night. The Fascists were moving on Madrid. China had declared war on Japan and her allies. Mussolini was helping himself to pieces of Africa. Hell, even auto workers were battling the police in Michigan. Trying to beat another human being unconscious for money seemed petty and futile.

There was also a good chance he'd get his own brains scrambled. He hadn't been in a ring for months and though he'd always kept up with his road and rope work, his timing was way off. Tonight he felt logy and slow on his feet. But he needed the money. Ten bucks for a win and five for a loss, Mendy had said on the phone two nights before. That was serious money. Too much money. Why so much?

"Mendy, I haven't fought since summer," Becker had said.

"Kid, this isn't the Garden, and you sure as hell aren't my first choice, but I'm in a jam and I need a ...I need somebody for Friday night. I'll go ten and five." Becker wondered what he'd been going to say. A sucker? A pug? "When you needed fights, I found 'em for you. Now I need a favor, and I'm willing to pay. Come on, college boy."

Becker had promised himself he was going to get out of this racket. For four years he had justified the club fights by the need to keep food in his mouth and cover expenses. But the so-called clubs had gotten seedier, the fights more brutal and the organizers more crooked. Once, he nearly lost his athletic scholarship when injuries from a Friday fight benched him for a Saturday football game. Now, his plans to finish school and become a teacher had run on the rocks. It was 1937 and the new year was not looking up. He was a college graduate one step away from the breadlines. No time to be choosy.

"Hell, Mendy, I need the money, and I know I owe you. I'm just saying..."

"So you gonna help me out or what?" Mendy said.

Becker paused, thoughts of a crushed nose or detached retina going through his head.

"Kid? You there?" Mendy said.

"Where are we going? Philly again?" Becker asked.

"Well, it's a little outside of town..."

Ninety minutes after crossing the river from Camden into Philadelphia, Becker and Angie had found themselves pretty much lost as they followed the taillights of Mendy's car into the darkness. Becker was driving his girlfriend's '32 Ford four-door and having trouble staying a safe distance behind the lumbering DeSoto. A light but steady snow was beginning to fall.

"Mendy drives like my grandmother," Angie said.

"Your grandmother drives?" Becker asked.

"She's been dead for nine years." Angie squinted as he tried to see out his side window. "So where is this place we're going to?" he asked.

"I got no idea. Mendy said to follow him, so I'm following."

"What's the joint?"

"Some lodge or athletic club. I don't know. Like Knights of Columbus," Becker said.

"They got Catholics way the hell out here? Another half hour we should start seeing Mormons."

"So maybe Moose...or Elk," Becker said.

Angie's brow furrowed.

"What is an elk anyway?" he asked. Becker looked at him from the corner of his eye, but Angie was straight-faced. Sometimes Becker didn't know when he was kidding.

"Like a deer, but bigger," Becker said.

"So what's a moose?"

"Even bigger."

"You ever seen one?"

"In Jersey? No, I never saw a moose in Jersey," Becker said. He wants to play, I'll go along, he thought.

"Think we might hit one on this road?" Angie said.

"Hey, we go where the money is, right?"

They were approaching some lights up the road and Mendy's car slowed to a crawl, finally turning into a gravel parking lot next to a long, one-story wooden building. There were about twenty cars and pickup trucks already in the lot. Above the door, a spot light shone on a sign made of painted plywood, half of which had been torn off. Only the letters "-odge" remained.

Becker parked at the back of the lot, away from the lights. By the time he and Angie had walked up to the building Mendy was already waiting, stomping the snow off his feet and trying to pull his overcoat closed over his bulging stomach. As usual, he was chewing on the unlit stub of a half-smoked cigar. Becker could always smell the cigar when Mendy was anywhere around, but rarely saw him actually smoking it.

"Nice place, Mr. Schechter," Angie said. Mendy glared at him for a moment but Angie looked back with simple-minded innocence. Mendy pulled Becker a few steps aside and whispered.

"Matt, who'd you say this guy is?" Mendy asked .

"That's Angelo. He's gonna be my corner man tonight," Becker answered. An actual corner man was almost unheard of in this low end of the fight game.

"Angelo who?"

"Vitale."

Mendy looked over at Angie and thought for a minute.

"From your old neighborhood?" he asked.

"Next street over."

"His mother is ...Auntie..." Mendy snapped his fingers twice but his gloves muffled the sound.

"Auntie Lena. Really it's Maddalena, but nobody calls her that," Becker said. Angie's mother was a figure of some stature in the neighborhood with a reputation as a midwife and healer for the people who couldn't afford a real doctor. Some thought she was a kind of witch because she could supposedly stop the flow of blood or relieve pain by laying on her hands. She often took in boarders, usually terrified women hiding from their husbands, but most of her money came from doing abortions.

Angie never talked about his father and Becker never asked.

"Hmm." Mendy took the cigar out of his mouth, spit and plucked loose shreds of tobacco off his lips. "Should know what he's doing." Then he frowned. "But tell him not to piss me off."

The room they entered smelled of stale beer, tobacco smoke and damp human bodies. There was a three-deep crowd at the bar but most of the tables were empty. It was dimly lit except for the center of the room where a makeshift ring had been set up. Becker and Angie walked over to it and stared, their heads cocked sideways. Becker chewed on the inside of his cheek. Angie shut one eye and held up his hands like a movie director framing a scene.

"I like it," he said.

"Who ever said they had to be square anyway?" Becker said.

It had only three right angles. The fourth had competed for space with one of the building's main support pillars and lost. Unlike a regulation ring, it was only about two feet off the ground but it seemed big enough to maneuver in and the mat was well padded despite the numerous stains and some taped-over tears in the canvas. A short, wiry man with a weathered face and thick grey hair was working on one of the turnbuckles. He looked up as Angie started pacing off the sides of the ring. He put down a wrench and walked over to them.

"You're the fighters?" he asked, noticing the disparity in size. Becker was a little under six feet and lean, Angie a little under five-seven and square-shouldered.

"Just me. He's the corner man. I'm Matt. This is Angelo." Becker started to hold out his hand but Angie beat him to it.

"Call me Angie. Good to meet you, sir. Thanks for having us out here," he said, gripping the older man's hand.

The man seemed surprised to be called "sir", and shook their hands self-consciously. "I'm Sam. I just work here," he said. "You boys alone or you got a manager?"

Angie pointed over to the bar where Mendy was talking with two men, waving his hands in the air and shaking his head from side to side.

"That roly-poly guy making friends at the bar," Angie said.

"Where do we change?" Becker asked.

"Come on, I'll get you the gloves too," he said. He showed them to a door at the back that opened into a store room full of folding chairs, broken tables and cases of beer, liquor and bar supplies.

"It ain't much," he said as he walked over to a stack of boxes in the corner. "Don't leave nothing in here you don't want to lose." After checking two or three boxes he found the one he was looking for and took out a badly worn pair of boxing gloves. The padding was misshapen, the leather faded and scuffed. Becker took them, checked the laces and made the mistake of opening them at the wrist to look inside. The smell that escaped snapped his head back.

"Seen better days I guess," he said.

"You got here first so I gave you the good ones," Sam said. "There's tape in here somewheres," he said, rummaging in the box. The man seemed nervous at playing the host.

"I got tape," Angie said, "and trunks."

"So when does this start?" Becker asked.

"Like I said, I just work here, but the other guy ain't here yet," he answered, shifting his weight from one foot to the other. "You boys OK for now?"

"Great. Thanks, Sam," Angie said with a tone and smile meant to put the older man at ease. "Sam, could I talk something over with you?" Angie put his arm around Sam's shoulder and walked him slowly out of the room, gesturing with his free hand and speaking in gentle tones as the older man listened and nodded slowly. The door closed behind them and Becker began taking off his clothes. A moment later Angie stuck his head in the door.

"The other guy just came in. I'll be back in a minute to tape you up," he said.

"How's he look?" Becker asked, immediately regretting the question.

Angie grinned. "Big, hairy and scary," he answered.

Becker looked across the ring at the other fighter, waiting for the bell to sound. I can't believe this guy is a light-heavyweight, he thought. I might be an inch or so taller, but he's about a foot wider and thicker. Like throwing jabs at a telephone pole.

Suddenly it came to him.

"Jankowski's Garage," he said.

"That's it," Angie said. "But they said the 'J' like a 'Y'. Like Yankowski."

"That's right, nobody could understand the guy, his accent was so thick," Becker said, his mind drifting. "What was that Polish thing the lady across the street was always saying to her kids?"

"Old lady Radtke? She could cook, couldn't she?" Angie thought for a minute, smiling to himself. "Yeah, something real funny sounding..."

The bell sounded, Angie pushed in Becker's mouthpiece and patted his shoulder.

"Go get him Killer. Give me just a little more time," he said.

No shame in taking a beating. His father's words echoed in his head again. Yeah, well not tonight Dad, if it's OK with you.

Becker moved in quickly, throwing the standard combinations, left-left- right, jab-jab-jab-right cross, then felt Jankowski step inside his reach and start again with short hooks to the body. Becker dropped his elbows and felt the close-cropped head moving in close, pushing against his chin, trying to open up his guard for an uppercut to the jaw.

Becker answered first with his own left-right hook combination to the temples, rocking Jankowski enough for him to slip out to center ring and start the process over. Left-left, left-left-right, jab and move, moving back and to his left, trying to stay oriented and out of the corners. Jankowski's eyes were still focused, still on the attack. Becker threw two more fast combinations and thought he saw the knees give slightly, but Jankowski shook it off and kept coming.

His mind drifted. What did Old Lady Radtke use to say to her kids?

Before he realized it, the odd-shaped ring had been cut off and Jankowski had him jammed up in the corner. Again he pulled his elbows into his ribs, covered his jaw and tried to absorb the blows to his midsection, letting them rock him from side to side, stealing short breaths between the punches, looking for a chance to land a hook and roll away again.

Just as his arms were starting to go numb from the relentless pounding, Becker sensed an incoming left hook and slipped it past his jaw, then another from the right passed harmlessly beside his head. Jankowski couldn't land a head punch but he didn't need to. The toll on Becker's ribs was going to finish him in minutes.

Becker saw Angie wrapping up his wagers, catching an occasional glimpse of the action in the ring, smiling, but paying little attention. Becker knew his friend had no doubts about the final outcome. He thought his old friend was some force of nature who slipped punches before he even knew they were thrown. He once saw a drunk take a swing at Becker while he was in the middle of a sentence. Becker instinctively moved his head two inches and didn't miss a syllable. The drunk spun himself around with his own momentum and landed flat on his ass before anyone knew what was happening. The barroom erupted in laughter as the drunk picked himself up and shuffled out the door. A couple patrons clapped Becker on the back as the barkeep poured him a free shot, but he just looked puzzled.

"What was that all about?" Becker said.

"You didn't see that guy? Angie asked.

"Course I saw him. Just didn't make anything of it."

"That's the point."

The sound of the bell echoed from some faraway place and Becker realized he had survived another round. He staggered to his corner, the ribs on his left side screaming every time he took a breath. He sat on the stool, crouched over, trying to hide the pain until he could slowly straighten out and sit up. He felt Angie toweling off his face and managed to open his eyes. The club manager's face was a foot from his and spittle was flying as he shouted.

"Nobody brought you out here to give us fucking dance lessons. If you two pansies can't do what you're getting paid for then it comes out of my pocket, and that means somebody's gonna take a wrench to your kneecaps before you get out a here. Get off your skinny ass and give me a fight." He turned and held his finger an inch from Angie's nose. "And don't even think about throwing in that towel."

Becker heard Angie muttering 'son of a whore' in Italian as the man waddled across the ring to Jankowski's corner to deliver a similar rant. He smelled the stench of a rotting cigar and seconds later Mendy appeared at Angie's elbow.

"Hey kid, can you take this guy?" he asked, a drop of saliva poised to drop from the end of his cigar butt.

"Mendy, what the hell do I know?" Becker watched the other corner. Jankowski was staring across the ring at him without emotion, ignoring the manager's screams, but the older man next to him looked cowed by the verbal onslaught. He said something in reply and was quickly shouted down. "How does it look?"

"It doesn't look good," Mendy said. He can't land one, but he really goes for the guts. You're landing plenty but they're all going onto his thick skull. Can't you open up that cut a little more? The one over his eye?"

"He ain't much of a bleeder Mendy," Becker said.

"Kid, listen. Either one of you goes down or there's gonna be trouble. These hillbillies are out for blood and one way or another, they're gonna get it. You hear me?" Before Becker could answer, Mendy muttered "Talk to him" to Angie and disappeared into the crowd.

"Can you do it?" Angie asked. For the first time, Becker detected a note of worry in his friend's voice and it unnerved him. Angie never worried.

"Is my ass really skinny?" Becker said.

"That's more like it," Angie said, the impish smile returning.

In reality, Becker didn't know if he could survive another round and suddenly realized that Mendy hadn't intended him to. It should have been over by now. He looked across the ring. Jankowski listened as the older man shouted into his ear but he never took his eyes from Becker. The bell sounded and he raised his glove to tap twice on his left jaw before rising. Was it a message or just an unconscious gesture? Was that a nod just before he stood up? To me or his corner man?

The two fighters closed and Becker put out the jabs, left-left-shoulder feint-left-right cross. Jankowski tucked his chin and stalked, taking the jabs on his forehead, ducking, crouching, plowing his way past the swarm of blows, but this time Becker let himself be pushed back into his own corner, covering up and rocking side to side with the rhythm of the blows. My only hope is to make him overconfident and careless, he thought. But why did he tap his jaw?

Again he sensed an incoming hook and as he turned his head just enough to let it slip past, he let his mouthpiece fall out and heard the crowd behind him bellow in anticipation of a coming *coup de grâce*. He took another ten seconds of body punches to his ribs, elbows and upper arms before locking up Jankowski's arms. The crowd booed and the referee shouted "Step away, goddamn it!" before Becker could turn his opponent enough to roll out of the clinch.

Again, Jankowski came at him. Again, Becker threw combinations as fast as he could but he was getting winded. He couldn't inflate his lungs without a searing pain in his ribs and he started to feel the panic of suffocation. He backed up but his heel caught on a tear in the canvas and his momentum carried him off his feet to the mat. An instinctive outstretched hand and curved torso broke his fall, allowing him to quickly rise to one knee. Expecting an eight count, he paused to get his breath but saw the referee shouting at Jankowski "Get in there! Finish it now!" Jankowski looked back in disbelief. "Get in there, you punchy bastard!" the ref shrieked. The crowd erupted in a feral roar. Jankowski moved forward hesitantly, his eyes moving from the ref to Becker.

Becker launched himself upward off his right foot and delivered a sharp uppercut between a raised guard to Jankowski's jaw, rocking him back on his heels to the edge of the ring. He steadied himself against the ropes with one hand and shook his head clear, then turned to face center ring, rocking slightly. Ducking his chin again, he raised his gloves and started to bull his way forward, but his left hand hung slightly lower this time, leaving his jaw exposed.

Becker couldn't miss the opening. He threw two left jabs, shoulder feinted a third and instantly rotated his hips and shoulder into a speeding right cross which landed like a cudgel just in front of Jankowski's left ear lobe. The head snapped to its right and the body followed in a lifeless pirouette.

Jankowski's chest hit the ropes first and he started to slide down and to the side, his arms limp. Becker made a reflexive step forward to catch him, but the referee pushed him back and watched the inert body crash to the mat. The crowd cheered and the ref raised his own hands in appreciation, as if it had all been his doing. He finally knelt beside the fallen man, pulled out the mouthpiece and turned the head to the side. Half-open, glazed eyes stared across the ring at Becker.

After the formality of the counting out and arm raising, the referee returned to Jankowski's motionless form, now being attended to by a local with a black bag who had turned the body over and was having little success with smelling salts. Probably a veterinarian, Becker thought.

His breathing returning to normal, he walked to his corner and put his forearms on the ropes. Hanging his head, he spit into the bucket and realized by the presence of blood that he had bitten the inside of his own lip. He started checking with his tongue for loose teeth. All accounted for.

Jankowski's supine form held the quiet interest of some spectators, but the crowd thinned as most drifted toward the bar. Becker caught glimpses of Angie several times as he settled up, finally sauntering up to the ring with a handful of cash which he folded over once and stuffed into the front pocket of his trousers.

"I thought that guy's head was coming off," he said as he started to loosen the laces on Becker's gloves.

"*Karaluchy pod paduchy,*" Becker said.

"That's it! Old lady Radtke! What's that mean anyway?" Angie asked.

"Damned if I know," Becker answered, his thoughts drifting. "She was a nice old broad. Wonder what ever happened to her?"

Angie glanced over Becker's shoulder.

"Still not moving," he said.

"Where's Mendy?" Becker said, trying to change the subject.

"He was talking to the manager for a while, but see those two heavies over at the end of the bar?"

The ring lights blinded Becker to most of the room but he could just make out two bulky figures, the only ones wearing fedoras.

"What about them?" Becker said.

"Mendy saw them, got spooked and got scarce. I haven't seen him since," Angie said.

"Mendy runs with a tough crowd, but he'd better not leave without paying me. I don't feel like chasing him down for my money."

"Get him another time," Angie said. "We hit it big on side bets."

"If I don't get it tonight, I'll never get it. Mendy's not going to hunt me down to pay me."

Angie took a towel from a canvas gym bag and tossed it over Becker's shoulders, then held the ropes as he stepped out of the ring and headed back to the store room. When they got there, the door was locked. Angie turned to survey the room and, catching Sam's eye, gave him a wave. The man dropped a cigarette, twisted the sole of his shoe on the butt and hurried over, pulling out his key ring.

"Sorry Angie, but I was keeping it locked like you asked," he said, holding the door and switching on the lights.

"Thanks, Sam. You're a pal," Angie said. "Say, you seen our manager anywhere?"

"He asked me to let him out the back door and not to tell nobody," said Sam.

"When was this?" Angie asked.

"About ten minutes ago."

"He didn't stay for the end of the fight?" Becker asked.

Sam shook his head, embarrassed to be delivering bad news. "But it was a real good fight Mister. Best I seen here," he said.

"Thanks Sam. You took real good care of us. This is for you." Angie pressed some bills into the older man's hand. "Wish it was more, but we did our best."

Sam stared down at the money, wide-eyed at his good fortune.

Becker watched the exchange as he pulled the tape off his hands and smiled to himself. With Angie, everyone had clean slate and a story worth hearing. Though he'd left school at sixteen, Becker had seen him talk to anyone from college professors to stevedores, businessmen and gangsters and immediately engage them with his charm and quick wit. Angie toyed with people who thought themselves smarter, tougher or classier but nothing made him more uneasy than to see an innocent pushed around, whatever his social standing. Becker was college educated and multi-lingual, but often wondered if Angie had the keener intellect and warmer heart.

Once again, Angie put his arm around Sam's shoulder and walked toward the door.

"Let's you and me take a look for our friend's car," he said.

When the tape came off his hands, Becker realized how sore they were. He washed the smell of the gloves off with some coarse soap at a small sink and let the ice-cold water run over his knuckles for as long as he could bear it. He then did his best to towel dry and get dressed, grunting with pain as the ache in his ribs made it difficult to bend forward. Dreading the simple necessity of putting on his shoes, he realized that he couldn't find them. Stolen, he thought. Of course they are. What do you think? The country's in a depression and people are stealing shoes. Something out of Charles Dickens.

He finally found them under a cart of folding chairs.

Angie stuck his head in the room.

"Nice and cozy?" he said.

"What?"

"Are you moving in here or can we get going?"

"Couldn't find my shoes, smart-ass. You find Mendy?"

"His car is gone," Angie said as he came into the room and handed Becker a wad of bills. "Your cut."

"The two heavies?" asked Becker, pocketing the money.

"Not here," Angie said.

"Think they're from Mendy's crowd?"

"They looked more mozzarella than matzo to me, but who knows?" Angie said.

Sam and the older man came in, supporting Jankowski with an arm over each of their shoulders. They laid him down on a makeshift table of beer cases with a blanket stretched across it. Sam started to unlace his gloves.

"I'll do that," said the older man. Sam looked across at Angie who answered with a nod and half-smile.

"I'll be going then," said Sam. "You let me know if you need any-thing." Angie opened the door for him as he left the room.

"How is he?" Becker said.

"Coming around," the older man said. "It takes time."

Becker debated what he should do next. He looked at Angie, who shrugged as if to say "Not my show", crossed his arms and leaned against the wall. He finally put out his hand. "Matt Becker," he said.

"Bernie Jankowski." The man shook his hand. "This is Joe." He gestured at the body on the table.

"You his father?"

"Uncle. His father passed last year."

"Sorry," Becker said. "That's Angie." Angie raised a hand and Bernie nodded in reply as he ran a damp cloth over his nephew's forehead and down his shoulders and arms. The fighter groaned and opened his eyes, squinting against the glare of the overhead light. His right hand came up to shade his eyes.

"Easy, Joe," said his uncle.

"We OK?" the fighter asked.

"Nothing broken. You got all your teeth and your eyes look OK," said Bernie. "How do you feel?"

Jankowski closed his eyes and clenched his teeth as if swept by a passing wave of nausea. "Help me sit up."

Bernie pulled him to a sitting position. He swayed as he tried to bring the room into focus. Becker looked at the breadth of his shoulders and thickness of his torso and couldn't believe he had squared off with the man. Jankowski finally made eye contact, first with Becker, then Angie.

"Matt Becker." Again he held out his hand, shaking the massive paw still wrapped in tape. "That's Angie."

"Joe Jankowski," he answered. "I know you guys."

"Yeah?" Becker said.

"You run that dice game across town there. On...what's the street...in that garage."

Becker was disconcerted by the notoriety. "We don't run it. Sometimes we keep an eye on it for somebody else," he said.

"My mistake," Jankowski said.

"Good fight," Becker said.

"You too." He held his chin and moved his jaw from side to side, as if to make sure it were still in place. "What kind of place they running here?"

"Not much like the boxing I know."

"Me neither."

"Bunch of animals," Bernie said.

"You really a light-heavy?" Becker asked.

"I told Mendy I lost some weight. I don't know how much. He said don't worry about it," said Jankowski. "Anyway, what the hell, right?"

"Yeah, what the hell." Becker paused, unsure of where to take the conversation. "Lucky I got that shot in or we'd still be there."

"Yeah, lucky."

"Hold on a minute," Becker said. He walked over to Angie and looked at him with his right hand out. Angie grinned back.

"Way ahead of you, as usual," Angie said. He put a thick sheaf of bills into Becker's hand. Becker walked back to the table.

"Don't wanna forget this." He held out the bills, his palm down. Jankowski and his uncle stared warily.

"What's this?"

"Your cut," Becker said.

"Of what?"

"They set us both up, right?"

Jankowski nodded and let out a humorless snort. "Damn right they did," said Bernie.

"But we got out of it, and made a small killing in the process. Anyway, it could've gone the other way just as well."

"Nah, I knew I'd never tag you good after the first round," Jankowski said. "I was never fast like you. I'm just a slugger."

Becker answered by pulling up his shirt and looking down at his bruised ribs. His ribcage looked asymmetrical, or was he imagining it?

Jankowski smiled for the first time. "I guess I got a couple shots in."

"Yeah, well, you got style." Becker pulled his shirt down and held out the money again. "So take it. Me and Angie never burned anybody in our lives and we ain't gonna start tonight."

Jankowski took the bills and held them up to judge their thickness before passing them over to his uncle. "Thanks. I guess I owe ya."

Becker shook his head. "More like somebody owes us."

There was an uncomfortable silence.

"Hey, do you guys speak Polish?" Angie said, walking over from across the room.

The three looked back with blank stares at the non sequitur.

"I do, but these kids..." Bernie said, jerking his chin toward his nephew. "Why, do you?"

"Me? Hell, no. I just want to know, what does *karaluchy pod paduchy* mean?"

Both men snickered and looked at each other. "I don't know," Jankowski said.

"It don't mean nothing," Bernie said.

"But it's Polish, right?" Angie said.

"It's Polish, but it's just nonsense words," Jankowski said.

"Nothing bad, right?" Angie said, hoping he hadn't offended anyone.

"No, Angie," Jankowski said, smiling. "It's like, what, I don't know. Like *fee, fie foe, fum.*"

Angie looked more bewildered than ever. "Angie, it's from an old fairy tale," Becker said.

Angie pursed his lips and twisted them to one side. "So if I meet a nice Polish girl, I can't use it to impress her?" he said.

"Only if she's five years old," Jankowski said.

"Just my luck," Angie said with exaggerated drama.

Smiles all around. The mood had lightened, the tension eased, as they all went along with the feeble joke.

"You boys got time for a beer?" Bernie asked.

"Sorry, we gotta catch up with Mendy," Becker said.

"Mendy's not here?"

"He took a powder after the fight," Angie said, all business now.

"Bastard," Bernie said.

"Not because of us," Angie said. "Some people he knows showed up."

"Forget it," Jankowski said. "We did OK, right?"

"It's the principle, Joe," Angie said.

Jankowski nodded, but looked intently at Becker and Angie, trying to make them out, not sure if this was some kind of con. "Damn few principles around these days," he said.

The men exchanged handshakes and leave-takings. "Maybe we'll have that beer back on the other side of the river sometime," Becker said.

"Maybe more than one," Bernie said.

"Count on it," Becker said. "Careful getting out of here. I'm not expecting trouble, but this doesn't seem like a real friendly place. Sam is letting us out the back. We'll get him to do the same for you."

Jankowski raised his right hand in farewell. "You boys go with God," Bernie said.

"*Karaluchy pod paduchy,*" Angie answered, closing the door behind them to the sound of laughter. " 'Go with God'. That'll be a first," he said to Becker.

They started to move through the crowd toward the back door where Sam was waiting. Becker winced at the pain in his ribs and tried to walk normally as he concentrated on putting one foot in front of the other.

"Matt, could you move your ass just a little?" Angie said.

"What's with you?"

"I figure sooner or later that asshole manager is gonna try to start his car. Then he's gonna check his engine and start looking for his distributor cap and while he's looking, he might start thinking about who pulled it out, not to mention who cut the valve stems off his tires. I don't think it'll take till spring to make a good guess."

CHAPTER 2

Becker knew he was tired enough to get himself killed. He tried to keep his eyes focused on the road ahead instead of the snowflakes crossing his field of vision. The snow was moving horizontally and traction was getting random as they moved deeper into the squall.

"You want I should drive?" Angie asked

"I got it. Thanks anyway," Becker said.

"You don't look like you got it," Angie said. "You just don't like my driving," he said with a sigh, as if he couldn't care less.

"I've had enough excitement for one night," Becker said.

Angie turned sideways in the seat and surveyed the car's interior.

"So, you living in this heap?" he asked.

"Not yet," Becker said.

Angie noticed a rifle case sticking out of a canvas bag on the floor of the backseat.

"What about the duffel?" he asked.

"My father's war souvenirs," Becker answered.

Becker's father was Jean-Baptiste, called Jean by his family or just John by the neighbors. The previous spring, he had collapsed while stoking the boiler of an inbound freight. By the time the engine pulled into the yards, the engineer had given him up for dead, but when some of the yard crew tried to pull his body out of the cab, they saw he was still breathing. They brought him back to the house in the back of his own truck. The local doctor prescribed bed rest and wait-and-see. He also told him to stop smoking the four or five dozen cigarettes a day which he could roll, seal and pop between his lips faster than the average man could tie his shoes.

After a few days he was up and about, puttering around the house, clowning and making a nuisance of himself. He teased his daughters in his native French, tried to cook but got chased out of the kitchen, drank too much wine at dinner and sang to his wife, Anneliese, who resorted to German or Yiddish for her scolding, both mock and real . Finally relieved of the long days of labor and short nights of fitful sleep, he seemed decades younger. Becker knew his father's mood could change from light-hearted to vicious in an instant and he kept his guard up, waiting for an explosion that never came. This was a different person.

Jean's older brother, Martin, started showing up at odd hours of the day and night to visit, saying he had time off from work. No one in the family seemed to know what exactly his job was and the subject was generally avoided. Becker once heard it described it as "union work" but there were no set hours and he often disappeared for days or weeks at a time. Becker remembered several occasions growing up when the police had searched their house late at night looking for him and many times when Angie's mother had been called in to stitch a wound, set a bone or once, to twist a dislocated shoulder back into its socket, but these events were never discussed within in the family.

Martin watched Jean warily, not content with what most saw as an improvement in his condition. Instead, his mood seemed to darken in the presence of his brother's robust bonhomie. One night when Becker was home from college on a weekend visit, he had descended the stairs silently and been unseen witness to a confrontation between the brothers.

In two swift movements, Martin had slapped a freshly rolled cigarette out of his brother's mouth and back-handed a glass of wine from his hand into the sink where it shattered.

"Petit con, c'est quoi ce bordel?" he said. You little asshole. What's all this shit?

Becker's father reacted in an instant of fury. Reaching his left hand to grasp the hair at the nape of the neck and placing his right hand on his brother's chin, he twisted Martin off his feet and onto the kitchen floor, holding him down with a knee to the chest and a hand at his throat.

Martin didn't fight back but reached up and patted his brother's hand before taking it from his throat. Jean slid his knee off his brother's chest and sat cross-legged on the floor, breathing heavily. Martin raised himself on one elbow and reached the other arm up to his brother's shoulder.

They spoke softly to each other, more like brothers than Becker had ever seen them, but he couldn't make out the words. He heard mention of their own father, who had died of a heart attack in his forties and one clear, emphatic statement from Jean-Baptiste.

"I can't wait out the end in bed, counting the cracks in the plaster," he said. "If it's coming, let it come."

Becker returned to college the next morning. Ten days later he got a message at his dormitory to call home.

His father had been found standing at the foot of the stairs wearing nothing but a t-shirt, unable to speak or walk without being led, his eyes staring straight ahead in terror at some private nightmare. The doctor said it must have been a stroke.

Becker returned to a strangely quiet house, the usual bickering between his mother and two sisters replaced by somber monosyllables and averted glances. His mother had moved her husband into Becker's attic bedroom, supposedly because it got more sunlight but more because she didn't want her daughters to see him weak and helpless. She took control of his care and dismissed any offers of help or expressions of sympathy, insisting that the girls go about their lives.

Becker was the only surviving son. His older brother, his parents' firstborn, had died of the flu in 1918. Becker's younger sister, Francoise, was a painfully shy high school student who despaired of her boyish figure and lack of self-confidence. She was a violin prodigy but saw her talent as something freakish and embarrassing rather than a source of pride. Becker was fiercely protective of her, once having broken the nose of an erstwhile friend who had referred to her as "flat as a board".

His older sister by three years, Denise, saw herself as the family executive officer. She managed the household, disciplined the younger children and was the *éminence grise* behind her mother's authority. She had recently begun a career as an elementary school teacher and it was in that role and tone of voice that she sat Becker down at the dining table and explained their father's condition. For the first time in his life, Becker pitied her for the responsibilities she took on herself.

Their father could move his limbs but had little strength or coordination. He couldn't feed himself and swallowing was so difficult that he often choked or coughed up his food. He had to be helped to the toilet, but the doctor warned that they should make preparations to deal with the onset of incontinence. He was a kind man and a family friend, later devastated with shame to discover he had made that prognosis well within earshot of the patient.

Becker had long ago become immune to his sister's patronizing manner. He ignored it, laughed at it or countered it with sarcasm. On that day he simply didn't care, instead staring captivated by her composure and regal bearing. She sat with the controlled posture of a ballet dancer, spine straight, shoulders back and chin up, long black hair held in a silver barrette and speaking in precise, carefully chosen words. She spoke German, the family's language for weighty issues, in her own elegant, feminine idiolect, effortlessly making the guttural sound musical, and as he listened, it occurred to him for the first time that his sister might be beautiful. But he still could not bear the contrived formality of the situation and was determined not to endure a lecture.

"Has he tried to kill himself yet?" Becker asked, matter-of-factly. The words struck his sister like a blow and he instantly regretted them. He cursed himself as her eyes filled with tears.

"Forgive me, sister." Becker took her right hand in both of his as she used the left to press a handkerchief to one eye, then the other. Her head moved side to side in silent denial, but Becker was sure he had his answer.

He remembered bringing a small plate of apple slices up to his room. As he opened the door, he smelled the sharp, sour odor of a sickroom. His father was already watching the door and greeted him by raising his hand a few inches off the bed.

"*Salut,* Papa," Becker said. "So, you decided to slow down now?"

Jean-Baptiste didn't speak, instead raising both hands slightly, palms up to indicate the bed and the confines of the room, as if to say "*Évidemment.*" Obviously.

"Can you eat?"

A slight puffing of the cheeks.

"You gotta eat." Becker put down the dish and pulled his father higher on the bed, sliding another pillow under his head. He then sat on the edge of the bed. One by one, he broke the apple slices into small pieces and placed them on his father's tongue.

"I feel like I'm giving communion," Becker said.

A glance at the ceiling. *Like they'd let you in a church.*

"Of course I forgot the wine."

A raised eyebrow and pursing of lips. *Just like you to forget the most important thing.*

"You've got to make my graduation you know. You get to see me in a robe and a funny hat."

A stare from a place deep inside. A sob without tears. Finally, a weary smile.

"So Papa, since I've caught you in a good mood, can I borrow twenty bucks?"

His father answered by raising ten fingers slowly off the blanket.

"I could make do with fifteen."

He raised the fingers of one hand.

"Ten?"

He closed the thumb and forefinger of his right hand to make a zero.

"Should've quit while I was ahead," Becker said with a shrug.

His father nodded sagely and tapped his index finger on his chest. *Me too.* He waved off the next offered piece of apple.

Becker set the plate aside and started to get up but his father fumbled for his hand, finally grabbing his wrist. He lifted his head, struggling to rise as he looked at his son in desperation, his lips opening and closing soundlessly as he fought to communicate some vital message. Finally, he let his head fall back to the pillow and drew deep breaths, exhausted from the effort, but the breathing turned quickly to a choking cough. Becker stepped forward and reached under his father's shoulders to turn the head and torso to the side as he waited out the crisis.

When the coughing subsided, Becker continued to hold him around the shoulders, rocking his body gently. His father's eyes stared at nothing, his face limp and expressionless even as Becker lowered him back to the bed and used a tissue to wipe the spittle from mouth and a damp cloth for the sweat on his forehead.

This visit was too much for him, Becker thought. Best to let him rest. He stood to go, searching his mind for the right words to leave with.

"I'll be back in a little while," he said. But when he reached the door, he turned and heard himself speak in English to his father, something he almost never did.

"Papa, I want you to know..." he said in a choked whisper. His father raised a hand and shook his head, cutting him off.

Becker knew that many times he had wished him much worse than this, how many times had he cursed the man for the years of whippings, drunken tirades and petty cruelties, the Jekyll and Hyde episodes of a tormented spirit. He couldn't escape the thought that he was responsible in some way for his father's agony. But the terror he saw now in his father's face showed the certainty he was suffering a punishment brought on himself and that demons long forgotten had returned for retribution.

Becker walked down the stairs with a burning knot in his throat. Reaching the foyer, he put his hands on either side of the narrow window next to the door and pressed his forehead against the cool glass. He heard his mother say his name from the living room.

"Mathieu." Few people ever called him that. The name appeared on his birth certificate and a few other official documents, but it had been her father's name and she didn't want it to be forgotten.

He prepared himself to console his mother but there was no need. He found her sitting in her favorite chair, knitting in her lap, with the usual cup of tea that smelled of whiskey. He walked into the living room but before he could sit down, she spoke sternly to him in German.

"You take those out of this house and keep them safe," she said, pointing to an army duffel bag in the corner of the room. "I don't want them here anymore. *Verstehen?*"

Becker walked over to the duffel. The barrel of a 1903 Springfield rifle was sticking out of the top. He removed it, opened the bolt and checked the chamber before setting it in the corner. Holding the bag open, he tipped it from side to side to examine the contents. Wrapped in towels he found a .38 Police Special and a Model 1911 .45. There were also several boxes of ammunition for each weapon.

Something was missing. Without thinking, he walked to the hall closet and found his father's cleaning kit under the clutter of the top shelf and a case for the rifle behind some shoes. He gently slid the rifle into the case and returned it to the duffel along with the kit. He knew his father would want these to have proper care. He often said they had saved his life.

Becker sat at the far end of the sofa. Little warmth remained between mother and son after years of bitter family arguments.

"Mama, what do you need me to do?" he asked.

"Go back to school. Be a teacher, if that's what you want. I will take care of your father. He doesn't want you to see him this way," she said.

Becker nodded, stood and went over to kiss her cheek. She turned her head, both of them unmoved by the ritual. He then went to gather his things for the short trip back to school. She saw him off at the door.

"You're driving her car," she said, her tone flat.

"She can't use it Mama," Becker said.

She looked away, shaking her head. "What kind of woman-," she said.

"Mother. Think real hard about what you're going to say next." Becker had no illusions about women as the weaker sex. He had seen the damage his mother was willing to do with the spoken word and had often wondered where such anger and cruelty came from. Whatever the case, he was in no mood for it tonight. He was ready to give much worse than he got, and he had been trained by a master.

"The Big War?" Angie asked.

"The Philippines," Becker said, his eyes on the road.

"The bag says 7th Cavalry. He rode horses, like in the movies?"

"He started out just shoeing horses. Then he spent some time chasing natives through the jungle, but he doesn't like to talk about it. He used to sleepwalk through the house at night, looking for Moros. He almost throttled me one night when I got up to take a piss."

"*Minchia*," Angie muttered, shaking his head. He looked through the windshield into the blackness. "Can you see where you're going?" he said.

"Just following the ditch and trying to stay out of it. I haven't seen a road sign since we left the lodge," Becker said.

"Whoa, there's a light," Angie said, pointing ahead and to the left.

Becker put in the clutch and coasted to a stop, rolling down his window to see better. There was a turn-off that led uphill into the woods on the left side of the road. He could see one set of tire tracks in the snow. About fifty yards up a large sedan was parked among the trees, parallel to the road with its headlights on.

"It's just sitting there," Angie said.

"Is that Mendy?" Becker asked.

"Doubt it," Angie said, " 'cause I'm pretty sure that's Mendy's DeSoto right there." Angie was pointing up the road, just within range of the headlights. Becker eased his car forward and saw that the DeSoto had been rammed from the rear. They had probably forced it into a skid and then overtaken it before Mendy could regain control, Becker thought.

"Maybe they're having a picnic," Angie said.

Becker's stomach was painfully empty. When was the last time he'd eaten? He looked from the road to the woods and back again, and tried to think.

"You don't like the shape of that steering wheel?" Angie asked.

Becker realized he had the wheel in a death grip and was unconsciously bending it toward him as the steering column squeaked in protest. With a visible effort, he released the wheel, wiped his sweaty palms against his thighs and turned a lifeless stare toward Angie.

"Don't look at me. I didn't do nothing," Angie said.

Becker reached into the back and took the Springfield from its case with his right hand, easing it over the seat as Angie ducked his head. He put the rifle barrel between his legs and reached again, this time feeling inside the duffel bag for a box of cartridges. He pulled back the bolt, filled the magazine, chambered a round and locked the breech. He reached one more time into the duffel and took out the .45.

"You keep this and wait here," he said to Angie.

"Right, Sarge," Angie said. "What am I doing? Hunting moose?"

"If this goes wrong, you gotta have the car ready to get us out of here."

"Goes wrong? Tell me how this can go right," Angie said.

"So what are you saying?" Becker asked.

Angie looked straight ahead and gave it ten seconds of thought.

"Mendy is with us," he said. "But in five more minutes it'll probably be finished anyway, so you'd better move your ass."

Becker nodded and got out, slowly closing the door until it clicked. Angie slid behind the wheel.

Outside it was eerily silent, the falling snow muffling all sound. Becker had hoped to approach through the trees but now saw that the roadside ditch and thick brush would make that impossible. Instead he moved up the narrow turnoff, using the tire tracks to avoid the ankle-deep snow and trying to orient himself by the faint glow of the headlights.

He had walked for less than a minute when he made out the shape of the big sedan through the trees. It had followed the turnoff up and to the right, parking near the top of a small hill. There were three figures in front of the car, two standing and one in a fetal position on the ground. Becker slowed, trying to place each foot precisely, knowing that any sound might give away his presence. When he judged the distance to be roughly fifty paces, he sidestepped left, reaching out until he felt a tree. Leaning against it to steady himself, he looped his arm in and around the rifle sling before grasping the fore stock and pressing the butt into its comfortable niche against his shoulder. He had known the weapon since he was twelve, cleaned it and fired it countless times. His father once joked that his son had used the Springfield more than he had. The night had gone suddenly and irrevocably wrong, but the feel of the rifle gave him a sense of serene clarity.

The headlights now gave a silhouette of the rifle sights in the foreground and the three figures at the center of a distant stage. One of the hoods from the lodge was beating Mendy with a crow bar, pausing between blows to bend over with his hands on his knees and chat with his victim. Becker couldn't make out the words. His partner was trying to warm his hands in his armpits, but would occasionally adjust something on his right hand and use it to deliver short, hard blows to Mendy's back, ribs and face. Becker guessed brass knuckles. From what he could see, Mendy's right knee had already been broken and the right arm was hanging shattered and useless. He was lying on his left side and facing away so Becker couldn't make out what other damage had been done, but he no longer had the strength to cry out. They were beating him to death.

From where he stood, the targets appeared nearly identical in their long overcoats and fedoras, but Becker judged the one with the crow bar to be the greater threat. He knew the assailant would have to rise for the next blow, so he waited, blinking to keep the snowflakes out of his eyes.

The man spat in disgust and rose, tapping the heavy piece of iron in this left palm like a beat cop with a nightstick. He stood at a slight angle to the line of sight so Becker aimed just forward of his left arm and gently squeezed the trigger. The .30 caliber cartridge roared in the stillness. Becker blinked and saw a spray of black mist behind the target as the bullet struck the left chest, exited the right shoulder blade and sent the body to the ground like a dropped marionette. Becker chambered another round.

The second man watched his partner fall with his mouth hanging open, not connecting the slap of the bullet's impact with the distant crack of the rifle. He took one step backward and felt a burning blade rip across his upper chest, spinning him around and off his feet to land face down in the snow beside the car. Winded by the force of the blow and fighting to draw breath, he pushed himself to his hands and knees, coughing blood.

Becker couldn't see the second target or know if his shot had missed. He chambered a third round and moved forward, trembling with cold and adrenalin. He listened for any hint of sound in the surrounding darkness but his ears were still ringing from the gunshots. A distant tapping in cadence with his pounding heartbeat became the sound of someone sprinting up the road toward him. He turned, bringing the rifle up again, searching for a target, then saw Angie stop in the middle of the road with his hands raised.

"Easy," he said. He knew Becker was operating on instinct and he wanted reason to take over before he took a bullet himself.

Becker put his index finger to his lips and waved Angie forward.

"Maybe one more," he whispered.

They advanced on either side of the car, its headlights now starting to fade as the battery weakened. They could hear Mendy moaning and trying to speak through swollen, bleeding lips. As they got closer, the sound of coughing and labored, liquid breaths reached them from somewhere out of sight. Becker circled to the rear of the car and Angie around the front, stepping between Mendy and the supine body. Angie didn't need to check to know it was dead.

The second man was sitting propped against the fender, his eyes straight ahead, his chest heaving. Becker stood just out of his reach and held the rifle on him.

"Finish it," the man said, blood dripping from his mouth as he spoke.

Becker saw Angie come around the front of the car but couldn't read his face in the fading light.

"I've got to check this guy for a piece," Becker said.

Angie stepped forward and aimed the .45 at the man's temple.

"So check," he said.

Becker patted the front of the bulky overcoat until he felt the butt of a pistol under the left armpit. He wondered why the weapon hadn't been drawn. Then, looking at the man's right hand, he saw the brass knuckles and the fingers bent at an odd angle. They must have forced his fingers back when he fell, Becker thought. His gun hand was useless.

He opened the overcoat and took out the pistol, a Smith & Wesson K-frame .38, dripping with blood. The front of the man's shirt and suit were also soaked. The bullet had entered high on the left chest, shattering the collarbone and exiting somewhere under the right arm. The rattle in the chest and the red, foamy spittle told of shredded lungs. Becker felt a brief sense of guilt at his failure to make a clean kill, but finished his task by checking the lower back, waist and ankles for a backup weapon.

"Matt, we gotta get out of here," Angie said.

"I know. See if you can get this heap started. I'll see if I can help Mendy."

Mendy was curled up on his side trying to hug his knees. He kept speaking to some unseen listener, incoherent mutterings through split lips and broken teeth. Becker tried to get his attention by gently rocking his shoulder, but he moaned louder at the movement. What am I gonna do with this wreck? he thought. The poor bastard is Humpty Dumpty.

"Mendy, we gotta move you," Becker said. No response.

The headlights dimmed as the car's engine turned over and caught, drowning out Becker's voice as Angie gave it some steady gas. Now the headlights blazed and lit up Mendy's face. One eye was swollen shut, the other blinded by blood from a two-inch split on his forehead. The nose had been smashed and the lips were ribbons of torn flesh. Becker took a handful of snow and tried to clean some blood from Mendy's one good eye. In a sudden convulsion that startled Becker, he coughed and spit out a mouthful of blood and teeth chips.

"Momsers!" he shouted.

"Yeah Mendy, that's the spirit," Becker said. He ran his hands down Mendy's body, trying to find other injuries. He moaned when his ribs were touched but otherwise lay still. One knee was obviously shattered, the other swollen up like a football and the right arm was broken in at least two places. He has to weigh two hundred pounds, Becker thought. Maybe the beating didn't kill him but me and Angie trying to pick him up should finish the job nicely.

Angie got out of the car. "What about Guido?" he asked.

Becker looked up. Angie's face looked ghoulish lit from below by the headlights.

"He needs a favor," Becker answered. Angie nodded and walked to the driver's side of the car. Becker heard a hushed voice, Angie or the wounded man, he couldn't tell.

"Ego te absolvo...," followed by a single shot from the .45.

"Hah!" Mendy said. "Momsers!"

Angie came back. "What's he saying?" he asked.

"He's saying 'bastards'," Becker said.

"Is he gonna make it?"

"Your guess is as good as mine. Do you think you can back Mendy's car up here without going in a ditch?"

Angie looked at him with ill-temper.

"Two minutes," he said. "You'd better worry about some farmer coming down this road before we get out of here."

"The only thing that might come down this road is a rat. This is the local dump," Becker said, pointing up the small hill into the darkness. "Can't you smell it?"

"I thought that was you," Angie said, "but I didn't want to say nothing."

"They were going to dump Mendy's body over the edge and down the hill."

"Momsers," Angie said.

CHAPTER 3

Twenty minutes later they were on the road back to Jersey. Becker was driving the DeSoto, with Mendy curled up in the back. Angie was following in the Ford. Snow was still falling and covering the tracks, blood and brains they had left behind. They had harvested a fortune, more than seven thousand dollars from the bodies before putting them in their car and sending it over the crest of the hill to roll sixty feet down into a ravine filled with garbage and thick brush. They had moved Mendy by pulling the collar of his overcoat, one foot at a time, until they had him at the open door of the car, where Angie had lifted his torso and Becker his hips to slide him onto the back seat. Mendy moaned and wept before blacking out from the pain. Becker almost envied him. His own ribs were screaming.

After putting some distance between themselves and the dump, Becker pulled into a roadside diner that was dark and closed for the night. He took an empty soda bottle from the rack next to the vending machine, rinsed and filled it from an outside spigot and used it to drip some water between Mendy's battered lips. He revived slightly and after coughing once, managed to get down a couple swallows. He opened his one good eye.

"Hot," he said.

Becker leaned over the front seat to turn down the heat. By the time he turned back, Mendy was unconscious again.

Angie watched from outside the car. "How is he?"

"Out," Becker said. "Other than that I don't know. You got any change?"

Angie gave him enough for a phone call. Becker went to the booth outside the diner and got an operator who made the connection. He heard it ring ten, twelve times, then a click and a distant voice.

"This better be good."

"Uncle Martin?"

"Mathieu? I can hardly hear you." There was a pause. "Is it my brother?"

"No Uncle, not yet."

"*Quoi donc?*" Martin said. So what is it?

Becker also switched to French and gave an abridged, newspaper-style version of the nights events, knowing Martin would want him to get to the point and express regrets much later, if ever.

"Are you talking about Sappy Schechter from Brooklyn?" Martin said.

"That's him," Becker said. "But nobody calls him that to his face."

"Call me back in twenty minutes."

They kept heading toward home, trying not to get separated or crowd each other on the snow-slick road. Headlights would bear down out of the blackness, blinding them with bright swirling snow and Becker's heart would pound as he searched for some point of reference to keep the car going straight in the whiteout. The cars would pass and he'd be left with the faint beams of his own lights and thirty feet of visible road.

Angie followed the taillights of the big DeSoto, fighting the dangers of too much wheel spin in high second, too little torque in low third and near zero visibility. The combination of sweat and melting snow on his clothes kept steaming over the windows. He had only his wool gloves and newsboy cap to keep the windshield clear.

By three in the morning they had reached Philadelphia and the blessed relief of street lights and visible landmarks. They found another phone booth at a closed filling station.

Martin answered on the second ring.

"You're late," he said.

"No phones," Becker said.

Martin read an address to him. Becker repeated it back.

"How long will it take you?" Martin said.

"We're just coming to the river, so about twenty minutes."

"Go to the middle of the block. Avoid the streetlights. Someone will meet you. They'll take Mendy and his car. Angelo should wait down the street or around the corner. Don't let anyone see that car. And Mathieu." Martin paused. "Don't introduce yourself."

The drive took only ten minutes, but when he pulled to the curb there were already two figures waiting just out of range of the street lights, their shoulders hunched against the cold. Becker cut the headlights, put on the brake, left the engine running and got out. He could see Angie pulled over far back at the end of the block. One of the figures opened the back door to check Mendy, the other approached Becker. As it drew closer, he could see that it was a woman, perhaps his mother's age, a woolen scarf covering her head and tied beneath her chin, another wrapped around her neck and pulled up to partially cover her face. She pulled it down but paused in an instant of recognition before speaking.

"Gut Shabbes," she said.

Becker was struck speechless. He didn't know the woman. Did she know him? Why was she greeting him in Yiddish? Was it Sabbath already? Of course it was. This whole thing had started on Friday night.

"How is he?" she asked. Becker was shaken, but tried to sound serious and controlled.

"Not good. Some broken ribs I think. Both knees smashed, nose, teeth, one eye in pretty bad shape. He might not make it."

"Who did it?" she asked.

"Don't know 'em."

"Italians?"

"Probably. Looked like."

"What happened to them?" she asked.

Becker shrugged and looked back toward Angie waiting in the Ford.

"What happened to them?" she repeated.

"Lady," he said. He looked at her face and realized that she was willing to go on all night like this. "They didn't make it," he finally said.

She took off her glove and held out her right hand. Becker instinctively did the same, but instead of shaking his hand she looked at the swollen knuckles and then raised it to her nose. She nodded. When she released it, Becker couldn't resist checking it himself. The hand smelled of wet wool, but also of gun oil and gun powder. Embarrassed, he put his glove back on.

"I gotta go. Mendy's wallet is in his coat. I took out fifteen he owed me," Becker said. "This is a third of what the other guys were carrying." He handed her some folded bills. "They won't be needing it."

The woman moved to the side to let the faint glow of the street-light fall on his face.

"Why the *mitzvah*? she asked.

"Lady, I gotta go. And this never happened."

"OK," she said, touching Becker's arm for a moment. "I don't know you."

"Yeah, I hope."

Becker pulled his cap low on his forehead, raised his collar, stuffed his hands in his pockets and walked back toward Angie. When he reached the Ford he turned and looked back. They were already gone. He got in the car and Angie looked at him.

"Everything OK?" Angie asked.

"You're kidding, right?" Becker said.

"Just an expression."

Martin smoked a cigarette at his kitchen table as he watched Angie and Becker devour the eggs and bacon he put in front of them moments earlier. He was gently rotating a mug of coffee in place on the table as he contemplated the scene.

"You remember that dead pigeon you brought home and wanted to bury in your back yard?" he said.

Becker paused to finish a mouthful of food. Then he reached for his coffee and took a sip, glancing once at Martin over the rim of the cup.

"Nope," he answered.

Martin smiled.

"What will you do?" he asked.

"Too tired to think," Becker said. "Ask Angie."

"Too hungry to talk," Angie said.

"Such mercy," Martin said. He took a drag on his cigarette and blew the smoke toward the window. "If Schechter dies, this is good. If he lives, sooner or later he'll have visitors and sooner or later he'll talk. He will give up your names."

"People got a funny way of living longer than you expect," Becker said, looking past his uncle.

"Not so much longer." Martin was quiet for a moment. "Do you know who these men were? His people or somebody else?"

"My people," Angie said through a mouthful of food. "Guaranteed. But what's the difference? Jewish mob, Italian mob – it's the mob."

"You know who Mendy is?" asked Martin, smiling at some secret joke.

Becker and Angie looked at each other, both shrugging. "He wasn't exactly straight, but I don't really know what he was into," Becker said. "He found me sparring at the Y one day and asked me if I wanted to make some money. I did maybe a dozen fights with him over the past year and a half. Some real dumps, but I always got my money."

"And the deceased? You get a name?" asked Martin.

"One had a driver's license, said his name was John Clark. It had to be a fake," Angie said. "If his name's Clark, then I'm Johnny Weissmuller."

"They had a notebook. Names, numbers, I didn't have time to go through it. They were probably collecting, for themselves or somebody else," Becker said.

"Can I see it?" asked Martin.

"Everything went in the river, along with the plates from their car," Becker said.

"*Tant mieux*." So much the better. Martin looked at the clock on the wall. It was a little after six in the morning. "We've probably got at least a day or two before the danger comes, but this place isn't safe. Even for me. You have a place you can go?"

"Gotta use your phone," Becker said.

Martin nodded toward the hallway. Becker walked to the phone and picked it up, trying to move out of sight or earshot of the kitchen but the cord was too short. Then he tried closing the kitchen door, but it caught on a hallway rug and he couldn't free it.

"No secrets in this home," Martin said.

Becker dialed and listened to it ring.

"Hello?"

"It's me," Becker said.

"Where are you?" she asked, yawning.

"In town, with my uncle."

"How's your dad?"

Becker never knew how to respond to the many polite, well-meaning expressions of sympathy or concern without sounding rude or cold. It took him an uncomfortable moment to choose a response.

"No news," he said. "Listen, Sandy." The use of her given name made her instantly alert.

"What is it?"

"I got in a little jam last night and I need a place to stay."

"So?" she asked. He often stayed there days at a time.

"Me and Angelo."

"So we'll have company," she said.

"Problem?"

"Not unless he's studying for the priesthood."

"Not even an altar boy," Becker said.

"Bring him out. This place is too big anyway."

"By the way, have you looked out the window this morning?" he asked.

"No. Wait a minute." Becker heard the phone put down and the sound of a curtain opened. She came back. "Good luck getting up the driveway."

"I think we can be there in an hour or two."

"I'll get out the good china," she said.

Becker smiled to himself. Everyone's a smartass, he thought.

When he returned to the kitchen, Angie was smoking a Lucky Strike. He looked up at Becker with raised eyebrows. Becker nodded.

"So I finally get to meet the widow?" he said.

"I thought you already met her," Becker said with a wink. After years of secrecy, Angie and Becker had been shocked to discover that they had both lost their virginity to the same neighborhood woman when they were in their mid-teens. She wasn't actually a widow, but an attractive divorcee twice their age.

Angie shook his head. "You know who I mean," he said, hoping this subject didn't get broached in front of Uncle Martin.

"Angie..." Becker started to say something about "Don't embarrass me" but stopped himself. He realized that he was looking forward to having Angie meet his girlfriend. They were his two best friends.

"Sit down a minute," Martin said. He leaned forward, elbows on the table, fingers laced around the coffee mug.

"I'm going to tell you what you already know," he said, looking at both of them. "You're halfway between this world and the next. You know who you're dealing with and they don't deal with people like us. You both need to disappear."

Angie and Becker said nothing.

"Have you got any money?" Martin said.

"We took what they had on them," Becker said. "I put Mendy's cut in his wallet. I've got what's left with me."

"Mendy's cut?" Angie said.

"He was with us. He's the one got smashed up. He doesn't get a cut?" Becker asked.

Angie tilted his head to one side as he took a minute to digest the simple logic. "So he gets a cut."

"I may need some of it. I'm going to work on finding you a place to go," Martin said.

Becker took a roll of bills from a zippered pocket in his coat and started counting them onto the table. Martin held up his hand when there was about five hundred dollars. Becker gave half of what was left to Angie.

"You know where I'm going. I should have been in Spain months ago. This has just forced my hand," Becker said.

"Why don't you just join the Legion? New identity. New passport. New home." Martin said with a half-smile as he put the bills in his wallet. Becker wasn't sure he was joking.

"Because I don't know what they're fighting for," he answered. "And I'm not sure they do either."

Martin looked at him. "Call me tonight. Don't go home. I'll take care of things at your house. Angie, you want me to call your mother?"

"I'll do it," he said. "She's gonna kill me. Or make me wish I was dead. I don't know what's worse," he said, shaking his head. Angie's mother was the only person who could put a scare into him. Come to think of it, Becker thought, the mothers are scarier than the fathers in this neighborhood.

The snow had stopped and the sun was shining on the bleached landscape as they headed out of Camden into the Jersey country-side. Angie folded his arms across his chest, put his head against the window and quickly dozed off. Becker fought to stay awake by re-playing the previous night's events and trying to figure out how it could have been different. It could have been worse, he thought. I could have slipped walking on the snow, they would have heard me and there would have been a fire fight. I could have missed. At that distance? Not likely. The bodies? We should have closed their eyes.

What was their connection to Mendy? Did he owe them money? Then why hadn't they emptied his wallet? Mendy still had a couple hundred there when I took out the fifteen bucks. Were they working for someone? Their car had New York plates and this had happened in who-knows-where Pennsylvania. How did they know where he'd be? Had they followed Mendy all the way there, and us too? If they had, how did I miss them? Too much snow. Most important, what did they know about Angie and me and what did their people know? How much could they find out? Did that woman know me?

"You wanna keep the noise down?" Angie said, his eyes still closed.

"What?"

"You're talking to yourself."

"Sorry."

"It's OK. More like whispering. Take it easy, we'll make it out of this."

"Sorry I got you in."

"It was your turn," Angie said.

Right. This wasn't their first killing.

Though he and Becker were the same age, Angie had left school six years earlier, in 1930. His mother was bringing in a small but steady flow of money, but Angie felt responsible for her and tried to leave the city to find work. His mother wouldn't have it. She owned her house outright, but she still needed to take in boarders as well as the occasional young women patients. She needed Angie to keep an eye on things.

So Angie stayed close to home, working whatever odd jobs he could find, carpentry, sweeping floors, day labor. He also started running a weekly dice game out of the garage of an abandoned house down the street. It prospered and soon expanded to three nights, attracting the attention of a low-level mobster named Siracusa who gave Angie a stern talking-to and demanded a cut. Angie didn't argue, especially since Siracusa helped smooth things over with the local beat cops who took no more than a reasonable percentage and soon became good customers.

All was going well, until an enraged husband tracked one of his mother's patients to Angie's house one summer night in 1933. Gaining no entrance by ten minutes of shouted threats and pounding on the locked door, he found a bicycle on the sidewalk and threw it through the front window. He then stepped into the parlor where Angie's mother put a straight razor to his throat and slowly backed him out the door.

Angie and Becker were walking down the street just as the man stumbled backwards down the front porch and onto the sidewalk. Seeing her son approach, Angie's mother folded the razor and slipped it into the pocket of her apron. Confronted by the three of them, the man stood white-faced and panting with his hand to the cut on the side of his neck, spitting out his words in a fit of righteous anger.

"You're a murdering bitch and you're going to die," he said to Angie's mother.

"You pay for the window," she said.

"You're going to die," he said, pointing at her. "And she's going to die," he said, pointing at the house. Turning, he squared off with Angie first and then Becker. They tried to look bored. The man got ready to spit and Becker got ready to drop him, but in the end he thought better of it and walked away at a quick pace.

Becker turned to Angie. "I believe him," he said.

Angie replied with a nod. "Mama?" he said, turning to his mother.

"Matteo," she said to Becker, ignoring her son. "Come in and have something to eat." Although she wasn't the least bit self-conscious about her accent, she had always spoken to Becker in Italian, most of which he understood but couldn't speak. He would answer in English, an arrangement that had served them well for as long as he could remember.

Later that night Angie and Becker sat on the porch, drinking coffee, keeping watch and chatting with passersby. They had covered the broken window with a piece of plywood and an old door they found in the garage. Angie had sent word out to cancel the night's game.

"You think she's OK?" Becker asked.

"She wouldn't say if she wasn't."

"Nothing the cops can do."

"Like we need cops around here," Angie said.

"Siracusa?"

"I can't bother him with this. He lets me operate because I bring in money, not headaches. This ain't his problem."

They sat in silence for the next half hour. The street slowly emptied of people.

"I'll stay around for a while," Becker said. Angie nodded and they went inside, but left the front door unlocked.

Sometime after midnight, they heard footsteps on the front porch followed by the turning of the doorknob. Becker and Angie stood in darkness on either side of the entrance. The door opened inward slowly, as if the intruder were expecting a creaking hinge to give him away. When it stood fully open, the streetlight cast the man's shadow across the foyer and Becker could see that he was holding a pistol waist high, like a western gunfighter. What an idiot, he thought. He thinks he's Tom Mix.

As the man stepped forward, Becker brought a baseball bat down on his forearm. He started to cry out, but Becker stepped behind him, kicked the door shut with his heel and moved to silence him with the bat across his throat, not realizing that Angie had already slid an ice pick into his chest one inch below the breastbone. They both held the body as it went limp and slumped to the floor.

They waited, trying not to breathe, listening for some sign that they had been heard, a shout, a police whistle or approaching footsteps. Nothing. Then a voice from the top of the stairs.

"Va bene?" Angie's mother said.

"Bene Mama," Angie said.

"Matteo?"

"I'm OK, Auntie Lena," Becker said.

The man's wife waited two days to report him missing. She explained to the police that he often disappeared and that she thought he must have a girlfriend. By that time, the tides of the lower Delaware River had carried his body out to sea.

"Since you're not going to let me sleep, I gotta ask you something," Angie said.

Becker waited a moment, trying to judge Angie's tone of voice. A lead-in like that could mean anything.

"Shoot," Becker said.

"Where are we going?"

"I can only say where I'm going. I'm not trying to tell you what to do," Becker said.

Angie mulled that over for a few minutes as he nodded to himself and pinched the bridge of his nose.

"You speak any Spanish?" he asked.

"I wouldn't go telling anyone I speak it. I've been working on it this year, but I need a lot more practice."

"You think you can do any good over there?"

Angie didn't know it, but the question cut deep. Since finishing college, Becker had been fighting with the question of what he might be good for. His family and friends always assumed that he'd end up as a teacher and to him, it seemed an honorable enough way to spend his life. But once in college, he was unable to adapt to the hierarchy. A working class student on an athletic scholarship who spoke foreign languages better than his professors was an open affront to the careerist academics who controlled his fate. In the end, they had told him that there was no place for "a man like him" in the profession of teaching. A man like me, he thought. The phrase echoed. He'd learned early that the best way to survive on the streets or dodge a beating at home was to keep a low profile. Now he'd run his life off the rails by getting noticed. Where did I screw up? And what did they mean by "a man like me"? He felt he should know - as if the answer were knocking at the door – but when he opened it, no one was there.

"I'm not doing any good here, and soon I'll just be bringing heat," Becker said.

"You and me both."

"Angie, maybe you're clean in all this. Maybe you can go on with your life."

"Matt, two hundred people saw me making bets at that joint. More people saw me than saw you, and they'll remember too," he paused, smiling " 'Cause I got their money." The smiled faded. "No, I gotta get away from here. If I stay, I'll just bring heat on my mother."

"Angie, I'm talking about going into a war," Becker said. "Fascists on one side, Communists on the other, You and me standing in the middle of the road, trying not to get run over.

"You mean someone might want to kill us?" Angie said, in his Shirley Temple voice. "Oh dear!"

"More like a whole lot of people with tanks and planes and machine guns."

Angie digested this. "This is the same mess you've been stewing about for the last six months?" he asked.

Becker smiled. "Has it been only six months?"

"Whenever you get into one of your moods, I figure it's gotta be the Fascists, the Wall Street big shots or your family." Angie paused, took a deep breath and sighed. "Told you. Reading all those newspapers isn't good for your digestion."

"I know I've been bending your ear off, but nobody else seems to get it."

"Forget it. I think we generally agree about who needs killing."

CHAPTER 4

Becker lost track of time and place, suddenly realizing he'd missed his turn. Not wanting to wake Angie again and judging the road slick enough, he put in the clutch, set the parking brake and eased the car into a gentle one hundred eighty degree skid. As it slid gently to a stop in the opposite direction he released the brake, let out the clutch and gave it a little gas, starting back toward the turn. From the corner of his eye, he saw Angie smile with his eyes still closed.

"Real smooth," he said and went back to sleep.

Sandra's house was a well-kept, turn-of-the-century fieldstone with a barn and storage shed which she used as a garage. It was connected to the road by fifty yards of gravel driveway lined on one side by crabapple trees, which were radiant in the spring and fall but little consolation in the dead of winter when the narrow passage was often rendered impassable by snow. There was still an old farm tractor in the shed which she used to plow or pull out stuck cars when things got bad. By a combination of luck, low gear and a practiced running start Becker didn't need it that day.

He pulled to a stop behind the house at nine in the morning and waved to Sandra's five year old daughter who was putting the finishing touches on a truncated snowman.

"Hi Uncle Matt," she said as Becker got out of the car. The snowman still held most of her attention.

"Uncle Matt needs a hug Sweetheart."

She faced him, brushed the snow off her mittens, flashed a heart-stopping smile and ran full tilt at Becker who swept her tiny form high above his head before drawing her down into his arms. She put her head on his shoulder and patted his back as he rocked her gently from side to side. Suddenly all business, she sat back in the crook of his left arm and pointed.

"Who's that?"

"April, this is my best friend Angie."

"Good morning to you little lady," Angie said, doffing his cap and making a small bow.

April chuckled but quickly hid her face in Becker's shoulder.

"April Darlin', your little ears are so cold. Let's get you a hat," Becker said.

As they approached the house the side door opened and Sandra came out onto the porch. She wore tan slacks and a faded plaid shirt with the sleeves rolled up. Her auburn hair was held up by a red bandana tied just above her forehead, She looked at the three of them for a moment and then took three long strides to reach her arms around Becker and her daughter.

"Hey Kid," she said, pressing her forehead to Becker's.

"Hey Lady," he answered. This was their standard greeting. Sandra was four years older than Becker.

They held each other until a giggle from April brought them to their senses.

"Sandra Ellis, this is Angelo Vitale," Becker said. His first sight of the woman had rocked Angie back on his heels and he had been staring dumbstruck ever since. He now seemed to be looking for somewhere to run, but Sandra's face brightened as she took his hand.

"Angie, right? I feel like I know you already. Call me Sandy, OK?"

"Ma'am," Angie choked.

"Nobody's called me 'ma'am' for a long time. Finally, I meet a gentleman," she said.

Angie seemed to stand a little taller, but he was still almost an inch shorter than Sandy. She put her arm around his shoulder.

"Let's get you boys inside. You look beat." Whispering to Becker, she said, "And you smell like a goat."

She offered food and coffee but what they really needed was a shower and some sleep. After showing Angie to the upstairs bathroom she returned to the kitchen and cleaned some of the cuts on Becker's face as he recounted the events of the last twenty-four hours to her in a hushed voice. They both kept an eye on April in the living room to be sure she didn't overhear.

"What are you whispering about?" she said.

"Be a good girl and let the grownups talk," Sandy said. She took Becker's face in both of her hands and looked in his eyes, trying to understand. Something terrible had happened last night but he appeared normal. He might have been telling the story of a minor traffic accident.

"Wait. Stop a minute," she said. "You killed these men?"

Becker nodded. "They were beating Mendy to death."

"Who's Mendy?"

"You know. Mendy Schecter. My manager." Becker started to realize how little he had told her about his club fights.

"Your boss?" She put more alcohol on a gauze pad and dabbed a little too hard at a scrape on his jawline. Becker pulled his head back reflexively but she held him by the hair and continued scrubbing at his face.

"He's not a boss. He's – just someone who set up boxing matches for me."

"A gangster?" Sandy asked.

"I don't know what he does when he's not doing fights, and that's the truth."

"So you killed two men for a stranger." There was an edge in her voice Becker had never heard before.

"Sandy. How well do I have to know a guy before I save his life?"

Her hands moved from his head and face to rest on both shoulders. Using him for support, she slowly let herself collapse into the kitchen chair next to him.

"Where are the bodies?" she asked. The fight had gone out of her.

"Sandy, anything I tell you puts you in danger. I've already told you too much."

"And you're leaving?"

"We're in a lot of trouble. That means all of our people are in trouble – even you and April."

"What kind of trouble are we in without each other?"

"The worst," he said, looking away, "but at least you'll be alive."

"Matthew," she whispered. She almost never used his full name. "Save my life."

She let him hold her in his arms but her body had lost all strength.

"Sandy, Darlin', I'm trying."

"You're the only father she knows," Sandy said, looking at April over his shoulder.

"She deserves better."

"How long?"

"Don't know yet. I may not know for a long time," Becker said.

"Spain?"

"Don't know that either," Becker said, afraid to confirm any information which might endanger her or someone else. "Martin is working on something, someplace no one will come looking."

"You've talked about it, but I never thought..." she said, now sitting motionless, her face a blank as she watched April playing. She never complains, Becker thought. I don't understand it.

Sandy's husband, David Edward Ellis, M.D., had been a promising young internist from a long line of doctors. He was devoted to his profession, considerate to hospital staff, kind to his patients and by all accounts, a thoroughly decent human being. But the study of medicine had given him little experience of women and he fell hard and fast for Sandy. She was twenty and half-way through nursing school when he met her doing volunteer work at the hospital. It was the spring of 1930.

They married the following autumn and went to live on the farm, not too long a drive from work and a place for him to keep a small stable. Riding had been the family hobby for generations and though David was barely adequate as a rider and had always felt a bit awkward around horses, he liked the upper-class culture that went with riding and didn't want to disappoint his parents by giving it up.

Two weeks after the wedding, Sandy's mother had been diagnosed with cancer. There was little that could be done for her other than vain attempts to ease the steadily increasing agony. Sandy's father spent an eternity at her bedside trying to give comfort and courage to the woman who had been his childhood sweetheart, often weeping, unwashed and unshaven for days at a time, unable to come to terms with the injustice of her suffering. She lasted five months, but she was gone long before she stopped breathing.

A month after her funeral, Sandy's father parked his car on the state highway, got out and walked in front of a truck. The troopers suggested that he was trying to remove some obstacle from the road but no one was sure. The driver of the truck had been hospitalized in shock.

April was born in the spring of 1931. The Depression had laid waste to city and country alike, but the farm was an oasis of normality. The Ellis family had managed to keep most of its fortune but David's private practice languished and his position at the hospital required more late hours and weekend work. Sandy quit school and was busy with the house and a newborn so they hired Becker's father to come in part-time to look after the horses.

Jean-Baptiste picked up extra money as a farrier, tending to what was left of the New Jersey gentry by taking his small truck through the surrounding counties, doing any necessary shoeing and grooming of horses for people too busy, indolent or infirm to do it themselves. His Model A pickup held a makeshift forge, anvil and the necessary tools and he was allowed access to the barns and stables where he would start work before dawn and often be gone before the owners had risen from their beds. When Becker became old enough, he started to accompany his father to help out and learn the trade. With his help, they worked faster, covered more ground, made a little extra and got home earlier. Later, when Jean-Baptiste was called in for weekend work at the railroad, Becker took over for his father.

By this time the Ellis farm was down to just two horses so he only made a brief stop once or twice a month. Unlike most of the other clients, Dr. Ellis was always there to greet him in the early morning, sometimes holding his young daughter. At first, he had wanted to be sure the son could handle the job as well as his father, but later he came just to watch and learn or to entertain his little girl before going in to work. Like his father, Becker had a quiet, assured manner with the horses which Ellis admired and tried to emulate, with little success. Though entirely in his element amidst the gore and suffering of a large hospital, he was a frail and doughy figure, intimidated by the size and power of the giant beasts. This was clear to Becker on their first meeting and though he had taken a liking to the doctor, he usually couldn't wait for him to leave because the horses seemed skittish when he was around.

In the January of 1933, Becker made his usual visit to the Ellis farm. The sun had been up for about twenty minutes when he arrived and with the driveway blessedly free of snow he was able to coast the last few yards downhill to the side of the barn next to the stalls and corral.

As he got out of the truck, he saw a small figure next to the fence. He shaded his eyes from the sun and saw that it was the daughter, bundled up in a winter coat, hood, mittens and tiny boots. She looked at him without expression. Becker called out twice for the doctor before walking over to the child. He was afraid she would run, but when he opened his arms to her, she allowed herself to be picked up.

Becker found the doctor lying face down next to the open gate of a stall, about four feet from the hind legs of the horse. He set the little girl on the ground a safe distance away.

"Just stay here, Honey. Don't move, OK?"

He felt the doctor's wrist and neck but found nothing. The eyes were open and the side of the head had been struck a killing blow.

Becker picked up the child and walked to the house. As he stepped onto the porch he could smell bacon cooking. He knocked, his heart pounding. The girl hadn't spoken or moved since he had arrived.

Mrs. Ellis answered the door in a housecoat and curlers, and Becker was ashamed at the first thought that came to him. My God, she's beautiful, and I've been stepping in horse shit.

"There's been an accident," he said.

There had been an argument between his mother and father over whether or not Becker should attend the funeral. His father thought it was the natural thing to do but his mother insisted it wasn't proper.

"They're not your people Mathieu. You just work there," she said.

"He was kind to me Mama. He never talked down to me."

"You think he was your friend? The rich *Mediziner*?"

"We're talking about good manners Anneliese, not the class struggle," said Jean-Baptiste, using the word *Klassenkampf*. His wife's face flushed crimson with rage and the two of them had at it in three languages for the better part of an hour. Nothing infuriated his mother more than her husband's failure to take her politics seriously. Jean-Baptiste thought all politics nonsense and amused himself by stoking her anger with sarcasm and non sequiturs.

"I won't have those people looking down on my son," she shrieked.

"But Anneliese, imagine all the free food he can liberate while he's there."

Becker's father came to his room later that night.

"Has the storm passed?" Becker asked.

His father answered with his habitual Gallic shrug and puffing of the cheeks. He was in the early, whimsical stages of drunkenness. "Have you got something to wear?" he asked.

"Hadn't thought about it," Becker said.

"Come on, let's see if you'll fit in my suit."

"You've got a suit?"

"I got married in it."

The suit smelled of camphor and was much too short in the arms. "Good God, my son is an orangutan," said Jean-Baptiste.

In the end, he decided to wear his best white shirt, a dark tie and trousers and cover them with an overcoat. His father loaned him his best dress hat, also too small, but Becker thought it might be a useful prop and brought it along. Arriving at the cemetery in his father's truck, and seeing the grandiose assemblage of late-model sedans it occurred to him that his mother may have been right - he was about to make a fool of himself. He parked out of sight on the far side of a small hill and made his way between the headstones to the grave site. It was a crystal clear winter morning and the sun warmed the small group of family, friends and colleagues who had gathered, but Becker didn't know anyone and didn't want to attract attention to himself. He stood apart, head bowed, with the hat held in front of him. He couldn't see Mrs. Ellis or her daughter. Am I at the right funeral? he thought.

The ceremony lasted about half an hour. Becker watched the group thin out slowly, eventually catching sight of Mrs. Ellis as she shook hands and embraced the departing guests. A woman about her age was watching the daughter as she drew pictures in the snow with a stick and sang what Becker thought was a Christmas carol, the solemnity of the occasion lost on her. Finally, only the mother, daughter and two other adults, apparently husband and wife, remained. Becker started back toward the truck.

"Mr. Becker," he heard her call. He turned and saw Mrs. Ellis coming up the hill. He walked down to meet her.

"Mrs. Ellis, I'm very sorry. My father couldn't come. He sends his condolences." He had rehearsed and revised the phrases over and over in his head. That came out all right, he thought.

"Your father?" she said. Becker suddenly realized that she had never met his father, just as she had never met him until the day her husband died.

"Your husband hired my father. I inherited the job from him," Becker said.

"I'm sorry. Is your father...?"

"No, he's fine. He just had to take other work."

"I didn't know. David always took care of the horses. I was never an early riser. She used to wake me at all hours," she said, glancing toward her daughter.

Becker didn't know what to say.

"I'm sorry to ask this now, but should I come at the usual time?" he asked.

She looked embarrassed. "What is the usual time?"

"I check in every other Saturday. I'm usually there and gone pretty early, unless there's a problem with the trimming or shoeing. I won't disturb you."

"So that means..."

"A week from this coming Saturday," Becker said.

"OK. Sure. I mean, yes please." She pulled the collar of her coat higher. "I wanted to thank you for...for that day."

"I didn't do anything," Becker said.

"No. God knows how long he would have...I mean, what would have happened if you hadn't come. You took care of April, and you told me and you called the police and waited while they took David and they asked you all those questions." She took a deep breath. "It was very kind of you." Her voice was steady, but she seemed unable to look at him or anything else for more than an instant.

"It's good of you to say that," he said. "Well, I should let you get back to your family."

"My family?" She looked back at the people at the grave. "Oh, that's David's brother and his wife."

"They from around here?" he asked.

"Boston."

"And your folks?"

"They passed away last year," she said, finally looking directly at him.

"Both...?"

She nodded once, but her eyes held his, trying to communicate something beyond language.

Now Becker looked away. "It's not right," he said, shaking his head slowly. " I just don't understand sometimes."

"Neither do I. I never will," she said. Becker heard sorrow but no self-pity.

The little girl called out as loud as she could.

"Mommy!" she shouted with all the breath in her tiny body. " Uncle Fred has to go to the bathroom!"

Becker watched in admiration as her mother executed a perfect double-take and rolled her eyes. "Her Highness is calling."

"Sounds important. I'll be out to your place next week. If you need anything before then, just call me or my father."

"Your number..."

"Oh, right." He searched his pockets for a scrap of paper.

"I've got a pencil here," she said, opening her purse and pulling off her right glove with her teeth. Becker reached out and took it gently from her mouth in an unconsciously intimate gesture. After she jotted the number on the back of a small notepad, he returned the glove to her. She smiled. "Thanks," she said.

"Maybe I'll see you on the twenty-eighth. But call if you need anything," Becker said.

The next week and a half passed very slowly. His studies seemed more banal, the professors more aloof and his classmates more puerile than usual. His other part-time jobs, life-guarding at the YMCA and waiting tables, didn't occupy his mind enough to keep his thoughts away from the Ellis farm.

On the appointed Saturday, he was up, shaved, bathed and out of the house well before dawn. He had purposely scheduled an earlier stop so he could arrive later in the morning when she would be more likely to be awake, but he saw no lights in the house when he got there and no one was waiting when he parked near the barn. He went about his work at a more deliberate pace than usual, occasionally looking up at the house for signs of life. When he could find nothing more to do, he carefully packed up his tools and started to walk toward the house. He stopped after half a dozen steps and went back to the truck. What am I doing? he thought. Her husband got his head smashed in right here two weeks ago. Of course she's not coming to the barn.

He started the truck, turned it around and started up the small hill toward the driveway. Just before reaching the first of the crabapple trees he heard a sound and looked in the rearview mirror to see her running, waving and trying to call above the noise of the engine. He stomped on the clutch and brake, throwing the truck into a slight side skid and shifting the forge, tool boxes and assorted tack to the front of the truck bed with a raucous clang.

"Are you OK?" she asked when he got out, looking at the truck as if she were expecting pieces to start falling off.

"Yeah, fine."

"I haven't paid you," she said.

"Oh, right." Becker realized that they hadn't paid him since before Christmas.

"I'm sorry, but I don't know how much it is."

Becker told her and followed her back to the house to be paid. She offered breakfast but he settled for coffee, apologizing for his work clothes.

"I'm really not dressed to be a guest in anyone's kitchen," he said.

"Don't say that. You're not a guest here. I hope you'll consider yourself part of the family," she said.

Becker didn't know what to say to that. He settled for "Thank you, Mrs. Ellis."

"Do you think you can call me Sandy, Mr. Becker? You're making me feel very old."

"Sure. I'm Matt."

They drank coffee together and it soon became apparent to Becker that she was desperately lonely and had probably been so well before her husband's death. Their hesitant small talk eventually became an exchange of life stories. With little effort, she persuaded him to stay for lunch. He did some minor repairs on a leaky faucet and a jammed window sash. He was amazed to discover that the doctor had no tools in the house, not so much as a claw hammer or crescent wrench. Becker didn't know how people could live in a house without tools. Maybe his mother had been right. These people were from a different world.

"David used to say he wasn't very handy around the house," Sandy explained.

"Well, I'm not much use in a hospital."

With the shared tragedy, the isolation of the farm and April as an innocent but attentive chaperone, they nurtured a chaste companionship. At first, he kept to his normal schedule, but he soon found some excuse to come every week, making the farm his last stop of the day and then doing odd jobs around the house or barn. After lunch, if weather permitted, they would go riding, one of them holding April on the saddle just behind the pommel. The girl became more and more comfortable with Becker and he found himself searching out small gifts for her during the week, picture books, dolls, pull-toys, anything to get a smile from her.

Becker didn't know what to make of his relationship with Sandy. He was used to indulging the coy, standoffish affectations of college girls, but her warmth, humor and good manners put him at ease one moment and off balance the next. His physical attraction to her was intoxicating and unnerving at the same time. He struggled to avoid staring as she moved across a room, drew a deep breath or brushed back her hair and silently reproached himself when he realized what he was doing. Don't make a fool of yourself, he thought. Her husband just died. She needs help, not heavy breathing.

More confusing was his growing awareness that she was watching him. He felt her eyes on him when his back was turned and often, from the corner of his eye, he could see her staring intently at him. He did his best to ignore it, wary of committing some decisive indiscretion which would put an end to his visits, once and for all. Instead, he directed most of his charm and affection toward April, who was quite pleased to be the focus of his attention. The two of them romped, played and embraced like father and daughter. As for Becker and Sandy, they had never so much as shaken hands.

April's birthday was, of course, in April. Sandy had a small party and invited some of the neighbor kids, their mothers and a couple aunts and grandmothers, the nearest of whom lived a half mile away. April didn't know the children well, if at all, and throughout the day kept asking her mother "Where's Uncle Matt?"

"Today is Wednesday, Honey. He can only come on Saturday. You know that. Don't you?" Several pairs of eyebrows went up among the adults in attendance but April, having just turned three, didn't see how the days of the week entered into it.

"Why?" she asked.

"Who is Uncle Matt?" asked one of the mothers. The room went silent.

Sandy took a deep breath before answering. "He's the man who found David in the stables. He takes care of the horses for us."

"You mean Becker, the farrier? The Frenchman?" another said. "He talks with an accent you know," she confided to the room at large.

Sandy knew they were talking about Jean-Baptiste and debated a moment whether to let it lie. She decided to take a stab.

"I think you mean the father. This is the son. He took over the job," she said. "And he speaks quite well."

"Oh, I didn't realize. And how old is the son?" the woman asked.

"I have no idea. I didn't think it was polite to ask." Sandy smiled, but her tone left no doubt that the topic was closed. The party broke up soon after.

As the guests were leaving, one of the grandmothers, a tall, big-boned redhead with sparkling green eyes put her arm around Sandy's shoulders and pulled her aside.

"Don't pay any attention to these old cows, Honey. I know that Becker boy and if you don't snap him up somebody else will. Hell, his father wouldn't be such a bad catch either, if I were a little younger."

The next Saturday, Becker had a long morning working with a horse and owner to correct the horse's single–foot gait. The consultation, diagnosis and corrective shoeing kept him busy from dawn until mid-morning. Then the owner insisted he stay for some coffee and sweet rolls, so he didn't get to the Ellis farm until just before noon. Once there, he pulled out a fresh bale of hay and was just about to cut it open when he caught sight of Sandy walking down to the barn from the house. Ten years of childhood ballet lessons had given her a precise step and roll of the hips that made Becker beg God for mercy and self-control whenever he saw it, but this time he was caught unawares and stood staring as she approached.

Sandy had watched as he put on a pair of canvas work gloves and effortlessly pulled a hay bale down from a stack taller than himself. As he now stood facing her, holding the cords of the sixty pound bale in one hand and a knife in the other, she wondered what he might be capable of. She saw gentleness and compassion every week as he played with April and showed subtle deference to her grief, tears and mourning. She also knew there was some combination of scholar and gangster hiding behind his reticent, old-fashioned chivalry. But at that moment, as she felt him watching her, she sensed the presence of something implacably lethal and became conscious of the sound of her own heartbeat.

Becker suddenly realized he was staring. He gave what he hoped was a natural smile and nodded in greeting, then tossed the bale back on the stack, closed the switchblade and put it in his pocket.

"Busy morning?" she asked.

"Over at the Woodburn place. Trying to make a single-footer into a trotter."

"I'm not sure what that means."

"Don't worry. I spent the whole morning with Bill Woodburn and I'm not sure he knows either," Becker said.

"Did I interrupt you?"

"Well, I guess not. I changed my mind about the hay. Do you smell that breeze?"

"Smell it?"

"It smells like spring. I think we should take the boys out to the pasture. Let them stretch their legs and have a picnic for the afternoon. It will do them good," Becker said.

"The boys...," Sandy laughed.

"Quiet," he whispered. "They'll hear you."

"The boys" were actually geldings, a nine-year-old named Mars and an eleven year-old named Lucky. Sandy helped him bridle the horses and walk them out to the pasture, a three-acre field enclosed by a white wooden fence of double two-by-sixes. Once through the gate, Becker set them off with pats on the rump and they trotted out into the open and began cavorting back and forth across the grass like colts.

Becker stopped at the truck on the way back to the house to get a change of clothes and clean shoes. He also picked up a small package.

"Is that for April?" asked Sandy.

"It's just a kids' book. I didn't wrap it very well I guess."

"It'll have to wait. Her aunt and uncle picked her up last night. They'll be in Philly for the weekend," she said.

"So it's just..." Becker's voice was uncertain.

"You and me," she answered on an up note, stepping out ahead of him with her long-legged stride. She reached the porch well before him and turned with fists on her hips and her weight on one leg. "Are you coming?"

As they stepped through the door into the kitchen, she turned to face him, putting one arm around his waist and holding the front of his shirt with the other. Becker felt the heat coming off of her, or maybe it was him.

"I want you to stay with me for a while," she said.

"As long as you want," he said.

CHAPTER 5

Sandy looked at him with an expression he couldn't read.

"Did you step in front of a truck last night, like my father?" she asked

"I don't know how else it could have played out."

"Did I?"

"Don't say that. That little girl means that you're meant to be alive and everything good in you goes on. Knowing that will keep me going."

"Were we meant to be together?" she asked.

"I know we were meant to love each other. I'm grateful for that much."

"I guess we lose this round."

"I'm sorry, Darlin'."

"It's not your fault. Nothing special about us. A lot of people have lost more. I should count my blessings. David did right by me," she said, indicating her surroundings by a glance and a brief wave of her hands.

"He left you...It's not my business," Becker cut himself off.

"His family was old money," she said.

Beats new money, Becker thought, sorry he had broached the subject.

They heard Angie coming down the stairs, noisier than necessary, and quickly drew the backs of their hands across their eyes, but he had tactfully paused in the living room to make small talk with April.

"Hey Champ," he said, coming into the kitchen. "Your turn in the shower. She's too sweet to say you need it but I ain't."

The hot shower washed all remaining strength out of Becker's body. His last memory was Sandy tucking him into her bed and closing the curtains against the mid-morning sun.

He woke to the smell of food. The room was dark but a faint light from under the door let him find his watch. It had stopped just after two, but he knew from the darkness it must be much later. He lay in bed and stared at the ceiling. Nightmare sounds, feelings and images of the last day ran through his head. Jeers from the crowd. Threats from the club manager. The sensation of his fist connecting with Jankowski's jaw and the sight of his body falling to the mat. His hands moving over the blood-soaked clothes of the man he'd shot. All of it was my doing, he thought. I'm responsible. He tried to take a deep breath but couldn't seem to fill his lungs. He threw off the covers, sat on the edge of the bed and squeezed his temples with the heels of his hands.

Is this what a few hours in a warm bed brings? he thought. An attack of self-pity? You're not responsible. You were just there.

When he switched on the light, he saw that Sandy had put out some clean clothes from those that he kept at her house. He dressed quickly and walked quietly out the door carrying his shoes, not knowing who might be asleep. He descended the stairs in three giant, reaching steps, avoiding the floorboards he knew would creak. He heard Angie talking and laughing in the living room but he went to the kitchen doorway. Sandy stood with her back to him, stirring something on the stove.

"Hey Lady," he said softly.

She started at the sound. "Jesus, how do you do that?" she said. "You're gonna give me a heart attack one of these days."

Becker unconsciously moved with as little sound as possible, a skill honed in a household where the volatile atmosphere that attended heavy drinking made going unnoticed the only sure defense. He knew that it unnerved people when he suddenly appeared out of nowhere, but he couldn't help himself.

"I thought someone might be sleeping," he said "What's cooking?"

"Chicken and dumplings," she said, turning back to stir the pot as Becker put his hand on her waist, sniffed her neck and inhaled her scent.

"Smells good," he said.

"That will have to wait," she whispered, leaning back against him slightly. She had bounced back from her earlier melancholy. Becker wished he could do the same, but he was pretty sure he could at least pretend.

"Is that The Phantom?" Angie called from the living room.

Becker walked to the living room doorway. Angie was stretched out on the floor, propped up on one elbow wearing pajamas and a bathrobe. His clothes were drying on the room's radiators. April sat cross-legged in front of him.

"What are you two up to?"

"I'm teaching her to shoot, uh, play dice. And she's killing me," Angie said.

They were using kitchen matches for money and April had a small pile in front of her.

"Did you get some sleep?" Becker asked.

Angie nodded toward a large armchair that had a pillow and afghan on it.

"Best I've had in weeks."

"He passed out there and I didn't have the heart to wake him," Sandy said from the door.

"I was quiet," April said proudly.

When dinner was ready April led Angie by the hand to the kitchen table and sat next to him, watching his every move in fascination throughout the meal. Periodically, Angie would pause to wink, make a face or otherwise clown to get a laugh from her. She was an easy audience.

After dinner they drank coffee and watched April serve imaginary tea and make conversation with a teddy bear she had seated at a small table in the corner.

"Is there someplace I can get a sundae or a malted milk around here?" Angie said.

"Still hungry?" Sandy said.

"My clothes are about dry. Thought I might take the little one down the road for a treat, just the two of us, give you two a chance to talk," he said.

"There's a drugstore in the village," Sandy said. "April Honey, you want to go get some ice cream with your Uncle Angie?"

April sprang from her chair and ran over to pull on Angie's arm, just as he was raising a coffee cup to his lips.

"Whoa, Princess! Take it easy, we'll get there," he said.

Angie changed into his clothes while Sandy got April ready. The four of them met at the back door. Angie zipped his jacket and put on his cap. Becker handed him the car keys.

"What's her bed time?" Angie said.

"Tonight is special. Any time is OK," Sandy said.

"I'm calling Martin at ten," Becker said.

"See you in about an hour and a half," Angie said. He took April's hand and they went out the door.

They finished their coffee as they listened to Angie warm up the car and move slowly down the drive. They heard it reach the road and slowly shift up as it headed toward the village. When it was finally silent, their eyes met. Sandy put her hand on his.

He followed her upstairs.

Becker tried to call Martin for twenty minutes but the line was busy. He looked over at Angie and Sandy at the kitchen table and shook his head.

"I guess we have some time to kill," Sandy said. She went to a cupboard, took out three short glasses and a bottle of Old Overholt, poured two fingers in each glass and passed them around.

"What a woman," Angie said, smiling, shaking his head and taking a sip.

"So who's your woman, Angelo?" she asked.

"No one will have me."

"I can't believe that," Sandy said.

"Sure they'll have him," said Becker. "At least from what I've seen."

"The professor here says I'm a bad one at heart," Angie said.

"Angie, knock it off." Becker turned to Sandy. "He likes to do this. I said he was a Bedouin, not a 'bad one'."

"Oh, I get it. So you have a harem?" Sandy smiled.

"No," Angie said, shaking his head. "Matt, you explain it to her."

"He likes to move his tent around once in a while," Becker said.

"Probably got wanted posters all over town," Sandy laughed.

Becker returned to the phone and called again. This time he got through.

"It's me," Becker said.

"*Ça va?*" Martin said. They continued in French.

"*On se débrouille.*" We're getting by.

"So, do you get seasick?" Martin said.

"I've never had a chance to find out."

"Some friends are taking a trip. Maybe I can talk them into taking you."

"When and where?" Becker asked.

"I'll fill you in later. Where are you?"

"In the country. Angie is with me."

"We need to meet up tomorrow," Martin said.

"I don't have a car."

"What happened to yours?"

"It stays here," Becker said. There was a momentary silence at the other end of the line.

"So I'll pick you up," Martin said. "Where is it?"

Becker gave him the address and a brief description of the location. He knew Martin would find the quickest way there, if he didn't know it already.

He hung up and turned to look at Angie and Sandy. They were both grinning.

"What?" he asked.

"I was just telling Angie, I like to listen to you", Sandy said.

"Sorry Darlin', it's my uncle," Becker said. Normally he considered speaking a different language in front of others to be the worst kind of bad manners.

"I don't mind. It's nice," she said.

"He's got more ways of talking than anybody I know," Angie said, turning to Sandy. "You ever heard him talk to those college types? He sounds like Roosevelt instead of my old buddy from the neighborhood."

"Oh sure. That's how he swept me off my feet. I even bought him a cigarette holder, but he never uses it," she said.

"You know he's got Kraut books in his car?" Angie said, talking as if Becker wasn't in the room.

"I know. Karl Marx in the original German," Sandy said.

"Hey, I read The Katzenjammer Kids in the original," Angie said, finally letting up. He knew that Becker was embarrassed by his other languages, though he wasn't sure why.

"Alright, already," Becker said, sitting down. "I've a couple Italian words for you, but there's a lady present."

Angie held up both hands in surrender. "So what did he say?" he asked.

"We're taking a boat trip."

"Where to?" asked Sandy.

"Someplace no one will think to look." Becker knew where they were going, but still hesitated to give Sandy any information that might put her in danger.

"When?" Angie asked.

"He's picking us up at nine. He wants us waiting at the end of the drive."

"I gotta call my Mom," Angie said. "This is gonna be murder." He got up and went to the phone. As he spoke to his mother in Italian, Becker and Sandy held hands and tried to look at nothing in particular. Angie's voice seemed distant.

After minutes of what sounded like defensive pleading and occasional bursts of anger, Angie's voice finally softened.

"Matt," he said, startling Becker out of his own worries. Becker looked up. "She wants to talk to you."

He walked over and took the phone. Angie gave an apologetic shrug.

"Auntie Lena?"

"Matteo? Did you boys do like Angelo says?"

"He's no liar Auntie, especially to you," Becker answered.

He wasn't sure what she said next but he thought it translated as "Are you boys going to come out of this?"

"We just want our families to be safe," he said. Wrong answer.

"Matteo, you save my boy," she said, raising her voice. Becker heard a sob, quickly stifled. "You take care of my boy and you take care of yourself."

"I promise Auntie."

He gave the phone back to Angie, letting out a deep breath as he returned to the table. Angie spoke only three more words, "Sì. Sì Mama," and then hung up.

"I'm supposed to take care of you," Angie said, coming back to the table and taking a pull on his whisky.

"Yeah? She told me to keep you away from cheap booze and floozies," Becker said.

Angie answered with a weak smile and a liquidly resonant sniff. He passed his sleeve over his eyes.

The three of then sat without talking, listening to the steam in the radiators. After a time, Sandy spoke as she refilled their glasses.

"This will just go to waste if we don't finish it. Angie, find some music on the radio. This is a 'Bon Voyage' party," she said.

They made the most of it.

Sandy woke up early and tried to keep herself busy fixing a steve-dore's breakfast. Becker and Angie shaved, showered and packed their few belongings. Becker was careful to wrap his father's .38 and the extra .45 clips in a towel. He also packed ammunition and a short rod, brush and oil from the cleaning kit. Angie still had the .45. The Springfield would have to stay behind.

The plan was to get out of the house before April woke up, but in the middle of breakfast they heard her tiny feet padding down the stairs one step at a time, bringing both feet to a complete stop on each step before moving to the next. She came to the door of the kitchen and stood rubbing the sleep from one eye with her tiny fist. Angie was seated with his back to her, but he turned and held his arms open. She climbed onto his lap and he began sharing his pan-cakes, one bite for him, one for her. No one had spoken a word.

"Are you going to play with me today?" asked April.

"Angie and Matt have to take a little trip", Sandy said.

"I'm going too," April said definitively.

"April, this is just a work trip for big people," Angie said.

April thought and chewed a bite of food for a minute, clearly dis-satisfied with that answer.

"I'm going to stay next to you until you leave," she said.

"That's good Honey. You stay right next to your Uncle Angie un-til he leaves."

At twenty to nine, Becker and Angie both looked at the clock, then each other.

"Is it time, Warden?" Angie said. Becker nodded.

"We're walking you to the road," Sandy said. Becker started to speak but she was already moving. Unlike any woman he had ever known, she could be ready to leave in an instant. As the men watched in amazement, she swept her daughter out of Angie's lap and into snow pants, coat, boots, scarf and a wool cap. The whole process seemed to take place in a minute and a half. Reaching for her own coat, she looked up with raised eyebrows.

"You boys coming?" she said.

Becker and Angie hastily shoveled in a couple more bites of food and took final sips of coffee while pulling on their own jackets. Soon, the four of them were hiking down the long, snow-covered drive, Angie carrying April on his shoulders, Becker and Sandy following.

They reached the end of the drive. Becker dropped his bag and put his arms around Sandy. She put her forehead on his chest.

"Darlin', you know I wish..." he began, choking on his words.

"I know," she said. "It's not our time."

They heard a car approaching and Becker looked at his watch. Uncle Martin, he thought. Always on time.

April had her arms tight around Angie's neck as he rocked her gently from side to side, patting her back. As Martin's car pulled to a stop, he set her on the ground and squatted on his heels to face her.

"Are you my best girl?" he asked. She nodded rapidly several times. "OK Sunshine, you take care of your Mom. Me and your Uncle Matt will be back soon."

Martin got out of the car, opened the trunk and threw in Becker's bag. He walked to the group but stood a few feet back from April so as not to startle her. His six-foot-three frame and dark eyes often put the fear of God into adults.

"Uncle Martin, this is Sandra Ellis. Sandy, Martin Becker."

"Mr. Becker," Sandy said, reaching out a hand.

"You call me Uncle Martin." He noticed her tears as he took her hand. "Don't worry now. We'll set all this right and get him back to you before you know it. Angelo, who's your new girlfriend?"

The rising sun was at Martin's back, creating a hulking silhouette but April squinted up at him with curiosity rather than fear. He crouched to look at her eye-to-eye, placed his right hand on the side of her face and muttered "*pauvre petite*" under his breath. April put her mittened hand over his and smiled.

Standing abruptly he made a dramatic gesture out of pulling back his sleeve to look at his watch.

"You boys get in the car," he said. "I'll talk to the lady for a minute."

Becker got in the front, Angie in the back. They both watched as Martin blocked Sandy from their sight, but they saw him take her right hand in both of his, nodding twice, shaking his head twice. He held her shoulders as he kissed her on both cheeks, then bent to kiss the top of April's head before stepping away to round the front of the car and get behind the wheel.

As the car pulled away, the young men each raised a hand to the window. Sandy held both hands over her heart and looked at Becker, her face streaked with tears. April smiled and waved frantically as if at a departing steamship.

When they had rounded the curve Becker heard Angie draw in a deep breath and let it out slowly.

"Jesus," he said.

"Yeah," Becker said.

CHAPTER 6

"What's the plan?" Becker asked.

"We stay away from train stations. I'm driving you to the city," Martin said.

"And then?"

"Papers. You need passports. I know someone that can help, but it will cost. Here," he said, handing over the money from the night before. "I didn't need this but you will."

"All my ID is at the house. How do I get a passport?" Becker asked.

"You want to come back to your life someday? Then you can't use your own name. Uncle Sam doesn't want you in this fight, and if you get in it, he might not want you back. Not only that, but maybe your real name isn't the best one for you right now."

"Do I get to choose my new name?" Angie asked.

"Don't know," Martin said. "I've never done this before."

"I want to be Rudolf Valentino."

"How about Rudolf *Gatsangu*? " Becker said.

Angie snorted once but counter punched. "How about Matt *Manogats*? Uncle Martin. What do you think?"

Martin's body shook with laughter but he managed to make no sound. He'd picked up enough of the Sicilian vulgarisms to get the jokes.

"I'll think of good names for you two – what is it – *stuppiau*,"

"Martin. Stick with English or French, or some New York *paesan* is gonna leave you in the river," Angie said.

They stopped in North Jersey for lunch before heading across the George Washington Bridge and downtown toward Hell's Kitchen. Martin stopped in front of a building with a sign which said, simply 'Hotel'. Becker and Angie looked up at the grimy exterior.

"This is it?" Becker asked.

"What's wrong with it?" Martin said.

Becker pulled out a wad of cash. "Uncle, we can do better."

"You're gonna need that before long," Martin said, shaking his head.

"We might be dead before long. Let's show a little class. Besides, I don't want bedbugs robbing us blind while we sleep."

"You got a point," Martin said.

They were hardly dressed for the Ritz, and Angie had no luggage so they settled for a slightly more genteel establishment farther uptown. It actually had a lobby, coffee shop and bar. Becker and Angie took one room, Martin another on a different floor, "Just in case there's shooting," he said.

They ate at a diner a couple blocks from Times Square and headed out for a stroll through the Theater District, but a razor-sharp wind soon had them searching for shelter in the nearest bar. Unfortunately, it was Sunday night and most places were either too rich for their blood or closed down. They ended up back at their hotel, tired, frozen and ready for sleep.

The next day, Martin was already gone when they knocked on his door at nine. He'd left a note at the desk that he had people to see and would meet them for dinner. Angie and Becker took advantage of the free time to buy some shoes and clothing. They were carrying more money than they had ever seen in their lives, but they used restraint in their choices, trying to be tasteful, practical and not noticeable. They also went to a steamship office to check on fares and schedules. On the way back to the hotel, they stopped at Abercrombie & Fitch to buy some alpine rucksacks.

Over dinner that night Martin talked.

"Tomorrow, I need you to meet some people. Volunteers, like you. Don't bullshit them, but don't be too generous with the truth either," he said.

"Do we need their permission to go?" Angie asked.

"No. You can go anywhere you want, but unless you want to fight the Fascists all alone you might want to make nice, or at least not piss anybody off."

"Can they keep us out?" Becker asked.

Martin broke off a piece of Italian bread and paused before taking a bite. "You're healthy, not too old, not too young, not blind. Sometimes I think you're deaf, but they need people. They'll probably take you."

"How about you?" Becker asked.

"I'm fighting the war here," he said. Becker knew that was true.

"I mean, if somebody finds out what happened on Friday, are you going to be safe?"

"Wouldn't know. I don't think I've ever been safe. Don't know what it feels like," Martin said.

The following morning Angie and Becker stood waiting in the corridor of a rented meeting hall in lower Manhattan. There were twenty or thirty other men of various ages from late teens to mid-forties, many unshaven and looking as if they had slept in their clothes. A few appeared pale, unhealthy or malnourished. The man on Becker's left had a rattling cough that sounded consumptive. There were a few folding chairs but most of the men sat on the floor or on canvas bags, duffels or produce sacks that might have contained all of their worldly possessions.

A half hour before, Becker had held Angie's place in line while he had gone out and returned with three packs of cigarettes which had been passed around to grateful hands. The air was now thick with smoke, the smell of human bodies and the stale breath of men with no food in their bellies.

Twice they had seen Martin walk in and out of the interview room as if he owned the place. No one spoke to him, but some seemed to recognize him, muttering and pointing him out to their companions. All made way for him.

Every ten or fifteen minutes, a gaunt, grey-haired man in wire-rimmed glasses would stick his head out of the door and wave in the next applicant. They never reappeared, indicating to Becker that they must be exiting by another door or the next step in the process. Soon, it was Angie's turn. He stood, squared his shoulders, saluted Becker and walked through the door. Becker tried to imagine what Angie's interview might be like. Several comical or bizarre scenarios came to mind. He was still mulling them over in silent amusement when he was tapped on the shoulder and beckoned.

He walked into an auditorium with a stage, podium and a tattered curtain. The audience area was a flat, hardwood floor which had been mostly cleared except for a long folding table in front of the stage, lit by the first row of house lights. There were three men seated there, talking with each other and making notes, seemingly unaware of Becker's presence. The man who had summoned him leaned against the stage, reading a newspaper. Becker took a quick look around. He noticed a lone figure seated in the shadows at the back of the room, smoking a cigarette, and though the face was hidden, he recognized Martin's brogans at the end of the crossed legs.

The man at the end of the table was about forty, with the build of a former athlete or soldier gone to pot.

"Comrade! Over here," he shouted, standing and pointing to a spot in front of the table.

Becker approached with what he hoped was a brisk, military stride and stood facing the table with his spine straight and his shoulders back, his eyes focused on a point above their heads. He tried not to think of Angie, knowing that if he did he might start laughing.

"At ease, Son," the ex-soldier said. "Name?"

"Sir," Becker said. " With respect, I'd prefer to keep my name confidential."

One of the others, an academic-looking man of about sixty in a worn tweed jacket looked up from a sheaf of papers.

"Young man, we need to call you something," he said.

Becker searched his mind for a *nom de guerre*. "MacCready, sir. For now."

The third interviewer, a short, sturdy figure with the scarred hands of a manual laborer and a distinctly Levantine visage spoke next. His voice was Brooklyn with a Yiddish lilt.

"Are you here with Rudolph Valentino?"

Becker smiled, then stopped himself and tried to show regret.

"Yes sir."

"So, MacCready. Any military training?" the first man said.

"No sir."

"Ever fired a rifle?"

"Yes, sir. I've been hunting since I was twelve."

"Can you hit anything?" he asked. Becker's eyes went cold. He looked at the man and saw a black mist spray between his shoulders and his body fall in a cold, snowy forest.

"Sir," Becker said.

"Any good with a pistol?"

"I know how to shoot," Becker said.

"You look healthy enough. Any medical problems we should know about?"

"No, sir."

"What happened to your chin?" the academic asked.

"I pick up some extra money by boxing. Just club fights sir," Becker said.

"Comrade," the academic said. "I know you're not a party member. Why are you volunteering?"

"I'm an anti-Fascist, sir."

"Will you follow the orders of the party?"

"Sir, if I am allowed to serve, I will follow the orders of my superiors." Becker considered that a dodge and wondered if they would.

The ex-soldier and academic nodded to each other. The man from Brooklyn looked straight through Becker.

"Why would you do that if you're not in the party?"

"I know this is a war, sir. If soldiers don't follow orders, other soldiers will have to pay with their lives. I don't want that on my conscience."

Becker considered it a sincere answer and it seemed to satisfy the interviewer. He nodded.

"You have any other skills we should know about?" he asked.

"I can..."

Martin interrupted from the back of the room. "I think we've heard enough. I'll vouch for this man also," he said.

"We have a group of volunteers boarding ship at the end of the week," said the ex-soldier. Something about Martin's presence made this man nervous. The other two pretended not to notice him.

"Transport for these two has been arranged," Martin said.

The three interviewers exchanged glances and shrugs. "Get whatever supplies you can before crossing the mountains. We can't be sure what will be available when you get there," said the ex-soldier.

"Yes, sir," Becker said.

"Good luck, Son. Perhaps I'll see you at Albacete," he said. He sounded dejected, as if he wanted to be there now, but couldn't.

Angie was waiting in the hallway when Becker came out, a cigarette in his hands as he leaned against the wall. He looked up, took a last drag, tossed the butt on the floor and twisted the ball of his foot on it.

They faced each other, neither wanting to be the first to speak. Angie raised his eyebrows and turned both palms up. Becker did the same.

"So?" Angie said finally.

"Mr. Valentino I presume?"

"No sense of humor, those guys."

"What'd they ask you?"

"Could I handle a gun," Angie said.

"And?"

"I pulled the .45, stripped it and put it back together."

"I guess that worked," Becker said.

"You should have seen their faces when I drew it. They're real nervous types."

"Still, Angie, we gotta do something about the name. We don't want people to come looking for autographs."

"How about Leonardo da Vinci?"

Becker tried to give him a stern look but Angie was doing his innocent routine.

"How about just Leonard or Vincent?"

Angie held his chin in his hand. "Is that first name or last name?"

"Pick it."

The door opened and Martin came out. He walked away from them to the opposite end of the hall and looked around the corner, then came back and nodded toward the stairway to the street. Together they exited the building into the bright midday sun and a blast of icy fresh air. They caught a cab back uptown and talked over lunch at the same diner as the night before.

"Never tell anyone your real name. Not even people on your side, people you think are your friends. They don't need to know it."

Martin spoke softly but they could hear every word, even over the noise of the restaurant lunch crowd.

"You two...," he said, shaking his head. "Too noticeable."

"Martin, you looked in a mirror lately?" Becker said.

"I'm not on the run. You are," he answered. He paused to take a bite of his sandwich and a sip of coffee. "When you get there, you have to find a way to get away from the group."

"What group?" Angie said.

"Any group you find yourself in. If you're in a group, sooner or later you'll stand out as different. Then people will talk. Once people start talking, there's no end to it."

"Why are we so different?" Becker asked.

Martin paused to chew a bite of his sandwich, swallow and take a sip of water. After a moment, he answered.

"Competence."

They looked at Martin, waiting for him to continue. Before he could, the waitress came by to refill their coffee cups. She was a slender Mediterranean sylph with radiant black hair and impossibly long eye lashes, her movements carrying the warm, cinnamon scent of fresh-baked apple pie. Angie flashed her a smile and stared in frank admiration, but she gave him no more than a polite nod. As she turned to walk toward the next table, he whispered a musical *"ma che bella"*. The words reached her and she looked back over her shoulder with a graceful toss of hair, half a smile and a softening of deep black eyes. Martin took in the scene, expressionless.

"You're going to meet people who simply don't know what they're doing. They resent people who do because they live in terror of being found out. If they outrank you, they'll do what they can to get rid of you."

"I've already met them," Becker said.

"I know," Martin said. "But now I'm talking about people who will take more than your career. These people will cost you your life. Stay somewhere beyond their notice."

Becker knew he was being warned, but Martin seemed to be speaking to himself, recalling painful lessons learned long ago.

"Tomorrow we get your papers," Martin continued. "Something that will get you out of the country. But consider getting others when you get to Europe or before coming back here."

"Back here?" Angie said, absent-mindedly. He was sketching something on the back of the paper placemat.

"Are you expecting a hero's welcome? Whose side do you think Uncle Sam is on in this war?" Martin said.

"Oh, we're neutral," Becker said, his voice flat.

Martin snorted in disgust, then saw Becker's face and nodded.

"Right. Neutral," he said. "And neutered."

Becker and Martin stood to leave. Angie ignored them and continued sketching.

"You staying for dinner?" Becker asked.

"Right with you," Angie said. He finished his sketch and turned

the placemat for Becker to see. It was a perfect likeness of the waitress looking back over her shoulder and smiling, her dark eyes
shining with life.

"Meet you outside. I'll get the tip," he said

Becker walked to the cashier where Martin had just settled the
bill. They both looked back to see Angie approach the waitress at
the servers' station and present the drawing with a little bow, his
hand over his heart. Her wariness at his approach became curiosity
and finally wonder as she realized that somewhere in the midst of
the sweat, steam and grease of a midtown diner there were eyes that
saw beauty in her that she would never see. Angie waited for her
reaction, his eyes downcast, his cap clutched in both hands and
shifting his weight from foot to foot. Becker expected a peck on the
cheek might be coming, but instead she held the drawing with one
hand and placed the other gently along his jaw line, raising his head
until their eyes met. Her lips moved but the words were lost in the
background noise. Angie didn't speak, but Becker noticed him
touch her hand with his for an instant before backing away nervously and leaving with a brief nod of his head and a deft toss of folded
bills on their table.

The next morning they crossed over to Brooklyn where Martin
flagged down a cab and directed it through a series of turns and
double-backs that quickly had Becker and Angie disoriented. They
finally got out at a corner, watched the cab drive off, and after
checking up and down the street, walked to an ageing brownstone
halfway down the block.

There was a basement apartment with its front door under the
stairs. Martin had Becker and Angie wait as he walked down and
rang the bell once. Becker couldn't see who answered, but he heard
Martin speaking in a language he couldn't identify. After a moment,
he looked up and gestured for them to come down.

They followed Martin into the apartment. Their host held the
door, gave a welcoming smile and bolted the door behind them. He
was a little over five feet, well past middle age, wearing trousers
pulled far up over a round belly, giving the effect of an unnaturally

shortened torso. His face had an elfin quality, with outturned ears, an upturned nose and wire-rimmed spectacles with extra lenses attached, like a watchmaker's. As Becker gave a deep nod in greeting, he saw that the man had answered the door holding a Mauser C-96 with a ten round magazine. He was now trying to keep it out of sight behind his right leg.

"Please," he said as they entered.

Removing some stacks of books and papers from a small sofa he indicated that Becker and Angie should sit. This they did and found themselves sinking into broken upholstery until their knees were nearly chest level.

"Think they ever lost anybody in this thing?" Angie said, flailing in an attempt to pull himself into a more comfortable position.

"Quit bitching and try to look amiable," Becker said with a fake smile.

"Sure. Sorry." He let himself sink once more into the cushions and crossed one leg over the other. "What's amiable?"

Becker answered with the sideways glance he used when he wasn't sure if Angie was putting him on or not.

The room was bisected by a yellowing curtain hung from a wire that ran wall-to-wall near the ceiling. Their host held it aside and motioned Martin through.

"Please," he said.

They could hear the two men speaking, Martin explaining, the other man interjecting an occasional question or affirmation. Becker listened for clues to the language but couldn't catch anything familiar.

"What the hell are they talking?" Angie said.

"No idea."

"Hah! That's a first."

Becker didn't like not knowing and he didn't want to ask Martin. He tried to raise himself high enough to take a casual glance at one of the papers or books scattered about the room, but they were all too far away. All he could see was that they were printed in the Roman alphabet, but sprinkled with unfamiliar diacritical marks. Just as he was about to start a mental checklist of possibilities the curtain was pushed wide to reveal a makeshift photo studio consisting of an adjustable office chair in front of a white sheet tacked to the wall and a portrait camera on a tripod. Martin was seated at a desk smoking a cigarette.

"Please," the man said, flapping his hand up and down in an incomprehensible gesture. Becker started to heave himself out of the depths of the sofa but the man held up a hand to stop him, pointing at Angie and flapping his hand again.

"Please," he said again, apologetically.

Angie smiled and nodded, putting one hand on Becker's knee and the other on the arm of the sofa to push himself up. His first attempt to rise failed almost before it got started. He tried again.

"What boat is this guy just off of?" he said through a teeth-gritting smile. Becker answered by putting one hand on his butt and pushing him to his feet.

"Hey. Did you just goose me?" he asked, straightening his jacket, all propriety.

The man motioned him to the chair. Angie sat in a slouch and pulled off his cap, running his fingers through his hair to make himself more presentable. His feet dangled, toes barely touching the floor.

"Please?" the man said, pantomiming a person sitting erect and facing the camera. He quickly looked through the view finder and came back to the chair, waving Angie off , making a quick adjustment and then waving him back. Angie faced the camera and smiled. The photographer looked truly dismayed.

"No cheese! No cheese!" he said frantically.

Martin finally decided it was time to speak.

"Don't smile Angie. This is for your passport, not your girlfriend's purse."

Angie tried to look serious.

"Just normal Angie, not constipated," Martin said.

That final comment didn't help. Angie looked at the floor for a minute, pinching the bridge of his nose until it must have hurt.

When he looked up, his face was unsmiling, slightly quizzical and looking straight at the camera.

"Please?" the man said. "One, two, three." He snapped the photo, momentarily blinding his visitors with the flash. He snapped one more of Angie before motioning Becker into position.

After the photos, Angie and Becker waited in the front room while Martin and the forger concluded their business. Becker took the opportunity to pick up a yellowed newspaper and try to make sense of the print. He had a fair idea of what the circumflex "š" on the page meant but couldn't imagine what the "ĭ" he saw there might represent. He felt irritated by his ignorance.

"You're gonna get wrinkles," Angie said.

"What?"

"You're looking at that paper like I look at the racing form."

"Can't make any sense of it," Becker said.

"Matt, I think it's old's news anyway," Angie said.

Martin and the forger came out from behind the curtain and the three guests were hurriedly ushered out. As he held the door, the little man repeated "Thank you, thank you, bye-bye, bye-bye". After the door closed, they heard it lock and the sound of bolts being thrown.

Angie shook his head in bewilderment. "So many locks. I didn't see anything in there worth grabbing," he said.

"Just him," Martin said.

"What next?" Becker asked.

"I'll come back tomorrow. No sense parading through the neighborhood again," Martin said.

"But what names?" Angie asked.

"I told him your ideas, but in the end, I think he'll use his own judgment. And thank God for that," answered Martin.

"You'll be Mr. Please. I'll be Mr. No Cheese," Angie said.

"Does he even speak English?" Becker asked.

Martin smiled. "When he wants, I think. But he's good at his job. Best work I've ever seen."

"What language was that?" Angie asked.

Martin walked in silence for half a block.

"Do you know where we are?" he asked.

"Brooklyn," Becker said.

"Where in Brooklyn?"

Becker and Angie looked at each other. Angie shook his head once.

"Don't know," Becker said. "Maybe ten minutes southeast of the bridge".

"So if I tell you the language, you'll know the description, nationality and general location of one of the most dangerous men in this city. How long would it take for someone to track him down with that information?"

Martin's tone suggested that his question was not an admonition but an exercise in tradecraft. Becker sorted through the possibilities. Angie spoke first.

"Somewhere between 24 hours and never."

"Martin nodded.

"I wouldn't argue with that, but safer to go with the lower estimate."

"But that guy's dangerous?" chuckled Angie.

Martin's face darkened. "With what he knows, a lot of people would be safer with him dead."

"So why isn't he?" Becker asked.

"Too many people need him, for now. But sooner or later everybody gets found so it's best not to be there when the devil comes knocking."

CHAPTER 7

That night, Martin didn't want them to eat out. He said they'd already been seen together too much so he sent Becker out for meat, bread, cheese, mustard and wine. When he returned, his arms were so full he had to knock on the door with his foot. Angie opened the door with the chain on, looked Becker up and down in silence, checked the hallway behind him and said, "What's the password?"

"Sorry, wrong room," Becker said, and turned toward the elevator.

"Oh, Jesus have mercy. I'm starving in here," Angie said, quickly opening the door.

Becker entered the room and saw Martin seated on the floor at the end of one of the beds, his legs stretched in front of him and a half-full ashtray at his side. He tried to imagine what Martin and Angie would have talked about in his absence and quickly hit a brick wall.

"Am I interrupting?" Becker said.

"Swapping lies," Angie said. "His are way better."

"The service in this establishment is deplorable," Martin said.

"Yeah, and they'll let anybody in here," Becker said.

They spread a newspaper on the floor and laid the food out on it. They had no utensils but each had pocket knives, Angie and Becker identical switchblades and Martin a razor-sharp, folding knife which he'd owned since his youth in pre-war Europe. Angie stared as it locked open with an ominous click. It wasn't spring-loaded, but it was longer and more well-crafted than the switchblades.

"I'll bet that has some stories to tell," Angie said.

Martin shook his head sadly, as if they were stories he'd rather forget.

"It skinned a few deer back in the old days. A lot of rabbits too."

"Any elk?" Angie asked, his eyebrows raised in hopeful anticipation.

Martin looked to Becker for a hint to Angie's meaning.

"Never mind," Becker said.

They ate in silence for a good quarter hour, putting cheese, sausage and roast beef between slices of dark rye, adding coarse mustard and washing it all down with red wine from paper cups. When the meal was finished, they folded the newspaper over the remains, wiped their knives clean with a damp cloth and reclined with their legs straight out on the floor, crossed at the ankles. Martin and Angie lit cigarettes. Martin offered one to Becker but he held up his hand.

"Bad for the wind."

"Matt, I don't think you'll be getting in the ring for a while," Angie said.

"Little tobacco never did any harm," Martin said.

The room became quiet. They soon became conscious of the hotel noises, slamming doors, muffled voices, water moving through pipes and the rising and falling sighs of the elevator going about its duties. The three men started shifting positions, fidgeting and looking around the room.

"Somebody say it, for Christ's sake," Angie said.

"I'd sell my soul for a cup of coffee," Martin said.

"Would sure help the taste of this cigarette. Just doesn't seem right to have one without the other," Angie said.

"So, we go out, we come back. We don't attract attention. This isn't a night on the town. You get coffee, I'll get a bottle," Martin said.

They took the stairs to the ground floor to avoid the elevator operator and went out the hotel's back door into an alley, following it toward the lights and flowing crowds of the street. Still in the shadows of the alley, they stopped and looked up and down the street. There was a shared sense of some unseen threat.

"We'll go this way," Angie said, cocking his thumb to the left. "My waitress will make us a fresh pot."

"Back in the room. Ten, fifteen minutes," Martin said. He turned right and was quickly lost in the crowd.

When they reached the diner, Angie's waitress was nowhere to be seen so they took two open stools at the counter. A middle-aged Greek with eyebrows nearly as thick as his mustache and curly salt-and-pepper hair came over from behind the register.

"Boys?"

"Just coffee, three to go," Angie said. "One black, two regular."

The Greek walked over toward the coffee pots which were nearly full. Recently brewed, thank God, Becker thought. He couldn't see asking this guy, probably the owner, to brew a fresh pot.

"Maggie in tonight?" Angie asked.

"She's around," the Greek said. "What, you don't want to draw my picture?"

Minutes later, they were standing at the register with the three coffees in a paper bag when Maggie burst through the kitchen door with a tray of dinner plates on her right shoulder. Angie smiled as he watched her gracefully weave her way between the tables. He tried to catch her eye, but she was too busy. Becker had never seen his friend smitten so rapidly, but he did his best to conceal his notice of it.

In an instant, Angie's expression blackened as he turned toward Becker.

"Trouble. We gotta move," he said.

Becker didn't look, keeping his eyes fixed on the Greek as he took an eternity to fish the change out of the cash drawer.

"Keep it," Becker said over his shoulder as he swept up the coffee bag and followed Angie through the door. They hit the sidewalk and broke right in long steps just short of a run. They could see the corner ten paces ahead of them.

"Angelo!" a voice called from behind them. Angie sped up, pulling ahead of Becker.

"Hey!" the voice called again, just as they turned the corner to the right.

"Who is it?" Becker asked between breaths. Angie replied with a worried look and shake of his head.

"Not now," he said.

Their progress was abruptly halted by a truck stopped in the sidewalk as it backed out of an alley, its driver and passenger sitting patiently in the cab watching the side view mirrors for a chance to move into traffic. A parked car blocked their way to the left and there was no way around the truck to the right. Maybe we can go under? Becker thought. Maybe not. We'll be screaming hamburger if they see an opening and those wheels start turning.

"Angelo, don't make me come after you," the voice said from the corner.

Angie gave Becker an apologetic look that showed grim acceptance of the inevitable as he turned around. For his part, Becker felt relieved not to have taken a bullet in the back.

"Sal? Is that you?" Angie said, feigning surprise.

"Who do you think?"

The strangely high-pitched voice came from a man taller and wider than Becker who apparently had no neck. His face was the color and texture of corned beef and, in spite of the cold, there was sweat on his forehead and upper lip. In dress and demeanor, he was a reincarnation of the men Becker had shot.

Angie moved toward him, arms wide, and the two men greeted each other with brief, bone-crushing hugs. Becker didn't know the play so he stood his ground and tried to look innocuous as he calculated their next move. Ignoring Becker, Sal took out a silk handkerchief and mopped his face, firing questions in Italian, which

Angie parried with shrugs and offhand gestures. As the exchange continued, Sal's composure returned and his voice and mood seemed to soften. He daintily folded his handkerchief and pulled aside the lapel of his overcoat to return it to his pocket, briefly revealing the butt of a large automatic under his left arm. Becker and Angie had left their weapons in the room.

Sal put a huge arm around Angie's shoulders and walked him back around the corner toward the restaurant. Becker followed a few paces behind, ditching the brown paper bag in the first trash can he saw. Sal never looked back at Becker or acknowledged his existence, but when they reached the restaurant, he held the door to be sure both younger men preceded him.

The Greek made no eye contact with the three men as they re-entered, finding a sudden interest in shuffling through old checks. They walked past the counter to the last in a row of four semi-circular booths where another well-dressed brute sat hunched over a cup of coffee. As he looked up, a burning cigarette remained stuck to the right side of his lower lip, sending a steady stream of smoke into his squinting right eye. He ignored it.

"Junior, this is my nephew, Angelo," Sal said.

"Yeah," Junior said, reaching out to shake Angie's hand. He too acted as if Becker were invisible.

Sal guided Becker and Angie into the booth and took the outside seat, effectively blocking the two of them in. After gesturing across the room for three more coffees, he resumed speaking to Angie in an odd mixture of English and Italian, switching back and forth between languages, seemingly at random. Becker caught most of it, but lost an occasional phrase or exchange to the Sicilian dialect.

"So you come up here to see the sights? Why not just cross the river?" Sal asked.

"Philly? It's OK. But Sal, this is the big city. Plus, nobody knows me here." Angie closed one eyelid at Sal. How does he do that? Becker wondered. He can wink without moving his whole cheek. Becker resisted the impulse to start practicing.

"Hey, Angie, I ain't nobody," Sal said.

"Sal, you know what I mean. You always told me, don't shit where you eat."

"You still got that thing with – what's his name?"

Becker had the feeling that Sal knew Siracusa's name and Angie's relationship to him perfectly well, but chose not to speak it aloud.

"A little action, not much," Angie said.

"Who's he with?"

"Sal, I don't know nothing about who's with who. I'm just a small fish in the ocean."

"So why are you so spooked?" Sal asked.

"Thought you was somebody else," Angie said.

"Me? I ain't somebody else. I'm your Uncle Sal."

"Yeah, but not for nothin'. When was the last time I seen you? Two, three years?"

Becker tied to see where the conversation was going, but his total exclusion made it difficult. Though seated between Sal and Angie, neither gave him so much as a glance. Junior sat quietly, sipping coffee and turning his head to blow smoke away from the table. Every few moments his heavy-lidded, blood-shot eyes scanned the room, coming back to fall on Becker. He looked bored.

"So why you stay in that little dump of a town?"

"My Mom is there. It's just her and me."

"You know people down there?"

"Sal, it's my hometown."

"You know a Jew named Mendy Schechter?" Sal asked, as if the answer meant nothing to him one way or the other. "Some people call him Sappy?"

Now it's coming, Becker thought. He tried to prepare himself, but he didn't know for what.

"Friend a yours?" Angie asked.

"Answer the question."

Angie stayed cool. His lips pursed and his jaw moved slightly to one side as he considered the question.

"Everybody knows a Jew named Mendy. Me, I know two. One is a bad dice player, owns part of a dry cleaning shop with his brother.

Ain't seen him since before Christmas. The other one used to come into town sometimes from Brooklyn. Placed bets with a bookie I know. Him I ain't seen since, I don't know, last summer maybe. Don't know their last names." Angie also spoke as if the answers held no significance. Becker studied his coffee and the signs on the wall, trying not to let on that he could follow what they were saying.

"He do fights?" Sal asked.

"Which one?"

"Brooklyn."

"Betting?"

"Booking."

"Don't know. He used to stay up on the north side someplace, up by the cemetery. Maybe he's got people up there. You want I should ask around?"

"The cemetery," Sal said with a humorless smile. He jerked a thumb toward Becker. "This one's a fighter?" he asked.

"I do horses," Becker said, speaking for the first time.

Junior raised his head and looked at Becker. "Ain't nobody talking to you." No malice, no emotion.

No one spoke for a moment until Sal looked straight at Angie, waiting.

"Like he said, horses," Angie said.

Sal looked doubtful. Becker looked little like a successful race enthusiast.

"He plays the ponies?"

"Sal, he puts shoes on them and brushes them down."

"Tell him to show me his hands."

Angie tipped his head slightly at Becker who showed Sal his hands, palms up, then down. Sal took one in his manicured fingers and ran a thumb over the knuckles, turning it over to inspect the callused palm. Most of the swelling from Friday night had gone and there was little to distinguish it from the hand of any other person who did manual labor.

Sal let go of Becker's hand and looked at Angie, drawing in a deep breath.

"Maybe some people wanna talk to you. Junior, go make a phone call. Tell him it's my nephew from Jersey."

Junior slowly put out his cigarette in the ashtray and took a sip of coffee before placing both hands on the table and laboriously shifting sideways out of the booth. Once standing, he straightened the creases on his trousers and adjusted the drape of his jacket before walking toward the phone booth at the back of the restaurant.

Angie assumed a look of mild amusement. "This guy Mendy owes somebody money?"

Sal looked at his nephew for a moment before answering but read nothing in his expression, gestures, posture or eye movements. The boy didn't show any sign of fear or nervousness and seemed to be enjoying the sight of someone taking things too seriously. Sal was starting to feel like a fool and wished he hadn't sent Junior to make the call. He also had a bad case of heartburn and needed to take a leak.

"Angie, I don't talk about our business. You know better than that. You should anyway. Didn't I ever teach you nothing?"

Nothing useful, thought Angie. He really wanted to make a wisecrack and had a few choice ones on hand but he was starting to feel like he might be getting on top of this thing and didn't want to blow it. I'll do my sincerity routine, he thought.

"So Sal, what do you want from me?"

"Maybe nothing. It ain't up to me. Junior comes back, we'll know. Finish your coffee."

As soon as Sal finished his sentence, he felt the barrel of a gun pressed against the back of his neck. He saw the two boys turn and look behind him.

"Don't turn, don't talk," Martin said. "Get up slowly and head for the back."

Sal's head started to turn. "Hey, we're just..." The barrel of the pistol snapped against his left ear, just hard enough to break the skin. The sharp pain made his eyes water and as he reached his hand up to assess the damage he felt a hand slide into his jacket and remove his .45. Damn, he thought, This guy knows what he's doing.

"I said don't talk. Start moving and everything will be OK. You can take the cigarette."

Martin's voice was soothing but his manner was alert and cautious. Pocketing Sal's gun, he moved away two paces to prevent a try for his own. He watched Sal look briefly at Angie and exhale wearily, ignoring Becker. Sal slid left out of the booth and stood, adjusting the waistband of his trousers over his stomach. He started to look Martin over, but the man sidestepped behind him and started gently pushing him toward the back door.

"We've gotta move fast Sal," Martin whispered in his ear. "It's not safe here. Stay ahead of me."

How does this guy know me? he thought. And what is that accent? Is this a hit or some kind of shakedown? The hell with it. He just doesn't know who he's talking to.

"Hey, easy friend. We got no problems here," Sal said. "I know the right people."

"That's right, but we can't talk here, Sal. Just keep moving. Angie, coffee. Mathieu, with me."

Martin and Sal walked down a small corridor past the restrooms, Becker following a few steps behind. They came to the phone booth. Inside, Junior's bulky form was wedged into the seat, his head tilted oddly to the side, his eyes half open and staring out the window. The bulb inside the booth had been unscrewed so there was little light and no visible wound.

Sal slowed at the sight, his heart starting to pound. Martin used the momentary distraction to grab his collar and shove him against the door.

"Gotta move Sal. Don't worry about your friend. He'll be OK," Martin said.

The door burst open from the combined weight of the two men and Sal stumbled two steps down into the shadows of an alley stinking of garbage and lit by an incandescent bulb over the door. He staggered forward a few steps as he regained his balance.

"Mathieu, keep that door closed," Martin said to Becker in French. Becker put his back against it.

Sal turned to face his captor who now stood about two long steps away. He tried to move his head to an angle that would let some light fall on the face. "You know who I am?" he asked Martin.

"Sure Sal. I've known you since 1933. You opened up my best friend's head with an axe handle behind the Union Hall in Newark."

"I don't remember. What was his name?" Sal said.

"The funeral was many years ago."

"Is that what this is about? Mister, it's just a job."

"I know," Martin said. His tone stayed soft, almost a bedside manner.

"Just tell me what you need. Like I said, I know people."

"I need to go now Salvatore."

Sal went pale and the sweat reappeared on his forehead. He looked hard at Martin and ejected an impressive wad of spit from between his tongue and front teeth. It landed six inches in front of Martin's shoe. God damn, Becker thought. I wish I could do that.

Ten seconds passed. Martin raised his pistol and shot Sal in the chest. The body fell straight backwards into the shadows, the shoulder knocking over a garbage can, adding its resounding clang to the echo of the gunshot. Before the sound faded, Martin stepped quickly forward and shot Sal again in the center of the forehead. He then patted the pockets and found one extra clip for the .45.

"Walk," Martin said. Becker pushed himself off the door and the two of them moved down the alley at a steady, unhurried pace.

It was less than ten minutes back to the hotel. When they opened the door to the room, Angie was sitting on the bed with one leg crossed over the other. He looked up in silent inquiry.

Becker gave a single nod, greeting or confirmation, Angie wasn't sure. Martin ignored the question and hung his overcoat on the back of a chair.

"Sal?" Angie said.

"Gone," Becker said.

"Like, left?"

"Like, dead."

"And Junior?" Angie said.

"Not expected to recover," Martin said from the bathroom, where he finished washing his hands and splashed water on his face.

"Damn sight better that way," Angie said. "He knows a lot of people."

Becker winced mentally at the phrase. "So he said. Was he really your uncle?"

"My father's second cousin, I think. Is that an uncle?"

"For lack of a better term," Becker said. "Gotta give him credit though. When my time comes, I hope I have the guts to go out like he did."

Martin came out of the bathroom wiping his face and the back of his neck with a towel. "When your time comes, you can hope there is someone like me to send you off," he said. He walked over to his overcoat and pulled a fifth of scotch from one of the pockets. "May I have my coffee now, please?"

"That Greek thinks we really like his coffee," Angie said, passing over a cup. "Six cups in twenty minutes."

Martin pulled up the room's only chair and sat down wearily. He lit a cigarette, added some whiskey to his coffee and took a sip. The bottle was passed around.

Becker resisted a powerful urge to ask for the whole story, but much of it was obvious. They had taken too long and Martin had come looking.

"You knew him?" he asked Martin.

"Years ago. Hired muscle. Didn't know or care what he was doing. Actually, he probably did as much work for the unions as against them."

"And Junior?" Angie asked.

"He was the other one?" Martin asked. Angie nodded. "Didn't know him."

Angie wanted to know how he had died, but didn't know how to ask. Becker beat him to it.

"How'd you handle him? We didn't hear anything."

"He got into the booth but he is too fat to close the door," Martin said. He left the story there, his eyes staring across the room at nothing as he exhaled a cloud of cigarette smoke. Becker imagined Martin's knife opening up the man's throat.

"Well I don't know about you but I came close to needing a change of underwear," Angie said to Becker.

"You were doing good. I was starting to believe you myself."

Becker was silent for a moment before turning to Martin.

"You took Sal's .45?"

"Why not?"

"I'm carrying a .45 and a box of rounds. Angie's got a .38., no extra ammo. How about-"

"Take it," Martin said. He tossed the automatic onto the bed near Becker. "Angie, give me the .38. I'll take care of it. But you'll need to pick up some more .45 rounds somewhere."

They drank and then drank some more. The tension flowed out of them in bursts of nervous banter and bad jokes, telling and retelling each part of their stories, what happened, what might have happened, what they should have done. Martin said little, staying with the same scotched-laced coffee he had started with and patiently listening as if enjoying a good story he might have heard before.

The scotch was now more than half gone. Becker reached for it to refill his cup but Martin picked it up first.

"One minute," he said. "Before you both pass out drunk. You grow weary of New York?"

"I was freezing my ass off, but it turned real hot suddenly," Angie said.

"A scorcher," Becker said.

Martin nodded in agreement. "Tomorrow I get your papers. Tomorrow night, you ship out."

"With the volunteers or on our own?" Becker asked?

"I know a ship."

Late afternoon of the next day they stood on a pier by the boarding ladder of a cargo ship, the *Russell Morgan*. The vessel was heavy laden with machine parts, bundles of brass rod and huge coils of copper tubing. The loading was finished, the pier quiet and the ship in repose, waiting to follow the tide out to sea. Martin gave Becker a folded piece of paper.

"You'll be met in Le Havre. People will get you to Paris and from there to the Spanish border. Go with the group and blend in, but this paper has two addresses that might be useful. One is your cousin in Troyes, the other is a friend of mine in Paris. You can count on your cousin to take you in. The other one is for trouble."

"Who is it?"

"An old comrade from the struggle. We owe each other. I'll let him know you're coming."

"My cousin," Becker said, searching half-remembered details of his family tree. "Where is Troyes?"

Martin stared at his nephew for an instant before he remembered that the boy had never been out of the country.

"A little upriver from Paris. You'll find it if you need it," Martin said. "Listen. There's something you need to know."

"Yeah?"

"Schechter."

"What about him?" Becker asked.

"You know what he does for a living?"

"I never thought I should ask. I know he just booked fights on the side, like some kind of hobby."

"You know why they call him Sappy?" asked Martin.

"I know he doesn't like it," Becker said.

"His specialty is to tie a man to a chair and beat him to death with a leather sack full of lead shot."

"For who?" Angie asked.

"There is a group in Brownsville. They do jobs for the Syndicate."

"I know the guys you mean," Angie said.

"I thought you should know," Martin said.

No one spoke for a time. The sky was grey and a light, misty rain brought the taste and smell of salt water. The clouds had brought an early dusk and most of the light came from the bridge of the ship and spotlights on the superstructure. A man appeared at the ship's rail and crooked his arm once, signaling for them to board.

"Martin-," began Becker.

"No goodbyes," Martin said, avoiding his eyes.

"I'm sorry you're left with this mess."

"You worry too much."

"Ain't that the truth," Angie said.

"Anyway." Becker held open his arms and Martin hugged him fiercely, kissing both cheeks and whispering in his ear.

"Stay alive, boy. But if you are going to die, die for a reason."

He embraced Angie in the same manner, thumping him between the shoulder blades with his massive palm.

The two young men started up the steep stairs of the boarding ladder. When they were halfway up, Martin spoke in an even tone that carried clearly through the mist.

"I'll check on your people."

They each waved once in response and continued their climb. Martin watched until they reached the ship's rail and descended out of sight to the deck. He stood there for a moment, taking in the scent of the ocean, the muffled sounds from inside the ship and the feel of the light rain on his face. He pulled a pack of cigarettes from inside his coat and lit one, looking up and down the pier for anyone who might be watching as he slowly exhaled the first fresh puff of smoke. When he realized he was totally alone, he muttered a curse under his breath, pulled up his collar, thrust both hands into his coat pockets and walked into the shadows.

CHAPTER 8

Becker and Angie fell asleep soon after the ship put to sea that night and slept until the following midday. They were lodged in a room with eight bunk beds but only two other occupants. One was a meticulously well-groomed negro from Chicago who introduced himself as Elsaw Brown. He had gradually worked his way east, looking for restaurant or hotel work until he fell in with some labor protestors who had persuaded him to join the cause. He spent most of his time reading the Bible or old copies of *The Daily Worker* and writing letters to his wife and son. He hadn't seen them for over a year.

The other roommate was a tall, sandy-haired farm boy from Wisconsin named Walter Lowry. He stood the first time they met, giving a firm handshake and a grimace for a smile, but their enduring memory was of him lying in his bunk, staring into space, tortured by homesickness and painful memories.

He had lost his father two years earlier when a tractor overturned. The family lost the farm soon after. His mother and younger sister went to live with an aunt while Walter hit the road in search of work. All he knew was farm work, but employers were usually impressed by his strong back and humble nature, both of which they exploited to the limit.

As Becker had expected, Angie soon got a crap game running with members of the crew. The captain made a token effort to put a stop to it but the crew protested, insisting that it was a harmless letting off of steam. Contrary to any known interpretation of the laws of probability, each believed himself either currently ahead of the game or breaking even and on the verge of a sudden winning streak. A firm believer in the adage that you could shear a sheep many times but butcher it only once, Angie made sure that the losers never lost too much, the winners played down their good fortune and everyone left the game looking forward to the next one. Such was the subtlety of Angie's genius. The captain quickly relented and even dropped in to roll the bones one night as a gesture of fellowship. His first few passes even produced a small handful of cash.

"Angie, how did you handle that?" Becker asked. "The captain looks like the ultimate hard case to me. I haven't seen him smile once since we got on this tub."

"Captain Polaski? He's not so bad," Angie said. "Plus he's in for forty percent."

"Forty?" Becker shook his head like he'd been tagged. "You must really like this guy."

"Matt. Seriously. I'm just killing time here. Not to mention, it's his boat. And I don't swim so good."

So Angie kept busy, but Becker was feeling slow, overfed and slightly claustrophobic. He found an isolated corner of the deck where he could shadow box, jump rope and do calisthenics for an hour every morning and evening, a practice considered by the crew to be anything from eccentric to slightly mad in the bitter cold and damp of the North Atlantic in mid-winter. After the first day, Brown asked if he could join in.

"I think we might have some hard marching ahead of us," he said.

Becker welcomed the company and Brown rarely slowed him down. He was an inch or two shorter than Becker and not as broad across the collarbone, but he was thick through the shoulders and his arms were corded with muscle, as if he had spent years swinging a hammer or pickaxe. Short on endurance, he needed frequent pauses at first to catch his breath, but he never quit or lost heart. They even tried a little open handed sparring which somehow turned into boxing lessons for Brown. Though he'd never been coached, he was light on his feet, had quick reflexes, and never had to be told anything twice. He picked up some basics but there was little they could do without gloves. Becker wondered if he could take a punch. One day, he found out by accidentally connecting with an open palm to Brown's chin. It rocked him back against a crate and he came away shaking his head and fighting to focus his eyes, but his guard was still up.

"Sorry, Elsaw. You OK?" Becker said.

"Just rang the bell a little. Don't you worry, Mr. Matt. I been hit plenty in my time. I'm still standing."

In spite of their attempts to keep busy, Becker and Angie always made sure at least one of them was keeping a close eye on their baggage, which had been reduced to the two alpine rucksacks containing all their remaining cash, the two .45s and the extra ammo. They knew the close quarters of the ship could lead to curiosity they couldn't afford.

One night, Becker lay on his bunk with his head on one rucksack and the other under his knees, trying to compose a letter to Sandy. It had stalled when he realized that it was unsafe to say where he'd been, where he was or where he was going. Lowry was snoring softly, occasionally mumbling in his sleep. Brown was on his own bunk, trying to concentrate on his reading.

"Writing to your girl?" he asked.

"Trying. Words don't seem to come."

"I've got the opposite problem. Too much carrying on about nothing," Brown said.

"I'm sure she doesn't mind."

"Guess not, but my missus was never much of a reader. That's why I always print my letters. Even so, I think she sometimes gets one of her friends to read them, so I got to be real careful what I say."

Becker wanted to ask if he'd ever received a letter from her, but thought better of it.

"You worried about where we're going?" Brown asked.

" 'Course."

"Scared?"

"Shitless," Becker said. Brown's face darkened for an instant and Becker realized he'd never heard the other man curse. Did I just offend him? he wondered. He considered an apology, but the moment passed.

"You done any soldiering?" Brown asked.

"No. You?"

"Don't know one end of a gun from the other. How about you?"

"Angie and me, we've done a fair amount of hunting since we were kids."

"Where was that?"

"Pennsylvania, New Jersey. Got up to New York State a couple times."

"Deer?" Brown asked.

"When we could get it. Probably more woodchuck though."

"Don't know how I'm gonna feel about shooting at a man," Brown said.

Images flashed through Becker's head. He squeezed his eyes shut and held his temples.

"Mr. Matt?" Brown sounded worried.

"Just Matt, OK? We're all comrades here, right?" It was the first time Becker had used the term and he felt like a pompous fool.

"Right. Sorry Matt."

"Me too, Elsaw. It's that raisin jack we were drinking. Gave me the damn-darndest headache."

Brown smiled at Becker. "Matt, you don't have to worry about cursing around me. I ain't no momma's boy. My wife just don't like it so I'm trying to stay out of the habit. And I try not to go taking the Lord's name in vain, if I can avoid it."

Becker looked over at Brown and smiled back, laughing at himself and realizing how little he knew of the man.

"Anyway, I don't know how I'm gonna feel about it either. But I'm guessing it'll make a difference if the other guy is shooting at you."

"Suppose so," Brown said, nodding.

No one spoke for a time.

"Can I ask you something personal?" Brown said.

"You can ask," Becker answered.

"How do you feel about going into battle?"

Becker put down his pencil and stuffed his barely started letter between the pages of a book.

"Plenty of places I'd rather be, but I think we're doing the right thing."

Brown nodded. "I guess what I'm asking...Are you worried about being afraid?"

Becker finally saw where this was going and found himself irritated by the need to face his own feelings. What the hell do I know? he thought. And who am I to be giving advice? This guy has to be older than me by, what, ten years at least. Doesn't he know that it's better not to talk about some things?

Becker wanted to find a way out of this conversation in a big hurry but had nowhere to run. He had to say something, and try not to sound like Civil War general. Every answer running through his brain sounded like either false modesty or adolescent bravado.

He answered with a short laugh that was meant to be warm-hearted but came out sounding tinny.

"I've been afraid my whole life," he answered. "Ask Angie. He'll tell you. I'm a born worrier, a natural pessimist."

"I'm afraid, I mean, I don't want to let down my comrades," Brown said.

"I don't either, but what really worries me is getting my nuts blown off," Becker said.

Brown seemed to go pale. Damn, Becker thought. Now I've done it. I was just trying to lighten things up.

"Elsaw, listen. When they start shooting at us, I'll feel better knowing you're there. You, me, Angie and Sleeping Beauty over there will back each other up and there will be other good people backing us up. We'll be scared, but we won't be alone."

Brown sat on the edge of his bunk, elbows on his knees, fingers laced, looking at the floor as Becker talked.

"Sorry to be preachy," Becker said.

Brown looked up and managed a smile.

"No, you're right. Thanks, Matt. It's what I needed to hear. I just can't think of much else since we got on this boat. You know, idle hands."

"And it's not the best weather for shuffleboard."

Before the trip, Becker had imagined long hours walking the deck during the voyage, deep in contemplation, hands clasped behind his back like a character out of Conrad or London, but it hadn't turned out that way. He was surprised to find himself intimidated by the expanse of rolling waves. The ship seemed a fragile intruder in the hostile grey vastness and he felt that the sea might suddenly choose to swallow the tiny vessel out of sheer brute malice. He had no fear of water and was a strong swimmer but the combination of cold, wind and infinite power awed him. He couldn't escape the thought that they floated above millennia of sunken ships and lost souls. Every time he stepped on deck, he felt like a schoolboy trying to avoid the biggest bully in the playground.

As the ship waited to enter port, Angie and Becker leaned on the ship's rail and looked at France for the first time.

"What are you thinking?" Angie asked.

"I'm thinking about how much I like dry land."

"Don't like boats?"

"Nothing against boats. It's the ocean that scares hell out of me," Becker said.

"Well, it was a good trip for me. I'm up a couple hundred."

"It's good to have a hobby."

"What've you been doing?" Angie asked.

"Working on my Spanish, getting a little exercise." Becker paused for effect. "And watching the bags."

Angie took the hint. "Oh yeah, here's your cut." He handed Becker a roll of bills. "Sorry you got stuck with that so much."

"It's OK. Like I said, it gave me a chance to study."

"Spanish? Don't worry about it. I heard it before. It's just Italian with the words messed up a little."

Becker's face twisted as he looked sideways at Angie.

"You don't think so?" Angie asked.

"Ange, if you think you can get by, I'm the last person to bet against you," Becker said.

He'll probably do better that I will, he thought. Becker, having grown up with three languages, often found himself speaking slowly and choosing words with great care. Angie, effortlessly made people want to understand him, and though he often carried on in rambling, convoluted narratives, they usually resolved themselves to listeners with sudden luminous clarity and plenty of humor. He couldn't tell a standard joke, often losing the sequence of the setup well before the punch line, but he had no trouble making people laugh with funny stories seasoned by sudden cadenzas of Sicilian dialect, bizarre street metaphors and malapropisms.

They were joined at the rail by Brown and Lowry.

"So what happens when we get into port?" asked Lowry, fighting back a yawn.

"We get a train to Paris and meet up with the other volunteers," Becker said.

"You talk this lingo?" Lowry said.

"I can get us on a train," Becker said, and left it at that.

When the *Russell Morgan* finally docked in Le Havre it was mid-morning. They bid their good-byes to the captain and crew, Angie the recipient of many hugs, back slaps and punches to the shoulder. Becker marveled at how he could take so much cash off them and leave goodwill behind.

"Simple," he said. "Everyone thinks they're half an inch from the big payoff. They'll try even harder on the return trip."

Becker was even more surprised to find himself, Brown and Lowry similarly embraced by some crew members.

"Kill some of those Fascist bastards for me," said one of the older hands. "I wish I was going with you."

"The first one's for you," Becker answered. The man slapped him on the shoulder and walked away, his eyes filling with tears. Wonder what his story is? Becker thought.

The passage through customs and immigration was uneventful. Most of the staff was busy with an enraged businessman who was trying to get his merchandise into the country. He must have been a man of some influence judging by the efforts of the assembled bureaucrats to accommodate him. The result was that the Americans were waved through with cursory glances at their documents, the two forged passports attracting no notice. Perfect, as Martin had predicted.

They emerged from the building prepared to search for a taxi but instead saw a lean, prematurely gray man in dark blue trousers, woolen jacket and cap leaning on the hood of a parked car, contemplating the butt of a Gitane. Becker got his first scent of the rich, spicy aroma of a French cigarette.

The man looked directly at Becker, smiled and made a barely perceptible gesture of beckoning with the hand holding the cigarette. Becker walked toward him.

"Mathieu?" the man asked.

"Just Matt. And you are?" Becker answered using the formal pronoun – verb combination. The man seemed mildly amused.

"Albert." He put the cigarette in the corner of his mouth and extended his hand. "Your uncle sent me."

"I see," said Becker, who in reality did not see at all. How had he known the time and place? Becker shook his hand anyway, noticing that the index and second fingers were nicotine yellow and the cuticles had the indelible dark stains of someone who spends their life working on engines.

"How did you know us?" Becker asked.

Albert shrugged and puffed out his cheeks.

"I got a cable. From Martin. He said Americans. A tall one and a short one. Tough guys." Albert used the word *costauds*, a term his mother despised, thinking it implied that someone was too simple-minded for anything but physical labor. He wasn't sure he appreciated the description.

"I look so American?" Becker asked.

"You?" Albert looked him up and down. "Frankly, you look like a *boche* school teacher. Your friend? Italian, one hundred percent. But the others? Yankees, no doubt."

Becker looked over at Brown, Lowry and some other volunteers who had come out of immigration. He had to agree with the assessment.

"Your companions, they speak French?" Albert asked.

"Not a word, as far as I know."

"Too bad. OK, we take two cabs. You in one, me in the other. But let's hurry. There's a train to Paris in twenty minutes."

Becker explained to the others and the four of them quickly divided their packs and suitcases, Albert helping the drivers strap some of the luggage to the roof racks of the taxis. Angie and Albert took the first cab, Becker, Brown and Lowry followed in the other.

The two cars got separated in traffic and the first pulled in front of the station perhaps thirty seconds before the second. As Becker's cab arrived, he saw Albert halfway out of the passenger side front door, one hand holding his midsection and the other wiping tears from his eyes. The driver stood next to the car, trying to reach for the suitcases on the roof rack, but making no progress as he stopped intermittently to put both hands on his knees and draw in deep breaths between hoarse, hacking coughs and wheezing bursts of laughter.

Angie stepped out on the curb straight-faced and businesslike, straightening his collar and lapels, first ignoring the hilarity around him, then wiggling one finger in his ear at the sound of Albert's comical, braying laugh. He reached for the roof of the cab, loosened the straps on the luggage and took a suitcase in each hand, effortlessly swinging them down to the curb. He then reached for his wallet and made a face.

"I got no French money," he said, walking back to where Becker was standing.

"Neither do I. Angie, what's with them? They're gonna bust their guts." Albert and the driver were now trying to hold each other up, each with a hand on the other's shoulder.

"They were teaching me some French. I think I'm picking it up. I taught them some Italian too," he said as if nothing were amiss.

Albert showed them a place at the station where they could change their dollars into francs. There was a large sign over the teller window that said *Change.*

"Who'd have guessed?" Angie said.

They changed a small amount of their winnings from the trip into francs. Most of what they had taken off the gangsters was still hidden in different locations, trouser waistbands, jacket linings and false double layers of canvas sewn into their rucksacks.

The group bought second class tickets and ended up in two separate compartments, Brown and Becker in one, Albert, Angie and Lowry in another. Brown and Becker took the window seats in the otherwise empty compartment but they were soon joined by a middle-aged couple and two small boys. Becker guessed the boys to be about eight and ten years old. They sat next to Becker and the parents next to Brown.

Brown was clearly uncomfortable about something. He had trouble making eye contact with Becker. He kept passing the back of his hand across his lips and then looking at his knees, sitting at attention, as if such a thing were possible.

"Elsaw, you OK?"

Brown tried to smile but it looked more like a death's head grin.

"Never spent so much time around white folks and them paying me no mind. Feel like there gotta be a storm coming."

Becker considered this for a moment and tried to think of something to say that wouldn't make things worse.

"Elsaw, I never had a negro friend. I hope I didn't-"

"It's not you, Mr. Matt."

"Elsaw, it's just Matt."

Brown nodded, then nodded again more emphatically. Finally he looked up at Becker and gave a half-smile. It was self-conscious, but a real smile nonetheless.

The woman had pulled some knitting from a bag and was calmly passing the time. The man leaned forward in his seat and looked first at Brown, then Becker. He composed himself, took a deep breath and spoke in overly-enunciated, schoolroom English.

"Where is your country?" he asked.

"Just go down to the beach, turn left and keep going," Becker answered. Brown's face started to turn purple.

"Eh?"

"We're Americans," Becker said, changing to French.

"Oh, but you speak French very well!"

Yup, Becker thought. One sentence so far. A regular Victor Hugo. Well, maybe this isn't the best time to practice being a smartass.

"You're very kind. I studied in school," Becker said.

"My boy studies in school, but I think he doesn't get it," the man said.

The boy looked up from his book with a pained *Here we go again* expression.

"It takes time, right?" Becker said to both father and son.

"I go to zee bo-agh-de. I wrrrite weez zee shall-ke. C'est tres utile n'est-ce pas?" said the older boy. It's very useful, isn't it?

"But I understood you just fine," Becker said.

The boy shook his head and went back to his reading.

"I saw some Americans once," the man said, like one bird watcher to another.

"Where was that?" Becker asked.

"Belleau Wood. You know, the war."

"I know the name," Becker said, waiting for him to continue at his own pace.

"Feels like not so long ago. We'd been in the trenches for years. Dead and half dead. The stink. *Les poilus.* You understand, *poilus*?"

"The hairy ones. The foot soldiers."

"That's it." The man looked quizzically at Becker. "You learned French in school, eh?"

"The Jesuits. Very strict." Becker's parents had little patience with religion in any form, but there had been few high schools to choose from and his mother insisted that a Jesuit education was the best available and she would settle for nothing less.

"Ah, that explains it."

Brown had been watching the exchange with is mouth hanging half open.

"Matt...Jesus Lord. You really can do it."

"Elsaw, relax. It ain't like I pulled a rabbit out of a hat. But don't go spreading it around, OK? Seriously?"

Brown took his meaning in an instant and shook his head in earnest. Becker turned back to the man.

"And Belleau Wood? If it doesn't trouble you..."

"Oh, yeah. The Americans." He smiled sadly and touched his forehead, scratching his hairline absentmindedly. "Like I said, we were four years in the mud, us and the *boche*. And here come these boys. Clean! No beards, no lice," he laughed. "Someone said they weren't ordinary soldiers. 'Marines' someone said. What does that mean?" he asked.

Becker considered the question and wasn't sure he had a good answer.

"They're naval soldiers."

"Like sailors?"

"In the old days, they would shoot rifles from...". Becker searched his memory for the word "rigging" but came up blank. "From up among the sails."

"Ah, so that's it."

"What?" Becker asked.

"These boys could really shoot." He paused for a moment and hung his head. "But it wasn't enough. They went into it like it was a football match. They died. Hundreds I think. The *boche* slaughtered them in the wheat fields. The machine gun fire, you know." He shrugged.

The man used the feminine noun *mitraille* for machine gun. How did the person who named such a lethal, merciless contraption determine that it should be feminine? Becker wondered.

"What's he saying?" Brown asked.

"He was in the Great War. Saw his first Americans there. I think he felt sorry for them."

"Don't get me wrong," the man said. "They learned fast and they kept coming. Hundreds, thousands every day. They taught the *boche* a lesson."

The wife and sons were rapt, as if hearing the story for the first time.

"My husband never talks about the war," the wife said.

"Thank God he came home OK," Becker said.

"Hah!" He pulled up a pant leg to show part of a prosthetic. "They got my foot, but it was a fair price. I'm not complaining."

"Where was that?"

"Amiens. A couple months later, I think. Near the end." Becker tried to assume an expression of what he hoped was due respect. In reality, he was trying not to think. The man saw his face and slapped his shoulder as if he'd told a bad joke.

"The bastards! If I'd known, I'd have gladly paid up sooner and come home!"

The wife spoke to Brown and Becker without looking up from her knitting.

"And you, Messieurs, you are going to the war?"

"Sightseeing," Becker said. "And I have relatives in Troyes."

"Oh, not so far then. And your comrade?"

Becker was caught off guard for an instant before he remembered the more ambiguous nature of the term 'comrade' in French, not so blatantly political.

"Oh, leave them alone woman! You know they are not free to speak as they wish," said the husband. It occurred to Becker that the French had a history of political intrigue far longer than America's. It was in their blood.

Becker turned to Brown.

"It's just small talk, but the cat is obviously out of the bag and she wants to know what brings you here."

"I'm fighting for freedom," Brown said, without artifice or drama. Becker considered how to translate the response.

"Freedom, Madame. You know, for the blacks in my country...," Becker said.

"One hears stories," the wife answered. "In any case, we will pray to God to watch over you and your companions."

"You're very kind Madame."

"And one hears that there are Germans in this quarrel. If you encounter them, it will do no good to show mercy. Remember that. Promise me." The woman looked up, her expression deadly serious.

"My wife was in Belgium in 1914," the husband said, as if that explained everything.

"I give you my word Madame," Becker said, not exactly sure of what he was promising.

Becker attempted to relate the basics of the exchange to Brown.

"What happened in Belgium?" he asked.

"I don't know. I'd just been born, but I guess I should find out."

"There are Germans in this?"

"You think the other side doesn't have their own volunteers?"

The husband reached into a cloth shopping bag and began taking out apples and sausages which he sliced which a pocket knife. He passed pieces to his sons and offered some to his wife who shook her head and continued knitting. He held out some pieces to Brown and Becker with a welcoming smile.

"I regret, we brought nothing to share," Becker said.

"Of course not. You just disembarked! But take it, it's no big thing. We're all together here."

Brown got Becker's attention with a gentle elbow to the ribs.

"Do you think it's OK to take their food?" he asked.

"Probably a bad idea to turn it down," Becker said. He and Brown both took pieces of food in their turn as it was passed around the compartment.

"My name is Matt MacCready. My friend is Elsaw Brown. We thank you for your kindness."

"I am Boucher. Etienne Boucher, and my wife Geneviève. My boys, Georges, he is twelve. And the younger is Gaspard. He is ten."

"A pleasure," Becker said. He had thought the boys younger and was glad he hadn't been asked to guess their ages. Now, if the father would just forgo that little game.

"You said 'Matt'?" the wife asked.

"Yes Madame. It is a nickname for Matthew."

"Not Mathieu?"

More trouble to deny the obvious or simply admit to smaller lies? Becker thought. I guess I can give up a few pawns.

"In fact, Madame, you are right. My given name was originally Mathieu. My parents were French."

"Of what region?" She showed polite interest, but Becker knew it was all going into the file.

"Burgundy Madame. They are both from Dijon." In fact, both parents were from Alsace, and grew up speaking both French and German. His mother's family also spoke Yiddish at home.

"Ah, that explains it. I would not have said your accent is typically Parisian. And what sent them off to them to America?"

The father had been growing increasingly restive during this exchange. He finally reached his limit.

"Geneviève, dear one. So many questions. This is their first day in France, and we are not the prefecture of police."

Becker admired the man's equanimity. In his own family, a verbal brawl would have broken out long ago. In this case, the wife simply took a standing eight-count and Becker took the chance to gracefully bow out of the interview.

"*Hélas,* Madame. They have never told me the precise reasons for their departure, but I know that it was necessity and not choice. I believe that the circumstances are painful for them to recall."

This produced an understanding nod from the wife, but Becker had his guard up, and he knew she knew it.

Most of the ride to Paris was spent in a companionable silence. They exchanged pleasantries and Becker made vacuous comments about the beauty of the countryside. The husband insisted that Becker address him as *tu* rather than *vous* in spite of their age difference, but Becker stayed formal with the wife, which seemed to please her.

About halfway through the trip, the younger of the boys patted Becker on the shoulder and asked "Are you a cowboy?"

"No, sorry. I'm not."

"But you are American?"

"Yes."

The boy seemed to think he'd gotten a raw deal.

"Sometimes I ride horses, but we don't have many cattle where I come from," Becker said.

"Do you shoot a gun?" the boy asked.

The husband seemed to find the exchange amusing, but Becker was startled when he noticed the wife directing a penetrating stare at him over her knitting. He recovered by focusing on the boy.

"My friend and I have hunted a lot of deer since childhood."

"No red Indians?"

"*Hélas,* not a one. Sorry." Becker had always hoped he'd have a chance to use the word "Alas" in English, but the opportunity had never presented itself. He felt a mild sense of satisfaction doing it in French, twice in one day.

"Please excuse him. It's the films, you know," the mother said.

"Deer, eh?" the father said with some interest.

"When we could. A lot of ..." Becker searched his mind for the word for woodchuck and came up blank. "...smaller things."

A memory came to him of his father patiently coaching him through a lesson in long distance marksmanship which had resulted in Becker hitting a woodchuck at nearly three hundred yards.

"You missed him by a mile," his father had said.

"I don't think so, Papa."

"No, he just took off. You scared him."

"Let's go see," Becker said. "Start counting from here."

They had paced off the distance in long, deliberate steps up and down rolling hills and across a small stream until they found the shattered carcass of the woodchuck behind the rotting log it had been sitting on. Its head and upper torso were nearly severed from its lower body.

"You really creamed him," his father said, shaking his head in disbelief.

"Not much left," Becker said.

"Too much gun," his father said with a glance at the Springfield, "but it's all we've got."

Becker wondered about his father, mother and sisters and how they were coping with his sudden disappearance. In truth, he felt a guilty sense of relief to be away from the agonizing spectacle of his father's suffering. And he knew that whatever his mother felt about her son, he was a constant reminder of the father's vigorous youth and his brother's sudden death. Better for him to be away.

"You and your comrade." That word again snapped Becker back to the present. "You've been friends a long time?" the husband asked.

"We just met on the ship," Becker said.

"And what did he do over there?" The man seemed to regret that the language barrier had caused him to neglect one of his guests.

Becker explained the question to Brown, deciding it was best to let him tell his own story.

"Did whatever I could do. Moved around a lot. Hotel and restaurant work mostly, when I could find it."

Becker passed on his response. The husband and wife waited patiently for him to continue, but Brown stared at the floor.

"It's been difficult since '29," Becker said.

"Everywhere," the mother agreed.

"And he hasn't seen his family for a long time."

The dangerous places an innocent question can lead, Becker thought. Polite chit-chat suddenly twists a knife in someone's gut. But the adults were saved by the younger boy, Gaspard.

"Are you staying at our place?"

Becker played for time by smiling sweetly at the boy as he repeated the phrase in his head in search of the correct nuance. He had used the expression *chez nous,* which Becker had heard used to mean anything from, "our house" to "our country" to "among us" and several other meanings that could not be determined out of context.

The parents looked at Becker, brows raised in anticipation, as if the question were clear as mud. Becker looked back like a grinning idiot.

"Pardon?" was the best he could manage.

The mother, who Becker already sensed was busy peeking in the windows of his brain, sensed his confusion and spoke first.

"We invite you and your friend to eat dinner and stay at our house for as long as you like," she said.

He listened in shock. His own parents had never invited anyone but a blood relative to sleep in their home, and damned few of those.

"What's up?" Brown asked.

Becker told him and watched as his eyes open wide with a mixture of fear and embarrassment. Becker wanted to tell him to get a grip on himself, but this was already becoming a scene and he didn't want to make it worse.

"Madame, Monsieur, please excuse us. We're not accustomed to such kindness." Becker spoke slowly, trying not to trip over his own tongue.

"One doesn't do such a thing in America?" the father asked.

How would I know? Becker thought. People in his neighborhood had an inherent distrust of strangers which they passed on to their children. New faces were always noticed and carefully scrutinized. People who had moved in three years ago were still called newcomers. Unrecognized passersby were given a wide berth and woe betide the innocent fool who asked a question or directions to the nearest green grocer. They might find themselves walking up a dark, rat-infested alley with no exit.

The members of his own family were studiously polite to strangers, once they had been determined to pose no threat, but none had ever been invited into their home. Some monumental betrayal in his mother's past had made her suspicious of those around her. She had no close friends, only co-workers and passing acquaintances. She considered his father's garrulous good nature to be a fatal character flaw which would someday bring disaster down on their heads and she often chided him for exchanging minor confidences with friends or admonished him on the dangers of "getting too close". Jesus, Becker thought, how did they ever get together, much less have children?

His father wouldn't hear a word against her. "You didn't know her when she was young," he would say. "She was a great beauty, more than I deserved. She saved me, made each day a gift. But something went out of her when she had to leave her homeland. The anger...she never forgave. And when we lost your brother. She thought there was something more she should have done."

"I don't remember much," Becker said. "Just being very hot and sick, but I remember her face looking down at me. Seems like she was there every minute."

"She was. But you were stronger, or luckier. Your brother – he had the sniffles before lunchtime. Dead the next morning."

The images and voices raced through Becker's head.

"So sad your face!" Boucher said. "Homesick already?" Becker was jerked back to the present, realizing he hadn't responded to the woman's invitation.

"Forgive me Madame, Monsieur. This is our first trip abroad. We've had little experience with such kindness but we are touched, truly." Becker watched their faces, trying to judge his next move. Parry, feint or disengage? "We are obliged to meet with other volunteers in Paris, but perhaps we could join you tonight, at least?"

"For as long as you wish," Madame Boucher said. "Who knows when you can get a good meal again?"

"*Bon*," Boucher said. "We'll see then, when we arrive in Paris and you meet your other comrades."

Becker explained the situation to Brown, who seemed relieved that an avenue of escape had appeared on the horizon. Previous commitment, Praise the Lord, he thought. One night, I can do one night. Dear God, please don't let me embarrass myself – or Mr. Matt – or offend these good people.

CHAPTER 9

The train pulled into the immense Gare du Nord station in the early afternoon and its passengers soon filled the platform. Becker spoke hurriedly to Boucher.

"I just need a brief moment. I must talk to the boss about the next step."

"Take your time. The boys need a visit to the *pissoir*. Me too, for that matter. We'll wait for you over there, by the tobacco stand. You see?"

Becker followed Boucher's pointing finger across the milling crowds. "Right. Just a few minutes, I promise. Elsaw, can you stay with these folks? I'm going to find out what's up. I'll be right back"

Brown already had his own suitcase in one hand and the Boucher's two suitcases in the other. The sinews in his forearms looked like bridging cable. His face was calm.

"I'll be here," he said. "No place else to go."

Becker scanned the crowd but couldn't see Albert, which surprised him because he stood almost a full head taller than most of the people there. By a stroke of luck he saw Angie and Lowry standing stock-still in the middle of a crowd, their faces upturned and staring wide-eyed at the interior of the cavernous building. They didn't notice Becker's approach.

"Angie, wake up," Becker said with a raised hand of greeting to Lowry.

"Hey, Matt. Look at the size of this place." Angie came out of his reverie. "How was the ride?"

"Like Thanksgiving at my house."

"Oh, sorry." He made a sour face.

"Where's Albert?"

"Out front checking on a ride. He said to come out when we were all here."

"Give me a minute," Becker said. He saw Brown and the Boucher family standing in front of the small tobacco and newspaper stand as promised. He did his best to assume an expression of disappointed resignation and walked toward them.

"Madame and Monsieur Boucher," Becker said with all the sincerity and formality he could muster, placing his hand on his heart. "It's a great disappointment to me after all your kindness, but I regret that we are obliged by – he had puzzled over his next choice of words – 'le chef' to accompany our group. We have no choice."

"Don't worry yourself, my son. It's duty, *n'est-ce pas*?" He held Becker's upper arm tightly, his eyes moist.

"It's bad luck, but yes. Duty." I haven't lied. Why do I feel so guilty? Becker thought.

"No misfortune in it Mathieu. One goes where the fight is," said Boucher.

"And may God watch over you and Monsieur Brown," said Madame Boucher. "You will both be in my prayers. You will translate to him for me?"

"Of course, Madame."

Boucher used his grip on Becker's arm to pull him down and whisper in his ear. "She means well, my boy. But in fact, God won't be there. You watch out for your own ass."

Both parents embraced Brown and Becker with kisses on both

cheeks, Brown fumbling the ritual somewhat before recovering. He did better with the sons, dropping to one knee to give them adult handshakes. Becker did the same.

They ran to one of the exits where Lowry was waving his tree-trunk arm at them and Angie was watching the crowd for anyone who might try for their bags. The four of them collected their luggage and exited to the street. The sight before them stopped them in their tracks.

Though hardly the most fashionable *quartier* of Paris, the scene before them was unquestionably foreign and what it lacked in elegance it made up for with a dizzying kaleidoscope of exotica. Transfixed in the middle of the sidewalk, they tried to take in the cacophony of car, truck and bus horns, the siren smells of baked goods, cheeses and cured meats and the haughty, insouciant sexuality of passing women.

After his brain registered the sound of a muttered curse, Becker finally snapped the others out of the trance.

"Boys, we're blocking traffic here," he said, spreading his arms wide and pushing them back against the wall of the station and out of the flow of pedestrian traffic. Once there, they all dropped their bags and enjoyed the show. Becker fell in beside Angie.

"So what do you think?"

"Stinks," Angie said.

He had a point. The intoxicating smells of food and scented women were nearly smothered by the stench of horse shit, human and animal urine, sweat and engine exhaust.

"I swear to God, I just saw an old lady take a piss in the gutter, right behind a parked car."

"I believe you," Becker said, downcast.

"Hey, don't take it personal," Angie said, smiling and sticking an elbow in his ribs. "If I took you to Sicily, *minchia*...God only knows what we'd see." Angie's eyes went back to the street. "Albert," he said, quietly, so only Becker could hear.

Becker turned his head, casually following Angie's glance. He saw Albert standing on the opposite sidewalk, partially concealed behind a black sedan. He was leaning forward to speak to a short, goateed man in a long overcoat and bowler. The man rarely looked at Albert as they conversed, instead letting his eyes roam the traffic and passing crowds. After a final word, which Albert had to lean closer and turn his head to hear, the man quickly opened the door and jumped into the back of the sedan.

Albert came around the rear of the car to the curb, where he lit a cigarette and calmly walked into the rushing traffic as if strolling down the aisle of a church. Becker's heart pounded as the man ignored blaring horns, swerving cars, screaming brakes and cursing drivers to make his way across the street to where they were standing.

"You always cross the street like that?" Becker asked.

"Like what?"

"Without looking."

Albert made a dismissive gesture with a wave of his cigarette. "You worry too much."

"I hear that a lot lately."

"Do you see that autobus over there?" Albert pointed down the sidewalk to where a small bus waited with its motor idling. It was about half full of men who were clearly volunteers, its roof rack holding a cargo of identical cardboard suitcases. "Your friends will go there, with the others. They will be taken to hotels and cared for before they go south. You and Angelo will come with me."

Albert looked at Becker's face and smiled.

"Please, I need you to explain to them for me. I speak little English."

"Angie and me?" Becker asked, his voice flat. Something about this he didn't like.

"Mathieu, we are not corsairs. This is not a kidnapping." He waited as Becker examined his face and looked in his eyes. He maintained his gentle smile.

After perhaps sixty seconds, Becker turned and explained the situation to the others.

"We'll meet up again in Albacete. Maybe before. Don't worry," Becker said.

"No crap games till I get there," Angie said.

"You guys take care of each other," Brown said.

"I'll remember what you told me, Angie. We'll be waiting for you," Lowry said.

Brown and Lowry hurried down the sidewalk to the bus. They spoke a couple words to the driver and someone got out to help them secure their suitcases to the roof. After stepping up into the bus, Becker could see that they were greeted warmly by the other passengers with handshakes and slaps on the back. If we meet again, Becker thought, we shall smile. If not, this parting was well made. Who said that? Brutus. Conspiracy. Betrayal. He turned to look back at Albert who was still waiting patiently.

Something else Brutus said. "Hide it in smiles and affability..." Becker thought.

He and Angie walked back to where Albert was leaning against a lamppost, watching the spectacle of the city streets, much as they had. He had just lit a fresh cigarette.

"Your uncle tells me, how did he say it? Ah, he said you are one who can 'do what is necessary'. He also said you have certain other skills."

"I don't know what you mean," Becker said.

"You speak German?"

"Yes, not like a *boche* schoolteacher, but yes."

"Without accent?"

"It's not for me to say. I've never been out of the United States."

Albert considered the answer as he slowly released a cloud of smoke.

"Martin believes you may be useful for a certain type of work," Albert said.

"A certain type."

"There are many ways to fight a war."

Becker suddenly realized he was giving information but getting nothing in return.

"How did you know us in Le Havre?" Becker asked. Angie heard something in his friend's voice and reached into his pocket for his knife.

"I told you. Martin sent a cable."

"May I see it?"

"I burned it," Albert said.

"Forgive me, but I feel a need for caution." Becker glanced at Angie and made a barely perceptible motion with his head. Angie glided smoothly behind and slightly to the side of Albert, his switchblade now open and held at his side. He moved his rucksack from slung on one shoulder to squarely on his back. Becker picked up his own and put it on as he spoke. They were both ready to move if need be.

"You're leaving?"

"Would you describe Martin for me?" Becker said.

Albert didn't miss a beat. "He is tall, taller than me. Perhaps one hundred ninety centimeters."

"I don't know centimeters," Becker interrupted. "Show me."

Albert held his hand parallel to the ground three or four inches above Becker's head. Becker nodded. "Please continue," he said.

"His hair is quite short, going gray the last time I saw him. It goes back here, like me." He pointed to his own receding hair line.

"Scars?" Becker asked.

Albert puffed out his cheeks, just like his father and uncle. Becker's older sister used to do a dead-on impersonation of her father making that exact expression. Becker started to laugh at the thought but quickly stopped himself. Albert noticed, half closed one eye and cocked his head to one side as he continued.

"Too many." He paused in thought for a moment. "Many here," he said, running his index fingers over the knuckles and the backs of both hands. "A burn here," indicating the left side of his neck, "and many small holes here," moving his hand over the left side of his rib cage. "Shrapnel. Oh, and this eyebrow has a space in the middle." He pointed to his left eye.

Except for the shrapnel scars which he had never seen, Becker would have given a similar accounting. But he wanted to know Albert better.

"Actually it's the other eyebrow."

Albert let out a single syllable of laughter. "Ah, you test me. No, professor, it is the left, because it was me who put in the stitches."

Becker ignored his answer. "And his wife?"

Albert shook his head. "Gone. Very tragic."

"The children?"

"There was only the one. She is with her mother." His voice had become as toneless as Becker's.

"Please forgive my rudeness. It is only caution you understand."

Albert said nothing. Becker reached into a pocket and retrieved the paper Martin had given him. He showed it to Albert.

"Do you know this man?" he asked.

"Well enough," he smiled. "It's me."

"But the name--"

"For now I am Albert. You'll permit me?" he asked, taking the paper from Becker's hands. He tilted his head back slightly and stretched out his arms to examine it more carefully.

"Such handwriting," he said, shaking his head. He tore the paper into small pieces, walked to the gutter and tossed it in, waiting until all the pieces had washed down the storm drain. "You have more things written down?" His tone was kind, not judgmental.

"Not now," Becker said.

"You remember the address in Troyes?"

Becker nodded.

"Recite it please."

Becker did so. He had read it many times on the voyage and knew it well.

"Bravo! From now on, writing is for schoolboys," he paused, "or *boche* schoolteachers. So, to business?"

"At your service," Becker said.

"And perhaps Monsieur Angie can join us?" Albert stressed the second syllable of Angie's name. Becker couldn't decide if it was insult or simply his accent, but it grated on his nerves. Angie paid it no mind.

"Angie, it's OK."

Angie moved to Becker's side, facing Albert with his usual curious half-smile.

"You're here for the Cause?" Albert said.

"Yes."

"And him?" he said, tilting his head toward Angie.

"Angie, he wants to know if you're here for the Cause," Becker said.

"I'm with him," Angie said to Albert.

Albert looked quizzically at Becker, missing the nuance of the phrase. Becker guessed that he had some English, but might never let on how much. Nonetheless, much could be told by watching the eyes.

"We're a team," translated Becker. "We have always backed each other up since childhood. We've been through a lot."

"And if you are killed?"

"I'm sure he would settle my accounts."

Albert looked Angie up and down. "He is of the underworld?" he asked, using the French term *milieu*.

"He can operate in both worlds. I can't," Becker said.

"Useful."

Becker heard some distant singing and turned to look down the street. The bus full of volunteers was pulling away into traffic, its occupants united in song if not key. It sounded familiar, but he couldn't place it and the melody was soon swallowed by the sound of traffic.

"There goes our ride," Angie said.

"So, Albert. The group has left and you've kept us here," Becker said.

"There are battles at the front. We need volunteers there. Those men go to Murcia to train. But there are other battles, few fighters, and no time to train. We need you here."

"For what?"

"Do you see the man in the car?"

Angie and Becker looked across the street at the silhouette of the man in the bowler seated in the back of the sedan. His hands rested, one on top of the other, on a cane or walking stick. The driver sat partially turned behind the wheel, watching them.

"He gives us the mission," Albert said.

"But what's the mission?" Becker said.

"Have patience. We don't talk here. We take a short ride."

Albert nodded at the driver of the sedan and held up his hands chest-high to show ten fingers. The car pulled into traffic and quickly disappeared. They then walked to the taxi stand and started to get into the first cab in line. Angie and Albert took the back, Becker walked around to the passenger side of the front seat but when he opened the door saw the seat piled high with newspapers and old food wrappers. The driver waved him off with a curse.

"In back! *Putain!*"

Becker decided to let it slide, pretty sure that the driver wasn't calling him a whore, just using an all-purpose expletive. He closed the door and got into the back, squeezing Angie between him and Albert. It was a tight fit with Becker and Angie holding their rucksacks on their laps. Albert gave directions and started to light another cigarette. Becker caught his eye.

"For the love of God," he said.

Albert looked him, then at the cigarette, finally sticking it behind one ear, all for nothing since the driver quickly lit one and filled the stale, humid, oxygen-starved air of the car's interior with smoke. Albert smiled to himself. Becker held his temples with thumb and forefinger.

It soon became clear that the cabbie was a dangerous fool. He treated the car as if he had some longstanding and impassioned grievance against its owner, accelerating toward stationary vehicles and slamming on the brakes at the last minute, taking corners on two wheels and using every opportunity to make the tires scream and leave streaks of scorched rubber on the road. He ran the engine to its redline in every gear and slammed the clutch violently when he shifted. He paid little attention to what was ahead of him, none at all to what was behind and maintained a scatological screed toward other motorists, pedestrians, cyclists and the world in general through clenched teeth and the blue-gray cloud of smoke from his cigarette. Something started to burn behind Becker's eyes. Angie sat stone-faced.

Albert sensed their discomfort and found it amusing for the first few blocks. Poor little Americans! he thought. First time in a real city. They'll learn the realities of life soon enough.

But Albert was a man who had long survived on his instincts. He soon became aware of something like a peculiar electrical charge radiating from Angie and Becker which he did not recognize as fear. He sensed the threat of violence and suddenly had a vivid recollection of himself crouching in the dark, a bayonet clenched in his fist and his heart pounding with the knowledge that there were enemy soldiers in the trench but he could not see them.

He was watching Becker closely but Angie moved first. In a motion too rapid to see, he had drawn his switchblade, snapped it open and pressed the flat of the blade under the driver's right ear.

"Tell him," Angie said.

"Doucement, Monsieur," Becker said. Gently sir.

"Eh? You filthy--"

Angie moved the scalpel-sharp blade a quarter inch, just enough to draw blood, but it was the tone in Becker's voice when he next spoke that sucked all the air from his lungs.

"And shut up."

The cab slowed to a more stately pace, the driver's eyes fixed on the road ahead, his mind not registering what he was seeing, petrified with the fear of turning his head. Becker thought he had best get control of the situation.

"Monsieur, the chestnut vendor. There, on the right," Becker said.

"Oui, Monsieur." The driver slowed to a crawl and eased the car around the vendor's cart.

"And watch your cigarette. You're going to burn your fingers."

"Oui, Monsieur." He stubbed out his cigarette in the overflowing ashtray as Angie took the blade from his neck, closed it and returned it to his pocket.

"We get out at the next corner," Albert said.

They all got out without paying. Albert and Angie waited on the curb as Becker walked around the car, handed his rucksack to Angie and approached the driver's window. He held out some folded bills made up of the fare and a generous tip.

"No Monsieur, it's not necessary," he said, waving a hand which already held a fresh cigarette.

"Go ahead. Take it," Becker said.

"No Monsieur, I couldn't."

"For the dry cleaning then."

The light went out in the driver's eyes. Did I use the wrong word? Becker thought.

"Eh?"

"There is just a bit of blood on your collar. Here," Becker said, indicating the place on his own collar and then pointing at the driver's.

The driver touched his neck and earlobe and then saw the blood on his hand. He had been too terrified to feel the breaking of his own skin. His face ashen, his lips a sickly purple, he reached out a trembling hand and took the cash from Becker, who then stepped back to join his companions on the sidewalk. The three of them smiled and waved goodbye in unison. The driver put the car in gear, popped the clutch, stalled, restarted and drove away.

Albert looked at Angie, then at Becker. His expression was unreadable.

"What is it?" Becker asked.

"Nothing. Do you mind if I smoke?"

Becker suddenly remembered one of the signs he had seen at the train station. *Défense de cracher.*

"Go ahead. But no spitting."

Albert snorted once. "It's this way," he said pointing toward a small side street. The three of them started off at a leisurely stroll, Becker and Angie trying to take in the sights of the nondescript, middle class neighborhood but finding little of interest.

"Reminds me of home a little," Angie said. "Just smells different."

"Not all bad though," Becker said. "I'm not sure I can walk past another bakery without getting something. I'm starving."

"Whatever you get, get me two."

"Albert, where are we?" Becker asked.

The Frenchman paused for a moment before answering, but decided it was better if young Mathieu started to learn his way around. "This is the 11th. We call it Bastille. You know 'The Bastille?'"

Does he think I'm an idiot? Becker thought. Well you might as well cut him some slack. I'm as much of a mystery to him as he is to me.

"Someone told me they took it down," Becker said.

"In fact, yes. They took it down," Albert said.

"But the neighborhood cleaned up real nice," Becker said.

Albert just shook his head.

After two blocks of watching their backs and making sure they were not followed they approached a small café or restaurant. Becker couldn't tell which. He could hear voices from inside and detect the faint odors of a kitchen and bar, but there was no sign above the door and there were curtains about head-high which blocked any view of the interior from the street.

Albert preceded them through the door, giving a pleasant "*Messieurs-Dames*" to a room almost devoid of patrons. It was now mid-afternoon and the lunch crowd had nearly all departed, the dinner customers still hours away. A grey-haired retiree sat at one of the smaller front tables reading some type of large, paperback technical manual and taking notes, oblivious to the rancorous verbal sparring of what had to be a married couple at the table on the opposite side of the door. The only visible employee was a heavyset, middle-aged man wearing a waist-high white apron behind the bar, wiping down the bottles on the shelf and carefully returning each to its assigned place.

"That's the owner. We're safe here," Albert said. "*Salut,* old friend," he said. The man had already identified him with a glance in the mirror. He raised his hand and continued his work.

"A red wine, *s'il vous plait,*" Albert said. "Anything for you two?"

Becker searched the walls for a chalkboard bill of fare or a menu on one of the tables.

"Breakfast was at dawn and we've had no lunch. Can we get some food?"

"Monsieur, there would not be anything left to eat?" Albert said.

The man looked doubtful. "A minute please." He walked into the kitchen and they heard the clanging of some pots and an ice box open and close. Then he stuck his head out the kitchen door.

"A little *choucroute* and some sausages. A little country bread."

Albert looked at Becker and Angie for a response. Becker nodded his head enthusiastically.

"What gives?" Angie said.

"We're getting some food. Sauerkraut, sausages and some bread," Becker said.

"If it's dead, I'll eat it."

Ten minutes later, the owner placed the steaming plates of food in front of them with more care and ceremony than the dishes called for, but this was France and this was food. He also lost his patience with the couple arguing in the front of the room.

"Monsieur, Madame, I beg of you. One cannot have peace? There are people here who are eating." Though his grammar was excessively formal to Becker's ears, the man's tone made short work of the dispute. The couple saw the simple logic of the statement and left, taking no offense.

The food was left over from lunch, the sauerkraut a bit salty from too long on a steam table, the sausages a little tough, and the small pieces of bread starting to go dry, but washed down with a couple bottles of Alsatian beer the food put a new luster on the day and swept away the stress of the cab ride.

The man from the sedan came in while they were eating, his driver following a few steps behind. The cane he carried compensated for a limp which originated in a misshapen left hip, whether injury or congenital deformity, Becker could not tell, but he could see the pain and effort on the man's face as he moved across the room. Reaching their table, he removed his hat and overcoat to reveal a well-tailored pin-stripe suit and a mostly bald head, the hair on the sides recently trimmed. He had round, black-framed spectacles and a thick, pure white goatee. He seated himself with some discomfort but still made an effort to put on a welcoming face for Albert and the younger men.

Becker saw no potential threat and focused on the driver. He was perhaps five-foot-ten with shoulders like a hod carrier. By his measured gait, placid demeanor, and instant evaluation of the room, its occupants and its exits, Becker knew him to be a professional.

"This is Jarek," said the older man. "He is my helper and protector. Some things I can no longer do alone."

Jarek gave Becker and Angie a cordial, even friendly smile. The old man continued speaking.

"Forgive me, but the rules say that I cannot tell you my name. So you must call me some theatrical nonsense. I am 'Alma'."

"I'm Matthew, or Mathieu, whatever you like. This is Angelo," Becker said.

"Pardon me, my friends, but I think that for this business too many names could be a bad thing," Albert said. "Whatever they are, we must try not to speak them too much."

"Especially mine! Hah!" said the old man, looking at Albert. " 'Alma'. Such nonsense." Albert only smiled wryly and puffed his cheeks in response.

Becker sensed the man was due some respect and began to make excuses for eating in front of him but Alma held up his hand and shook his head.

"Please Messieurs, continue. You've had a long journey. Jarek and I have already lunched."

Still, Becker and Angie hurried through their last bites of food and quickly wiped the plates with pieces of bread. The owner appeared, swept up the plates with one hand and passed a damp cloth over the table with the other. Becker considered it presumptuous to ask and made a silent prayer that coffee would be offered. Angie spoke up without hesitation.

"There wouldn't be any coffee, would there?" he said.

Albert smiled and made a sweeping gesture which encompassed their surroundings.

"After all, it is a café, is it not?"

Shortly thereafter, two *cafés crèmes* were placed in front of Becker and Angie. Alma drank tea, Albert stayed with the wine which he had not touched and Jarek drank bottled water.

Angie stared for a moment at the delicate little cup in front of him, one eyebrow arched, sniffing like a hound.

"This is coffee?" he asked.

"So they said," Becker said.

Angie raised the cup to his lips, half draining it with his first sip.

"Try it," he said.

Becker did. His first taste made him wonder how much else he had missed during his twenty-two years and if he would ever live long enough to catch up. Well, he thought, even if I never have another cup, I had this one. I can't imagine anything ever tasting better.

"You gentlemen speak English. Yes?" Alma said.

Becker looked at Albert for some hint as to how to respond. His eyelids closed slowly, once.

"Yes," Becker said.

"If it is agreeable to you, may we use that language? My French is awkward and I don't wish to be misunderstood. Forgive me, comrade," he said to Albert.

"I can follow," Albert said in accented but easily understandable English. "If I cannot, I will speak."

Jarek paid no attention. He had opened a paperback book and pretended to be thoroughly absorbed.

"What do you know of the progress of this war?" Alma said.

"We've had no news for some time," Becker said.

The old man let out a deep sigh. "We held Madrid, in spite of what you may have heard elsewhere, but both sides paid dearly. They try to advance, we hold them back. We try to advance, we are beaten back. A few meters of ground are gained and lost. Of course, there is much slaughter. But it is our good fortune that defense requires fewer resources than offense, for it is resources that are our biggest problem."

"The embargo succeeds?" Becker said. In the natural order of things, one interlocutor is likely to adapt his speech patterns to the other's. In this case, Becker followed the older man's lead. Alma seemed not to notice, but Angie picked up on it now that they were speaking English and bit his lip to avoid grinning outright.

Alma considered Becker's question.

"No trains of course. Many ships get through, some are sunk or diverted. Much of the equipment we get is out of date or unusable. Weapons with insufficient ammunition. Worse, weapons with the wrong ammunition." He snorted in disgust. "These people seem not to notice that a seven millimeter weapon will not take an eight millimeter – what is the word – projectile."

"Cartridge," Angie said, beginning to feel sympathy for the old man.

"Cartridge, yes. That is the word. We buy aeroplanes that we feel are suitable, but at some point before delivery, new motors are exchanged for much older ones. And what good is a plane without guns?" He pulled out a handkerchief and mopped his brow, though the room seemed cool enough to Becker. "It is a complicated business to acquire arms and we have few experts. Some of our 'experts' appear to have been working for the fascists or themselves. We are often swindled."

"And Stalin?"

"Ah," Alma said, pausing to compose himself. "Comrade Stalin I believe truly wishes to aid the Cause, but for his own reasons does not wish to be seen aiding us. His agenda is unclear to me. Hitler and Mussolini, on the other hand, openly support the Fascists."

"So what do you want from us?" Angie said in a totally unaffected Jersey accent. Alma squinted for a moment and Albert looked puzzled.

"Comment?" Albert said. What did you say?

"What do you want us to do?" Angie repeated slowly, as if to the hard of hearing, embarrassed and irritated that he had not been understood.

Alma smiled at him.

"Monsieur speaks what is on his mind. Quite direct. Of course, this is the American style. Very well." He stopped and brought the handkerchief to his mouth as he was seized with a violent fit of coughing. Jarek held his arm and placed a hand on his back until it passed.

"As I said, we are short on resources." He continued in a strained voice. "One vital resource we lack is intelligence. In too many cases, we must depend on the NKVD, and as I explained, Comrade Stalin has his own priorities. We need operatives."

"But surely the party--" Becker said.

"They mean well. We have many volunteers. Many marchers. I'm sure many would give their lives. Many will. But too many faces are known, where they live, where they work, their families. And these men are workers, not...not what we need."

Angie patted Becker on the arm and put his hand up to whisper in his ear.

"Am I getting this? Is he asking us in on some caper?" he said.

"Let's give it a minute," Becker said, under his breath. "I think he's getting to it."

Alma continued. "One of our senior men took a large amount of money to Belgium for the purpose of buying arms. Polish rifles. He met a contact of ours in Liège some weeks ago. All seemed to be going well. He left for Antwerp to arrange shipment and disappeared. The money also disappeared, of course. He has recently surfaced here in Paris. Why, we don't know, but it was a foolish course of action. He was seen and his identity confirmed."

"Maybe he's got a broad stashed here," Angie said. Alma's eyebrows nearly touched for an instant as he tried to catch the meaning, but he chose to continue.

"He now travels with protection. Two bodyguards, possibly three. We think they are German. Very competent, very professional. It would most certainly be impossible to confront him in the open."

Becker waited patiently, sitting back in his chair, on hand on each thigh, a look of polite attention on his face. Angie delicately sharpened the ash of his cigarette to a fine point on the edge of an ashtray. Alma continued to perspire while Albert and Jarek watched the Americans. The first one who talks, loses, Becker thought.

Alma spoke first. "Naturally we would prefer to have the arms, but one begins to wonder if they ever existed at all. In any case, we need the money, or as much of it as we can recover."

"How much money are we talking about?" Angie said.

"In pesetas?" Alma asked.

"In dollars," Becker said. "I'm sorry, but we are unfamiliar with pesetas."

Jarek's voice startled the group. No one had heard him speak and everyone assumed his mind to be elsewhere. His English was good, but heavily accented. Becker couldn't begin to place the origin.

"The money was originally in gold, but it was too difficult to transport. In Belgium, he changed it to pounds sterling or possibly American dollars. We believe he is holding between fifty and sixty thousand pounds," he said.

"So what are we talking here?" Angie said.

Jarek pulled a pencil from his coat pocket and scribbled some numbers on a napkin.

"Approximately..." He paused, trying to find the correct words, but finally put the napkin on the table in front of Becker and Angie and pointed to an underlined figure with his pencil. "This much."

"Two hundred and fifty thousand. A quarter of a million dollars," Becker said.

Jarek took back the napkin and quickly confirmed the numbers and calculations with Albert in French.

"So this becomes a dangerous business," Becker said. How do I get around this 'direct American' nonsense? he thought. Someone needs to get to the point.

"Somebody's gonna die before this is finished," Angie muttered under his breath. Thank you Angie, Becker thought.

"That is certainly possible," Alma said, looking Becker in the eye.

"And why us?" he said.

"You are not known here, and you were recommended as men of – some ability."

"Our role?" Becker asked.

"That is for you, Albert and Jarek to decide among you."

"How many people know about this besides us?" Angie asked, patting his pockets for another cigarette. Again, Becker gave silent thanks for Angie's willingness to speak his mind.

"A fair question," Alma said. "There is my party contact in Liège. When this man disappeared I contacted him. He put out the word."

He paused to take two deep, wheezing breaths.

"In brief, many people in many countries know he is missing. Only the people in this room know he has been found."

"You're telling me that Albert found him and contacted you?" Becker said.

"That was the procedure," Alma said.

"The party contact doesn't know he's here?" Angie said.

"Only the people in this room."

"Albert," Becker said. "No one in Paris?"

"Ah, there we had luck." Albert grinned as if telling a great joke. "His mother lives in the 14th. I went there and asked about rooms to rent in the building next door. Dear lady. She invited me in, gave me tea and biscuits. I was there for two hours but she eventually started to brag about her children. One thing led to another. She gave me the name of his hotel."

Everyone looked at Becker and he looked at each of them in turn. Alma appeared enfeebled and out of his element. Albert perched like a carrion bird. Jarek sat with one elbow on the back of his chair, the other on a table, his formidable shoulders hunched as he held the napkin daintily in front of him. Angie seemed entertained as he looked at his friend and raised one eyebrow. How did I get to be the foreman of this crew? Becker thought. This is my first day on the job.

"Are we agreed that all word of this affair stops here?" Becker said. All heads nodded, but Becker turned to Albert and said "Understood?" in French, just to be sure.

"*Bien entendu*," Albert said.

"We all know how to keep silent Monsieur," Alma said indignantly. Albert focused a tired stare on the old man. Of course, old comrade, he thought. That is why our cause is rotten with informers. Becker noted Albert's reaction but decided there was nothing to do but let the matter lie.

"Gentlemen, sorry to interrupt," Angie said. "Just so there is no misunderstanding. We all know how this ends?" No one answered.

"I regret comrade, meaning no disrespect, that we must make preparations in private," Albert said to Alma.

Becker felt guilty for their treatment of Alma. Earlier, he had imagined him as some behind-the-scenes puppet master but now he had shrunken into himself and looked more like an overwhelmed bookkeeper, sick with worry over misplacing the firm's money.

"*Eh bien, Messieurs,* I leave you now," he said, using his cane to push himself to his feet.

"You are at the same residence?" Albert asked. Alma nodded. "I must ask you to remain there until this affair is finished, and not to report back to the Republic. It is imperative that no one knows we are moving against him. Not our people, not theirs."

Alma nodded as if receiving a mild reprimand. Becker wondered what history lay between the two men.

Jarek stood and moved a chair aside to let him pass. "Let me get my coat. I will drive you."

"You're needed here. I think I can manage to find a taxi at this hour and you may need the car."

The old man turned to shake hands with each member of the group before leaving.

"I fear we won't see each other again. Time quickly runs out," he said.

Becker smelled the sour odor of death on him, just as he had on his father, but wasn't sure how to respond.

"Oh no," Becker said. "*À la prochaine fois.*" Until the next time.

Alma shook his head. "May it not be soon." He walked toward the door but turned before reaching it as an afterthought occurred to him. "You are kind, my young comrade. But kindness will not serve you well in this affair. The time comes to be hard. *Adieu.*"

CHAPTER 10

The four of them watched him close the door softly before pulling their chairs around one of the tables. They were the only patrons left in the late afternoon, but Albert checked the kitchen before sitting down.

"We are alone. The owner catches a nap at this hour. His wife is out. Shopping probably. The daughter, who knows? Mathieu, Angie, you have met Jarek. He is Czech, but he has good German and you have heard his English. As for his French, well..."

Jarek smiled at the taunt and responded with a mild French vulgarity. "Albert likes to joke. Welcome to the Cause," Jarek said.

"Albert," Becker asked. "What's this business about his name?"

"It's a long, dull story," he answered, but seeing the wariness in Becker's eyes, he decided it was a story best brought out in the open. "The members of his network have changed code names several times, which in itself is not remarkable. The nonsense begins when some member objects to his code name. At one time they were using the names of birds, but naturally someone detected a hierarchy in the animal, pardon, the avian kingdom, and meetings

138

were given over to pettiness about whether someone was a black-bird or a, a-" Albert snapped his fingers, three times in search of the English word. "What is it Mathieu- '*moineau*'?

Becker himself was momentarily stumped, but suddenly the word was on the tip of his tongue. "It lives in a barn?"

"No, no," Albert said, impatiently. "Not swallow." But Albert's answer flipped some mental switch and Becker suddenly remembered.

"Ah, you mean 'sparrow'" he said.

"That's it! *Moineau!* So you can imagine..."

"Ah, well. There's always something," Becker said.

Angie elbowed Becker in the ribs. "What inning is it?"

"*Moins* means 'less'." Becker said.

"Sure," Angie said.

"I'll explain it to you later," Becker said.

"Don't bother," Angie said. He was sketching an image of the Sphinx on the paper placemat, which at second glance turned out to be a caricature of the mythical creature with a perfect rendering of Jarek's face, holding a paperback between his giant paws and waiting with a quiet, impassive serenity which Becker realized he would never know in his lifetime.

"So what about Alma?" Becker asked.

"So the network decided that they would all assume the names of Paris metro stations." Albert said.

"And Alma is a neighborhood of-?" Becker wasn't sure how to express the thought. Disrepute?

"Alma is not the problem. Napoleon is the problem," Albert said.

"Damn right," Angie said. "He shot the nose off the Sphinx."

Everyone stared at Angie, startled at his sudden contribution to the exchange. He looked up from his drawing, embarrassed. "Didn't he?" he asked Becker.

"So they say. I don't know if it's true," Becker said.

"He doesn't believe anybody," Angie said to the group.

"So what about Napoleon?" Jarek said.

"He had a general named Kléber, which is also a metro stop in the 16th *arrondissement*," Albert said.

"He came to a very disagreeable end in Egypt, I understand," Jarek said.

"So what's the problem?" Becker said.

"Some Russian in the Brigades has chosen to operate under the same name. Now we have two Klébers in two different countries. God forbid we should ever need to meet in the 16th," Albert said. He let out an exaggerated sigh of exasperation.

"And Alma is also a metro station?" Becker said.

"Actually it's Alma-Marceau, in the 8th," Jarek said. "But things are already complicated enough, are they not?"

"That ain't the half of it," Angie said, passing his drawing across the table to Jarek. "Here, keep it. I left your nose."

Neither Jarek nor Albert had been paying any attention to Angie's sketching and they both stared at the drawing with shock growing quickly to an amused fascination.

"Oh, Monsieur-" Jarek began.

"Call me Angie."

"Call him Toulouse-Lautrec, isn't it not true? Mathieu, did he not draw on the tables in just such a way?" Albert's dour sarcasm quickly turned to openhearted mirth as his donkey-like laugh echoed off the walls and his tears flowed. But his laughter quickly turned to a hacking cough and back to laughter again.

Jarek just sat shaking his head, his rough-hewn face split with a self-deprecatory smile. "In fact, Monsieur Angie, I wish that I could have such a nose."

"Forget it. Just passing some time," Angie said, mildly uncomfortable at having drawn attention to himself. "Are we gonna talk some business here or what? Albert, you want we should get a doctor? Or maybe a priest?"

"Angie, please. I beg of you to have mercy," Albert said, wiping his eyes with a handkerchief. Finally giving up, he walked behind the bar, turned on a faucet and splashed water on his face. He came back to the towel patting his face with a dinner napkin. "Twice in one day you do this to me. Still, little enough laughter these days."

Jarek looked at Angie. "From my heart, I thank you my friend," he said. "Truly. I only wish my wife...Well." He folded, the paper with some ceremony, placed it in his shirt pocket over his heart and patted it twice.

"So. To business," Albert said. "Tomorrow we must arm ourselves."

"With what?" Angie asked.

"Pistols. We are in the middle of Paris. I fear that cannon will not do."

Angie looked at Becker with his usual raised eyebrow. Becker looked back and cocked his chin slightly. Angie nodded once, as did Becker.

"We have pistols," Becker said.

"How many?" Jarek asked.

"Just two."

"Ammunition?"

"Some. More would be better."

"What type of pistols?" Albert asked.

"Automatic. Colt, .45 caliber," Becker said.

Jarek and Albert exchanged glances, slightly wide-eyed.

"Ah, cannon," Albert said. As I said, we have little use for cannon here in Paris, but I will try to find more cartridges."

"And the plan?" Angie said.

"We have a safe house, here, on this street. There is an apartment. For now, you should sleep. We will try to get a look at our friend when he goes out for dinner tonight."

"What time?" Angie asked.

"We will go a little before nine."

"Dinner?"

"Ange, people eat late here," Becker said.

"What if he eats at the hotel?" Angie asked.

Albert shook his head. "The hotel is modest. They have a small dining room for breakfast but no dinner. He and his watchers are obliged to get food elsewhere. I think we will see them tonight."

"*Messieurs,*" Jarek said, overly polite, "One might not see the cannons?"

Angie reached for the rucksack at his feet, pulled it onto his lap and unfastened the straps. He then gazed into space as he reached his hand deep into the heavy canvas, feeling his way past the tightly packed clothes. With a low grunt, he pulled hard with his right hand and pressed down with his left to keep the bag's contents from spilling out, finally extracting a triangular fold of worn terry cloth. He placed it gently on the table, returned the rucksack to the floor and unwrapped the weapon, dropping out the clip, locking back the slide and checking the breach before handing it to Jarek. Jarek took the pistol gently in his hands, admired the finish and also checked the breach before snapping the slide forward.

"Much used, but well cared for," he said.

He turned in his chair and held it out at arm's length in his right hand, supporting it with his left. He sighted on a lamp across the room and dry fired, the click of the hammer echoing in the silence of the room.

"There are two of these?" he asked.

"I have one just like it," Becker said. "But prettier."

"Magazines?"

"A total of five. This means that one weapon only has one extra clip."

"And, forgive the question, you have some experience with the weapon? I'm sorry to ask," Jarek said. Albert listened hard for their answer, wanting to be sure he caught any nuance in their tone.

A mental image came to Becker. Warm afternoons in the summer and fall, cloudy, overcast days in winter, firing scores of rounds at cans, bottles, pieces of wood. Firing until the ammo ran out. Firing until their teenage hands were bruised and aching from the recoil. Then searching through the forest undergrowth for ejected cartridges and taking them home to reload by hand.

Becker directed his answer at both older men. "Anyone can miss a target. You know this. A sudden movement, a gust of wind, so many variables. But we are both quite competent within the effective range of the weapon."

Albert and Jarek took a moment to digest the answer.

"You are not the American cowboys one sees in the cinema," Albert said.

"Not hardly," Angie said, expressionless. Becker looked at his friend's face and wondered what mental images were playing out behind it.

"I regret," Jarek said, handing the pistol back to Angie. "It was not my intention to treat it as a plaything."

Becker dismissed the need for an apology with a brief shake of his head and a smile. "So, not for playing. Albert, do we intend to kill these men?" he said.

"The guards, as I said, are professionals. I fear they will not simply put up their hands."

"There are four of us. It would be better to have more weapons," Becker said.

"I think I can get at least one more," Albert said.

"And what about this man. The target, what is his name?"

"He calls himself Garza. This one, I would like to speak to. Just a few words. Failing that, we would like to recover the money."

"And if the money can't be recovered? If it's in a bank, or some other safe place?" Angie said.

Albert shrugged. "For us, this is the fortune of a lifetime. All our lifetimes. In the grand scheme, Stalin sits on a giant pile of Spanish gold."

"All of it, in fact," Jarek said.

"And after?" Becker said.

"His theft has caused the death of many comrades. No court will give us justice. Plus, he will know our faces," Albert said.

Jarek spoke softly, his eyes on his coffee. "And if innocents see our faces?" he said.

The group was silent.

"He is on the top floor of this hotel?" Becker said.

"We don't know, but I would be if I were him," Albert said.

"And there is an elevator?" Again, they nodded.

"So we approach by stairs and elevator simultaneously. Once in the elevator we cover our faces," Becker said.

"A neck scarf, like the cowboy movies?" Albert said, smiling.

Becker gave him a look of ice-cold irritation. He had long ago grown tired of the cowboy references. Albert took his meaning.

"Pardon," he said.

"Something less likely to fall off, like a balaclava or a ski mask," Becker said, half to himself. "You can obtain such a thing?"

"Or make it ourselves," Jarek said.

Angie patted Becker on the upper arm to get his attention.

"Matt, I'm with you on this, but I'm not going in there blind, especially with two stone killer Krauts backing him up. I want to know this layout backwards, forwards and sideways," he said to Becker in rapid English.

"We need to watch these men, to make a surveillance, without being detected," Becker said.

"Not to worry," Albert said. "We have a delivery truck which we park across from the hotel. The back is covered with canvas. Small holes are cut in the side. They cannot be seen by passersby. We watch through the holes." Albert sighed deeply, shaking his head. "Truly, this is most tedious. It will be a relief to have some help."

They all sat in silence with their thoughts for a time.

"Is it possible for us to get a room on the top floor?" Becker said.

"Even if we could, if one of us were seen going into the room, I fear it would alert the bodyguards," Jarek said.

"True," Becker said. "We need someone to rent the room for us. Someone who will not arouse suspicion."

"We ask for a top floor room?" Albert said. "This itself is suspicious."

"So we pay off," Angie said.

"Pardon?" Jarek said. Albert's face also went blank.

"If you wanna use somebody's spot, then you gotta cut them in," Angie said, slower. The point was obvious to him, but he showed no impatience at having to explain.

"Cut them?" Albert said, confused.

"Angie means that we need someone at the hotel to help us. We should pay them for their help," Becker said.

"And for their silence," Jarek said.

"This is how it is done..." Albert searched his mind for the term, finally giving up, switching to French and cocking his thumb back over his shoulder. " ...over there?" He used the expression *là-bas* , meaning literally "over there", which suddenly started the old Great War tune running through Becker's head. He smiled at the absurdity of it all, in that he was now "over here".

"Business is business," Angie said with a smile. Becker now cringed mentally, worried that this blatantly capitalist approach would put off the other conspirators.

"I would prefer to work with comrades," Albert said, his face suddenly darkening.

"We work with what we got," Angie said.

"Perhaps such a person has already been paid," Jarek said.

"Then we pay more, and we stick this in his ear," Angie said, picking up the .45.

Jarek nodded knowingly, but Albert was in unfamiliar territory.

"How much?" he asked.

"What's a life worth in Paris these days?" Angie said, like he was asking about the weather.

"Worth?" Albert said, pronouncing it "worse". This was a word he didn't know.

"Worse than what?" Angie said. Jarek's face had also gone blank. Only Becker caught the source of the sudden derailment. God help us, he thought. How much time, toil and human life had been wasted through the ages over confusion like this?

"Hold it a minute," Becker said to Angie. He switched to French and spoke to Albert and Jarek. "He asks the value of a man's life in Paris."

"And what does that mean?" Albert said. Jarek looked at the Frenchman with impatience.

Albert responded with the standard Gallic shrug and puffing of the cheeks.

"Excuse me," Angie said. "I gotta take a – Matt, ask them where's the john."

Albert pointed to a curtained doorway at the back of the dining room. Angie grabbed his rucksack and headed toward the door, making an instant's eye contact with Becker. While he was gone, Albert and Jarek made forced small talk about the restaurant's owner and when he might be back. Becker watched them, sensing that some change in authority had occurred once the conversation had turned to the prospect of violence.

Angie reappeared silently and sat down, careful to return the rucksack to its place between his feet. He handed a small roll of bills to Albert, who hesitated a moment before taking it, sliding it between his ring and center finger and quickly counting through the bills with his thumb and index finger. When finished, he flipped the opposite end of the sheaf of notes to the front and repeated the process. Angie and Becker watched the technique. They had always counted money hand to hand, like dealing cards. This was something new.

"Five hundred," Albert said.

"Can you change this to francs, or something less conspicuous?" Angie said.

"Less...?"

"Noticeable," Becker said in French. Albert nodded his assent.

"Then we start with this tonight, on the night manager," Angie said.

"We still need someone to rent the room. Someone who will not alert the guards. A woman, if possible," Becker said.

"I know a woman," Albert said.

"Not flashy. Someone who does not attract attention."

"My mother," Albert said.

The other faces at the table went blank.

"Don't worry. She is of the Cause, since a very long time. She knows this type of affair. She will play the role as necessary."

"We can't hide her face," Jarek said.

"What's another old woman in Paris? Even the young begin to look old these days," Albert said.

"So tonight, we identify the targets, and the manager," Becker said.

"Perhaps he is just a simple clerk," Albert said.

"Even better. Tonight at work, we grab him for a chat. Tomorrow, we rent the room when he comes on duty. When they leave for dinner, if they leave, we move to the room on the top floor. Perhaps we can finish this tomorrow night."

Albert stood, as if to adjourn the meeting. "For now, rest." He handed the American money to Jarek. "You know someone...?"

"I'll deal with it. It is no problem," he answered.

Becker and Angie spent the rest of the afternoon and early evening in the garret room of a five-story, walk-up building down the street. It was modestly furnished with two cots, an armoire and a small table with a wash basin and water pitcher. The toilet and sink were on the next floor down. There was a shower on the ground floor operated by a pull-chain which released ice cold water. Nonetheless, both men made the trip and suffered the ordeal of washing up and rinsing in the freezing torrent.

When Becker finally lay down to get what sleep he could, he found that the cold water had left him strangely relaxed. He was content that everything that could be done, had been done. The afternoon sun warmed the room and made him drowsy. His last memory before falling asleep was of Angie, standing at the window with a cigarette, blowing smoke out toward the gray rooftops of Paris.

At ten o'clock that night, Angie was watching the front door of the hotel from a line of one-by-three inch slits cut in the canvas back of the delivery truck. They were camouflaged by lettering indicating that the truck was the property of *Fournier & Sons*. He heard a sound from his companions and looked down to see Becker and Albert sitting on piles of furniture padding with a flashlight and a deck of cards on the floor between them, whispering, trying to find a card game both of them knew. Jarek was stretched out with his hands behind his head, smiling at their predicament. Angie rubbed his eyes with his knuckles and looked back to see a tall, fair-haired man in a dark overcoat exit the hotel and stop to light a cigarette. He looked every bit the well-dressed gentleman out for an evening stroll, enjoying the fresh air as he chose which way to go, but his eyes took in everything in a one hundred-eighty degree arc. Angie saw him look directly at the truck.

"This is it. Kill the flashlight."

Becker switched off the light in an instant and took up position next to Angie. He saw the man look up and down the street before signaling to his companions in the lobby with a waist-high wave of the hand.

"Here they come," Becker said. "Albert, do you want to see?"

"I've seen them three nights running."

"I'll look," Jarek said, putting his eyes to a third slit.

The target emerged followed by the second bodyguard and the three men walked to their left down the street, the first guard a few paces ahead, the second pausing occasionally to look for anyone following.

"I see someone in the lobby," Jarek said.

Becker and Angie looked but saw only the desk clerk.

"Can't see anyone," Angie said.

"Gone now. Maybe just a bystander."

"If the lobby is empty, we should go now," Jarek said. It had been decided that Jarek and Becker would confront the clerk, Becker because he had a weapon and spoke French, Jarek for his intimidating physical presence.

They checked the street before pushing aside the roll-up flap at the back of the truck and starting across toward the hotel. Becker entered the lobby first. The clerk had both elbows on the desk as he read a newspaper. He didn't look up.

"Pardon, Monsieur. I need a room," Becker said as Jarek swiftly glided around the front of the desk to step behind it from the far side. He was light on his feet despite his size.

"How many-"

The clerk felt a slight caress of wind at his side and started to look up just as Jarek grasped his left wrist, twisted it behind his back and shoved him against the counter directly in front of Becker, whose .45 was now pressed firmly to the center of his chest. Becker spoke softly and with impeccable politeness.

"We are sorry to trouble you, Monsieur, but may we have a few private words?" he said.

The clerk, a pale, balding man in his mid-thirties with a slender frame and a slight paunch nodded in terror.

"Please, Monsieur. My family," he said.

"Yes, your family," Becker said, in sympathy. "Is that the office?"

"Yes."

"Let's go there," Becker said.

Jarek had guided the man through the door before Becker could round the front desk and join them. He entered a small, windowless room that smelled of mildewed paper and cigarettes. Its furnishings consisted of an old file cabinet, a battered wooden desk and an office chair. The rest of the wall space and most of the floor were covered with stacks of rotting paper in the form of invoices, receipts, tax forms, and other office refuse as well as piles of old magazines. Becker picked one up. It was about fishing.

"So you like to fish, Monsieur?" Becker said.

Jarek had seated the man in the office chair, where he sat staring at a stack of papers in front of him, afraid to look either man in the face.

"Not me. *Le patron*," he said. Now they knew they were dealing with an employee and not the owner.

"Me, I never cared for it," Becker said.

"Please explain that I am sorry for the delay. Please tell him I will get the money. I swear to you I can get it soon. Please do not kill me." The words spilled out of the man well before Becker and Jarek could make any sense of them. They exchanged puzzled glances.

"Go on," Becker said, at a loss, but concealing it. He had the gun after all.

"My brother, my brother-in-law. He will give it to me," said the clerk.

"Your wife's brother," Becker said in a tone of steely disbelief.

"No, no. My sister's husband. He has it. He will give it to me."

"He said this."

"My sister swore to me."

"You swear to me. Your sister swears to you. Everyone swears. But no one is paid. This unfortunate man still waits for his money," Becker said.

The man was weeping now, still staring down at the papers on the desk, waiting for a bullet in the back of his head. His nose began to run. Jarek took a tissue from a box on the desk and gave it to him, never taking his other hand from its place on the clerk's shoulder.

"How do you call yourself?" Becker said.

"Bozzoli."

"Ah, yes. Monsieur Bozzoli of the Hôtel Charles. Well, if it were in our interest we might speak on your behalf. If you can give us your cooperation, perhaps some new arrangements can be made. You may even earn some money."

"You will help me?" said Bozzoli.

"We will help each other," Becker said, with all the kindness he could muster.

"How can I help you?"

"Speak when I tell you and be silent when I tell you. Do not question us. Do you agree?"

"I agree."

"Three men left here a short time ago. Do you know them?"

"The two *boches* and the Spaniard?"

"What name is the Spaniard registered under?" Becker asked

"Lopez."

"Where is their room?"

"They have two rooms, connecting. Top floor."

"Take that pencil. Make me a plan of the top floor. Indicate their rooms," Becker said.

"What are you going to do?" asked Bozzoli.

"Don't speak. Draw. Clearly please."

Jarek put a piece of paper in front of Bozzoli, who took a ruler from the desk drawer and began to sketch, his hands trembling. He struggled to understand what was happening to him. One moment he had been enjoying a quiet night at the front desk with a newspaper. The next he was being tossed about like a child by a silent beast and threatened with a pistol the size of a field howitzer. And the one who spoke. His accent. French, but not Parisian, certainly. A Corsican? No, too polite, very civilized, very educated. But something frightening in the politeness. Like that butcher of a dentist his wife sent him to. Always the gentle voice, then the agony. He wiped his sweating palms on his thighs and tried to draw a deep breath. It wouldn't come. The monster's hand on his shoulder was like a vise. The closeness of the room was suffocating.

"Monsieur, I beg of you," he said. "I cannot move."

Jarek looked at Becker, who blinked once in assent. Jarek released his grip but remained at Bozzoli's side, his arms crossed as he watched the progress of the drawing.

"Calm yourself, Monsieur Bozzoli. We have little time," Becker said.

Bozzoli finally pushed the finished drawing to the side of the desk for his captors' inspection. It showed the adjacent rooms about halfway down the hallway almost opposite the elevator.

"Stairs?" Becker said.

Bozzoli drew small rectangles at each end of the corridor.

"Are there vacant rooms on this floor?" Becker asked.

"I believe there are."

"Show me."

"I must check the registration."

"Go, but be quick. And please, no foolishness," Becker said.

Bozzoli tentatively began to ease himself out of the chair, trying not to look right or left, fearful he would meet the eyes of his killers, but Jarek grew impatient and grasped his arm to lift and twirl him around and out the doorway to the desk. He looked at the registry book, mail boxes and key rack before rushing back to the desk, his eyes still downcast.

"These are vacant." He drew three neat circles on the floor plan.

"We want this one," Becker said, pointing to a room two doors down on the opposite side of the corridor.

"Immediately, Monsieur," said Bozzoli.

A montage of possible scenarios flashed through Becker's mind. The plan is to wait until tomorrow, he thought. What if this guy's real bookie shows up and breaks his legs? What if he goes home, spills his guts to his wife and she breaks his legs? More likely. Maybe the targets have already paid him off to warn them and they'll be gone tomorrow night. What if he just breaks from the strain in the next twenty-four hours? What if I break worrying if he's going to break?

"Shall I get the key?"

Becker realized that he had been staring into space and that both Jarek and Bozzoli were waiting for an answer. But he needed time to think.

"Patience, Monsieur. Let us first make our position clear. Please give me your wallet."

Bozzoli frowned, but handed over a sweat-stained billfold. Becker examined the contents.

"This is your current address?" Becker said. Bozzoli nodded. "And you live there with...?"

"My wife and my son. My mother in-law is also staying with us until she is better."

"Your mother in-law is not well?"

Bozzoli nodded, his eyes still fixed on the desk blotter.

"It is a pity. Illness in the family. Difficult, is it not?" Becker said.

"Yes, Monsieur."

Becker took a huge sheaf of franc notes, about half of what Jarek had exchanged, put it between the folds of the wallet and placed it on the desk in front of the clerk.

"Please accept this as a token of our good will."

Bozzoli eyes widened as he looked at the money, but its appearance did little to cheer him.

"Now listen carefully," Becker said. "We have business with these *boches* and the Spaniard. If you interfere, you will be silenced. Permanently. Colleagues of ours will also visit your family. Understood?"

"Yes, Monsieur."

"If you cooperate, it will be to your advantage." Becker was unsure of how to phrase the next question without giving away his ignorance. "Do you understand how much your debt has grown with the passage of time?"

"I fear it is nearly twelve thousand francs by now."

Becker now wished he'd been less generous with the payoff. "You are optimistic," he said. "But have courage, Monsieur Bozzoli. You are already well on your way to clearing your debt."

"Yes, Monsieur. Thank you, Monsieur. But, forgive me. You are not from Rossi?"

Becker had been waiting for something like this, but how show he answer? Was Rossi a place or a person? He exhaled slowly, his eyes cold with a look of weary impatience.

"Monsieur Bozzoli, you disappoint me" he said. "Time grows short and I thought you understood that you were not to ask questions. Perhaps you are not the man to assist us after all."

"Forgive me, Monsieur." Bozzoli's eyes were moist with tears.

Becker made a dramatic display of looking toward Jarek for counsel. Jarek played along and shook his head sadly, like a doctor telling loved ones "Sorry, he didn't make it." Bozzoli was stricken.

"I swear to you! On the Virgin! I will help you, anything you ask!"

Becker looked at his watch. "Bozzoli, Bozzoli, Bozzoli. You try our patience, but as I said we are short of time. We can discuss Rossi later. Understood?"

"Understood, Monsieur. Yes, Monsieur."

"Now think very carefully before you answer this next question. Is there a third *boche* in the room now?"

Bozzoli's lower lip trembled.

"Monsieur. There is a third foreigner who comes and goes. I don't know his nationality but he has some acquaintance with these men. A man of some authority. He may be in the room. But honestly, I don't know."

"Have you ever spoken to him?"

"He looks at me and I am afraid to speak."

Becker betrayed no emotion, but in reality the clerk's words caused him to feel true fear for the first time that night. A riot of obscene curses echoed inside his head. Shooters ahead of them and behind them, one in a locked room. And a gelatinous, sweating schlemiel as our back-up. Get a grip on yourself, he thought. You can always piss yourself later. The show must go on. He drew in a deep breath and exhaled a bored and weary sigh.

"So. Just as we thought. Now, Monsieur. I want you to sit in this chair until I return. Try to relax. Do not speak to this gentleman unless he speaks to you and in that case do exactly as he says. If a customer rings the bell, you may get up and deal with them in the usual manner. How long does Lopez usually spend at dinner?"

"Not long. Perhaps two hours. The *boches* do not drink. I have the impression that they press him to return early."

"Then we won't trouble you for long. For now, wait here and I will return in five minutes." Becker made eye contact with Jarek. His face showed alertness but no apprehension, though Becker had a sense that they had both drawn many of the same conclusions. The big Czeck nodded once and allowed himself a grim smile. Becker slid the .45 into his belt at the small of his back, covered it with his coat and walked out of the office.

Before heading to the truck he walked toward the back of the hotel to check for another entrance. He found a door in an alcove at the end of the main corridor and pushed it open. Odors of garbage and sewer gas assaulted him. He walked down two steps into an alley, turned left and found that side of the hotel blocked off by a high wooden fence. It would take a flawless running leap to reach the top, grasp the edge and pull oneself over. Anyone fleeing in this direction would find it difficult to manage on the first try and likely to be interrupted by a bullet on the second.

Looking up, he saw there were fire escapes for each of the rooms on that side of the building providing access to the alley on the other side of the fence. Another way out. Or in? Could someone get up the fire escape without attracting attention? How would they find the right room? He considered the problem as he turned to check the other end of the alley. He saw that it ran to the end of the block and into a main thoroughfare. The hell with this, he thought. I don't need the exercise and I don't have the time.

Returning to the hotel's back door, he found it had locked behind him. After jerking the door handle twice in frustration he took a deep breath. Stay cool. There's no time for self-recrimination. But don't make the mistake again. He started for the end of the alley in a comfortable jog, one hand on his .45 to keep it from bouncing out of his belt, reaching the street in less than thirty seconds. Turning right, he approached the truck from the rear and noticed smoke coming from the tail pipe. He looked quickly under the flap and found the back of the truck empty. They must have gotten cold, he thought. He walked to the driver's side window and tapped. Albert's head snapped to the left, his face frozen in shock. He recovered when he recognized Becker's face and rolled down the window, releasing a billowing cloud of cigarette smoke. Becker saw Angie on the passenger side, grinning.

"It's the Shadow!" he said.

"*Putain merde,* you scared me." He took a long pull on his cigarette and slowly let out the smoke. "So, *ça va?*"

"*Ça change,*" Becker said. "We do this tonight."

"What's happening?" Albert said.

Becker looked at his watch. It was already twenty five minutes since he and Jarek had entered the hotel. "If we wait, we risk too much. The clerk is shaky and there is a third guard somewhere. We could come back tomorrow and find them gone – or waiting for us."

Albert spat out another obscenity under his breath. "You're right," he said. "Too much waiting. Good for them, bad for us."

Becker knew that he and Angie both had their pistols and extra clips, but that still left them possibly out-gunned.

"Albert. This afternoon you said you could get a weapon. Did you get it?" Becker said.

"It's in the back."

"Let's see it. Angie, keep an eye out."

In the back of the truck, Albert unwrapped a roll of padding and produced an ancient double-barreled shotgun, sawed off to a little over three feet long. He handed it casually to Becker, who grimaced when he saw the condition of the weapon.

"Shine that flashlight over here," he said to Albert as he began to examine the patient. There was dust anywhere not recently touched and many traces of corrosion. The joints squeaked in pain as he opened the breach and pulled out the shells. Holding them to the light, he saw that the casings had gone gray or yellow with age. Turning them, he could make no sense of the markings on the brass head. He ran his thumb over the ends. The primers appeared intact.

"How old are these?" Becker said.

"No idea. The gun is not mine."

"You have more shells?"

Albert reached into his coat pockets and found three more. Their condition was no better, but two of them appeared to be of a different type.

"What kind of shot?" Becker asked, growing exasperated.

Albert shrugged.

"When was the last time this was fired?"

Another shrug. Albert looked at the cold appraisal in Becker's eyes, feeling like an errant schoolboy and despising himself for it. All these questions. So I am not a one for the killing, he thought. I'm not a gangster, but I have always served the cause, risked my life, taken many beatings from the *flics*. What has this young pup done?

Becker closed the breach, pulled back both hammers and dry-fired both actions once. There were cobwebs in the trigger guard which he blew out. He opened the breach again and looked down the barrels, seeing some remnants of expended gun powder but no obstructions. Throughout the process, he had sensed the growing Albert's growing irritation and searched his mind for some way to defuse it.

"I'm sorry to have startled you before. I should have signaled in some way."

"It's not a big thing," Albert said.

"I went out the back door to check the exit and got locked out like a fool. I had to circle the block."

"Ah, so that's it."

Becker let his shoulders slouch. "So, Uncle," he said. "What are your thoughts?"

He calls me Uncle? Thought Albert. Well, his father, his uncle and I...old comrades.

"About what?"

"Will we make it out of this?" Becker said. Please don't shrug again, he thought.

Albert shrugged. God damn it, Becker thought.

"It could happen. What are you worried about?"

"None of us know this *quartier*. Do you?"

"Around here? Like the back of my hand. I used to have a girl-friend who lived – ah well, that's old history."

"If we come running out of that hotel, can you get us out of here?" Becker said.

"You mean to have me wait out here?" Albert's voice carried the first signs of real anger.

"Albert. Perhaps it is not my place to say this, but you are the on-ly one of us who is not expendable."

"And what does that mean?"

"If you are killed, who will get the money to the Cause? How will Angie and I get to Spain? And if you are dead, the Party will hold us responsible, is it not so?"

Albert said nothing. He switched off the flashlight. Both men stood silent in the rays of streetlight that shone through the slits in the canvas.

"And you have a wife and children," Becker said.

"My daughters are almost grown," Albert said, his anger fading away. I was wrong, he thought. This one has a good heart, but there's something hard in it. God help me if I have to tell Martin I got this boy killed, and me without a scratch. "But my wife would miss having someone to complain to. Enough. I take your meaning. So what is it you want?"

"Watch for us. Be ready. And when we come out, get us to safety."

"Consider it done," Albert said. "What about the money?"

"If it is there, we'll get it. If not, we'll find out where it is," Becker said. "Provided there is anyone left alive to ask."

"And your plan for inside?"

"Still working on it, but we need to clear the room and watch for the return of Garza and his *boches*. I'm sorry to ask you Uncle, but we need this gun."

"Go ahead."

"It will leave you with nothing out here," Becker said.

"I get by on my wits," Albert said, his confidence returning.

"You'll have to teach me that sometime," Becker said. "Shall we begin this?"

"Let's go."

Becker rolled up the shotgun in the padding and they both walked back to the cab. Albert waited as Becker spoke to Angie through the window.

"Anything?"

"An old couple went in about five minutes ago. Just civilians I think," Angie said.

Becker nodded. "Ange, it's you me and Jarek inside."

"About time. My ass is going to sleep here."

"If I see them coming, should I sound the horn? As a warning?" Albert said.

Becker paused for a moment. What a dumb idea, he thought. "It's more likely to warn them, and we may not hear it anyway," he said. "I know this is hard, Uncle. But you are our escape, and if they come out, it means we have failed. You will have to chase them down."

"Right," Albert said, taking the door handle with his left hand and shaking Becker's with his right. "Good luck then, Mathieu."

Albert watched the two young men cross the street, their athletic step and the supple power in the movement of their torsos so different from the bent and broken shuffle he saw on the Paris streets every day. They reminded him of Martin. Are we the same species? he thought. What time is it? Almost eleven. Garza will be back soon. We'll find out soon enough what they're made of.

"Let's get away from the truck fast," Angie said.

"Why?"

" 'Cause I left a little present for Albert in the cab."

"What are you talking about?" Becker said.

"Matt, I just cut a deadly fart about ten seconds before you guys came back. I can't help it. Sauerkraut always does that to me."

"God help him. He could be blind when we get back. You pass mustard gas."

"Yeah, well it serves him right for those cigarettes he's been murdering me with. You know he lights the next one off the last one? I couldn't breathe in there."

"Nasty habit. I told you," Becker said.

"Hope he doesn't light up for a couple minutes. He'll blow himself to kingdom come."

"Well, he wished us luck."

"Why isn't he coming?" Angie asked.

"Getaway driver. Plus I'd rather have you and Jarek watching my back."

"Yeah, well luck ain't got nothing to do with this," Angie said under his breath when they were halfway across the street.

"Ain't that the truth. Angie, listen. We think there may be a third Kraut in the room now, but we can't be sure."

Angie paused in thought for an instant. "So we take him out first?"

"I think we have to, but we have to figure out how."

The two men walked directly to the office where they saw Jarek waiting behind the clerk. Bozzoli was still seated at the desk, his eyes fixed on an out-of-date calendar in front of him. He appeared to have gone into some tranquil form of shock. Becker unwrapped the shotgun, opened the breach and handed it to Jarek.

"This is from Albert. The best he could do," Becker said.

Jarek took it dolefully. "I already saw it. Perhaps it will fire," he said.

"And these," Becker said, handing over the three extra shells. "If we need more than that, we'll already be dead."

Becker turned to Bozzoli and put both hands on his shoulders. "Now, Monsieur Bozzoli. We would like to telephone Lopez's room."

"Telephone? We cannot. There are no phones in the rooms. The guests must come to the lobby to make calls," he said.

"And to receive? You take a message to the room?" Becker said.

"Sometimes, but I cannot leave the desk. I usually just put the message in the box."

Becker thought for a moment. "And where is the fuse box?"

"In the basement."

"Be specific. I don't have all night."

"Down the back stairwell. Open the door, straight ahead four or five paces. It will be on the wall on your right."

"Much better," Becker said. "You have a flashlight here?"

Bozzoli pointed out the office door to the front desk. There was a flashlight on the bottom shelf. Power outages were not unusual.

Becker looked at Angie, cocked his head toward the door. Angie headed out the office door, picking up the flashlight as he went, and walked toward the back stairwell.

"Five minutes. The lights may go out." Becker said to Jarek, who blinked once in agreement.

There were two incandescent bulbs to light the entire basement, but they found the fuse box without difficulty, just where Bozzoli had described it. Opening it, they found twenty-five cylindrical fuses arranged in rows of five, far fewer than the number of rooms in the hotel, indicating that one fuse must serve more than one room. Each fuse had a small piece of tape under it with a number scribbled on it, most of them faded or illegible.

"You're kidding, right?" Angie said.

"Seems perfectly clear to me," Becker said.

"Why not just cut all the power? Won't that flush him out?"

"And if it doesn't? We go in blind?"

Angie looked at him but said nothing.

"Let's try this," Becker said. He began removing and replacing one fuse at a time from the bottom row, gently unscrewing each one all the way before rotating it clockwise back into place.

"Matt. For Chrissakes be careful. I didn't bring no marshmallows."

On the third fuse, the basement light went out. Becker screwed it back in and the light came on. He ran his finger across the top row and looked at Angie.

"So if that was us, you figure these are the top floor?" he asked.

"Makes sense," Angie said.

Becker unscrewed all the top row fuses and looked at his watch. It was eleven-ten. Garza and the guards had left at ten. What had Bozzoli said? Two hours for dinner? Less than two hours? More?

"Angie, here's what I think. You stay on the ground floor, out of sight. Watch for Garza and the Krauts. If they show, you run like hell up the stairs. Beat the elevator, let us know, and we'll all take them on the top floor. Jarek and I will try to take the Kraut in the room before they get back."

"Might work," Angie said, but his tilted smile and raised eyebrow said otherwise.

Three minutes had passed. Becker screwed the top floor fuses back in before leading Angie upstairs to the main corridor alcove at the back of the ground floor.

"What do you think?" he said to Angie. Is this a good place to wait?"

Angie looked around the corner. "Best we can do, I guess. Just make sure you don't cross my line of fire."

"This door only opens out, so no one will surprise you from that side. But it locks by itself, so don't leave unless you're planning to stay gone," Becker said.

"Glad you told me. What if I'd gone out for a leak?"

Becker turned to go back to the office but Angie stopped him. "Matt. What about the fire escape?"

Becker looked at his friend. He hadn't forgot. He just didn't have an answer.

"I was hoping for two men to rush the Kraut upstairs. If someone watches the fire escape, that leaves us a man short," Becker said.

"Albert?"

"That leaves no one in the truck and still one gun short."

Now Angie searched for an answer. He shook his head. "It sure ain't perfect."

He returned to the office and found Jarek and his charge just as he'd left them, though Jarek was clearly getting bored. Becker's eyes scanned the room until he saw a manila file folder. Picking it up, he ripped the back off and placed the blank cardboard in front of Bozzoli.

"Write as I tell you. 'Our excuses for the inconvenience. We are having minor electrical problems. Back in five minutes.'"

Bozzoli did as he was told, producing a graceful continental script. Becker propped the sign against the registry book on the front desk. Looking across the lobby, he saw two chairs next to a small table with a lamp, a notepad and a telephone. That must be where the guests make their phone calls, he thought. He walked over to the table, pulled the phone and lamp from their wall sockets and took both to the office.

"Monsieur Bozzoli. You have a handkerchief?"

Bozzoli produced a sizeable piece of cloth from his trouser pocket. Clean, thank God, Becker thought.

"Monsieur, it is with great regret..." Becker said. He cut the cord from the lamp with his knife and looked at Jarek who responded with a single, knowing nod. Jarek put the shotgun down on a stack of magazines, took the cord and proceeded to bind Bozzoli's hands to the vertical wooden slats at the back of the office chair while Becker shook out the folds of the handkerchief and marveled at its dimensions. This thing could double as a beach towel, he thought.

When Jarek finished, he stood, picked up the shot gun, and stood at port arms, but with the breach still open. The man knows how to handle a firearm, Becker thought. Where did he learn that?

Becker spoke to Bozzoli. "Where is the master key?"

"Desk drawer. It has a blue tag."

Becker opened the center drawer and found the key in the front pencil tray. He put it in his pants pocket.

"Now, again Monsieur, I must ask you to forgive me. It will only be for a short time." Bozzoli looked bewildered.

Becker opened his own mouth very wide in demonstration. "Your mouth. Open, please."

Bozzoli opened his mouth and Becker stuffed the handkerchief inside. He then took a roll of office tape and ran it three times around the clerk's head to secure the cloth in the man's mouth.

"You can breathe?" Becker said.

Bozzoli nodded, but his eyes were full of panic.

"Good man. Now, patience. One of us will be back to free you in a short time."

Becker took Bozzoli's floor plan from the desk and motioned to Jarek that they were leaving but Jarek held up his hand. Putting down the shotgun. He grasped the office chair by both of its arms and slowly tipped it over, gently lowering it to the floor until the chair and its human contents were laying on their sides. As he stood up, he pointed to the wheels on the bottom of the chair. Becker smiled at his forethought.

As he passed the front desk, Becker checked the floor plan against the room keys hanging in front of the letter boxes. There were two keys missing from the fifth floor row. Those guests must be in, he thought. And the third guard? He's locked in, or he has his own key. Or he can pick the lock if he needs to. Or, best of all, he's not there.

Jarek followed Becker to the back alcove. "We're going up," he said.

"Break a leg," Angie said.

"Whatever you hear, don't come up."

"Got it." Angie didn't make eye contact, keeping his eyes on the front door.

CHAPTER 11

Becker took the stairs two at a time. Jarek tried to keep up but by the third floor he was falling behind. Becker made it to the fifth floor, opened the stairwell door to check the hallway and waited. There was a garish, red carpet with a fake oriental design going threadbare in front of the elevator and wall-mounted light fixtures at three points on each side of the hall. He smelled cigarette smoke. Fresh, not stale. He closed the door when he heard Jarek's footfalls coming up the last flight toward him.

"*Pardon*, but if I move too fast, it makes much sound." He looked Becker up and down. "You move lightly. How much is your weight?" he whispered.

Becker hadn't stepped on a scale since the previous summer, when he'd been a trim one eighty-five. But the last days had taken some weight off him.

"In kilos, I'm not sure. Perhaps eighty-three or eighty-four. You?"

"A bit over one hundred, plus or minus." He smiled. "Plus, I think."

"It suits you," Becker said. Jarek answered with a bow.

"I'm going to knock on the guests' doors and ask about the electricity, loud enough for our friend to hear. Hopefully, he'll hear me and it will give us an excuse to get him to the door," Becker said.

"I'll watch here. Signal me when you're ready," Jarek said.

Becker looked at Bozzoli's diagram one last time, stepped into the corridor, and walked purposefully toward the rooms at the far end. His skin tingled as he passed Garza's room but he did his best to ignore it. He came to the door of 501. Top floor, front room. Did they choose it or just get it by chance? he thought. He knocked three times. No response. He knocked again.

"Oui?" A man's voice. "Who is it?"

It's Matt Becker from Jersey, he thought. We're going to shoot up the joint for a few minutes, so get under the bed.

"I beg your pardon, Monsieur, but there was a brief electrical outage. We are checking all the floors to be sure there is no serious problem."

The door was opened by a middle-aged man in pajamas, wearing reading glasses. His breath smelled slightly of cigarettes and alcohol.

"The lights went out for a few minutes, but they're on now," he said.

"Oh, good. We don't think it's serious but we have to be sure. I didn't wake you?"

"I was reading," the man said, holding up a book, his finger between the pages to hold his place. Becker saw the author's name.

"Mallarmé," Becker said.

"Poe actually. His translation. *The Raven.*" The man smiled. "Then the lights went out. Then a knocking at my chamber door. Funny, is it not?"

"Ah, Monsieur. I regret to say, Lenore won't be coming."

"Nevermore?" the man said, smiling.

"Nevermore," Becker said, shaking his head sadly sharing their little joke. Probably a salesman. Lives his life in thousands of hotel rooms just like this one with no one to talk to.

"Too bad."

"Very sorry to trouble you at this hour, Monsieur. Good night, then," Becker said.

"No trouble. Thank you. Good night."

The door closed. Not a bad sort, Becker thought.

The second door didn't go so well. After the third knock he heard a woman's voice, fearful and agitated, followed by the hoarse bellow of a drunk woken from a sound sleep.

"What is it?"

Becker raised his voice to be heard through the door. "I beg your pardon Monsieur. There was a power outage. We are checking the guest rooms to be sure that all is well. For safety, you understand."

"Get lost, why don't you! We're sleeping," roared the man. Then the sound of the woman's voice again, but Becker couldn't make out her words. "And why don't you shut your big snout," responded the man.

"*Pardon* Monsieur! Good night," Becker said, louder than necessary in cheery tone of unctuous servility.

Jarek had watched both performances from the stairwell door. He now saw Becker point at the two doors of Garza's connecting rooms and wave him forward. As he padded soundlessly across the carpet, Becker realized that this critical point in the action had not yet been planned out and there were only seconds left. He signaled his intent to Jarek in an exaggerated pantomime. I knock on this door, he gestured, drawing the .45. You? Cover the other door with the shotgun. This door opens? We rush it. That door? We shoot.

Jarek took position three feet from Becker, pressed his back to the wall under a light fixture and brought the shotgun to his shoulder, pointing it at the far door. He didn't look at Becker, but nodded once to show he was ready.

Becker held the .45 in his right hand behind his back and knocked with his left, the same three taps he had used on the other doors, but he couldn't seem to hear them. Time slowed. How long before I knock again? He looked the watch on his left wrist. When he looked up the door was open four inches. The room lights were off and the curtains drawn but Becker made out the spectral features of a face level with his own, obscured by the darkness.

"What is it?" The voice was no more than a whisper.

"I beg your pardon, Monsieur," Becker began.

Jarek turned quickly from his place under the light, bringing the shotgun to bear on the door but betraying his presence by casting his shadow across the opposite wall. The door slammed shut and immediately shattered into splinters as a fusillade of pistol rounds shredded the wood at waist level. Becker took one step left and answered with three shots from the .45, blowing holes big enough to put a broom handle through. So much for rushing this door, he thought as the sound of his own shots echoed in his ears.

Becker tossed the master key to Jarek and pointed at the other room door. "On three," he said.

Jarek waved away the key. "Don't need it," he said, moving toward the far door.

Five seconds passed. Jarek looked over from the door and nodded. Becker held up his left hand and counted off on his fingers, one-two-three, turned the handle and swung the door wide, dropping to one knee and raising his gun as he entered. No shots. He heard Jarek hit the other door once, twice before it slammed open against the wall followed by another burst from an automatic weapon and the simultaneous roar of the shotgun. Becker hit the light switch, revealing an empty room but the door to the connecting room slightly ajar. He moved toward it and put his back against the wall, trying to find a target but seeing only darkness. I need light or I'm the only target, he thought. Light switches are near the door.

He quickly backed away and ran out into the hallway. He saw Jarek with his back against the wall next to the door, the breach of the shotgun open as he fumbled in his pocket for more rounds. His face was pale.

"Bad round," he said, holding up one of the yellowed shells before throwing it on the floor in disgust.

"How many are there?" Becker asked.

"Just one, but he has some kind of *machinenpistole*," Jarek said.

"Christ Almighty," Becker said.

"Don't worry," Jarek said. "Shoot fast, empty fast."

Becker took Jarek's place against the wall, but face first. Transferring the .45 to his left hand, he reached his right inside the door and turned on the room light just as another bullet crashed into the wall an inch from the switch, jolting his mind into a whirl of calculations. This guy can shoot, he thought, but that was a different weapon. Almost took my thumb off. Small caliber automatic. How many left? Is the machine gun empty or has he put in a new clip? I would have heard the old one hit the floor. Maybe not. I'm half deaf right now.

As the ringing in his ears faded, Becker heard the sound of motion inside the room. A chair scraping the floor, curtains thrown open and the squeak of the latch on the huge door-like windows. They opened side-to-side, not vertically like American windows, and were held shut by a swiveling latch connected to a vertical rod with hooks at the top and bottom, securing the shutters at three places. The window obviously hadn't been opened for months and the shooter was having a rough time of it. He's going for the fire escape, Becker thought.

"Stay in your room!" Jarek said, in French. Becker saw Jarek pointing the shotgun down the hallway at the man from 501 who had leaned his upper body out the door to see what was happening.

"Oui, Monsieur," he answered.

"Lenore show up yet?" shouted Becker, but the man had already pulled his head inside.

There's only room in this door for one person, and I've got the only dependable weapon, Becker thought. Hearing another squeak of protest from the window latch and using the doorjamb to cover the left side of his body, he extended the .45 into the room as he looked around the corner. The shooter was wearing a long black overcoat, billowing outward in the wind from the open window. He had one foot on a chair and another on the window ledge as he prepared to step out onto the fire escape. Becker hesitated. If I miss with this, the bullet could kill someone two blocks away, he thought.

He took careful aim and fired once at the center of the black form. It dropped from the chair to the floor behind the bed. Becker kept his gun on the point where it had dropped from sight and noticed the odd-shaped form of the automatic weapon on the bed. Why isn't he shooting at me with that? he thought. Suddenly, the small automatic appeared and fired three more rounds, two passing harmlessly out the doorway and the third crashing into the doorjamb, sending sawdust and splinters into Becker's face. He staggered back into the hallway, his left forearm held against his eyes as he tried to clear his vision.

Left eye clear, he thought. Right, can't open it. Hurts like hell. Blood, but not too much. Sounds of movement from inside the room. Last chance.

He went back to the door and tried to focus. He saw the black folds of the overcoat disappear into the darkness of the fire escape followed by the sound of a body tumbling down the iron steps to the next floor landing. There was a large bloodstain on the window ledge. Becker ran to the window and aimed the pistol out and realized he couldn't see a thing but was presenting a perfect target for anyone below. He pulled his head in, closed the window, secured the latch and drew the curtains. He then checked the other room to be sure its window was locked.

Returning to the hallway, he saw Jarek sitting on the floor staring at the opposite wall, the shotgun in his lap. "Are you hit?"

Jarek looked up and nodded in resignation

"Where?" Becker asked.

Jarek said nothing, instead waving his index finger aimlessly at his upper body. Becker knelt and pulled the big man's coat open at the lapels. He'd been hit in the right shoulder, just above the left hip and about five inches below his right pectoral muscle. The first two wounds were bleeding, but not much. The last had soaked his sweater, trousers and the carpet on which he sat.

"You said something to that guest before," Jarek said.

"Yeah. Just a joke," Becker said.

"Strange time for a joke." Jarek smiled.

"Just hysteria."

"Say a joke now," Jarek said.

"In a minute." Becker took out Bozzoli's floor plan and checked for the empty room. He saw the one they had originally hoped to use just across the hall. He walked to the door, opened it with the master key, turned on the light and propped the door open with a chair.

"Can you get up?" he said when he got back to Jarek.

"My sister made this sweater," he answered, slowly getting his legs under him. Becker locked his right arm in the armpit and put the other around Jarek's back, helping to pull him up. An agonized moan escaped from between clenched teeth as he rose. With Becker's support, he made two steps toward the vacant room before his knees buckled. With every muscle in his back, legs and arms screaming, Becker managed to drag the man's dead weight into the room, get his upper body onto the bed and pull his legs up. He was unconscious. Becker checked his neck for a pulse. Still alive.

He took two towels from the bathroom and placed them on the bleeding hole in Jarek's abdomen. That's pointless, he thought. They're soaking through. And the blood isn't stopping.

Pulling his switchblade, he made a small slice in the end of the bedspread and began ripping a long strip from the fabric. When he had separated about two meters, he stopped and cut the strip away. He then ran the band of cloth under Jarek's back and tied the towels snugly against the wound. Best I can do for now, he thought. I have to get downstairs.

He stepped into the shooter's room and took the machine pistol from the bed. No sense this getting into the wrong hands, he thought. He had never seen anything like it. It looked like a children's toy, half the size of the rifles he had grown up with. The stock was made of wood but the ventilated barrel and precision-made breech were steel. The truly odd feature was that the magazine projected sideways, feeding the chamber from the left rather than below.

With some trouble, he was able to remove the magazine and clear the chamber. The magazine had two rounds left. Might as well keep it. Can't leave it here. He took off one sleeve of his coat and slung the strap around his neck and shoulder, letting the weapon hang at his side, hidden when he pulled the sleeve back on. He put the magazine in his pocket and quickly looked around the room for anything dangerous, incriminating or useful. His eyes fell on a thick black belt laying across a chair. What is it with Germans and black leather? he thought. He walked from behind the bed and picked up the belt. He found it attached to two thick, rectangular leather pouches, each holding three magazines for the machine pistol. Finders keepers, he thought, but I've got to get back to Angie. He threw the pouches over his shoulder and left the room.

"Angie! Don't shoot, it's me," Becker said as he descended the back stairwell. No answer. "Angie!" His voice was a loud whisper. Still no response. He felt panic building and tried to fight it. What if Angie's hit? Or dead? How do I tell Auntie Lena? He stopped between the third and second floors to put a new clip in the .45. Just as he pushed in the clip he felt a sudden wave of nausea. He took a deep breath to steady himself but as he exhaled he felt his control going. He bent forward and heaved, vomiting once onto the carpet.

Well, glad that's over with, he thought. He continued down, holding the big automatic in two hands at arm's length ahead of him. Reaching the ground floor, he opened the door wide, crouched and looked for a target in the main floor corridor. Nothing.

"Angie?" he said in a normal voice.

"In here," Angie answered quietly.

The voice came from a room to Becker's right, its door six inches ajar, a faint light coming from inside. Becker pushed the door open, the .45 still sweeping side-to-side, looking for a target.

He saw a small dining room with about four deuce tables on each wall and three four-tops down the center. Three men were seated at the first four-top, Garza in the center and the bodyguards on either side. Their hands were flat on the table as they stared at Angie, and now Becker. Angie stood out of reach of any possible lunge for his gun, aiming it at each of the men in turn. He didn't look at Becker.

"Matt, I'd like you to meet Mr. Garza and..." He paused. "Two Krauts that give me the willies."

"They look comfy. Have you taken their orders yet?" Becker said.

"I didn't know how to say 'Get on your knees'." Angie looked at the magazine cases hanging from Becker's shoulder and couldn't make sense of them.

"Saddle bags? You know they hang horse thieves 'round these parts."

"What were they carrying?" Becker said. Angie pointed to one of the smaller tables where two small automatics lay side-by-side . He walked over and picked one up. He tried to focus on the lettering on the side of the weapon but his vision was till clouded by wood chips and blood. He made out the words *Waffenfabrik Mauser* on one side and the number 7.65 on the other. Vision was slowly returning to his right eye, but there was something in it and he kept blinking, trying to clear it.

"Only two?" Becker said.

"Garza didn't have anything I could see, but I haven't patted them down."

"You are English?" Garza said, in heavily accented French.

Becker pointed his pistol at the man. "Don't speak."

"I am not Garza! My name is Lopez!" the man pleaded.

Becker aimed at his head. "Don't speak. I won't tell you again."

Angie took the opportunity to get a good look at Becker for the first time and noticed blood everywhere on his clothes and small scratches on his face. "Are you hit?" he said under his breath.

"Not my blood," Becker said.

"Jarek?"

"Not good. He's upstairs."

"The third Kraut?"

"Gone. Out the fire escape." Becker quickly pocketed his .45 and picked up one of the Mausers, using it to point to the floor in front of the table. "You three, on your knees, here. Do it now."

They hesitated and the two bodyguards made eye contact. One gave a barely perceptible nod. Becker shot him in the ankle. So much for making a run at us, you schmuck.

"Do it now," Becker repeated. "Hands behind your head."

The wounded man slid to the floor first, all color drained from his face as he bit fiercely into his lower lip. The other bodyguard knelt next to him but Becker waved him to one side.

"Make a space. Monsieur Garza, in the middle," Becker said. "Angie, can you keep one eye on the hall and the other on my back here?"

Angie moved to the dining room doorway and leaned against the doorjamb. "We're covered," he said.

"Someone comes in, OK. But nobody leaves the hotel."

"Got it. You OK here?"

"Maybe, but if one of these guys drops me somehow-"

"I drop him," Angie said.

All three men were now kneeling on the floor in a row, the wounded guard's face defiant, Garza's blank with shock and the second guard's wary and alert.

"Monsieur Garza, you have money which belongs to the Cause," Becker said.

"I don't have money! There is no money!" said Garza. Becker saw the second guard's eyes dart toward his employer for an instant.

"Where is the money?" Becker said.

"There is no money!" Garza repeated. Becker turned the Mauser toward the wounded guard and shot him in the face. The bullet entered just under his nose, crashed through the jawbone and severed the left carotid artery as it passed out the back of his head. A geyser of blood shot three feet into the air before he fell backward into the table and knocked over a chair as he fell onto his left side. One leg twitched and a wet, gurgling noise escaped the hole in his face for the few seconds it took him to die.

Becker now pointed the pistol at the second guard. "Monsieur Garza, time grows short. Where is the money?"

"I tell you, there is no-"

"It's in the room on the fifth floor," the guard said.

"Where in the room?" Becker said.

"Under the floor.".

Becker backed away from the men. "Monsieur Garza, you will lie face down on the floor please. If you move, my friend will kill you," he said. "You," he gestured to the guard. "Get up. We are going to the elevator."

Becker stayed a safe distance behind the man as they walked past Angie and out into the hallway, pocketing the Mauser and drawing the .45 on the way. When they came to the elevator, Becker could see that it was already on the ground floor.

"Wait," he said. "You will press the button. When the door opens, do not turn around. You will enter, kneel and press your forehead against the wall, keeping your hands behind your head at all times. If you make any other movement I will fire into your bowels and leave you to die. *Verstehen?*"

"*Ja.*"

It struck Becker that he had inadvertently switched to German when addressing the guard. The guard seemed to make nothing of it, but he knew it couldn't have gone unnoticed. He remembered Martin's admonition about identifying the forger and cursed his carelessness. But what will he make me out to be? Becker thought. English, like Garza had? German? French? Maybe he had confused the issue enough that he might be able to let this man live.

When they reached the fifth floor, Becker backed halfway out and stood with his right foot against the elevator gate to prevent it closing. There were two women and a man in their night clothes arguing at the end of the hallway.

"Get back your rooms!" Becker shouted. "In twenty minutes you can come out."

The group stared, their mouths hanging open in shocked silence. "Move!" Becker shouted, louder this time. The group scurried into two different rooms.

Becker backed out of the elevator and put his left hand on the gate to hold it open.

"Stand," he said to the German. The man quickly got his feet under him and stood.

"May I turn?" he said.

"No. When I tell you, you will back out slowly. I will hold the gate and you will keep your back to me at all times. If you turn toward me or make a move for the gun I will fire and continue firing until you are dead. *Verstehen?*"

"I understand."

"Now," Becker said. The guard backed up slowly. When he had cleared the door, Becker let it close and stood back a safe distance. "Stop," he said. "The money is in this room or the other?"

"This room. Lopez's room."

"Enter. It's not locked."

The guard opened the door, stepped into the room and stopped. "Continue. To the far side of the bed. Keep your hands behind your head and do not turn around." Becker followed him into the room and locked the door behind him.

"Turn," Becker said. The guard did so. His face showed alertness but no fear. "Where is it?" Becker asked.

"Under the floor."

"Lopez told you this?"

"He didn't tell us. We found it ourselves. The idiot thought we didn't know. There are not so many places to hide money in a hotel room. Our orders were to retrieve the money if anything happened to Lopez."

"His name is not Lopez," Becker said.

"I know." The man shrugged. "It's just habit."

"Get the money now," Becker said.

"I have to move the bed."

Becker considered this. "How far?" he said.

"Perhaps one meter toward you."

"Do it now. You can put your hands down."

The guard got into a low crouch and pushed on the side of the bed frame until he had cleared the necessary space. He then knelt on the floor with his hands resting on his thighs. Becker moved sideways keeping his back against the wall and using his hip to push the dresser toward the bathroom door. This gave him a view of the floor in front of the German and a better field of fire. He could see that two of the floorboards had been pried up, pounded back into place and damaged in the process. They no longer fit flush with the rest of the floor.

"Open it up," Becker said.

The German tried to get his fingernails under the edge of the boards to pull them up but they were wedged in tight enough to prevent him getting purchase.

"I need some tool," he said.

Becker wanted to avoid giving him any type of edged weapon. He quickly scanned the room, looking for some substitute for a knife. He saw small toilet kit laying open on the dresser with slots that held a safety razor, nail clippers and nail file. He took the nail file and threw it on the bed within reach of the German.

"You're joking," said the guard.

"Get to work," Becker said.

The German put the edge of the nail file between the boards and tried to move them but the file bent on the first try. While the German was busy in the attempt, Becker took the opportunity to get his own switchblade out of his pocket and hold it in his left hand. The German looked up at him.

"This is pointless," he said.

"What did Lopez use?" Becker asked.

"Who knows? Ask Lopez."

Some note of condescension in the German's voice irked Becker. "You're right. But I'll need to put a bullet in your head now before I bring him up here and I'm a little pressed for time. This is a last chance to save your life." Becker tossed the switchblade, unopened, onto the bed. "Listen carefully. Open the knife and use it to lift the boards, but do not turn your eyes toward me. If you so much as look at me while that knife is in your hands I will kill you. Understand?"

The German nodded, took the knife and snapped the blade open. Both floorboards were up in seconds.

"Close the knife and push it across the bed toward me."

In a moment, the switchblade was safely back in Becker's pants pocket.

"Is there a weapon in there?" Becker asked.

"I don't know," said the German.

"If it were me, I would put a pistol in there, just for emergencies. In any case, I want you to take out the money and put it on the bed. If I see a weapon of any kind, you know what will happen."

"I know." The German put a hand on each side of the hole in the floorboards and peered in. "There is a bag on top. I will have to take that out first." He reached in and produced a small, expensive-looking leather grip which he tossed on the bed. Then, using his left arm as support, he reached deep between the floorboards with his right to produce several bundles of five pound sterling notes and American one hundred dollar bills which he placed on the bed next to the bag.

"That's all?" The German nodded. "Where is the rest?"

"Lopez has lived well these past weeks. He also needed to pay us and give some to his mother."

"You were paid well?" Becker said.

"I have no complaints."

The German had no way of knowing who Becker was or what information he had, so his lies must have seemed plausible, but Becker knew that a large part of the money was missing and that it certainly had not gone to Garza's mother or high living. But he had no time to get the information out of the German, even if such a thing were possible. He knew the man's main reason for bringing him to the room was to separate him from Angie so he could kill him and make his escape.

"Replace the floorboards and the bed please." The German quickly laid the floorboards in place before pounding each with the edge of his hand. He then pulled the bed back to the original position. "And put the money in the bag."

The German made an elegant display of efficiency as he lined the bundles across the top of the grip which was already half full of assorted papers and official-looking documents. When all the money was packed and the bag was full but not bulging, he zipped the top closed, buckled a single strap across the top, picked up the bag at both ends and threw it with all his strength at Becker's face – lunging after it to get his hands on Becker's .45.

Becker cocked his head effortlessly like he was slipping a punch and the bag barely grazed him as it passed over his left shoulder, crashing into the mirror above the dresser. The German followed a split second behind, taking giant steps across the bed with both hands outstretched and shouting an earsplitting "Ahhhhh!" in a further attempt to distract Becker from taking aim and firing. But for Becker, the scene moved in slow motion, puzzling and oddly familiar, like something he might have read in a book or seen at the cinema years ago. When the hands were two feet from him, he moved his left arm in a giant semi-circle, sweeping the German off balance as he crashed the butt of the .45 against the man's left temple. The body dropped like a stone and lay in a twisted heap at the foot of the bed.

Dumb shit, Becker thought. Do I look like I'm just off the boat? Well, I guess I am just off the boat, in a manner of speaking. Now what? I put a bullet in his head? He put his hand to the man's neck and detected a pulse. He also heard a groan of pain and, glancing down, saw that the man had broken both bones of his right wrist in the fall. One had broken the skin. This guy is definitely having a bad night. Best to leave him and get out before he wakes up. I bet he'll be surprised to wake up in this world.

Becker took the grip from the floor and walked out the door, crossing the hallway to the room where he had left Jarek, half expecting to see the room empty and that the big man had already made his way downstairs. He opened the door and saw him lying on the bed, his barrel chest rising and falling as he drew deep, painful breaths. Becker guessed that each breath caused his diaphragm to press on the wound, causing excruciating pain. Both hands were crossed over the makeshift field dressing, but it had done little good. There was blood everywhere.

"Jarek."

His eyes opened halfway and turned toward Becker.

"We have to leave you. If we move you, it will surely kill you. We'll call an ambulance as soon as we can get to a phone."

His breathing slowed. *"Ça ne fait rien,"* he said. The ambiguity of the phrase troubled Becker. It's nothing? It does nothing? Don't worry about it? It doesn't matter? The man knows he's dying and this is how he goes out? Becker knew he wouldn't have survived the gunfight alone and felt he owed the man something.

"Thank you for saving my life," Becker said.

Jarek's eyes turned toward the ceiling. *"Ça ne fait rien,"* he repeated. His breathing stopped. Becker checked for a pulse at his wrist and his neck. Nothing. The eyes were still open. He reached up his left hand and tried to tenderly ease the eyes shut, like he had seen in the movies, but the left one put up some resistance. In the end, he used his thumb to push the eyelid down, but as he took his hand away he thought he saw it slowly coming up again. Sorry, friend, Becker thought. When you meet your maker, you may be winking at him.

He patted down Jarek's body for identification and found nothing. He then covered the body with the other half of the bedspread, picked up the shotgun from behind the door and walked back to Lopez's room.

The German was coming around, slowly pushing himself into a sitting position against the dresser and gaping in disbelief at the torn flesh and protruding white bone of his right wrist. His pallor, drooping eyelids and shallow breathing and told Becker he was going into shock. Seeing the life go out of Jarek had made up his mind. He took one of the Mausers from his coat pocket, dropped to one knee and fired a single round through the man's right ear. Louder for me than for you, he thought.

What time is it? He looked at his watch. Eleven-forty. Damn. Is there a beat cop who stops in around here? No shooting from downstairs. If there'd been trouble, Angie would have warned me. He made a quick check of the dead man's pockets. He found a few francs, a German passport issued the previous summer and apparently good until 1941 and a German driver's license. Becker took all of them.

He found Angie just where he'd left him, his back against the doorjamb, glancing back and forth from the dining room to the main foyer.

"Any action?" Becker said as he started emptying the other German's pockets.

"One old geezer came in. Got off the elevator at the third floor. Nobody tried to leave."

"Do me a favor."

"Yeah?" Angie showed only curiosity. Becker never asked for favors.

Becker handed Angie the Mauser and nodded toward Garza, face down on the floor. Angie replied by holding up his .45. Becker shook his head.

"Quieter. And we need the rounds," he whispered.

Angie gave a deep nod and took the Mauser, checking the chamber as he did so. He walked over to Garza's prone form. "We'll be leaving now. It's been nice meeting you Mister Garza."

"The pleasure was mine," he answered automatically.

Angie straddled Garza's torso, pulled his head back by the hair and fired two quick shots into the base of his skull.

"Now check his pockets and let's get the hell out of here," Becker said, keeping one eye on the hallway and front door. He heard Angie wrestling with Garza's lifeless form between the tables.

"Matt, he doesn't look heavy, but I can't turn this guy over." Becker new there were few things more uncooperative than a dead or unconscious body.

"Put both his arms over his head."

"Matt, he's pretty dead. I think it's too late for artificial-"

"Angie, just do it."

Angie pulled Garza's arms straight out above his head. "Now hold his wrists and roll him," Becker said. The body rolled smoothly onto its back.

"Hah! Great trick. Where'd you learn that?"

"I was a lifeguard in a past life. Toss me his wallet and any papers."

"Jesus, the guy's got three wallets," Angie said, throwing over a worn brown leather billfold, a passport case and a long, zippered black leather case that looked like it was meant to be carried in the inside breast pocket of an expensive suit or overcoat. Becker stuffed them all in his coat and trousers pockets.

"Keep the cash," Becker said.

"Nice little piece," Angie said as he gave back the Mauser.

"Keep it."

"Matt, I already got the other one. One more and I'll start to clank when I walk."

"Like you got problems?" Becker opened his coat to show the machine pistol.

"What the hell is that?" Angie said.

"Damned if I know. Now let's move. We gotta get out of here."

"You got that right," Angie said. They both headed for the front door.

"One minute, let me get this poor guy loose," Becker said.

"Who?" Angie said.

"The clerk. Can you wrap this thing up again before we walk outside?" he said, tossing the shotgun to Angie.

"Got it." Angie caught the weapon casually with one hand and found the piece of padding from the truck on one of the foyer chairs.

Becker opened the door to the office and switched on the light. He saw Bozzoli lying on his side, tied to the chair just as Jarek had left him.

"Monsieur, as I promised-" Becker began.

Becker saw Bozzoli's eyes staring straight ahead, strangely bloodshot, his face frozen in a contorted expression of panic. He quickly tore the tape from around his head and pulled the handkerchief out of the open mouth but the cloth seemed to take forever to emerge, like a silk scarf from a magician's sleeve. When the mouth was empty it stayed open, the eyes continued to bulge, the face remained frozen. Becker checked for a pulse a found none. He looked on the desk and saw Bozzoli's wallet, the sheaf of bills still protruding from it. The cops will get those, Becker thought. He took them.

"Let's get out of here," he said to Angie as he returned to the hallway.

"How's he doing?"

"Dead."

"By who?"

"We had to gag him. He swallowed it," Becker said.

"Poor bastard," Angie said.

They walked toward the truck and saw both that both cab windows were open to keep the windshield free of steam, but the usual fog of cigarette smoke obscured Albert's face and made his expression impossible to read. The engine was running, the truck ready to go.

"Front or back?" Angie asked.

"I'd better take the front. I have to give Albert the box scores. Plus, I'm not sure Albert will want to see you right now."

"Oh, yeah. The sauerkraut. Well, check on me once in a while. It's gonna be freezing back there."

"Cover up. Use the padding." Becker said.

The cab was warm but the air was a fetid miasma of cigarette smoke and every noxious odor the human body could produce short of actual decomposition. Becker threw the leather grip in on the floor, but couldn't bring himself to actually get in. Another wave of nausea rolled over him but he steadied himself against the open door, clenched his teeth and swallowed back a mouthful of bile.

"Come on!" Albert said. "You're letting out the heat!"

"Albert, did you eat *choucroute* today too?" Becker asked.

"What's that supposed to mean?"

"Nothing. For the love of God, could you put out the cigarette? It stinks in here."

Becker imagined the Gallic cheek puffing as he got in but didn't look Albert in the eyes, instead rolling down the window and letting the icy breeze blow on his face. Albert put the truck in gear and moved into traffic.

"I didn't see Jarek," he said.

"Jarek isn't coming," Becker said. "Is there anything to drink?"

Albert reached behind the seat an produced a half-full bottle of red wine. Becker pulled out the cork and sniffed the contents before taking a sip. He swished it around in his mouth and spit it out the window before upending the bottle and taking a long swallow. It was rough and strong but better than nothing.

"You're a sight," Albert said, noticing the Becker's blood-soaked clothes and the scratches on his face as they passed a well-lit intersection.

Becker said nothing.

"Are you injured?"

"Something in my eye. It burns." Becker paused and looked at his clothes. "It's not my blood, I don't think. Jarek...I left him in one of the rooms."

"That's the money?" Albert asked, looking at the bag on the floor. Becker nodded. "All of it?"

Becker turned his face from the window and looked at Albert, his face waxen and blood streaked, his grey eyes black in the flickering shadows of the cab.

"What?"

"Is that all the money?" Albert said.

"Maybe not. Let's go back and check," Becker said, his voice flat and his face turned to stone.

"Go back? Now? Are you serious?" Albert looked back and forth from Becker to the street ahead.

"This time I'll wait in the truck," added Becker.

There was a long silence between the men. Becker watched as they passed the street scenes of Paris nightlife. It was nearly midnight but the cafés and restaurants were full. A deep weariness settled over him. Angie should be up here seeing this, he thought. I should be curled up in the back.

"Forgive the question, my friend. I spoke without thinking," Albert said.

"*Ça ne fait rien.*" Jarek's agonized whisper echoed n Becker's head.

"What did you say?"

"Jarek's last words to me. '*Ça ne fait rien.*' Did you know him?" Becker asked.

"Not really. I saw him with Alma a few times over the past weeks. He needed someone big enough to carry him up stairs. He seemed a good enough fellow. Always reading." Albert paused, needing to know but afraid to ask. "Mathieu, what happened in there?"

"There was a third *boche*, as we feared. He shot at us through the door, with this." Becker pulled aside his coat to reveal the machine pistol.

"What is it?"

"You know what a Thompson is?

"A what?"

"A Tommy gun. From the cinema. You know, da-da-da-da."

"And you weren't hit?" He shook his head. "You've got the luck."

Do I tell him that the shotgun misfired, leaving Jarek a sitting duck? Becker thought. No reason he should know. Nothing to be gained by it. "We broke in, but he was ready for us. More shooting. He made it out the fire escape, but I know he was hit. A lot of blood. I hope he bled to death in a gutter."

"I saw him leave the alley. He was injured, holding his side. I wanted to follow, but-"

"I glad you didn't. You'd be dead now. This one knows his business and we need you here."

"And Garza?" Albert asked.

"Mr. Garza stayed silent to the end. But one of his guards was willing to give up the money to save his life," Becker said.

"So, *l'addition*?" What was the bill?

"All."

"And Jarek," Albert said.

"And an innocent."

"Who is innocent?"

"The clerk." Becker recounted his dealings with Bozzoli and how he died.

"It couldn't be helped," Albert said. "It's not your fault. It's the war."

"He has a family. And he owes money. I want to get the money I promised him to his wife. Can you do this for me?"

"You have the address?" Albert asked. Becker recited the address he had memorized from Bozzoli's identity papers.

"I can find it."

"This is important to me Albert," Becker said.

"I take the responsibility." Albert tried to choose his next words with care. "Mathieu, these deaths, they are not your fault. You must not punish yourself. It serves no purpose."

But Becker's head had fallen forward on his chest. He was fast asleep.

CHAPTER 12

The next day, Albert climbed the winding staircase to the garret room of the safe house at nine in the morning, doing his best to balance a small coffee pot, two *cafés au lait* and a baguette on a small tray. As he made a turn, the baguette caught the banister and splashed half the contents of one of the cups before falling to a small landing two flights down. He uttered a fervent obscenity which echoed through the stairwell before he set the tray on the floor and dashed down to retrieve the baguette.

The bright sunlight of the garret had gently awakened Angie and Becker at dawn but neither had wanted to leave the warmth of their beds, despite the growing awareness of a cavernous void in their stomachs.

"Matt. You awake?" Angie said in a loud whisper.

"Nope. Out cold."

"Somebody's coming up the stairs," Angie said.

"Let 'em come," Becker said. Before going to bed they had locked and bolted the door. Considering that a feeble gesture, they had moved the room's only substantial piece of furniture, an ancient, towering armoire, in front of the door to act as a barricade.

"Yeah, but I smell coffee," Angie said.

Albert tapped gently on the door.

"Albert?" Becker called.

"Yes, it's me. I'm alone."

"Give us a minute, will you?"

Albert listened to the sounds of bare footsteps and furniture scraping across the wood floor followed by the bolt being drawn and the key turned. The door finally opened on the sight of the two of them standing in their underwear, bloodstains still covering the front of Mathieu's t-shirt.

"I brought you some breakfast," Albert said.

They put the tray on a chair between the two beds and Angie immediately picked up the baguette.

"What the hell is this?" he asked.

"It's bread," Becker said.

"Kind of hard." He tapped it against his palm. "You could beat a man to death with this thing."

"Give it here," Becker said. He tore the bread into two equal portions and gave one to Angie. "Just try it. Maybe you'll like it."

Albert sat on one of the beds and watched in bemused silence as they slathered layers of butter and marmalade on the bread before rending off huge mouthfuls by biting down on the leathery crust and twisting their heads like wild beasts.

"Kind of chewy," Angie said through a mouthful of food. Noticing Albert's expression he added, "But real good."

"You said you had business today. What is it?" Albert asked.

"Uncle, we are carrying money. It's our own, we brought it from home, but it is too much to be carrying into a war. We need a safe place to keep it. I was thinking of going to a bank, getting a safety deposit box," Becker said.

"It becomes clear. You watch those rucksacks like mother hens."

"Can you find us a bank? Dependable, but where we will not attract attention?"

Albert sat in quiet contemplation, watching swirling dust motes do silent battle with his cigarette smoke in the morning sunlight from the garret window.

"This money is for emergencies, is it not?" he asked.

"We may die there, Uncle, but we can't depend on it."

Albert nodded." I take your point, and your idea is sound, but I think the money would be better placed nearer the fighting."

"You have a suggestion?"

"Tonight, we leave for Toulouse. It is not a big city, nor is it small or insignificant. But it is not so far from the border as Paris. If you need to get out of Spain in a hurry, your funds will be much closer. The disadvantage is that they will be in the obvious direction of your escape." He paused to take a deep pull on his cigarette. "But this cannot be helped."

"Agreed. Please excuse me," Becker said. He quickly explained Albert's suggestions and the reasons behind it to Angie, who nodded approvingly at the simple common sense of it.

"We gotta start thinking more logistical, not just tactical," he said.

It was the kind of statement from Angie that always hit Becker like a flashbulb going off in his face. Maybe Angie is really some higher form of being who just keeps me around for his amusement, Becker thought. He plays this tough, ignorant-but-streetwise thug as a game, just to make fun of the rest of us.

"Good point," Becker said.

" 'Course it is," Angie said. "But where the hell is Toulouse? And, no offense, the name kind of gives me the creeps as a place to keep money." It took Becker a second to realize he meant the French pronunciation which sounded like "to lose" in English.

"You'll get over it." But Becker realized that apart from the fact that it was in a southerly direction, he wasn't really sure where it was either. He always mixed up Toulouse and Toulon, but he knew one of them was a seaport. Maybe they would be going by ship? He thought. It sure beats marching and climbing through the snow. Becker handed over a piece of note paper and a pen from his pack on which Albert scribbled a crude map of his homeland. All the borders and coastlines came out as straight lines connected by sharp angles.

"Paris, here. Switzerland, here. Spain, the Pyrenees, here," he said as he pointed with the pen. "Toulouse, here, not so far from the mountains."

So much for another ocean voyage, Becker thought. But, come to think of it, a lot of the ships headed for the Republic were ending up on the bottom of the Mediterranean. An image of himself treading oily water, surrounded by debris and floating bodies while a U-boat machine-gunned the survivors flashed through his mind.

"Which brings me to our next task for today," Becker said, pointing to his shoes next to the bed. "We can't cross the mountains in those, much less go into the trenches."

"Get dressed. We'll get the boots. But Mathieu, as one who had been in the trenches, let me suggest that you worry about socks as much as boots. I'll meet you downstairs in thirty minutes. No doubt, you want to shower. Again. Like good Americans." He left the room, shaking his head in exasperation.

"What the hell was that all about?" Angie said.

"He says we gotta worry about socks, not just boots. And he thinks we wash too much."

"That's 'cause he's got no sense of smell. Another week in this town and I'm gonna lose mine, or drop dead. One or the other."

Becker lost a coin toss and had to bear the icy blast of cold water first. He headed down the winding staircase to the first floor carrying soap and a towel. At the bottom of the stairs he saw the landlady, whose florid but friendly face split into a broad smile at the sight of the American who actually spoke French. Still, she spoke to him like he was eight years old.

"Good day, Monsieur," she said, a little too slowly. Does she think I'm deaf or just stupid? Becker thought.

"Good day, Madame," Becker answered. " I hope we are no inconvenience? You have been so kind."

"Certainly not!" she insisted. She looked at the soap and towel. "Monsieur will take a shower again?"

"Yes Madame. There was some filthy business last night and-"

"No need to explain. Please, make yourself at home." The gentle face turned adamant for an instant before she started to climb the stairs. *Why am I explaining?* he thought. *She must be a veteran if she's watching this place for Albert.*

"Thank you, Madame."

The woman paused on the third step. "By the way, you've had no problem with the gas?"

"The gas?" Becker said.

"For the water heater."

"Actually, it's a little different than we use over there. If you have a moment, I want to be sure I don't make a mistake."

"Certainly not," she tut-tutted. "One could blow up the building! If Monsieur will permit me, I will show you. It's getting old, like me, and has some funny little tricks."

Out of sight behind the shower stall was a gas operated water heater which had to be turned on and lit with a kitchen match. It had a nasty habit of going out, in which case the soaking wet user would have to exit the stall, switch it off, wait for any accumulated gas to safely disperse and then re-light it. But Becker finally got it running well enough to enjoy rinsing the soap from his hair and body with warm water.

As he walked back to the room, he tormented himself over whether to tell Angie about the water heater. He finally decided that there's no point in a practical joke if the target never finds out.

"You gotta be shitting me," Angie said after he learned the truth.

"Angie, I swear to God, I just found out myself."

"The last shower I took there, my nuts went north for the rest of the day."

"Come on, I'll run you through the drill. Try not to blow up the building," Becker said.

"Yeah, after all this, I blow myself up taking a shower."

By the end of the morning they had each found some sturdy boots, a half dozen pairs of thick hiking socks and some woolen caps. They also went to a used clothing store and replaced their nondescript gray, city topcoats with heavy, leather fleece-lined jackets which reached to mid-thigh, belted in the middle and had a multiplicity of pockets, both large and small. They were well scuffed and faded in places, but the leather was sound and rugged.

"I feel like Eddie Rickenbacker in this thing," Angie said.

"Angie, it's January, for crying out loud. And we're walking into the mountains."

"Still, I feel like a *chooch*." His frown changed to his usual playful grin. "Think I could get a flying helmet and goggles in this joint?"

"Don't forget the silk scarf," Becker said.

"Yeah, right. So I'll go out like Isadora Duncan. Forget about it."

Albert tried to make some sense of their conversation with his limited knowledge of English and almost thought he had the gist when he heard Rickenbacker's name, but gave up when the subject turned to the modern dancer. He wanted to ask what they were talking about but was certain the explanation would only make it worse. Do all Americans talk so much nonsense, he thought?

They walked away from the store with Becker shaking his head to himself. Angie knows about Isadora Duncan? he thought. Never underestimate Angie, and don't be such a condescending bastard.

Their final stop was a used bookshop. A small bell rang as they entered and walked on a creaking floor between ceiling-high stacks of hard and soft cover books of all types and ages. They came to a counter at the end of the room where Albert greeted a man who could have been his twin except for his distinctly North-African features. He embraced Albert warmly and shook hands with Becker and Angie, but no names were exchanged and no offense taken.

After the cursory formalities, Albert reached into his pocket and produced a single cartridge and set it on the counter. The shop owner picked it up, adjusted his glasses, and examined it with a practiced eye.

".45 ACP," he said, half to himself. "Don't see many of these."

"Do you have any?" Albert asked.

"You have an American .45? I can give you a good price."

"Unfortunately, this is for a friend. I wouldn't even know what a .45 looks like."

"Well, give me few moments to check. I'll see what I have."

Angie and Becker appeared to browse the aisles on opposite sides of the shop but Becker stayed close enough to listen carefully for signs of trouble and protect Albert at the counter while Angie positioned himself to cover the door.

The man returned quickly, a broad smile on his face. *"Voilà!"* he said. "You're in luck." He put four twenty-round boxes on the counter.

"Émile!" Albert called. "Could you put down the girlie magazine and come here for a moment?"

Becker walked sheepishly to the counter. "It was just a novel, Uncle."

"Your nephew?" said the shop owner.

"The son of an old comrade. No real nephews, I'm afraid. Just nieces." Albert slid one of the boxes open and extracted one of the cartridges. "Émile. What do you think?"

Becker examined the cartridge from every possible angle, then took two more from the box. "I beg your pardon. The light is so much better at the window." The older men nodded and proceeded to chat about old days, an old neighborhood and old friends. Becker took the cartridges down the side aisle to Angie and gave two to him.

"What do you think?" whispered Becker.

Angie rolled one cartridge back and forth in his palm before holding it up in his fingertips and checking for the primer for corrosion. He did the same with the others.

"Can't find a damn thing wrong with them," he said.

Becker walked back to the counter and replaced the cartridges in the box. "They look fine. You wouldn't know how old these are, would you?"

"They're American, as you can see. My guess is that some doughboy sold them here at the end of the war."

"Well, as you said, we're lucky to find any at all. We'll take them," Becker said. "How much?"

The man named a figure which meant nothing to Becker but its rising intonation indicated it was a testing of the waters rather than an ultimatum. Albert answered with an amount about twenty-five percent lower which was accepted with a shrug and a smile.

"Done," the man said, already taking some brown paper and twine from under the counter and preparing to wrap the purchase.

"Pardon, but perhaps you could help us with one or two other things," Becker said.

"How can I be of service?" His manner turned formal and businesslike.

"Nine millimeter, parabellum?" Becker said.

"As much as you need."

"About forty rounds," Becker said. The man was back in an instant with two boxes.

"Something else?"

"I guess we are finished, unless, you wouldn't have any of these would you?" Becker held up one of the 7.65 rounds.

The shop owner took the cartridge in his fingertips and twirled it around. "For the little *boche* pistol?" Becker nodded. "Where did you get it?"

"From a little *boche*."

The man's lips pursed in self-reproach. "Forgive me, not my business. A moment please."

He returned with four more boxes of 7.65 cartridges, considerably newer than the .45s.

"Please take these as a gift for my friend's nephew." He found a cardboard container and arranged the various ammunition boxes inside, filling in the voids with crumpled newspaper before wrapping the whole package with twine, handing it across the counter to Albert and quoting the total price. Becker gave him a handful of franc notes.

"Your change. Just a moment please," the man said.

"Please, don't trouble yourself for a few francs. We are all friends, is it not so?" The last phrase stopped the man's breath in his throat as he searched Becker's face for its true meaning. He saw only a warm smile – and bitterly cold eyes.

"I have one of the pistols if you are interested. A German naval officer sold it to pay for his girlfriend's – medical problems."

"Not necessary, thank you," Becker said. "But thank you for your help and your kindness." He took the package and headed out the door.

"I'll be just a minute, Émile," Albert said.

"Take your time, Uncle. We'll just have a cigarette." Angie and Becker closed the door gently behind them.

"Your nephew, he knows his weapons?" asked the store owner.

"Better than me," Albert said.

"And their use?"

"Better than me."

"He has good manners. So many young people today-" The man had begun to perspire. He took out a handkerchief to wipe his forehead.

"True. His mother raised him well," Albert said.

"His mother? I should light a candle for the father."

The man stopped himself at the very instant that the words *And who is his father?* were about to pass his lips. "Albert, forgive me for saying this, but your nephew – something is not quite right."

Albert raised his hand. "I know what you're saying, but you've only seen one side of him. There is death around him. But I honestly believe that it will be death for our enemies."

"He is of the Cause?"

"And he has proved himself," Albert said.

"They are going south, he and his friend?"

"Perhaps," Albert said.

"May God watch over them."

"If He just stays out of their way, I think that will suffice."

They drove through the heart of Paris, Angie's face pressed against the window glass or sometimes actually hanging out the window to watch the wonders pass by. They crossed the river and headed northwest along the Champs-Elysées until they came to the Arch of Triumph and Angie frantically insisted that Becker translate his request to negotiate the organized bedlam of the traffic circle one more time so he could get a second look at the tribute to Napoleon's victories. Albert's response was a combination of laughter and good-natured cursing, but he was quick to acquiesce, accelerating with many exaggerated appeals to the mercy of the Blessed Virgin as he inveighed against the incompetence and general torpidity of the other motorists.

When they arrived at their destination, Becker reckoned their location to be somewhere in the northeast part of the Paris but still within the city proper. He had been hoping to see some sign or remnant of one of the medieval doors or *portes* of the city but he had not and was sure he would have noticed. They were in a residential neighborhood of elegant townhouses and expensive cars. Becker was grateful that they were driving Alma's sedan and not the *Fournier & Sons* truck they had used the night before.

"Is *this* where he lives?" Angie asked.

"No," Albert said. He didn't elaborate.

The three of them walked to the next block over from where they had parked and Albert took the lead as they mounted a flight of white marble steps. Something Becker had never seen outside the cinema, a young woman in a maid's uniform, answered the door. She took no notice of their working-class attire, addressed Albert with formal verbs and delivered the French equivalent of "And who may I say is calling?" with absolute aplomb and courtesy. Angie made a great show of bowing and taking off his cap to the maid as they entered. Becker noticed and whispered to Albert.

"Under no circumstances, give Angie anything to draw with," he said.

Albert looked from Angie to the maid and then to Becker, finally giving a deep single nod and a conspiratorial smile.

They were led into a study with a bay window, an elegant sofa and chair suite at one end and a massive, ornate wooden desk the another. Walls of bookshelves lined the space in between. Alma was seated at the desk reading a book, but he stood quickly as the maid announced his guests. He was wearing the same suit as at their first meeting.

"Monsieur Albert and his associates," she changed effortlessly into English.

"Gentlemen, please sit down. What a pleasure. I didn't expect the pleasure of seeing you again. Coffee, tea?" Alma looked at a vest pocket watch. "An aperitif? It's getting late."

"Just coffee. Another late night, I'm afraid," Albert said.

"So how much did we recover?" Alma said. Albert did not respond but ceded the floor to Becker.

Becker rose and placed the leather grip at Alma's feet. "This is everything we found. There are several bundles of British one pound and five pound notes which I have not counted. Also, American dollars in twenty, fifty and one hundred dollar denominations, a little over eighty thousand dollars in total. But it seems that much of the original amount cannot be accounted for, even considering the cost of Garza's expenses and protection. "

"And Jarek?" Alma asked.

Becker's mood had darkened when that question had not been the first order of business, but he quietly reasoned with himself that his emotions were soon to be his worst enemy. He set them aside in a special file for outstanding accounts, hoping he could manage to misplace it one day.

"He was shot. He probably saved my life, but we had to leave his body for the police. He had no incriminating documents on him when I left him," Becker said.

"He was dead when you left him?" Alma said.

"There was a wound in the abdomen, here," Becker pointed to his own body. "And two other places. But this one, I could not stop the bleeding. I believe that he felt no pain at the end."

"That, at least, is a blessing," the old man said.

"He mentioned a sister," Becker said. "He had a family?"

"She died in childbirth last year. He hardly ever spoke of it." Alma raised his eyes and looked at Becker. For him, this death was just another in a multitude.

"And the child?"

"It did not survive. The conditions were most severe. I believe they were in a railroad car at the time. Jarek was with her, but there was little he could do." Alma's thoughts were far away, but he finally looked back at Becker. "I'm surprised he mentioned her to you."

"There was some delirium at the end," Becker said.

"Garza and his guards?" Alma asked.

Becker didn't know how to phrase it so he simply shook his head.

"Just as well," Alma said. "The committee could waste a lifetime dealing with this embarrassment and there would still be no resolution. This solves many problems."

"But not all," Becker said. Alma's eyes went up. "There was a third guard, different from the others, more dangerous, more professional and heavily armed. We wounded him, possibly a fatal wound but we can't be sure. He escaped and we didn't have the means to pursue him."

"What do you suggest?" Alma said.

"Whatever this man's mission is, either it has failed or it is not yet finished. You and your comrades should take measures to protect yourself."

"Don't worry, young man. Your concern shows the kindness of your heart, but we are well protected. You needn't concern yourself."

Becker said nothing for a few moments. The maid had come and gone, oblivious to Angie's most charming smile, apparently indifferent that he had stood when she entered the room. But Angie maintained his customary optimism. Just the sight of a pretty girl was enough to brighten his day. Becker, however, felt that he had failed to get his point across.

"Comrade," he said to Alma.

"Yes, my boy," the old man answered, stirring milk into his tea.

"Look me in the eyes," Becker said. His voice was a saber drawn slowly across a whetstone. Alma looked at him.

"It is not my intention to be kind. You believe that you're protected?"

"Yes."

"I mean no disrespect, but consider carefully before you answer me," Becker said.

"Of course."

"If I set out to kill you, what would be the result?"

Clouds passed in front of the late afternoon sun and the room took on a noticeable chill as Alma considered his answer.

"I'm sure I could not stop you," Alma said.

"The man that escaped us is infinitely more dangerous. I saw his eyes. I urge you to take this threat seriously."

Alma set his tea cup on the table, put his face in both hands and sighed deeply. Becker wondered if there might be tears, but in the end he simply rubbed his eyes before looking up.

"For me, it is that I have lost the desire to go on. But you are quite right. There are others who need to be watched and moved. I will set this in motion immediately."

"I would be grateful," Becker said. "This is the man who killed Jarek and I am sure that he is as dedicated to his cause as we are to ours. And I fear he may be a much better killer."

"I understand," the old man said. "And I know that you doubt my understanding, but I assure you that I know the danger. This is not my first battle. I will not be in this house tonight."

Albert and Becker both nodded.

"Would you like us to take you somewhere?" Albert said.

"Best that you not know where I will be," he replied.

"But it's your car."

"To do with as you wish. It's no longer safe for me to drive, especially at night," Alma said.

"You seem to get around well enough," Angie said, trying to brighten the mood.

"Ah, yes. True enough. But I've been known to lose consciousness behind the wheel of late, which is most disconcerting to my passengers, not to mention any pedestrians in the vicinity."

"Fortunately, I generally pass out before I make it to the car," Angie said with mock seriousness. "And by that time my female companions seem disinclined to revive me."

Becker's eyes widened at Angie's sudden change of dialect, expecting that Alma would have no idea what he was talking about, but to his surprise, the old man's face broke into a wide grin. Angie had won him over long ago and Becker hadn't noticed it.

"Ah the fickle heart of woman," Alma said, with mock sadness.

"Ain't that the truth," Angie said.

The small group of comrades finished their coffee while making small talk. Both Albert and Alma tried to be optimistic about the war, but Becker sensed that there was a much broader and more dangerous conflict at the core of their concern. Angie and Becker listened, showing polite interest, but contributing little. The events of the previous evening were still too much on their minds. The topic turned finally to the weather and all knew that the meeting was drawing to a close.

"Before you go, I wonder if I could ask you to do me a small service," Alma said, as he rose slowly from the sofa and used his cane to walk stiffly toward the desk. The others also stood.

"Certainly," Becker said.

Alma took a plain white envelope from the top of a pile on the desk and handed it to Becker. It was thin, possibly containing a single sheet of letter paper, and sealed with a illegible signature across the flap as a perfunctory guard against tampering. There was no address on the front, only a six-letter cipher written in block letters.

"It is a simple code, but it will do for the intended purpose," Alma said.

"Which is?" Becker said.

"I would be very grateful if this were to reach the military commander of the International Brigades."

Becker considered the request. Who the hell am I to be asking to see the military commander?

"Monsieur," he said, shaking his head slowly, "I will of course do my best, but I have no authority, that is, I'm in no position to-"

"If you do your best, then that is sufficient. I understand that it may never reach its destination. If it doesn't, no harm is done. The contents are meaningless to anyone but the commander. But please, remember that it should go to the *military* commander. I would prefer that it not go to André Marty."

"I will make every effort," Becker said.

"If you cannot meet with the commander, please pass it to the most senior military officer you encounter."

"Whom shall I say it is from?"

Alma frowned as he considered the question, tugging gently on his chin with his left hand. After a moment he appeared to come to a decision.

"You may say that it comes from Department Five in Paris. I think it better not to mention this name that I am using." He shook his head disdainfully. "As you know, I don't like it, but it was not my choice."

They started south that night, with Albert driving, Becker navigating and Angie curled up in the back, using a rucksack for a pillow.

"Albert, on this map it looks like we have the better part of seven hundred kilometers to travel, probably more," Becker said.

"Basically, yes. I'd say that's so."

"And how long do you think that will take us?"

"Approximately?"

"OK."

"I have no idea. I've been east and west in this country, especially east. You know you're family is from-"

"I know."

"I've been to Normandy for vacation a few times. But all of that has been by train. Driving? Mostly in the city. I've never driven farther than Chartres."

"Chartres? You saw the cathedral?" Becker asked.

Albert gave him a blank look. "No, I missed it."

"Everybody's a wiseass," Becker said under his breath in English, but Albert had no trouble with his tone of voice.

"It's something to see, but I don't go in for all that religious crap." he said.

Becker reminded himself that his father, Martin and many of his friends were rabid atheists, an occasional source of tension in a family with so many Jewish blood relatives and in-laws. To his knowledge, no one in his family had ever seen the inside of a synagogue, but he often heard religious references pop up in the clan's crossbred lingua franca of Yiddish, French, German and English. At least he now knew where Albert stood.

They headed generally south and west, trying to steer clear of the highland massif that occupied the south-central part of the country and stay near the west coast where they hoped the roads would be flatter and straighter and they could make better time. Albert and Becker suppressed their longings to stop and explore the cities of Orléans and Tours and made a doomed attempt to explain their historic significance to Angie, but Joan of Arc, Charles the Hammer and the Moors meant nothing to him

"Did they ever make it into a movie?" Angie asked from the back seat, making no effort to conceal his boredom.

"Yeah, Minnie Mouse played Joan of Arc," Becker said.

"What about Noah?"

"Different Arc," Becker said.

"What's a Moor?"

"Basically, they were Spanish Arabs." Becker cringed inwardly at his own over-simplification.

"Bedouins?"

"Angie..."

"You're making all this up, aren't you," Angie said.

"Why do you always talk in nonsense?" Albert said, frustrated at his inability to catch their drift.

"Albert, it's just word games, to laugh at, stupid jokes," Becker said, switching to French. "Since we were children. He thinks I'm too serious, too proud of my schooling. So he teases me. Really, he's the smarter one. He just thinks teachers are fools."

"He's not far wrong."

The morning sunlight brought warmth to the back seat and Angie eventually drifted back to sleep.

"And what about you?" Albert asked. "You were going to be a teacher, is it not so? Like your mother and sister? I heard you were at a good school."

"I was at a good school, but perhaps the wrong type of student."

"Ah, you made a bad choice of necktie?"

"I don't think my necktie was the problem," Becker said to the window. Albert's question had sent his mind hurtling back in time to the same questions he tried to put out of his mind. Where had he gone wrong? He studied, he worked, he played by the rules. How had he attracted so much ill-will?

"I wasn't speaking literally." There was a moment's pause. Finally, Albert took his eyes off the road and looked at Becker. "So?"

Becker considered the question and couldn't find an answer that was sufficiently evasive without being rude. There was still a long ride ahead. He decided to come clean.

"It was no one thing. First, I wanted to be a French teacher, but my French was better than theirs."

"This I believe," Albert said.

"And German. It was the same. You know my mother."

Albert made a sound of dread. "I fear for the child who makes a mistake around her. She's not so easy on the adults either as I remember."

"And one of the professors had a boyfriend," Becker said.

Albert took a minute to digest this, his upper lip folding up toward his nose.

"And what did this have to do with you?" he asked.

"The boyfriend had a gambling problem and got himself in debt to the wrong people."

"And they sent you to collect?" Albert's tone was cheery, as if he finally understood.

"Long story. The people went to a friend of Angie's. The friend asked Angie to talk to me." Becker had a clear memory of the night Siracusa had showed up as they were wrapping up the dice game.

"Hey college boy," Siracusa said. It was a common insult, used to suggest someone had aspirations above their true station or thought they were smart but didn't know the score. Becker said nothing, but stood to face the older man still holding the shotgun he used to provide security for the game. Angie looked on, his teeth clenched.

"You know these names?" Siracusa continued. He showed Becker a crumpled piece of paper. Becker tucked the shotgun under his arm and turned the paper to the light.

"I know the second one. He's a professor at the school. The other one I don't know," Becker said.

"Put that thing down, you gonna talk to me." Siracusa pointed at the shotgun. It was already open at the breach. Becker dumped the shells into his palm, put them in his pocket and set the shotgun on a crate.

"Like I said," Becker answered, handing the paper back.

"They're both sissies. The first one is a degenerate gambler. He owes some people a lot of money. We think the other one doesn't know, but might bail his boyfriend out if he did. They're citizens, so nobody wants to put the arm on them. But they will if they have to."

"What do you want from me?" Becker said.

"Figure it out, college boy."

"Spell it out, so I get it right."

"Are you talking shit to me?" Siracusa's voice seemed to drop to a whisper.

"No, but this isn't what I do and you know that. I need to know exactly what you want if it's going to get done." Becker watched Siracusa's face and body movements. He was nervous and obviously under pressure. Angie had once described him as a "medium size fish", powerful enough to protect Angie's game and run his own operations but not yet a big-league player in the underworld. Becker sensed that he was under pressure from someone stronger, or perhaps had made a promise that he wasn't sure he could keep.

"Go to the professor. Tell him his boyfriend is in trouble. No threats, but tell him something bad might happen."

"That's it? Just the message?"

"Make sure he gets it," Siracusa said. "I don't wanna come back here."

Becker said nothing. Siracusa stared at him, trying to read something in his face while keeping his own intimidating but it didn't seem to be working. He buttoned his overcoat and turned to leave.

"Somebody get me out a this dump," he said to no one in particular.

"He tries real hard," Angie said when he had gone.

"Is this on you?" Becker asked.

"I guess now it's on both of us," he answered.

Becker made an appointment to see the professor and managed to get a meeting two days later. The professor started off their conversation in French.

"*Eh bien,* Monsieur Becker. May I ask why you have requested this meeting? This is a very busy time for the faculty."

Becker's instinct told him to answer in German. He knew the professor had adequate German, but wasn't sure how much. And the door was ajar. He didn't know who else might overhear their conversation.

"I am told that that this person is an acquaintance of yours," Becker said, handing a paper with the boyfriend's name and a dollar amount next to it across the desk.

"I know him," said the professor, quickly folding the paper as he stood and crossed the room to close the office door.

"I have been asked to inform you that he is in financial difficulty. The situation is quite serious."

"Is this some kind of threat?"

"Certainly not. I even don't know the details. I am only passing on the message," Becker said.

"Who do you think you are, coming in here?" There was a note of condescension in the man's voice that grated on Becker's nerves.

"I'm only a messenger. But I am quite serious. And so are they." Something in Becker's voice and manner made the man's head recoil as if he'd been slapped. "Thank you so much for seeing me. I won't take up any more of your time."

He had hoped that was the end of it, but later that week he was summoned to the professor's office. The man's secretary handed him a bulky manila envelope as she cradled a telephone between her head and shoulder.

"He's out until Monday, but I'm supposed to see that you get these. He said that was all of it." She whispered, holding one hand over the mouthpiece.

"I'm sorry. All of...?"

"The research you asked about."

Once in the hallway, Becker leaned against the wall and unfastened the flap of the envelope. It was a standard academic model with a string looped around two cardboard posts. Inside was a thick mailing envelope. He reached his hand in and pinched it between his thumb and forefinger. Money. About two inches worth.

The next Friday night, Becker stood on a street corner as Siracusa's 1934 Cadillac pulled up. He noted that it was only a coupe and that Siracusa was driving himself, not chauffeured. I guess that's what a "medium size fish" does, he thought.

"What the hell is this?" Siracusa asked, taking the envelope Becker passed through the window. Becker didn't bother to answer. "Nobody asked you to collect."

"I didn't ask to collect. He just gave it to me."

"The boyfriend?"

"The professor," Becker said.

"Is it all there?" Siracusa asked.

And how the hell would I know, Becker thought. Do you even know?

"I didn't open it."

"Right." A hint of relief showed on Siracusa's face, as if he'd been absolved from some annoying social obligation. He looked at Becker and started to extend his hand but quickly realized that with his bulk he would never get his hand out the window. Instead, he drew his thumb and forefinger around the outside of his mouth.

"Well. You done OK," Siracusa said, quickly putting the car in gear and pulling away.

"Thanks." Becker's gratitude was drowned out by the sound of the Cadillac's engine.

"And that was the end of it?" Albert asked.

"Not exactly. The boyfriend confronted me on the street about a week later, screaming like a madman. He was shouting that I had humiliated that dear, sweet man. He made quite a scene."

"And it would have been bad form for you to knock his head off in public." Albert was chuckling to himself at the thought.

"About a week after that I received a letter from the chairman of the education department saying that because of questions about my character and known associations with criminal elements I would have to withdraw from my education courses or face expulsion from the university."

Albert's shoulders slumped as he took one hand from the wheel and drew it his palm across his forehead, over his right eye and down his cheek.

"Oh, Mathieu. And this finished it for you? This one asshole?" Albert said.

"There was no way to fight it. It was true, after all. I do associate with 'criminal elements'."

"You received your diploma? They didn't take that from you."

"Finally. History major. Not much use, I'm afraid," Becker said.

"You wanted this so much? To be a teacher?"

"I like kids. I couldn't think of anything else I'd be good at."

"I'll bet you could make the class shut up. Just give them that face of yours. They'd piss themselves."

"What face?"

"Like when you were talking to Alma," Albert said.

"I just thought he didn't understand the danger," Becker said.

"Well, you got his attention in a hurry." Albert let out soft, wheezy giggle, but soon his face went dark. "Bastards. Maybe someday when this is all over you should go back and there should be a settlement of accounts." Becker loved the French expression *réglement des comptes* much better than the English "settle the score" in its implication that the bookkeeping had been botched and now needed to be set straight.

"It's a pleasant dream. I often think about it. But there's no sense in me trying to make the crooked places straight."

"Forget Isaiah. Not even God can do that. Just burn the place down."

At four in the morning, Albert finally let himself be persuaded to give up the wheel. They pulled to the side of the road and consulted the map together until Albert was reassured that Becker knew where they were going. Once in the passenger seat, Albert remained in his customary vulture-like posture, silently evaluating Becker's every shift and turn of the wheel until gradually the tension went out of him and he slumped against the window.

It was the dead of winter and the nights were long. When dawn came it brought a light spray of freezing cold rain. It had been raining on and off since they arrived in the country but they had yet to see a single snowflake. Becker found it incomprehensible that any rain could be so bitterly, bone-chillingly cold without turning to snow, but with the rain as a light mist he was able to keep the car at going at a steady speed, accustomed as he was to driving on snowy roads and sudden patches of black ice.

The farther they got from Paris, the more useless their maps became. Often the roads indicated on the maps had not yet been built, were unpaved, in serious disrepair or dangerously narrow. Cars were still such an oddity on country roads that many drivers paid little attention to which side of the road they were on or how fast they were going, Albert in particular. Becker was frankly terrified of his recklessness behind the wheel but knew that the older man needed to assert himself in some way in the presence of these young foreigners. A challenge to his driving skill would be an unbearable affront to his masculine dignity and Becker had no idea of how to go about it.

About halfway through the trip, Becker was awakened from a sound sleep by a teeth-rattling crash of metal to find the car gracefully pirouetting down the road, nearly airborne, at a speed that turned the view from the windshield into a surrealistic charcoal landscape of elongated trees, shrubs, and deserted farmland. The car came gently to rest in perfect alignment with the side of the road, like a child's toy set in place by the hand of Providence. Becker gathered what remained of his wits and looked at Albert. He was staring straight ahead, his face bloodless and his eyes staring into a world beyond. Both elbows were locked as he kept a death grip on the wheel.

"Albert," Becker said, touching his arm. "We're alive. All's well."

Albert took several deep breaths and released a stream of curses that would seem mild by English standards but in fact reached an impressive level of both blasphemy and vulgarity in French. Becker made mental note of those he could catch.

Albert got out of the car with murder in his eyes, looking for the other car. Becker looked in the back seat to see that Angie was still asleep and got out to chase after Albert, but he hadn't gotten far. He was standing in the middle of the road, staring at the damage. The big Citroën had been lightly side-swiped across both passenger doors, somehow leaving the huge protruding front fender untouched. The rear fender was bent dangerously close to the tire and would probably hit it when they went over the next bump in the road. Becker had seen worse. How'd they miss the front fender? he thought. Albert must have swung the wheel at the last second.

The other car, a black two-door coupe with a strange resemblance to a '32 Ford was about one hundred meters down the road with both rear wheels in the ditch. They walked toward it and saw that its front fender was nowhere to be seen, the rear fender had flattened the tire beneath it and the passenger door was jammed shut. The driver was holding a handkerchief to a cut over his left eye, but having little luck staunching the bleeding. During the walk to the car, the color had returned to Albert's face and the civility to his manner.

"You are not injured Monsieur?" Albert asked.

"I can't get out," the man said, still dazed.

"Don't move," Becker said. He circled the car and entered through the passenger door, immediately switching off the ignition. He checked the man's legs and feet, and found no apparent injuries, but the front of his shirt was stained with blood. He tried to get the window down, but it wouldn't budge.

"Albert," he called through the window. "Is there a first aid kit in the car?"

Albert's response was to shrug, puff his cheeks and jog back to the Citroën. In a moment he returned holding a small metal box with the customary red cross on the cover.

By now, Angie was awake and surveying the scene. He came around the front of the coupe and stood by the door.

"I dreamt we hit an iceberg. We were going down with all hands."

"Glad you could join us," Becker said.

"Matt, I'll do the cuts. You help Albert with the tire," he said. Becker saw this as a sensible division of labor and went out to help Albert bend the rear fender away from the tire.

Angie quickly cleaned and closed the cut and managed to get the man out the passenger door. He gently eased the man to the ground on the side of the road, where he sat holding his head in his hands as if fighting a terrible hangover. Albert, Angie and Becker soon had the spare tire put on and the engine running but after Angie took the car a couple hundred yards down the road he came back shaking his head.

"Something is wrenched loose in the suspension. Wherever he's going, he ain't gonna get there," he said.

Becker translated. "Monsieur, your car is not safe to drive. We're going that way," he said, pointing toward the Citroën. "Is there someplace we can take you? Perhaps to a doctor? That cut needs stitches."

The man looked down the road at the Citroën and shook his head. "But we're going the same way."

"The crash spun us around," Albert said. "Several times. Really, I'm not sure what happened, but we were going the other way."

Becker guessed that Albert had been going too fast and too near the center of the road. When he saw the other car, he locked the brakes, sending it into an uncontrollable spin. It was a miracle the big sedan hadn't obliterated the little coupe.

"I live in the next village. If it would not be too much trouble," the man said.

"Angie," Becker translated, "we're taking this guy home."

"Come on Mac," Angie said as he got the man's feet under him and started walking him toward the Citroën. "We're taking you for a ride." He winked at Becker as he passed and whispered, "Never thought I'd get a chance to say that to someone."

Albert insisted that Becker take a long-overdue turn at the wheel and they rode in silence for several miles.

"I can't believe this place sometimes," Angie said from the back seat.

"Why's that?" Becker said.

"So here these two guys almost kill each other in a head-on crash and they're calling each other 'Monsieur'. Back home, they would have finished each other off and someone would have found the bodies when they saw buzzards circling."

The man was unconscious when they entered his village so they stopped at a small café to ask directions to a local doctor. Two patrons took charge of the patient, carrying him with his arms over their shoulders past a small fountain to a building on the other side of the square, muttering a mixture of solace and admonition to their senseless cargo.

Other townspeople came out to admire the car and commiserate with Albert over the damage. Angie and Becker tried to remain inconspicuous but they were soon fending off invitations to come into the restaurant, have lunch and recount the adventure. The entire incident appeared to be the event of the decade and would no doubt be the subject of much retelling and embellishment. Becker imagined the Citroën eventually changing to a Rolls-Royce or a coach-and-four. But by a silent meeting of worried glances, the three of them agreed that this type of delay could come to no good end.

"Alas, my dear friends. We are obliged to decline your kind offer. It is my sister you see, in Perpignan. She...well, I don't wish to trouble you with our family tragedies but we must get there as soon as possible," explained Albert.

Surprisingly to Becker, there seemed to be a firm consensus on the best route out of town. In the past, they had found such small villages to be ideal places to get lost. They would enter on a main national artery and soon find themselves exiting on what later turned out to be the trail to a cow pasture. So they began to ask locals for directions. It generally took considerable greeting, inquiring after each other's health and other small talk before the point of the exchange was arrived at, which Becker found strangely endearing given the curt, informal yet neighborly nature of American discourse. A typical exchange would begin by Becker slowing the big sedan until the passenger window was slightly in front of the intended quarry.

"Bonjour Monsieur," Becker would begin.

"Good day, Sir. And how are you?"

"Very good, and you?" Becker would reply.

"Oh, it goes well enough. But the weather is foul, is it not?"

"Well, it's the season. Pardon me, I don't wish to trouble you, but..."

"It's no trouble."

"You're very kind. Is this the road to Brive-la-Gaillard?"

"Well, I suppose that if one continued in this general direction, one might arrive at Brive-la-Gaillard, or thereabouts," he would reply, with much massaging of the chin.

"How long, would you say?"

"You have relatives in Brive-la-Gaillarde?" the gentleman would ask.

"We're trying to get to Toulouse."

"Well, if you stay on this road, you can't go far wrong."

"Monsieur, as you say, the weather is quite bad. Might one take you where you are going?"

"Oh, but you are very kind! And in such a fine automobile! How does such a young man come to driving such a thing?"

"It belongs to my wife's father," Becker would reply.

"And I am the father's brother," Albert might add, dourly, depending on how much sleep he had lost.

Several times they were invited to lunch or dine with their new traveling companions. Twice they accepted and once took advantage of their hosts' hospitality to sleep on the floor near the hearth of an old country farmhouse. The trip was becoming more of an odyssey than any of them had anticipated and Becker and Albert began to despair of ever reaching their destination, though both were careful to keep their concerns from the other.

CHAPTER 13

One morning, something brought Becker to sudden consciousness and he realized Albert had patted his upper arm to wake him.

"My turn?" Becker said.

"We've arrived," he replied.

Becker looked out on a city street and saw they were parked next to a bank, but since it was hardly past dawn, there was no sign of life.

"I think this capitalist monstrosity will serve your purposes," Albert said.

Becker looked at his watch. Six-thirty. "What day is it?" he asked Albert.

"I don't know," he answered. "You boys have some money, right?" Becker nodded. "I think we need some sleep, and a good scrubbing. You can't walk into a bank looking like that."

"Yes, but can we check into a hotel at this time of the morning?"

"We've driven all night to reach my sister with the mysterious misfortune, is it not so? What is so strange?"

"Well let's not keep her waiting," Becker said.

Later that morning, Angie and Becker stood outside the bank. They had found a respectable hotel, the Hôtel Splendide, bathed, breakfasted and dressed in the best clothes they had. Still, they felt foolish walking into the bank dressed as hikers and carrying the rucksacks. But the clerk who took care of them seemed to take no notice other than to comment once again on Becker's accent, asking if he was from Paris. They rented a small safety deposit box, put most of the money they had left and kept a few hundred dollars for emergencies. They concluded their business as quickly as possible. In less than thirty minutes they had said their goodbyes after shaking hands with the clerk, manager and assistant manager. At least there was no kissing, Becker thought. Still, way too much attention. If Martin were here, I'd get an earful. Don't get noticed, he would say. But how else do you rent a safe deposit box? Should I go out and buy a suit? I should have come alone and left Angie at the hotel. It dawned on Becker that he wanted Angie's trust more than he cared about security.

"We take this to war?" Angie said, showing Becker the safe deposit key in the palm of his hand.

Becker looked at him but said nothing.

"Give it to Albert?" Again, Becker looked at him and said nothing. "Forget I said it."

"Let's take a walk," Becker said.

It was a cool morning, but the sun was strong and washed their minds clear of much of their fatigue. Becker stepped into a *tabac,* a small tobacco shop, and bought a tin of pipe tobacco and a newspaper. When they came out, he pried the lid off the tin and emptied the contents into a storm drain but kept the wax paper from the pipe tobacco and tore a six inch square off the newspaper. He then wrapped the key in the wax paper and newspaper, snapped the tin shut and put it in his pocket.

They crossed to the right-hand sight of the road and walked along the next block until Becker was able to flag down a passing cab.

The driver greeted them politely, but as they exchanged the usual pleasantries, Becker realized he could barely make sense of the man's dialect.

"I beg your pardon, could you repeat that?" Becker said.

"I said, 'You're from the city, is it not so?" he repeated, not unkindly.

"Uh, I'm from the east. Lorraine actually. My brother in-law here is from Italy."

"You don't say. Rome?"

"Down south, Abruzzi."

"And you speak Italian?" asked the driver.

"Oh, no. Well, just a little. We're studying English at the university."

"What university?"

The cab still hadn't moved and Becker was becoming concerned that soon he might lie himself into a corner he wasn't prepared for. Can't a person just get from one place to another without telling their life story anymore?

Angie gave him an elbow to the ribs and smiled. But his next words were through clenched teeth.

"Did you just tell this hack I was from Abruzzi?" he said.

"Sorry, it's the first thing I could think of. I didn't want to tell the truth."

"Why not just say I'm from Norway, for Chrissakes. Abruzzi. Don't ever tell my mother. She'll put a curse on you. Make your balls drop off."

"Do you think you could take us for a little drive along the river. We'd like to see a little countryside," Becker said to the driver.

"North or south?"

"Let's try south."

The cab traveled along with the driver pointing out points of interest in his incomprehensible Languedoc accent. Becker imagined them to be the locations of past assignations with the local lasses or places where he had rolled unsuspecting tourists like themselves. Angie sat with his arms crossed and fumed.

Finally, Becker saw what he had been hoping for.

"Well, Monsieur. I suppose we'll get out and enjoy a walk along the river and catch some sun. There's been precious little of it on our trip."

"Here? We're pretty far from town."

"So we'll enjoy a brisk walk back. Good for the constitution," Becker said, thumping his chest. He probably sounded a bit mad, which suited his purposes. He leapt from the car, stretched his arms wide, did a few quick jumping jacks and sprinted in place. Angie got out like he was walking to an execution, preferably Becker's.

Once paid with a generous tip, the driver's mood seemed to lighten. He carefully pocketed the cash, wished them a pleasant hike and then spotted an oncoming truck heavy laden with farm implements and empty crates rattling toward town at barely thirty miles an hour. He laid in wait with his engine idling and waited until the last possible second to make a screeching U-turn in front of the truck, a maniacal grin contorting his features as he looked back toward the havoc in his wake. The truck's driver, a boy slightly younger than Becker and Angie, slammed on his brakes, stalled and lost a few of the crates and some tools from the back of the truck, but seemed resigned as he put on the parking break and got out.

"They're all crazy," said the boy as they helped him pick up some scattered bits of his cargo.

"Who's that?" Becker said.

"The cab drivers. They're all gypsies you know," the boy explained.

"How do you know?" Becker asked.

"One just knows."

Becker had never seen a gypsy and didn't think he's recognize one if he did. But he'd heard plenty of statements like the last one. He was becoming convinced that the natural state of humanity was for everyone to hate everyone else – it was only a matter of degree. He was still trying to figure out what the people of Abruzzi had done to the Sicilians, or vice versa. He did know that the worst indiscretion of all would be to ask.

"Do you both have your wallets?" asked the boy.

"I think we're OK," Becker said, quietly amused at the thought of someone trying to get Angie's wallet.

You're not from around here?" the boy asked, noticing Becker's accent.

"No, up north. Just passing through," Becker said.

"To Spain?"

"Just passing through," Becker said.

"Just as I thought," he said. "Don't worry. I won't tell. I'd be going myself but my parents need me here. They really do." He seemed to need Becker's understanding.

"Family comes first," Becker said. Was that just a convenient platitude or did he really believe it?

"Your companion. He is French?"

"Italian, but one of the good ones," Becker said, looking for an excuse to change the subject. "Do you think the truck will be OK?"

"I suppose so, but she never starts on her own. Do you think I could trouble you for a push?"

"No trouble," Becker said, grateful for the level ground. "Hop in."

"What's up?" Angie said.

"We're gonna push start him."

Angie took a joyful, childlike pleasure in starting up any machine. He waved Becker into position at the left rear of the truck and he took the right.

The truck was soon crawling down the road at the same pace as before and Becker was sure it would reach its destination before spring. The boy waved his hand and shouted as he drove away.

"Watch out for the damned...!" His last words were carried away by the crunch of a gear shift but Becker had no doubt as to their general intent. Watch out for everyone.

"So, Matt. I'm so glad you brought me out here. Is this a nature hike or what?" Angie said.

Becker had already crossed the road and was walking back toward town. "Sorry about the Abruzzi thing. I'm just trying not to give out our pedigree to every Joe we meet."

"Yeah, forget it. It's just my father was Abruzzese, and everyone in the family warned my mother not to marry him."

"What's wrong with them?"

"Damned if I know. One guy I know, he's Abruzzese. My Mom still uses his *maltagliati* recipe, so how bad can they be?"

Becker's mouth started to water as he remembered Auntie Lena's cooking and the dish made from shrimp and the odd-shaped, leftover pieces of homemade pasta that remained after cutting the traditional shapes.

They walked on for a couple more minutes. Neither spoke.

"So anyway," Angie said.

"We're hiding the key," Becker said.

"OK. Where?"

"First, do you know where we are?" Becker asked.

Angie looked up and down the road, ruffling the hair at the nape of his neck. "Couple miles outside of town, south side, next to this big river."

"You know the river?"

"I can read it, but I can't say it. But what difference does it make? How many jumbo-sized rivers they got around here?"

"You gotta point. Anyway, it's La Garonne. Some people around here say it like 'Garonna'."

"So where's it go?"

"More like where's it coming from."

Angie gave him a puzzled look.

"Same place we're going to," Becker said.

"Up those mountains?"

"That's about the size of it."

"And the key?" Angie said.

"I don't want to give it to Albert."

Angie nodded. "Yeah, I figured that. OK guy, but a bad risk and we got no leverage."

"So it has to be somewhere not too far from the border and near a landmark we can both find."

"So I found the river. Now what?" Angie said.

"See that marker?" Becker pointed to a *borne kilométrique*, a small concrete stone with a semi-circular top marked with numbers indicating the road and the distance from some central city landmark.

"The mile marker?"

"Yeah, basically. The use kilometers over here. They call it a *borne kilométrique*."

"Savages," Angie said. "What's a *borne*?"

"It means 'a piece of stone with numbers on it'."

"So you're telling me it's a *gomesegiame*," Angie said, counterpunching with 'whatchamacallit'. "We bury it here?" .

"You could find it if something happened to me, right?" Becker said. Angie crossed himself unconsciously.

"Easy enough. South on the main road on the west side of the river."

"Got a better idea?"

"Got no ideas. No bananas neither. Let's dig," Angie said, already reaching into his pocket for his knife. Becker held up a hand to stop him.

"You watch out for whatever comes down the road. I don't want any attention. I'll start," Becker said.

Angie kept watch while Becker sliced away a neat piece of turf and used his switchblade to go down about a foot.

"Stop," Angie said.

"What," Becker said.

"The plan's basically right but we got a couple problems."

"I can tell you one right now," Becker said. Angie tilted his head, waiting for a punch line. "About two hundred dogs have already marked this spot."

Time lost all meaning as they both convulsed in laughter. Angie even dared to sniff Becker's hands, which only made it worse. A passing motorist slowed to watch them, tears pouring down their faces, and then sped away.

"Gypsies! Run for your lives!" Becker said, choking the words out between peals of laughter.

When they finally recovered, they were both sitting cross-legged on the grass, a little cold but enjoying the mid-day sunshine.

"OK, so dogs. That's one problem," Becker said.

"Gypsies," Angie said.

"Ange don't start. We gotta meet Albert at five."

Angie spoke soberly. "This is city property, or county or what-ever it is around here, right?"

"Yeah."

"So they send a crew out to paint the stone and we're screwed."

"A crew could kill half a day out here painting this stone," Becker said.

"A crew of Amish. A crew of Italians could be here a week. They'd sniff that box out for sure."

"I take your point. What else?"

"See that river?" Angie said.

"Kind of hard to miss it," Becker said, seeing where Angie was leading.

"Coming down out of those mountains? In the springtime?"

Becker continued nodding, the picture making his idea seem madness.

"You ever see the Delaware go over the banks in the spring?" Angie asked. Becker whistled silently to himself with a twist of his head. "That box could end up, I don't know, where does this river end up?"

Becker wasn't sure. Bordeaux? He thought he knew his French geography but suddenly realized that a lack of geographical knowledge could get him killed someday.

"So. We take a little climb up the hill?" Becker said.

In the end, the box was buried a good twenty meters up in the woods beside the road, two feet down, under layers of loose rocks, gravel and dirt. They did their best to burn the location into their memories using the road marker and some other landmarks.

"Think we'll ever find this again?" Angie said.

"Think we'll be alive to come looking?" Becker said. Angie spit and said nothing.

They walked back to the city and got slightly lost when they reached the outskirts. It was past noon, they were starving and short on patience so rather than try to find their way back to the hotel, they decided to fortify themselves with some lunch. A matronly woman of indeterminate age gave them a warm welcome at the first restaurant they came to, though several of the male patrons gave them looks of undisguised suspicion or contempt. They must take us for gypsies, Becker thought.

Their hostess seated them at one of the few open tables, far in the back near the toilet. Martin would like this, Becker thought. Near the rear exit, good view of the room and no one at our backs.

"The gentlemen would like water or wine with their meals?" asked the woman in a sing-song voice, as if she were addressing her grandchildren.

"Angie, water or wine?" Becker said.

"Both," he answered, which sounded like a good idea to Becker.

"We'll have both Madame. Pardon, but we know little of the local cuisine. Could you recommend something?"

The woman seemed taken aback. "Oh, but Monsieur, today there is only the *cassoulet*." Becker noticed sideways glances from several of the other patrons.

"That sounds wonderful. We are in luck! Merci Madame," Becker said. The woman seemed relieved to have avoided an embarrassing moment with some ignorant out-of-towners as she walked quickly to the bar and picked up identical carafes of water and red wine with one hand and stuck four fingers into four glasses with the other. Seconds later she was pouring the water and wine at their table.

"The meal will be here right away," she said before walking back to the kitchen and shouting "Two more!"

"When do we get a menu?" Angie said.

"We don't," Becker said.

"Another one of those joints? Angie said. "Don't tell me it's sauerkraut again."

"Do I look suicidal?"

"So what is it?"

"I have no idea," Becker said. He was enjoying Angie's discomfort and Angie knew it. It was rare for Angie to be the straight man in their relationship, and Becker wanted to milk it for all it was worth.

"Does it have a name, smartass?"

At that moment, the woman returned with two steaming bowls piled high with a casserole of beans, pork and other meat that Becker couldn't identify. The slightly spicy aroma was intoxicating.

"*Bon apétit, Messieurs*," she said.

"Thank you Madame. It looks wonderful."

"So much the better," she replied over her shoulder before busying herself with other customers.

"I'll take yours Ange, if you don't like it." Angie's eyes snapped once toward Becker, his cheeks bulging like a squirrel's as he wolfed down his first mouthful.

It was the perfect soul-soothing dish for empty stomachs far from home on a cold January day. The meat was tender, the beans rich and varied in size and texture, the vegetables fresh and not overcooked and the spices like exotic drugs to palates rendered numb and torpid after too much tasteless, hurried and stale food eaten during their time on the road. As for the wine, they neither knew nor cared about its type or lineage, only that at that moment, it was the best they had ever tasted.

"First I've seen you smile since Paris," Angie said.

"Yeah," Becker said. "Too much time to think."

"Not healthy."

"Amen to that."

"Wish my Ma was here to taste this," Angie said.

"She'd be back in the kitchen giving them pointers," Becker said.

Angie smiled, nodding in agreement. "Probably. But she'd love this stuff. What's it called?"

"I'm not sure I caught it," Becker said. "I think she just said 'casserole'."

"Well I can't much argue with that." Angie made an exaggerated frown. "Matt, old pal, I thought you spoke this language."

Here we go, Becker thought. I knew this was coming sooner or later. Angie wants to play. "Angie. Where's your family from?" he said.

"Sicily. Some little town up in the hills. I never been there."

"What? You mean we go to Palermo, you can't tell me the best place to get *pasta fagiole*? And you like those beans so much. Maybe find me a nice local girl?"

"Alright already, I hardly ever been out of Jersey, except up to the City," Angie said.

Becker took a softer tone. "Ange, honest to God, sometimes I'm just treading water here. That cab driver today? He could have been speaking, I don't know, Chinese."

"You ever listen to the president on the radio? I think he's soused on bathtub gin. I don't know what he's talking about half the time. 'Course I would be too if I had to spend the rest of my life on wheels. Where's he from anyway?"

"Not sure. New York, upstate someplace, where people got money."

"So are we getting coffee?" Angie asked.

"I want to get back to the hotel and get a couple hours of sack time before tonight. I don't know what Albert's signing us up for but I'm willing to bet it doesn't involve sleep."

"Sleep. Has a nice sound to it," Angie said.

The days of travel, the morning's exercise and the satiation of the meal all combined to knock them out once they found their way back to the hotel, a task they decided to let a cab driver do for them. Angie commented that he'd taken more cab rides in the last two weeks than he had in his whole life and was considering making it a regular habit.

Becker was awakened by a distant tapping. He reached for his .45. He heard the noise again. Angie slept on, oblivious. It was pitch black outside and he had a sudden fear that they had missed their appointment by hours and would be taken for incompetents or slackers when the word got out. Looking at his watch, Becker saw that it was just before five. He heard a voice in French.

"Mathieu, it's me."

Albert had come to waken them. Becker went to the door with the .45 in his hand and stood well to the side.

"Albert?"

"It's me. I'm alone. All goes well."

Becker let him in, noticing that Albert also had his hand inside his jacket on the butt of a pistol. He looked at Angie.

"He's alive?"

"He can sleep through anything. Are we late?"

"Probably not, but we'd best get going. Fifteen minutes?"

"That'll do," Becker said.

He shook Angie into semi-consciousness before heading for the bathroom for a quick wash up. He decided there was no time for a shave. When he got back to the room, Albert was sitting comfortably, smoking a cigarette, one leg crossed over the other as he watched with mild amusement as Angie struggled to get dressed and awake.

"If you'll forgive me, I think you should shave. It will be your last chance for a while. Also, I don't want you to embarrass me," Albert said.

"Embarrass you?" Becker said.

"I drive a Citroën. My acquaintances are customers of large financial institutions." He paused for effect and assumed a dreamy look. "I'm a gentleman."

The assertion was so out of character that Becker snorted once and fought back a face-splitting grin. Nonetheless, he dropped his jacket and rucksack and headed back for the bathroom, quickly soaping up and running a safety razor across his face, drawing blood in three places in his haste. When he had rinsed and toweled off he went back to the room where Angie looked at him apologetically.

"Matt. Can I use your razor? Mine's at the bottom of my bag," he said before getting a good look at Becker's face. "Jesus, what was this? You look like Caesar on the Senate floor."

"Old razor, and I was in a hurry. Here, take it," he said, handing the razor to Angie. "It's really done for now anyway."

Angie's beard was like steel wool and even shaving twice a day did little to help.

Albert looked sternly at Becker. "You watch those cuts when you get in the field."

"Yeah, I want to look my best when I get captured and shot," Becker said.

"I'm not joking, boy." Albert hadn't used this tone with Becker before and he felt his hackles start to rise.

"What the hell got into you?" Becker asked. Albert's sudden change from farcical to sullen caught him off guard.

"If those get infected, you'll be lucky if you don't die in the mud, with your comrades stepping on you or using your body for cover. You wash, before and after and every chance you get." Becker looked in his eyes and saw a deep melancholy, contrasting with the rebuke in his voice. God only knows what he's seen that I haven't, he thought.

Angie came out of the bathroom looking like a schoolboy ready for his first day of classes. His hair was slicked back, his face scrubbed and there was a small wad of soap behind one earlobe. Albert picked up a towel and spoke as he wiped it off.

"Take everything. We won't be back here. All the weapons and ammo. Especially bring that – thing – that you picked up in Paris. And all the magazines," Albert said. "Here," he said, tossing a long canvass duffel on the bed. "I thought this might help."

Since the machine pistol was a better part of a meter long, it was too big for their rucksacks, which had no spare room anyway. Then there was the weight. Becker guessed the weapon itself to be a little under ten pounds and each thirty-two round magazine to be a little over a pound. They had seven magazines. Becker began to appreciate the more irksome aspects of military adventure.

Angie seemed to have regained his playful good humor along with his full consciousness. "So who gets to schlep this bag over the mountains?"

"We'll take turns," Becker said, not quite convincingly.

"The hell with that. I didn't bring home this plumber's nightmare," Angie laughed. "Plus you're twice my size."

"Yeah, remember that," he parried, half-heartedly. He knew that, lifelong friendship aside, Angie had no fear of him whatsoever. Like most men he associated with, Becker evaluated the potential physical threat posed by other men he encountered. It was a simple matter of survival in the world where he grew up. He immediately knew some people were dangerous by virtue of size, strength, speed or temperament. Others were harmless for similar reasons. But there were many that defied evaluation. Angie was one of those and Becker was his opposite. Becker knew that for some reason, he often frightened people unintentionally. They thought him angry when he was not or expected physical violence when the idea had not entered his mind. But not Angie. Becker knew that his friend was capable of, even adept at, violence. But no one ever expected it. And Angie knew what Becker was capable of but seemed to have no fear of it whatsoever. Why?

As for the machine pistol he had already resigned himself to carrying it as far as he could before disabling the weapon and leaving it behind. He had disassembled and reassembled it repeatedly during their journey and was confident that he understood the workings of the mechanism, but he didn't know the effect of the recoil on full automatic. He remembered the line of splintered holes that appeared in the hotel door in Paris. Nearly straight. The shooter must have had a powerful grip on the stock, he thought. Probably locked against his ribs by his right arm. He had found the selector for single shot and considered forgoing full auto altogether. Maybe I should just leave it there, he thought. But then what the hell is the point? Maybe short bursts, three or four rounds. If I hold down this trigger too long I'll be standing there like a fool with ten pounds of empty Kraut steel in my hands while somebody fills me full of holes. Thirty-two rounds in this magazine. He knew because he had emptied and refilled each one during the ride. How long would it take to empty one? Becker counted in his head "one, one thousand, two, one thousand, three, one thousand..." Three seconds? A little more or less? Well, even if I don't fire it, it'll scare the hell out of anyone who sees it pointed at them. Maybe that's the point.

A short while later they were heading toward the outskirts of Toulouse. Albert was driving. To Becker it seemed they were still too far from the border to attempt crossing into Spain that night, but he hadn't seen Albert all day and didn't know what might have developed.

"We make the crossing tonight?" Becker asked.

"Not tonight. Tomorrow. Daylight is better," Albert said.

Becker had visions of himself slipping in the darkness and plunging into an abyss where his mangled corpse would lay forgotten for all eternity.

"Can't argue with that. So who's our guide?" Angie asked.

"Guide?" Albert kept a straight face, but his tone held the promise of an impending punch line. "He's an Englishman."

"An English guide?" Angie said. Becker turned sideways to catch sight of Albert's face when a passing light shone on it. He was enjoying some private joke.

"Oh, do not have fear," he said. "He has been over these mountains many times."

"At least we don't have to worry about the lingo," Angie said.

"Don't bet on it," Becker said.

They drove for twenty minutes through the darkness before finding themselves beside a chain link fence perhaps two and a half meters high. Albert slowed the car slightly and Becker could make out a large grass field and the silhouettes of two large buildings with semi-circular roofs and several smaller buildings and huts. When Albert made the turn through an open gate and started to speed across the grass toward the buildings Becker realized they were at an airfield.

"Airplanes!" Angie said. Becker squinted into the darkness and saw the shapes of three small biplanes tied down on the grass past the hangars.

Albert brought the car to a stop in front of one of the smaller buildings, the only one with a light above the door. It appeared to be an office of some kind and had telephone wires running into it. There was a man sitting outside the door smoking a cigarette, his chair tipped back on two legs as it leaned against the wall. He looked at the car without any hint of interest. Albert started to get out. Becker put his hand on his arm.

"OK, Uncle. No jokes now. What's the story?" he said.

Albert grinned, highly pleased with himself for having played the game so long.

"The movement is bringing an airplane into Albacete tomorrow. That is the pilot. You are the passengers," he said.

"We're *flying* into Spain?" Angie said, a note of alarm in his voice. Albert nodded.

"It's not even seven o'clock," Becker said. "What are we supposed to do here all night?"

"Guard the plane," Albert said. Becker couldn't discern whether this was an order, a simple statement of fact or both. "Can I get out now?" Albert asked, his good humor instantly returning.

They all got out of the car and walked toward the office. As they approached, the man tipped his chair forward and almost lost his balance as he stood up.

"You're Albert?" he asked. Becker could smell alcohol from a good distance. Cognac? Probably.

"Yes, Monsieur *le capitaine*," Albert replied smartly, extending his hand. "And you are...?"

"Downes," the man said as he shook Albert's hand. Becker watched the man's face and imagined the thoughts racing through his head. I know I'm drunk. You all know I'm drunk. I shouldn't be drunk, but we're all pretending I'm not.

"Matt MacCready," Becker said shaking the man's hand. "And this is Angelo."

"Kenneth Downes," he replied. He shook Angie's hand, but looked at him for a moment with his head cocked. "Italian?"

"U.S.A. Pal. Born and bred," Angie said, smiling. "And you can call me Angie. Everyone does. Say, are you a real captain?" Becker hoped Angie wasn't going to start teasing a helpless drunk who would hold their lives in his hands come tomorrow.

"Ah, that explains it," Downes said, reassured. "What?" he asked, confused again.

"Albert called you 'captain'," Angie said.

"No, not really. Well, I was a lieutenant, briefly mind you, in the last war." Downes suddenly realized he was on the defensive, a situation he was unaccustomed to, especially with Americans. Time to reaffirm the order of things. "So are you young lads going to look after my machine for me tonight?"

Albert looked at Becker and Angie for their answer. Angie said nothing, smiling, but openly looking Downes over like a used car. Becker turned his back and walked to the car, returning with the machine pistol, snapping in a magazine and coking the bolt as he approached. Angie reached into a shoulder holster and pulled out his .45 and cocked it. Downes blanched under his ruddy complexion.

"Now see here," Downes began, not sure what was happening.

Becker stood with the machine pistol hanging casually from his right hand and stared at the pilot until he was certain the man was thoroughly brought to heel.

"Show us the machine," Becker said quietly. He loathed being talked down to. He'd recently developed a particular distaste for being referred to as 'young'.

"Right," Downes said. "Follow me."

The next building over was one of the hangars. The group followed Downes in a side door where he soon managed to find the switch, flooding the room with light. In its center, squatting like a football lineman, was an olive green, low-wing monoplane with four windows along the fuselage and a single, huge radial engine in its nose. To Becker, it seemed in repose but not inert, possessed of some sentient spirit, alive with savage energy, eager to be out of its cage and back in its element. I am not this ugly, graceless piece of wood and metal, it said. Free me. I perform wonders beyond your earthbound imagining. The group watched in silence, except Downes, who barely managed to muffle a resounding belch.

"That thing flies?" Angie said.

"It does," Downes said. "Rather well, in fact."

"It looks kind of, I don't know, chubby," Angie said.

"What's 'chubby'?" Albert asked Becker. Becker explained the term in French.

"Ah, well, she's no ballet dancer. That's for sure," Albert said. Downes made a face. He knew something disparaging was being said in a language he didn't understand.

"What is it?" Becker said, as he walked toward the plane, trying to hide his stunned fascination, the machine pistol slung across his back.

"Gentlemen, allow me to introduce the Lockheed Orion, Model 9D, which, though not thing of beauty to the uneducated who see her on the ground, is actually faster than greased lightning. And wouldn't the Fascists like to get their hands on that!" Downes said indignantly, though much of the dramatic effect of his presentation was lost in his difficulty pronouncing the word 'that'."

The group suddenly noticed a low humming and turned to see a form curled up on a row of crates, snoring peacefully. His back was to them but they could see a woolen cap and a leather coat being used as a blanket.

"Who's that?" Becker asked.

"That's my mechanic," Downes said.

"Does he have a name?"

"Name's Burdon. Knows this plane inside and out. Knows just about any engine inside and out."

Albert drew Angie and Becker to one side.

"That plane needs to survive the night, intact. I'm taking these two," he cocked his thumb toward the pilot and mechanic, "to a place of safety where I can be sure he doesn't get himself killed or too drunk for tomorrow. Right now, he's as valuable as the plane. We have asked the man in the office to go home and he has gladly accepted. You two need to watch. Make sure no one gets to her."

"You mean, to switch the engine?" Becker remembered Alma's story about the difficulty in getting planes.

"I don't think there is another engine for this plane. There are very few, perhaps less than a dozen. And some of those have surely been lost by now."

"This Downes," Angie said. "He's a combat pilot?" He made no effort to hide his incredulity.

Albert puffed his cheeks. "I'll believe he's a pilot when I see that thing disappear over the horizon."

"Thanks Uncle. I feel so much better," Becker said.

"You asked. I told you," Albert said.

"Downes. I can't decide if that name is lucky or unlucky. For a pilot I mean," Angie said.

"Albert," Angie said. "Who are we protecting this plane from? I mean, what kind of visitors can we expect here tonight?"

Albert looked at Angie and bit his lip. The he walked toward the plane and stared as if seeing her for the first time, lost in thought. He turned suddenly and walked back. He spoke his slow, precise English to Angie.

"We don't know enough. These planes are known to exist. Someone might have seen it fly in today, but that was in the early morning. A pilot to steal it? It only takes one, this plane."

"Ah, my friend, this airplane takes a bit of skill to get into the air. It's not something that just any cadet could get into the air without mishap," Downes said.

"So, sabotage," Becker said.

"Possible. A grenade would make an inferno of this building and this machine," Albert said. "Gunfire? Into the engine or fuel tank? Either a disaster here or perhaps later all of you crash into the Pyrenees." He paused, shaking his head and looked down at Becker's machine pistol. "Please. If you're going to have a shootout-"

"Don't shoot at the hangar," Becker said. "We get it."

"Yeah, but who?" Angie said.

"That's a fair question. I wish I had a good answer," Albert said. "The French Fascists, they're as fragmented as the Spanish Left. Hard to imagine them agreeing on anything, much less mounting an operation, but the situation is constantly changing. There is an embargo, and some of the rich pigs have influence with the police. They could impound the machine."

Albert paused, rubbing his hand back and forth over a two-day growth of beard. "Still, I can't imagine the police of Toulouse rousing themselves in the middle of the night to come down here and make trouble. But let's not forget our friends in Paris, like the one you stole that machine pistol from."

"He didn't steal it. He found it," Angie said.

"Make sure you shout that real loud when they show up looking for it. And remember, shout in German," Becker said.

Now they were all silent, with nothing to do but look at the plane. Becker looked around the hangar. The front door was closed, but he saw no lock.

He pointed toward the door. "Locked from the outside?" he said to Albert.

Albert, Becker and Angie walked outside and saw a sturdy padlock on the outside of the hangar door.

"Key?" Becker said.

They followed Albert as he went into the office to speak to the night watchman. A moment later, Albert was waving a key ring at them through the window. He waited while the man found his coat, gathered up his few belongings and walked outside to a small motorbike.

"Excuse me, Monsieur," Becker said.

"Yes, Monsieur?"

"Is there another entrance to this field?"

"At the other end." He pointed into the darkness. Becker saw nothing. "Way over there, you see those two lights?"

Becker made out two small lights the better part of a mile away and realized that they must be replicas of the ones over the gate they had entered on this side a half hour ago.

"Locked?" Becker asked.

"Open now, but I will lock it on my way out. I live over that way," the man said.

"You will cross this field in the darkness on that motorbike?"

"That is something to fear?" the man said, mildly amused.

"Well, I'm sure you've done it many times," Becker said.

"We check the field once or twice a day for debris or obstructions. Tree branches, rabbit holes and the like. They're hell on the undercarriages," he explained.

"Ah, I see," Becker said. "And the keys to the gates?"

"I keep one for each, and there are duplicates in the desk."

"Thank you for your kindness, Monsieur. Good night."

The man didn't actually doff his beret, but he seemed to rearrange it in a form of leave-taking. He did wave and flash a yellowed smile as he hit the throttle on the bike and sped into the darkness of the airfield.

As soon as he was gone, they heard the doors to the office and the hangar open almost simultaneously. Downes stood in front of the hangar, doing his best to hold up the unconscious mechanic without falling over himself. Albert, in front of the office, looked at them sternly and pointed at the Citroën.

"Come on then, Burdie. Time to go for a ride with the nice froggy gentleman and then get a good night's sleep," he said as he dragged the mechanic over to the sedan, opened the door and threw the man headfirst into the back seat. He then folded the legs into a position that would allow him to close the door and slammed it mercilessly.

"Bloody Geordie wanker," he said just before getting in the front passenger seat.

"What did he say?" Albert said.

"I have no idea," Becker said.

"But it was English," Albert said.

"I still have no idea," Becker said, in all sincerity.

Albert turned to the two of them. "I'll be at that gate just before dawn. If I get really motherly, I may call on the office phone." He looked at his watch. "Let's say two AM. If it's an emergency, I'll let it ring twice and call back."

"Uncle, I'll try to stand near the office at two, but it's unlikely anyone will be near that phone. And all these lights? They are going out as soon as we lock that gate behind you."

Albert nodded.

"Do you think the watchman really locked that gate like he said he would?" Becker said.

"He's one of ours," Albert said. "Why do you think he left you here alone all night?"

"Well, that saves one of us a walk," Becker said.

"Watch the sky and the gate toward morning. I'll be here just before dawn and you'll need to let me in. I want that thing in the air as soon as the sun breaks over the hills," he said.

"Wait," Becker said. Albert and Angie watched as he ran into the office, opened the desk drawer, took something and came back. He held up three keys, each clearly labeled.

"This gate, that gate and the hangar," Becker said. "You take them. Lock us in and let yourself in tomorrow. This way, even if someone gets in and stops us, it will delay them getting the plane."

"Your friend," Albert said to Angie. "He's a, how do you say it, someone who thinks the future will be bad. *Un pessimiste.*"

"A pessimist," Angie said

"Oh, same in French," Albert said.

"You have no idea," Angie said.

CHAPTER 14

They watched Albert get into the Citroën and drive out the gate, suddenly feeling isolated and exposed.

"We don't even know how big this place is," Angie said. "You could hide an army out there in the darkness."

"So let's put out all the lights," Becker said.

"Great. Then I have to go back and tell your mother how I shot you because I thought you were a French Fascist and she'll cave my head in with a frying pan. Then my mother will shoot your mother. The streets will run red with blood. They'll have to call out the militia-"

"OK, Napoleon. Let's hear your plan."

"Is that a short joke?" Angie said.

"No, it was a military genius joke," Becker said. "So what's your master plan?" Becker was ribbing his friend, but in truth he valued his opinion.

Angie walked in a small, irregular circle, looking at the gate, office, hangars and the distant stars of light at the far gate.

"How's this. This gate we know is locked. We kill all these lights, gate, office, hangar. We leave those on," he said, pointing to the lights at the far gate. "If someone comes in that way, we'll see them coming. Then, we post ourselves as lookouts near the hangar. If someone shows, we move into the dark and ambush them."

By midnight they had been guarding the hangar for the better part of four hours and had realized they would never make it through the night. The temperature continued to drop, so they each started taking fifteen minute breaks every hour warming themselves at a kerosene heater inside the office. They had brought sandwiches and water but nothing hot to drink and the night's chill was working its way deep into their bones. They tried to focus on the tiny, distant lights of the far entrance but the effect was so hypnotic that they had both caught each other falling asleep several times.

"Now this is adventure," Angie said. "Facing the darkness, freezing my ass off and falling asleep."

"Angie, if you were coming for this plane, when would you come?" Becker asked.

"Coming to steal it or coming to burn it?"

"Pick one."

"To steal it, I come at dawn. The guards are sleepiest and I need the light. To destroy it or sabotage it, I come now. It gives me more time. But why destroy it?"

"They've got no one to fly it or fix it," Becker said.

Angie was quiet for a moment, staring across the field. "You think that gate is really locked?"

"It's locked, or the manager's playing for both teams or he's dead."

"Watch," Angie said, pointing.

On the far side of the field, a truck with a canvas-covered back was speeding across the road, no other traffic to deter its passage. It slowed to a stop in front of the gate and they saw motion and shadows but couldn't make out the number of people or what they were doing. Then they clearly heard the truck's two front doors slamming followed by its engine revving in low gear as the headlights swept with the turn and the truck pulled through the gate and started across the field toward the hangar.

"Batter up," Angie said.

"Angie, if there are more than two or three, we can't capture them."

"If there are more than two or three, they're here for trouble anyway. But we've got to keep any shooting away from the hangar."

"When they get stopped, I'll be out there." Becker pointed toward the darkness of the field. "They'll have to return fire in that direction. Just make sure they don't get the hangar door open."

"Matt, please don't cut me up with that thing." Angie gave the machine pistol a sour look.

"I'll be lucky if I don't cut myself up," Becker said.

Becker looked for the best route to cover, but when he turned back Angie had disappeared. Throwing the machine pistol across his back, he sprinted what he guessed to be fifty meters into the darkness and lay flat on the grass of the airfield, sure that he was invisible to anyone near the hangar or office.

The truck had picked up speed as its driver became accustomed to the terrain but it slowed again as it neared the small cluster of buildings, executing a small final turn to bring its headlights directly on the center of the hangar door.

"Where are the damned lights?" a man asked in French as he got out of the cab. The man was wearing some type of leather uniform coat with a peaked cap.

"You should have asked the watchman," the driver answered as he got out of the truck.

"Too late now," the first man said. Both men laughed. The watchman was dead? Becker thought. "I'll find the keys and get the door open." He walked into the office and returned in seconds. "There's someone here," he said to the driver, drawing a small automatic from his coat pocket.

"How do you know?"

"There's a heater. It's lit," he answered. "Hey you in there! Get off your asses and keep watch!"

Four men get out of the back of the truck. Becker couldn't make out faces or clothing, only that they were wearing heavy coats. Two held rifles, one a shotgun and the third appeared to be using two hands to shoot himself in the groin with a small caliber automatic as he fought to get it loaded and cocked. He finally managed to rack the slide and stood holding the weapon at waist level as he peered into the darkness.

The man in the peaked cap produced a key from his coat pocket and approached the center of the hangar doors. The padlock was at shoulder level. As he inserted the key into the lock, the right side of his head exploded, his body dropped like a wet dishrag and Becker heard the report of Angie's .45. An instant later, the truck's driver took two rounds to the chest, pushing him back to fall seated on the truck's running board before tumbling headfirst to the ground.

"What's happening?" one of the men shouted.

"They're shooting at us!" said another.

"But from where?" said a third.

The man with the shotgun fired a round through the office window and another into the darkness between the office and hangar. Don't shoot at the hangar, you schmuck! Becker thought. I hate to shoot him in the back, but this guy has got to go.

Becker stood up. He knew he couldn't be seen, but the muzzle flashes would give him away so he got ready to move. He put the stock to his shoulder, grasped the wooden hand grip, and fired a four round burst. The man with the shotgun tripped as the impact of the rounds pushed him forward to the ground where he coughed once and lay still. Becker sidestepped left as the remaining three men turned away from the hangar and dropped flat on the ground. The riflemen each fired a single round into the darkness, far wide of Becker's position. The man with the pistol fired off four wild shots before one of the others stopped him.

"Save your ammo, you *petit con*! You don't know what your shooting at!"

Twenty-eight rounds left in the magazine. Again, Becker brought up the weapon and fired four rounds at the rifleman on the right. He saw the rounds hit two meters behind the target. Twenty-four rounds. He fired another burst and saw the rounds impact the body. He was still taking fire from the other rifleman and the rounds were getting closer to him. He fired two bursts at the prone figure and the firing stopped. The man with the pistol stood and ran away from the bodies next to him toward the hangar, firing blindly toward the buildings. A single shot from Angie's .45 spun him around in mid stride and he sprawled face-down in the dirt. One arm was useless, but he pushed himself over onto his back with the other, his chest heaving. Angie strolled slowly out from the shadows toward the fallen man.

"Don't fire toward the hangar!" Angie said, just before shooting him once through the center of the chest.

Becker drew his own .45 from the shoulder holster beneath his coat and walked toward the truck. The man with the shotgun had died from two rounds in the in the upper back. One of the riflemen had lost the top of his skull and what remained glistened shiny red in the moonlight. The last man had taken two rounds in the legs and at least one in the lower back but he was still breathing, muttering Hail Marys. Becker squatted next to him, held his hand and repeated the prayer with him twice.

"*...Priez pour nous, pauvres pécheurs, maintenant et a l'heure de notre mort.*"

As the man paused to take gasping breaths, Becker pressed the .45 against the base of his skull. At the last minute, he changed his mind and fired between the man's shoulder blades. No sense blowing the man's face off for no reason, he thought.

Becker's ears were ringing so he didn't hear Angie approach. He jumped a little when he spoke.

"Are you OK?"

"I didn't get hit," Becker said.

"What was he saying?" Angie asked.

"Hail Mary's."

"And you?"

"Same."

Angie nodded and looked at the bodies. "I was afraid I'd find you lying out here," he said.

"They never saw me," Becker said.

"I guess that thing works."

"It works."

Angie stood with his hands on his hips and surveyed the scene. "So who are these guys?"

"They ain't the Rotary Club."

"Is that guy wearing a uniform?" Angie said.

"Let's check it out,' Becker said.

It was more like a costume. The body was clothed in tailored tan jodhpurs tucked into high riding boots and a black leather jacket that reached to mid-thigh and had a distinctively military cut to its collar. Angie picked up the blood-splattered hat with two fingers and held it in the light, trying to read what was written around the inside of the brim.

"Italian," he said.

"Papers?" Becker asked, as he picked up a ring with the airfield's three keys on it.

Angie made a quick check of the pockets before standing and shaking his head. They checked the other bodies. None were carrying papers or identification of any kind.

"Well, at least they got that right," Angie said.

"Some consolation," Becker said. "Listen, there's something I've got to do and I've got to do it now."

"Check the gate?" Angie said. Becker nodded. "Go ahead. I'll keep our friends company."

Becker jumped in the truck and headed for the far gate as fast as he dared in the pitch blackness. Well before reaching it, he could see that it was wide open. Getting out and walking over to the gate, he saw the heavy chain hanging loose with the padlock hooked through one of the links, opened with the key still in it. He pulled the gate shut, ran the chain through the gate frames and secured them with the padlock. As he walked away, a thought occurred to him. He returned and broke the key off in the padlock. He drove slower this time as he returned to the hangar. Angie was sitting on the chair in front of the office, smoking a French cigarette.

"I think I'm developing a taste for these things," he said.

"No kidding. I could smell it from halfway across the field," Becker said.

Angie seemed surprised. "I thought you liked how these smell," he said.

"Yeah, I'm just used to you smelling like Lucky Strikes," Becker said.

Angie looked at the bodies lying on the ground. "So, time for some heavy lifting?"

"If we don't, I'm afraid it will make for a bumpy take off."

Neither man moved. The corpses near the hangar were clearly visible, but the others were shapeless mounds in the darkness of the field. It was suddenly very cold.

"What a mess," Angie said.

"Carnage," Becker said.

"Six."

"Right. I noticed."

Angie took no offense at the sarcasm. "How'd we get out so clean?"

Becker shook his head. "Because we didn't think it would be easy?"

"Maybe." Angie tipped the chair forward and stood, stretching his arms over his head. He launched the cigarette butt into the blackness with his thumb and first two fingers. "Poor bastards never knew what killed them."

They discovered that the back of the truck had bench seats on each side that folded up to make more cargo space so they had plenty of room for the job at hand. Angie took the shoulders, Becker the feet and they swung the bodies up and into the back of the truck. Then one of them would climb in and straighten the body so another could fit beside or on top of it. They were finished in less than fifteen minutes. The two of them stood looking at the six bodies, stacked like so much scrap lumber.

"Maybe we should think about daytime work," Angie said.

"Second thoughts?"

"Just that I've been working nights for a long time."

"How many days since we got to this country?"

Angie thought for a few moments. "I don't know exactly. All that driving kind of mixed me up. I was half asleep most of the time."

"It hasn't been a week."

"Definitely not," Angie said.

"A lot of dead bodies," Becker said.

Angie looked over at his friend. "You said we were going to war, right?"

"Right."

"I'm pretty sure this is what they do in war. Except usually you don't have to clean up. You feeling guilty?"

"Feeling cold. Let's get the truck behind the hangar and get warm."

In fact, Becker felt little, and that made him wonder what he was turning into. He felt anger at the forces that had made him a killer, but satisfaction that, so far, he had been so adept at it. Don't be a child, he thought. You think you've seen war? You don't know what war is.

Albert's call came a little after two.

"*Ça va?*"

"We had some visitors," Becker said.

"How many?"

"Six. They came in a truck. No uniforms, but the leader was wearing boots, riding pants and a leather jacket. He had a leather hat. It looked like some kind of uniform."

"Armed?"

"It wasn't a social call," Becker said.

"You and Angie?"

"We're fine."

"And the visitors?"

"In the truck, behind the hangar. They got in through the other gate. They had the key. I think the night manager might be dead."

"I can't leave these two to check, but I can make a call," Albert said.

"How are they?"

"Dear God, they snore. It's like artillery."

"Good. You're on guard. It keeps you awake," Becker said.

"A few hours until dawn. I'll see you soon."

"Right," Becker said.

"Keep your head down," Albert said.

"Albert, we had our party. You're the one who should watch out. I don't know where you are, but you'd better be damned careful when you try to leave."

"You're right. I'll call in some help," he said. "See you soon." He rang off.

"Wait, Albert-" Becker was going to ask him to bring some food in the morning, but now it was too late.

By early morning, Becker had given up all hope of ever being warm again and had resigned himself to a peaceful death from hypothermia. He stood a thirty minute watch beside the hangar while Angie dozed in the office and tried to glean some remnant of heat from the kerosene heater which had run dry an hour before. Unfortunately, the office was drafty as a barn and not nearly as comfortable.

Becker heard the office door open. "What time you got?" Angie said.

Becker looked at his watch. "A little after six-thirty."

"What time is dawn anyway?"

"It's the end of January."

"So, a little before lunchtime," Angie said.

Becker let out a snort. "I never cared about it before. 'Course, I don't think I've ever been this cold before."

"Let's at least walk a little. It'll keep the blood moving."

They started walking in a large oval from the hangar down around the parked biplanes past the hangar and back to the gate, slowly gaining speed as their joints limbered up. They soon realized they could see their own breath by a faint light appearing on the horizon.

"Gotta be soon now," Angie said.

"Angie, have you ever been in a plane before?"

"Nope. You?"

Becker shook his head. "How do you feel about flying?"

"Hey, I'll try anything once." He considered the implications of that statement for a moment. "With a couple exceptions."

They heard a car approaching but saw nothing. Their walk turned into a two hundred meter sprint for the gate, each of them taking cover on either side of the small office shack.

"If that's not Albert, it means he and the pilot are dead," Becker said.

"Yeah," Angie said, out of breath.

"So we take out whoever is in the car, destroy the plane and use the car to get out of here." Angie nodded, still trying to get his breath. "Hey old man," Becker said. "You gotta lay off those coffin nails."

"Right boss," he wheezed. "It's just that after the Olympics last year I kind of let myself go. But you should see me pole vault."

They recognized the big Citroën as it slowed and came to a stop on the far side of the road, two car-lengths from the gate. The driver's side door opened and a man got out, immediately putting both hands behind his head and walking in slow, measured strides toward the gate.

"Mathieu. Angelo. All is well. Don't shoot." It was Albert. His voice carried clearly in the stillness of the icy morning air.

"The pilot and mechanic are with you?" called Becker.

Albert turned his head and spoke to the car's occupants. Downes and the mechanic got out and stood with their hands up. Damn it, Becker thought. I forgot the mechanic's name already. Well, he was out cold last night anyway.

"What's this bloody nonsense?" Downes said.

"No one else?" Becker said.

"No one," Albert said.

"You have the key. Open the gate," Becker said.

Albert waved the mechanic forward as he walked to the gate and started to unlock the gate, but the cold had frozen the lock and the mechanism defied Albert's increasingly frantic efforts to turn the key.

"Don't force it!" said the mechanic. "If the key breaks, we're buggered for sure."

He elbowed Albert aside and tried to persuade the padlock to cooperate. Albert backed off. He's a mechanic, he thought. Let's see what he can do.

"Come on now, there's a good girl," he said. "Oh, bugger." He walked back to the car and came back with a rolled up newspaper, the end of which he lit with a match taken from a box in his pocket. The tightly rolled paper produced a small, smoky flame which he waved back and forth under the lock, while holding the key tightly in his left hand to warm it. After two or three minutes of mild heat , he put the key in the lock and opened it easily.

The mechanic and pilot held opposite sides of the gate as Albert pulled the car through and parked in front of the office. They then closed the gate and locked it behind them.

The mechanic walked purposefully toward the hangar to check on the plane. The pilot leaned against the car hood and lit a cigarette. Angie and Becker came from behind the office and approached Albert.

"Albert, tell me you've got some food and hot coffee," Angie said. Becker expected him to add 'or I'll shoot you' since he still held the .45.

"Oh! Pardon. One minute," he said, genuinely apologetic. He trotted back to the car and returned with two cylindrical rolls of newspaper and a thermos bottle. "Excuse us," Becker said, cocking his head toward the office. "We need food."

"Bon appétit," Albert said. "Where is the lorry?"

They were already walking toward the office but Becker broke stride to point toward the back of the hangar. Taking a flashlight from his pocket, Albert sighed deeply and began to walk slowly in that direction.

"What lorry?" Downes said. Albert ignored him, but the pilot pushed his considerable bulk off the hood of the Citroën and tried to catch up to discover the source of the mystery.

Becker and Angie cleared the office desk and unwrapped their food. The thermos was full of hot *café au lait*. The newspapers were wrapped around baguettes sliced and stuffed with sausage, tangy yellow cheese and dark mustard. The bread was fresh and still slightly warm. They tore into it like starved predators. For minutes, the room was silent except for the sound of frenzied chewing and the gulping of hot coffee, until finally they were able to sit back in their chairs and pause for breath.

"Good," Becker said.

"Almost worth the wait," Angie said.

"We'd better slow down."

"Better yet, take some with us." Angie nodded in response and started to wrap the remainder of the baguette when he suddenly stopped and squinted at something outside the window.

"Hey, what was the mechanic's name? I forgot it already," Becker said.

"What the hell," Angie answered.

Becker turned in his chair to look out the window but it was so steamed up he couldn't see. He grabbed the machine pistol and walked outside with Angie following close behind.

Downes was on his knees with his hands behind his head, facing the field. Albert stood behind him, one of the small Mausers in his hand. It was pointed at the back of the pilot's head. He's standing too close, Becker thought.

Becker spoke to him in French. "What's going on?" he said.

Albert replied in English. "This one follows me to the lorry and looks inside. He is shocked. He doesn't like what you do. He doesn't like us. I think he does not like this work."

"You killed those men?" Downes said, turning his head toward Becker.

"Yes."

The answer struck him dumb for minutes. Finally, the words stumbled out of his mouth, his voice breaking. "Was that necessary? Those were men, not animals. Their bodies are stacked in that lorry like – just so much meat." Becker wasn't sure, but he thought he saw tears on the man's face. "There's a boy in there. Can't be more than sixteen."

"He got off more rounds than any of the others. He was a good soldier," Becker said.

"Bollocks!" Downes replied. Becker mulled it over, wasn't sure of its real meaning, but got the idea. Downes was terrified.

"Sir, those men came here to kill us and destroy the plane. They were heavily armed," Becker said. "Albert, what about the night watchman?"

Albert made a gesture of running his thumb across his throat from ear to ear.

"They murdered the night watchman to get the key to the other gate. They would have killed us too," Becker continued. "Eventually they would have come for you."

"How many men are in that truck?" Downes asked.

"Six."

"And you killed them? You two?"

"We used the darkness for cover," Becker said.

"Bloody Yanks. Cowards. I want no part of this."

The mechanic came out of the hangar and stood back a safe distance from the group. "She's ready as she'll ever be, but we need to get the door open and push her out," he said.

"We have a small problem," Angie whispered to the mechanic.

"What's that then?" He didn't seem particularly concerned that the pilot had a gun to his head.

"Six men came here last night to burn the plane and kill us. We killed them," Angie said. "We put the bodies in their truck. It's behind the hangar."

Angie's gun was drawn but pointed at the ground. The mechanic gave it an unconcerned look and walked back behind the hangar to look. He returned and stood next to Angie.

"There were six of them sir," he called out to Downes. "I saw at least two rifles and a shotgun."

"Stay out of this Burdon!" Downes shouted, his voice cracking.

Angie turned to the mechanic, transferred the .45 to his left hand and held out his right.

"Oh, sorry, I'm Angelo Vincent. Call me Angie," he said.

"Dickey Burdon. Friends call me Burdie." They shook hands casually, as if waiting on a train platform.

"This pilot, Downes. A friend of yours?" Angie asked.

"Me? Don't know the man, but he seems a bit gormless. He just needed someone to handle the big radial and his regular was off somewhere, so it's me got the job. Acts the posh officer type, but I think maybe he's just putting it on."

Angie struggled with the man's dialect and accent but he got the general gist.

"What this about the radio?" Angie said.

The man looked cock-eyed at Angie for a minute before comprehension dawned.

"No, mate. 'Radial', not radio," he said. "The engine."

"Sorry, Pal. I still don't get it," Angie said.

"She's got nine great bloody cylinders in a circle, like this." Burdon made a circle with his hands. "And the pistons go in and out, instead of up and down," he said, gesturing frantically with his hands acting as the pistons.

"Get out of here," Angie said, fascinated.

"Whey-aye, it's true mate. Come on, I'll show ye."

"I think we'd better stay here for a minute," Angie said.

The two of them made small talk about engines and cars, sometimes sharing a laugh at their respective accents and misunderstandings, but they quickly recognized each other as cut from the same cloth.

"Sorry to ask this Burdie, but are you, uh, carrying a weapon?" Angie asked.

Burdon unzipped his jacket and held one side open to reveal the butt of an enormous revolver in a shoulder holster. The barrel appeared to be at least six inches. Angie's eyebrows went up.

"What the hell is that?" he asked.

"It's a Webley, Mark 6."

"Never heard of it," Angie said. "What's it fire?"

".455."

"No offense Pal, never heard of that either. Has he got the same thing?" Angie said, cocking his head toward the pilot. Burdon nodded.

"Matt." Angie raised his voice only slightly, but the sound carried. "He's got a piece."

Becker had been pacing back and forth on the grass, trying to make a decision which would not overplay his hand or get himself into something he couldn't get out of, once again shocked to find everyone waiting for him to make a decision. He was groggy from lack of sleep and growing angrier by the minute.

"Albert, step back one meter." His voice was harsh and commanding. Albert stepped back, his face like a chastened schoolboy's.

Becker walked forward and patted the front of Downes' coat until he felt the butt of the revolver, then drew it quickly from its holster and stepped away. Beautiful weapon, he thought. A top-break revolver. It opens like a shotgun and ejects the spent cartridges. Heard about them, never seen one. What am I going to do with it? I'm carrying too much iron right now. No time for this.

"Mr. Downes. Stand up please," Becker said. "You can put your hands down." Becker gestured to Albert to back off. He put the Webley in his belt at the small of his back and walked over to face Downes, whose face was pale and streaked with tears.

"Could I ask you to walk with me for a minute?" Becker said, starting off toward the office without waiting for an answer. Downes quickly caught up. When they were out of earshot of the others, Becker turned and looked the pilot in the eye.

"You flew in the Great War?" Becker said.

Downes nodded.

"Did you see combat?"

Downes looked at the ground. "It was too late. I got my wings in 1918. I got assigned to a squadron. Then, the armistice."

"Sounds like you caught a break," Becker said. "My understanding is that flying was not very good for your health back then, and the Krauts knew their business."

"Damn right about that. But I wanted to do my part and nothing came of it." He paused. "All these years, living with that. It eats away at you."

"Have you ever seen a dead body before?" Becker said.

Downes raised his eyes but still couldn't meet Becker's. He said nothing.

"It's a hard thing. Changes your thinking, changes something in here," Becker said, tapping his chest.

"Who are you people?" Downes said.

The question took Becker aback, something he had no time for.

"What do you mean?" Becker said.

"You and the other one." He pointed at Angie, who was laughing at something Burdon had said. "How do you do this?"

"We grew up in a bad neighborhood," Becker said, growing impatient. "Listen, Mr. Downes. You wanted to do your part. Today is your chance to show what you're made of." He looked at the sky and his watch. "The sun will be up very soon. You have a choice. Fly this plane to Albacete with us or stay here."

"And if I choose to stay?" Downes asked, already knowing the answer.

"We have to burn the plane," Becker said. "You, your mechanic. What's his name?"

"Burdon."

"Right. You and Mr. Burdon, I don't know what will happen to you. You can't come with us and if the other side catches up with you-well, it will be quick."

Or, Becker thought, they might want information. In which case, it will be slow. Better not to get into that.

Downes said nothing, but looked at the horizon to check the sun's progress. The tension had gone out of his face. He reached into his jacket pocket, took out a pint flask made of tarnished silver and took one swallow.

"Sorry, bad manners." He offered it to Becker, who also took a swallow. It was cognac, and it burned its way down his throat. Becker did not return it.

"So?" Becker said.

"We'd best get moving," Downes said.

"One minute." Becker called Albert, Angie and Burdon over.

"All's well. Just time for a quick belt." Each man took a healthy swig from the flask as Downes started to protest, finally crossing his arms over his chest and smiling as Angie and Albert both coughed after downing the fiery liquid.

When the flask came back to Becker, he up-ended the remaining contents onto the ground and passed it back to Downes.

"Don't worry. I hear the Spanish make a passable brandy," he said. "Angie, Albert, Mr. Burdon, could you get our gear in the plane?" The three were moving before he had finished speaking. He turned to Downes.

"Shall we get the hangar door?" Becker said.

"Let's hope for a more cooperative lock," Downes said.

"Amen to that." Becker started for the hangar.

As they approached the doors, Becker pulled the key from his coat pocket and showed it to Downes.

"Feeling lucky?" he said.

"Not particularly, but I'll give it a go," Downes said. He took the key, slid it in the padlock, squinted his eyes shut for an instant and turned. The lock opened with a click on the first try.

"Maybe that's a good omen," Becker said with a dry smile, noticing that Downes had one foot in what appeared to be brain tissue and skull fragments. He hoped it would go unnoticed.

Each man took one side of the huge sliding doors and began to pull. The rollers on which they moved shrieked in agony and defiance as Becker and Downes used both hands and all their strength to move them, finally putting their backs against the edges and pushing with their legs until they had opened to their full extent.

Downes was bent over with his hands on his knees, wheezing for breath when they finished.

"Well, that just about did me in," he said as Becker approached.

"Me too. I pity the poor bastard that has to close them again," Becker said.

Burdon stood by the door on the right wing of the plane and called to Downes. "She's packed, fueled and ready to go sir. Just have to push her out a bit."

"Push her out?" Becker said. "Why don't we just, you know, drive her out?" He instantly regretted the complaint, but cold, lack of sleep, violence and the final confrontation with Downes had sapped his judgment. Now he had to worry about that too.

Downes was about to respond when he looked at Becker's face. He would have guessed him to be forty had he not known differently. He looked like a man just back from the dead, his eyes sunken into their sockets, the pale skin stretched tight across his cheekbones, the lips blue with cold. He quickly decided to rephrase his churlish answer to Becker's question.

"I wish we could, but that's a five hundred and fifty horsepower engine. She puts out quite a blast. We'd make a hell of a mess of the hangar, which I don't really give a damn about, but we might accidentally blow some debris into the aircraft, and she's a touchy little bird. Have to treat her like a lady."

"Right. Bloody stupid question," Becker said. *Did I just say 'bloody'?* he thought. *Christ, I need some rest.*

Downes noticed and smiled. "We'll have you speaking the King's English in no time, uh, mate." He paused and put a fist to his mouth as he cleared his throat. "Beg pardon," he said. "Sorry, but I was a bit under the weather yesterday and I'm afraid I've forgotten your name."

"Matt MacCready. For now," Becker said, extending his hand.

"Oh, right. *Noms de guerre* and all that. I'm Kenneth Downes," he said, shaking Becker's hand. "I heard Albert call you 'Mathieu'. You're French?"

Becker smiled. "Sometimes. Just call me Matt. I don't always remember to answer to the other one."

"My friends call me Kenny." He paused and pulled up his collar against the cold. "Matt." He paused again, but Becker was willing to wait it out. He needed this man. "Matt, I feel I should apologize for my-"

"Kenny?" Becker said. "It's forgotten." He wanted to say more, but now Becker found himself at a loss for words.

"I feel such a damned fool."

"Then maybe you're the sane one," Becker said. "In another time and place I think you would have been in the right."

Downes found himself looking at bloodstains on Becker's hands and wondered again to himself, Who are these people and what are they made of?

"Are we gonna push this monster out of here or what?" Angie called.

With men pushing on each wing it still took a bit of cursing to get the plane moving but once the wheels were turning they soon had her out onto the grass and it took little effort to swing the tail around until she was pointed down the field. When the job was finished, everyone lit cigarettes except Becker. He watched as they performed the well-practiced ritual and for a moment envied them the obvious pleasure and relief it gave them. Plenty of time to pick up more vices, he thought. For now I guess I'll stick with alcohol and cold-blooded murder.

Angie walked to the front of the plane and looked into the cowling, trying to take in the marvel of the radial engine as Burdon had explained it. Albert walked to the car and sat on the hood, drawing deeply on his cigarette between spasms of coughing. Downes and Burdon were suddenly deep in consultation. They waved Becker over.

"A lot of shooting here last night?" Downes asked, then shook his head. "Damned stupid question. Of course there was."

"A bit," Becker said. But it was all over very quickly."

"I've been all over this girl and I can't find a single bullet hole," Burdon said. "But what do you think?" he said to Becker.

"We took positions that would keep the firing away from the hangar as much as possible. Two men died in front of the doors but the shots were fired parallel to or away from the building. But I can't make any promises. One of the – visitors fired some wild shots," Becker said. "Where they went or if they penetrated the hangar?" He shrugged.

"Nothing for it," Downes said. "Let's get her in the air. We'll know soon enough if anything is amiss. I'll get things started."

Becker and Angie jogged over to the car and embraced Albert.

"Better you than me," he said looking toward the plane. He had been preparing himself for this farewell and had searched for ways to joke his way through it. I'll probably never see these boys again, he thought. I don't want them to see me in tears on this day or any other.

"No taste for adventure," Becker said. Both men tried to hide a sudden swell of emotion.

"What are you talking about? I let you drive didn't I?" Albert looked over at Burdon and Downes. "These English. I like the mechanic. You think the pilot can do the job?"

"He'll get us there," Becker said. "What about you?"

"Back to Paris, but I think I'll sell the car and take a train. Angelo, can you keep watch on this one?"

"I'll do my best, Uncle." Angie's voice was hoarse. For once, he didn't have a wisecrack.

"I'll wait until you're in the air. I want to see if she really flies," Albert said. "Now, no more goodbyes please. I despise bourgeois sentimentality. Get out of here. The sun's coming up."

Back at the plane, they started to climb onto the right wing to reach the small entry hatch, but Burdon stopped them. They noticed he was holding a fire extinguisher taken from the hangar.

"Wait until she's started up," he said. He looked up at the cockpit and made a swirling motion with his right hand. They heard some clicks from deep inside the engine cowling followed by the sound of a man taking a punch to the solar plexus. The propeller made a half turn. The clicks and sound repeated. On the third try the engine started, the propeller began spinning, and the front of the plane suddenly became a fearsome, screaming vortex of elemental power. Becker and Angie each stepped back, but Burdon moved side to side in front of the plane, ducking his head to look for smoke or leaking of the fluids that were the plane's life's blood. He came back to his original position and slowly moved his hand in a faster circular motion.

The engine's sound turned to an ear-splitting whine as Burdon ran back to the hangar to place the extinguisher inside the door. Running back to the plane he shouted something and waved Becker and Angie toward the plane. They scrambled up the steep slope of the wing and just before entering the hatch, Becker saw Burdon turn and give Albert a wave and an exaggerated military salute.

Inside they found six passenger seats and saw the lower half of Downes' body in the raised pilot's seat. There were four windows on each side of the plane and Angie went for the last seat with the best view, but after securing the hatch Burdon quickly directed them to two seats over the forward part of the wing and motioned for them to fasten their seatbelts. He took a position crouched in the narrow space next to Downes, where he could see the instrument panel and its arcane profusion of gauges, lights, switches and dials. Becker watched him frowning in concentration as Downes slowly raised the engine speed to a tornado-like roar. He pointed to one of the gauges and nodded once. A little more power and they felt the plane start to move, its undercarriage rumbling over the irregularities of the grass airfield. The vibration rattled the plywood body of the plane, made their heads bobble like rag dolls and seemed to go on forever. Becker looked out the window and was alarmed to see that they were moving slowly toward the far side of the field a mile or more away. Why? He started to reach inside his jacket for his .45 but quickly realized there was nothing he could do with it other than make a fool of himself.

The jostling, squeaking, pounding journey ended in a graceful pirouette and Becker briefly saw a hint of sunrise pass across one of the windows as the plane turned and came to a stop.

Angie leaned over to shout into Becker's ear. "Are we driving to Spain?" Becker answered by turning both hands up and raising his shoulders, mimicking one of Angie's signature gestures. Angie answered by flicking his fingers across the underside of his chin, twisting his pursed lips to the side and looking out the window. Becker noticed he was trying to conceal a smile.

Burdon and Downes were shouting at each other, their words lost in the blast of wind and noise from the engine. Each gestured at a gauge or two before coming to some agreement. Burdon nodded once and they felt the vibrations as the plane started to move again, the engine much louder this time, rising in pitch, the pounding of the undercarriage more violent as the speed increased. Becker tried to guess how fast they were going but found himself at a loss. Seventy? Eighty? More? His hands sweated as he gripped the armrests and looked straight ahead. I will not close my eyes, he thought. If they can do it, I can do it. He looked at Angie. His eyes were closed and his lips were moving.

Becker felt the tail of the plane come off the ground and suddenly the pounding from the wheels seemed to lessen. A few more seconds and it stopped. Becker realized the plane had left the ground but now the vibration was replaced by a low groan from deep in the body of the plane. The bowels of the aircraft seemed to be in the midst of some excruciating torment punctuated by painful spasms and seizures. He looked forward at Burdon who sat stone-faced but strangely composed. After less than a minute, the episode passed and Burdon nodded to Downes. Becker let out a deep breath he had been holding as he realized he had just heard the undercarriage retracting and locking in place.

Burdon came back to the cabin and sat sideways in the seat just forward of Becker's. He had to shout to be heard. They both leaned forward to listen.

"You lads alright? You looked a bit green for a minute there," he said.

"Why the long drive? I think I lost some teeth," Angie said. Burdon gave him a puzzled look but soon took his meaning.

"The wind. All airplanes take off into the wind." He made sweeping illustrative gestures with his hands as he spoke.

"Engine alright?" Becker said. Burdon frowned as if any answer might put a hex on their journey. Well, sailors were supposed to be superstitious, Becker thought. Why not fliers?

"All the gauges are OK," he answered. "But she's a good lass, for a Yank." He winked. "Never had a bit of trouble with her."

"How long?" Angie asked.

He shrugged. "About three hundred miles, two hundred miles an hour. Long enough for a nap." He smiled and patted Becker's shoulder. "You lads get some rest. I'll let you know if we're going to crash." He walked back to his perch next to Downes, smiling at his own wit.

Becker saw Angie shaking his head and mouthing the lament they had both used a thousand times. "Everybody's a wiseass."

CHAPTER 15

Becker and Angie had been looking forward to enjoying a view of the earth from thousands of feet in the air but they soon passed through a layer of haze and spent the journey looking down at a fluffy carpet of clouds that extended to the horizon. The thrill of that scenery soon faded and the warmth of the cabin combined with the powerful, mesmerizing drone of the engine soon had Becker's eyelids growing heavy.

He felt a pat on his arm and Burdon was speaking close to his ear.

"We'll be coming into Albacete soon. Seatbelt," he said, pointing. He took the seat in front of Becker and fastened his own.

Becker fastened the belt and moments later felt his ears pop and his stomach tighten as they descended through the clouds and haze. When they broke into the clear, they saw a grayish brown landscape of flat farmland with occasional rolling hills and felt the plane make two gentle banking maneuvers in as many minutes. Becker realized that Downes must have made the entire flight using no more than his compass and dead reckoning and that this was almost certainly not the first time he had made this trip. How many aircraft of how many different types had he ferried to the Republic since the start of the war?

Hearing the landing gear lower and lock in place, the passengers prepared for a beating similar to the one they had taken on takeoff but instead they heard the sound of a single tentative skid followed by that of the wheels rolling on a smooth surface as the plane once again became earthbound.

"Is this the airfield?" Becker shouted next to Burdon's ear.

"Concrete," he replied. "Very handy in wet weather. If this was grass, everything would be grounded when it rained."

The plane taxied to an open area on the field, away from the other aircraft and Downes brought the engine to a low idle. Burdon rose from his seat and spoke some quick words to him before heading to the rear of the plane.

"Give us a minute," he said. "I have to find out where they want us to put it." He opened the door, stepped out onto the wing and spoke to someone outside as Becker and Angie tried to see what was happening out their windows. He saw that a small group of Republican soldiers had sprinted across the field and taken up guard around the plane but he couldn't determine how many.

Burdon was back in a moment.

"They want us to leave it here," he said as he walked back to the cockpit to tell Downes. They soon heard the engine shutting down and the propeller coming to a stuttering halt, the sudden absence of sound making them realize that their ears were ringing.

They gathered up their belongings and checked to be certain nothing was left behind. Downes took a small leather document case from his duffel and, following an unspoken protocol, the others waited for him to exit first. He tossed his bag through the small door and then squeezed his unwieldy frame through after it, followed by the rest of the passengers.

There were four guards around the plane and two other soldiers with rifles at port arms waiting for them as they climbed down off the wing. One of the soldiers, apparently having no English motioned for

them to follow him. The other fell in behind as they walked toward a row of single-story buildings next to the hangars at the edge of the tarmac.

The soldiers led them into one of the buildings which consisted of a single row of offices along a narrow hallway. They were directed to a small waiting area of low wooden benches near the entrance where Burdon and Angie promptly sat and lit cigarettes. Becker, the machine pistol slung across his back, decided to stand, as did Downes. The soldiers slung their rifles, but remained on either side of the group. Becker couldn't determine if they were being guarded or escorted.

"Don't know why they can't get proper chairs in here. The last time I sat on one of those benches after a flight I thought my back was going to break," Downes said.

"They usually keep you waiting long?" Becker asked.

"Depends on who's here. One of the colonels is a friend. We've downed quite a few drinks together actually. But his adjutant is a pain in the arse. Likes to make you wait just to lord it over you, if you know what I mean. And his English is mostly gibberish."

One of the doors halfway down the hall opened and a head appeared. The face broke into a smile.

"Señor Downes?"

"Colonel Torres!" Downes said, snapping to attention and saluting dramatically, more in greeting than military formality. The Spanish officer came into the hallway and walked toward them. He was medium height and slender. Becker first judged him to be in his early thirties but as he came nearer the group the grey temples and lined face put him closer to fifty. He carried himself well, walking with a precise military step, his left thumb hooked in his belt, his right hand extended in greeting to Downes. Becker noticed that the man's uniform had a loose fit and guessed that he had recently lost weight. Well who hasn't? he thought with a mental shrug, noting that he had tightened his belt a notch in the past week.

Downes and the officer shook hands before turning to the group.

"Gentlemen," Downes said, "Colonel Torres of the Air Force of the Republic of Spain."

Angie and Burdon quickly stubbed out their cigarettes in a near-by ashtray and stood, not quite at attention. Becker tried to square his shoulders somewhat but immediately felt foolish, knowing that his clothes and the machine pistol made him look more criminal than soldier.

"Señor Burdon I know," Torres said, with a quick nod, but his face darkened as he looked at Angie and Becker, turning his head slightly to see what kind of weapon Becker was carrying. "And these gentlemen are?"

"These men are volunteers. They have been guarding me and the plane. Mister MacCready and Mister Vincent," Downes said. "Colonel, I assure you, without these men I would not be here and neither would the plane."

"There was trouble in France?" Torres said. Downes nodded solemnly. "Gentlemen, please come into my office," Torres said, equally grave.

Torres dismissed the two soldiers and escorted his guests into an office spacious enough to accommodate his large desk, a table with four chairs and a sofa which had obviously been slept on regularly. The table was strewn with files and assorted paperwork which Torres quickly gathered into his arms and dropped onto a similar pile already on his desk.

"Gentlemen, please excuse...," he searched for an appropriate word and finally settled for "...all this," indicating the condition of the office with a wave of his arm. "Please be comfortable. I regret to say that we have had no coffee or tea for some days now. There is only wine."

"That'll do for me," Downes said cheerfully as he took off his jacket and tried to position his considerable rump on one of the wooden chairs. Torres looked at Becker, who was standing near the window, the weapon slung on his back making it difficult to take off his jacket or sit down.

Becker knew it was still well before noon but was wary of giving offense by refusing. Better to look like a drunk or a prig? he wondered. He tried for a polite but noncommittal response.

"Very kind of the colonel," he said. Angie and Burdon, at opposite ends of the sofa, nodded in silent agreement. Torres opened the door to an adjoining office, spoke some rapid Spanish to an unseen subordinate and left it slightly ajar.

"Please, Señor," he said to Becker. "Your weapon and coat." He mimed the act of taking off a jacket. "It is necessary to be comfortable."

Becker nodded self-consciously, took the machine pistol from his shoulder and set it, stock down, in the corner where it would not fall. Torres took his coat and Downes' and hung them on a coat rack by the door. As he walked back, he looked in the corner and then at Becker.

"Señor will permit me?" he said, pointing toward the corner.

"Of course, Colonel," Becker said. He had already removed the magazine, which now protruded slightly from one of his trouser pockets. Picking up the weapon, he checked the breach, made sure the bolt was on safe and passed it gently to Torres.

"German, yes?" he said, turning it from side to side, examining the markings and mechanism.

"Yes sir," Becker said.

"Caliber?"

"Nine millimeter."

"And the...," he frowned, once again searching his mind for the correct term as he tapped the magazine mount with his finger and looked at Becker.

"Yes sir, the magazine goes there," Becker said.

"You have a magazine?"

"Yes, sir."

Torres returned to his examination but held out his open right hand. Becker's mind raced. This is just what I need, he thought. A loaded machine gun in an office full of people. Can I get out of this? Probably not. He's a goddamned colonel and I need his good will. Colonel or not, if he chambers a round I'm hitting the floor.

Becker took the fully-loaded magazine from his pocket and placed it gingerly in Torres' hand. The colonel looked at it, held the weapon at his waist and poised the magazine just outside the mount.

"It goes here? To the side?" he said.

"Yes, sir," Becker answered, his heart pounding as he anticipated the insertion of the magazine.

"And this weapon is a, how do you say, a small *ametralladora*?"

"Yes, Colonel. A machine gun. Really a machine pistol," Becker said. "Only a nine millimeter."

Torres lowered the weapon without loading it. Thank God, Becker thought. He heard Angie release a long, deeply held sigh of relief from across the room as the colonel set returned it to the corner and gave the magazine back to Becker.

"How did it come to you?" he asked, a note of wonder in his voice.

"It is from a German secret policeman."

"A gift?" Torres said, smiling.

"No, sir."

"You killed this man?" Torres asked.

"Possibly. I know he was badly wounded. He escaped and left this behind. I thought it might be useful."

An orderly brought in an earthenware pitcher and five small glasses held in the fingers of one hand. He set them on the table, poured a half-glass of red wine into each, saluted the colonel and left the room. Glasses were passed over to Angie and Burdon. Torres, still standing, raised his glass.

"Gentlemen, to the Republic!"

"The Republic!" the others responded in unison.

Torres sat at the table with Becker and Downes. "And was it useful?" he asked, looking at his wine glass."

"Yes, sir. Very useful."

"In France?"

"Yes, sir."

"There was an attack on the airplane?" he asked, looking at Downes.

"Some men came last night," Downes said, his eyes on his wine glass.

"Who were they?" Torres asked.

"We don't know. They wore no uniforms and carried no identification. One of them may have been Italian," Becker said.

Torres rubbed his eyes and pinched the bridge of his nose for a moment. "It becomes more and more difficult. True, Mister Downes?" he said.

"I'm not complaining," Downes said. "These lads did all the work. Burdon and I slept well all night. All I did was fly, and she's a beauty Colonel."

Torres face brightened briefly. "Beauty? The airplane is fast?"

"Very fast," Downes said, smiling.

"A gentle beauty, I hope?" Torres asked. "So many beauties give..." he tapped on the center of his chest.

"Heartbreak?" Downes said. "Not this one. You will like her. Burdie, hand me that case, will you?"

Burdon had been holding the leather document case Downes had brought with him. He passed it over to Angie, who passed it on to Downes.

"These are the documents for the aircraft," Downes said, handing the leather case to the colonel. Torres opened the flap of the case, peered inside and quickly found two sheets of paper which he laid side by side on the table. The one on the left appeared to be technical specifications for the plane. He squinted at the words on the page.

"I have seen this name, but please tell me how to say it properly," he said to Downes and pointing to a word on the page.

"Lockheed," Downes said. "The company name."

"And this?" Torres pointed to another word.

"Orion."

"And what is 'Orion'? A bird perhaps?"

Downes face went blank for a moment. He looked to Becker for help.

"A constellation," Becker said, but no light appeared in the colonel's eyes. He decided to try it with a Spanish intonation. "*Una constelación?*"

"Ah, yes," Torres said, turning toward Becker. "And which *constelación?*"

"The Hunter?" Again, Torres looked at him without comprehension. Becker reached his arm over his head and used his index finger to point out three imaginary stars. *"Uno, dos, tres?"*

"Ah yes! *El cazador!*" Torres said. Becker was relieved. He was about to try a Spanish version of the French word *chasseur*, which he now knew would have only made matters worse. Good God, he thought. How are we ever going to fight a war this way?

"Se habla Español?" Torres asked.

Becker shook his head. *"Yo no lo hablo. Pero yo sé algunas palabras."* I don't speak it, but I know some words.

Torres raised one eyebrow skeptically. *"Creo que estas hablando ahora."* I think you're speaking it now. Perfect, Becker thought. I'm trying to tell him the truth and he thinks I'm pulling his chain.

The Colonel returned to perusing the documents on the table while reaching into the pocket of his tunic for a pen. When he finished the first, he turned to the second, ran his finger quickly along four lines of typing, signed at the bottom with a dramatic flourish and handed the paper across the table to Downes.

"Thank you, Colonel," Downes said. He folded the document, put it in his shirt pocket and buttoned the flap.

"So, gentlemen," Torres said. "What are your plans?"

"Me and Burdon will spend a night or two here. Then, make our way to Barcelona and find a ship back to England," Downes said.

"You will stay at the usual *pension*?"

"If the landlady will have us. We made a bit of a mess last time." Downes looked momentarily sheepish.

"If you have a problem, tell her to call me here," Torres said. "And these gentlemen?" he added, indicating Angie and Becker with a gesture.

"We have come to volunteer for the International Brigades," Becker said.

"So you will be going to the barracks?"

Becker realized that with everything he'd had to occupy his mind in the last week, his thinking hadn't progressed that far.

"May I ask for the Colonel's advice?"

"Well, you must go to the barracks at some point, but it is a most unpleasant place. It is on Calle de la Libertad. My driver can take you there, but I must tell you that he speaks no English."

"That would be very kind," Becker said. He saw the Colonel's eyes stray to the machine pistol in the corner of the room. "Forgive me, Colonel, but may I ask for your help in a difficult matter?"

"Of course," Torres said, warily. No fool, he knew some transaction was in the offing, but he was curious to see how Becker would finesse the proposition.

"I'm afraid that this weapon is not suitable for a foot soldier in the International Brigades. But possibly an officer like the Colonel would find it useful. May I leave it in your care?"

Torres clasped his hands over his belt buckle and leaned back in his chair, smiling.

"Certainly, Señor. But you will need its return in the future?"

Becker shook his head slowly. "I leave it for the Colonel and for the Republic."

"*Muchas gracias,*" Torres said with finality. He had closed the deal. "If there is anything I can do for you gentlemen..."

Becker took Alma's envelope from his jacket on the back of the chair. "Pardon me, Colonel," he said.

"Yes?"

"This was given to me by our contact in Paris. It is for the senior military commander of the Brigades." He handed the envelope to Torres, who examined the writing on both sides.

"Ah, yes. General Kléber."

"This is our first time in Spain and we have no contacts here. Could the Colonel assist me in getting this message to the General?"

"And this is from...?"

"Department Five, in Paris," Becker said, quietly, as if he knew the words held great significance.

"Department Five. Of course." Torres nodded meaningfully. In reality, he had no idea what Becker was talking about, but Kléber was a general and he was a colonel. "Please excuse me for a moment." He got up, went in to the adjoining office and closed the door. The four men waited in a silence periodically broken by the sound of Downes slurping his wine.

"You know, he's right Matthew, old boy. Those barracks. A bloody hellhole," Downes said. "You should come to our place. She can never keep all the rooms filled. Not at the prices she charges."

"Right, mates. Come on, we'll make a night of it," Burdon said.

Becker looked at Angie, but couldn't read his expression. "Ange?"

"Hey, Matt. I'm with you. You call it," he said.

"Kenny, I think we're supposed to be soldiers now. Recruits anyway, who don't know the ropes yet. I think we'd better report in, or the boss might get pretty sore. Even worse if we spend the night on the town."

"Don't know the ropes, eh?" Burdon said.

"I pity the poor Fascist bastards that meet up with you lads," Downes added.

Torres returned and closed the door behind him. "General Kléber is not in Albacete now, but I have given the letter to one of my best officers. He also has a pass which will get him through all checkpoints. I think this is the best way for the letter to reach the General."

"I'm grateful Colonel," Becker said.

"It is nothing," Torres answered. "But gentlemen, I regret to say that my car is not available. My driver will have to take you into town in one of the lorries."

"That will be fine Colonel. You're very kind," Becker said.

Torres frowned. "It is not secure. Please be careful. Sometimes grenades are thrown into trucks by the Fascists."

After a half hour of small talk and more wine the colonel looked at his watch.

"Gentlemen, I regret...," he began.

"Right, Colonel," Downes said, rising and finishing his wine with a resounding gulp. "We'll be off then. Can't keep the ladies waiting." His mood had brightened and his face was pink and glistening.

As the group made their way out the door, Torres gently took

Becker's arm. "Señor. Could I speak to you and your friend for a moment?" he said. Downes and Burdon looked toward them. "These gentlemen will meet you outside," Torres said.

"Right," Downes said. "Come on, Dickey. Let's give the military their privacy." When they had gone, Torres closed the door.

"Señores, you are carrying passports?"

"Yes, sir," Becker said. Angie nodded.

"You know that when you arrive at the Brigades, they will take your passports. You may have difficulty getting them back." The two Americans exchanged worried glances.

"We didn't know," Angie said.

"Señor Marty, he is the Supreme Commander of the Brigades. He has a great fear of spies. Trotskyites. Counter-revolutionaries. And to be frank, he has little affection for the American volunteers. He is French, you understand. Please be careful."

"Is the Colonel saying we are in danger?" Becker asked.

An expression of profound grief and weariness passed over Torres' face. "Even the loyal can be denounced. My own wife was denounced for being a school teacher. My sons tried to save her. They too are gone."

Becker and Angie bowed their heads momentarily. "We are sorry for the Colonel's loss," Becker said. "The injustice."

"As you say," Torres said, his eyes unfocused. "The injustice." There was an uncomfortable silence as the colonel patted his pockets for cigarettes, finally realizing they were on the table. He turned away from them as he picked up the pack, lit one and drew the smoke deep into his lungs. When he faced them again, his face was calm. He extended the pack to his guests, who declined with a shake of their heads. "So. May I see your passports please?"

Becker and Angie took the documents from their rucksacks and handed them over.

"Vincent." Torres smiled. "Quite new." He paged through Angie's before turning to Becker's. "How do you say this name?"

"MacCready," Becker said.

"And what manner of name is that?"

"Scottish, sir."

"These are your real names?" Torres asked with a direct gaze.

"No, sir. Only the Christian names."

"It is common for the volunteers." Torres closed the passports and held them at his side. "Señores, I will ask you to leave these with me. I will put them in the safe in my office. If you need them, you may come here and I will return them to you. If I am not here, I will leave instructions for my staff to return them."

"And if the Brigades ask for them?" Becker said, hoping he didn't sound impertinent.

"You must tell them they were confiscated by the Republican Air Force when you arrived. A matter of security. I will give you a receipt. If anyone questions you, tell them to contact me. I will deal with them."

Becker looked at Angie briefly, but could read nothing in his face.

"Thank you, Colonel," Becker said. "I believe this is a great kindness."

"It is nothing. I regret it is the only kindness I can offer. Please excuse me a moment." Torres executed a military about-face and walked into the adjoining office. He returned in moments holding two small Republican Air force documents with their names, passport numbers and his ornate signature on them.

"These should satisfy the Brigades' staff," he said.

"Colonel. You have been very kind. I wish we could return...," began Becker.

Torres shook his head. "It is not necessary. Now, the lorry is waiting."

He walked them out the door of the staff building, across a small gravel parking lot to the waiting truck. A fine mist of rain was beginning to fall. Downes and Burdon were already seated inside the canvas-covered cargo area, partially obscured by a haze of cigarette smoke. The driver standing next to the truck quickly tossed his cigarette and saluted as they approached.

"Here I must say goodbye." Torres reached out to shake their hands. "Senor Mac-. Forgive me. Your Christian name is Matteo?"

"Yes, sir."

"And Angelo?" The "g" came out slightly guttural, but Angie paid it no mind.

"Yes, Colonel."

"*Vayan con Dios*, Matteo and Angelo." Torres looked stricken, but maintained his composure. "I hope to meet again in better times."

Becker summoned the courage to try his Spanish. "*Hasta la proxima vez*," he said, shaking the colonel's hand. Torres managed a weak smile.

"Very good! I knew you could speak Spanish." He saluted Downes and Burdon who, unable to stand in the back of the truck, remained seated and returned his farewell with a wave.

Angie and Becker boarded the truck and tried to get comfortable on the hard wooden benches. Torres spoke to the driver and then pointed at the canvas flap at top of the truck.

"You must close this! Remember the grenades!" he shouted as the engine revved. Becker and Angie quickly jumped up to loosen the ties which held the flap in place. As the canvas rolled down, they caught a final glimpse of Torres walking slowly back toward the staff building, his head bowed.

"He doesn't think we're gonna make it," Angie said.

Becker nodded slowly at his friend but said nothing.

CHAPTER 16

The trucks had moved out of the Albacete bullring around midnight, packed tight with American and Irish volunteers. Few had room to sit. Most stood and fought the rocking of the chassis and the swaying press of bodies, trying not to set off a domino cascade of falling men which would send the truck tipping into a ditch or over some precipice. Their newly issued rifles were pressed between knees or clenched in one hand as the other searched for handholds on the frame supporting the canvas canopy. In spite of the close quarters, the men were chilled to the bone by steady drafts of icy night air.

After the second hour, they came to realize that there would be no rest stops and no allowances for normal body functions. Those desperate for relief struggled past elbows, shoulders, rucksacks, ammo packs, Mills bombs and a tangled mass of ill-temper to the rear where they tried to keep a precarious balance as they relieved themselves off the back of the truck.

Angie and Becker had been the first onto the truck and now they regretted it. They were among the few who had found seats but hours on the hard wooden benches had left their buttocks and lower backs in agony. The cold air from the front of the truck blew through the space where two sections of canvas were tied together through grommet holes, easily piercing the meager protection of their woolen caps and delivering an aching, burning numbness to the exposed skin of their faces. For an hour they had been taking cover behind their Great War vintage French helmets, holding them to the right side of their faces like vaudeville song-and-dance men.

"Why don't they just make this thing a convertible?" Becker said.

"What are you complaining about? I'm in the front. The cold air has to go through me to get to you," Angie said.

"But you're hot-blooded."

Angie gave a snort and said something under his breath. "Which way we going anyway?"

Becker took his compass from his pocket. "Can't see it now, but the last time I got a look it was generally north or northwest, but we've made a couple detours. Can you see anything?"

Angie peered through the gap in the canvas. "Sometimes I see the shadow of another truck but nobody's using their lights much."

"Blacked out."

"When is the full moon?" Angie asked.

"I think we missed it."

The truck stopped suddenly and at least two dozen bodies lurched in unison toward the front with a collective groan and a chorus of cursing. Some fell to their knees on the truck bed to be piled on by their comrades. Others had feet or hands tread upon or faces struck cruel blows by slung rifles. While the men were still picking themselves up, the truck started again with a jerk followed by a series of convulsive throes from its tortured clutch, throwing the bruised and aching mass toward the rear.

"He's waking up all my lice!" came a voice from deep inside the pile.

"The bastard's doing it on purpose!" shouted another.

"Think so?" Becker whispered to Angie.

"Did you get a look at the driver before we got in?" Angie asked.

Becker shook his head. "I think he's more of a mule driver, and I pity the poor damn mules."

"I guess that's about par for this course," Becker said. The whole Brigade operation had seemed a comedy of errors since they arrived. Bureaucracy, incompetence, frequent shuffles of leadership and little or no real training. Angie and Becker had yet to meet another volunteer who had ever fired a gun.

Angie looked at him with mock indignation. "What are you comrade? Some kind of Trotskyite?"

"You'd better stow that crap, brother. You don't know who's listening," said a strong Brooklyn accent on Becker's left. The face was hidden in shadows, but the glow of a cigarette showed a stubble of beard beneath an oft-broken nose. "They're shooting malcontents."

"They're gonna need a lot of bullets," muttered Angie. "Not to mention someone who knows how to shoot."

"I'm telling you. Mark my words," the voice continued. "Someone posted a caricature of André Marty on one of the bulletin boards. The mustache, the gut, the beret and screaming his head off. Funny as hell but the Brigade staff is out for blood. They say it's 'subversive elements.'"

"Some people got no respect for authority," Angie said.

"Thanks, friend," Becker said, knowing it was Angie's drawing and hoping to change the subject. "Hey, comrade. Can I hold your cigarette for a second? I just want to use the light to get a look at my compass. I think we turned after that last stop."

The cigarette moved toward Becker's face. He felt for the hand, carefully took the tiny, hand-rolled butt in his fingers and held it over the compass long enough to get a reading.

"We turned again. A little north of west," he said, passing the cigarette back to its owner.

"Do you think this guy knows where he's going?" Angie said.

"I think he's just following the truck ahead of him."

"Matt, I've been looking and I can't see a truck ahead of him." Angie sounded more annoyed than worried, but as the driver briefly turned on his lights, Becker saw that Angie was right. In the momentary sliver of light, he also saw that Angie's face was pale and drawn, his jaw clenched and his eyes squeezed shut.

"What is it?"

"My guts have been doing the Charleston since we left Villanueva this morning."

"You got the trots?"

"I swear, Matt. If I never see another plate of *fraggiol'* again..." He was cut off by a pain which doubled him over. There had been a steady diet of beans in oil which had played havoc with the volunteers' digestion, but Becker also suspected a fair amount of dysentery was making the rounds.

"Hold on, Ange. We gotta be there soon." Angie nodded but said nothing.

Five minutes went by before Becker heard Angie's sharp intake of air. He was bent over, hugging his midsection. "Ange?" Becker put his hand on his friend's back.

"Matt, I think I'm gonna crap my pants."

"If you gotta do it, go ahead. The way this place smells, I think a few guys already have."

Becker considered it a feeble response, but Angie turned his head to give a weak smile. In fact, the truck had the usual sour reek of human bodies and damp wool but anything more pungent would make it intolerable.

"Matt. Get me off this goddamned truck. Now." Angie spoke in a tone he had never heard before, instantly sweeping any indecision from Becker's mind.

"Can you sling your rifle?" he said. Angie nodded.

Becker slung his own on his right shoulder, took a handful of Angie's jacket in his right fist and picked up both their rucksacks with his left. Using them as a ram, he pushed into the crowd.

"Make a hole! I got a sick man here," Becker shouted.

"Who are you shoving?" said an irate voice.

"Move your ass before I put a bullet in it," Becker replied. In fact he had no way to reach his .45, but the sound of his voice convinced enough of the listeners.

"One side here."

"Let 'em through, comrades. Sick man here." Becker recognized the sound of Elsaw Brown's resonant bass. They had met up the week of their arrival and had tried to stay together as much as possible. Brown always pulled more than his own weight and never complained, something Becker wished he could say about himself.

As they reached the back of the truck, Becker moved Angie ahead of him. They could see the vague outline of another truck about thirty yards behind, both vehicles moving at about ten miles an hour as they inched slowly up a steep grade in the darkness.

"Can you make the jump?" Becker said.

"Don't know," Angie said between gasps.

Becker grasped the collar of Angie's jacket. "I've got you. Make the step. If you fall, be sure to roll or that other truck..."

"I see it." Angie squatted with one leg as his other foot found the trailer hitch frame and Becker helped take his weight. He took a long step to the ground and stumbled once but didn't fall, quickly moving to the side of the road. Becker caught up with him in seconds. Hearing footsteps, he turned to see that Brown had followed them off the truck.

"You there! Get back in the truck!" came a voice from the cab of the second truck as it flashed its headlights. But the three men had already moved to the side of the road and were lost in the darkness. Afraid to lose sight of the leading truck, the second continued on.

Angie forded the roadside ditch and disappeared into the knee-high brush. Becker and Brown dropped their packs and tried to stretch the stiffness out of their aching shoulders, backs and legs as they waited for their eyes to adjust to the darkness, but no adjustment came. They saw faint flickers of light reflecting off clouds miles away and twice discerned the flashes of the truck headlights as they moved up the road in the distance but their immediate surroundings were a blackened, starless void.

They heard Angie's voice from the bushes. "Blacker than three feet up a chimney out here."

"You OK, Vincent?" Brown said.

"Who's that?"

"Elsaw."

"Brown? What are you doing out here?" There was a note of defensiveness in Angie's voice. It was one thing for him to hold Becker back, but quite another to inconvenience a relative stranger.

"Mr. Matt is looking after you and I'm looking after him," Brown said. There was a moment of quiet, only the faint whisper of a light, misty rain from the low-hanging clouds.

"Fair enough," came Angie's reply. "Either of you got a flashlight?"

"Not me," Becker said.

"Nary a one. You lose something out there?" Brown said.

"I didn't lose it. I just put it down and now I can't see it." Angie's tone was a clear warning against asking what 'it' was.

"Take your time. We're not going anywhere," Becker said, imagining Angie's chagrin at being thought a screw-up. He suspected it was the rifle that had gone missing, compounding the error, and in turn making any offer of help even more unwelcome.

"Matt. Say something so I know where you are," Angie said.

"I'm here. Can you hear me?"

"Have you moved since we got off the truck?"

"Maybe a yard or two to your left," Becker said.

"So move back," Angie said. Becker reached out to touch Brown's shoulder and walked both of them back two long steps.

"Done. I think this is where you moved into the brush."

"Now keep talking for a minute. I'm going to follow your voice back," Angie said.

"And say what?"

"Something intelligent."

"One, two, three," Becker began. He heard Angie's footsteps in the brush and saw the flash as he struck a match and quickly cupped his hand over it.

"That's good. I'm impressed," Angie said. "Keep it up." Becker could hear Brown's stifled chuckle.

"There was a young lady of Exeter, so pretty the men craned their necks at her. One was even so brave, as to take out and wave..."

"Got it," Angie said. They heard his pace quicken as he moved through the brush to the road. They sensed more than saw his approach, aware of his breathing and the rustling, rattling sounds of his clothes and equipment.

"What was it?" Brown said. Becker cringed mentally, hoping Angie wouldn't bristle at the question.

"My book," Angie answered naturally.

"Must be a good book," Brown said.

"Could be. It's in Spanish," Angie said. "But it's the best damned toilet paper I've had since we got off the boat."

Realization dawned as Brown and Becker uttered heartfelt grunts of understanding. The rarity and value of such a mundane commodity was obvious, as was Angie's reluctance to leave it lost in the brush. European notions of toilet paper had been slow to catch on among the American volunteers and eventually even the Spanish analogue had come to be in short supply.

"Think we'll ever catch up with the trucks?" Brown said as they started down the road three abreast.

The implications of the question instantly smothered any possibility of conversation, all of them beset by the same anxieties. Where were the lines? How far did the trucks have to go? Would they find themselves isolated and exposed when the sun came up? Would they come to a crossroads and not know where to turn, walking blindly into a rebel machine gun? Would they catch up with their regiment only to be shot or imprisoned as deserters? Worst of all, would they arrive after the battle was over to find their comrades dead or maimed, having done nothing for the Cause?

"We'll probably find the trucks in a ditch and get there just in time to help push them out," Angie said.

"That would suit me fine," Brown said.

They walked in silence, the fatigue and rhythm of the march dulling the pain of their anxieties. The darkness left them nearly blind, but they were just able to make out the shadow of the few yards of road before them and the faint outline of a rolling horizon. Becker tried to listen for signs of life but could only hear the rattle of canteens, Mills bombs and ammo packs coupled with the pounding of their footfalls and the friction of cloth on cloth as their limbs moved back and forth. Each sound was a rasp on his frayed nerves.

"Stop," he said finally. Angie and Brown waited. Becker tried to find a way to phrase his next words in a way that would convince but not offend.

"You wanna borrow the book?" Angie said.

"We're making too much noise," Becker said.

"Mr. Matt, nobody's said anything for a half mile. You just got the willies," Brown said.

"Listen to him Elsaw." Angie's mind had been elsewhere but he instantly realized that Becker was right and that his friend was hearing what they were not.

"There's no light out here. No wind, no birds, cars, trucks, voices. Only us. Hundreds of pounds of humanity and assorted junk stomping down the middle of a dirt road in the open. Anyone could shoot us dead with their eyes closed."

Becker was suddenly embarrassed by his indignant tone. He wanted to know if he was getting through but he couldn't see his listeners' faces.

"So what do we do?" Brown asked.

"We start by getting rid of everything we can and strapping down the rest," Becker said. Brown and Angie had four Mills bombs each, dangling from belts and shoulder webbing. Half of them went in the ditch, the others into coat pockets. Becker and Angie both took their .45s from their packs and put them in shoulder holsters under their jackets. Canteens were put into rucksacks and the empty spaces in ammo packs were stuffed with odd bits of clothing.

The entire refit took five minutes. When they were finished, Brown and Angie stood sheepishly looking at Becker, as if for inspection.

"We don't sling the rifles. We carry them," he said.

"Matt," Angie said.

"Angie. Every step we take, the butt of the rifle hits one of us in the ass. You can hear it half a mile away."

"It's gonna get heavy."

"Probably."

"So can we get going now? It's going to be time for breakfast in a few hours and I want to be there," Angie said.

"Yeah, we go," Becker said. "But we spread out, single file, at least five, no, make it ten yards between us. The sun won't be up for a few hours yet, but we should be getting some light soon so we won't lose each other. And for God sake, walk softer. You guys walk like Krauts march."

Brown and Angie stared wide-eyed at the admonition, but Becker had already started off down the road and they realized that they could barely hear his footsteps.

"He does walk kind of quiet," Brown said.

"He's had lots of practice," Angie said. "Go ahead, I'll bring up the rear."

The procession was noticeably quieter and all three men had become hypersensitive to their own sounds and those of the surrounding darkness. Wind in the trees, the movement of a small animal in the brush, the sound of small arms fire miles away, even the sound of light rainfall on the road ahead all created a vivid three dimensional environment from what had been an impenetrable shroud.

Angie was not given to narcissistic introspection but the noise from his abdomen and the sensation that someone was slowly pulling a tire chain through his guts kept reminding him that they were lost on this road because of him. He wondered if Becker were angry at him, but eventually dismissed the notion. For Becker, intent was everything. If Angie had been malicious or thoughtless, their friendship might have ended right there, permanently, possibly even violently. Years ago, Becker's father had tried to explain to Angie in his broken English that his son was fiercely loyal but also a *rancunier*. It took Angie some time to comprehend that this referred to a person who held longstanding grudges. As a Sicilian, this was something Angie could understand, but unlike a Sicilian, Becker was not sensitive to slights. In fact, he had a blind spot that often left him unaware he had been wronged or insulted. This was a mystery to Angie, something that made his best friend unpredictable to him, even after all the years of their friendship. As for tonight, he figured Becker was more irritated by the noise than the inconvenience.

In fact, Becker was worrying about mistakes and incompetence, his own and others'. He felt the weight of the rifle in his hand and decided it was nothing like his father's Springfield. Too light, it felt like a piece of junk. When they had unloaded the crates in Albacete someone had said they were Remingtons, but he hadn't been able to make out the manufacturer's name stamped anywhere on his weapon, only some kind of double-eagle insignia which he didn't recognize. The ammo was 7.62 mm, which he knew to be roughly .30 caliber, but he had never fired it and didn't know what to expect. In any case, the rifle was still slimy with cosmoline, in spite of his best efforts to clean it. He had used the better part of his remaining gun oil to clean out the action and barrel, but he dreaded actually discharging a round and causing an explosion which would rip half his face off.

And why did their so-called convoy consist of only two trucks? Even with his limited view, he knew they had left the bullring in Albacete with a group of more than a dozen mismatched vehicles. Had they gotten lost, fallen behind or was there a reason for taking a different route? He took out his compass. The road they were following was taking them almost due west, but for most of the trip they had been heading north or northwest.

Becker stopped and turned. His companions also stopped, keeping their distance but close enough to make out his form in the darkness. He could see the first hints of daylight on the horizon behind them and realized they were silhouetted on a slight rise in the road. He gestured with his arm and lowered himself to one knee. Brown and Angie did the same. Becker's heart pounded in his ears for an instant but he calmed it with slow, deep breaths.

Some message was trying to reach him from below his level of consciousness but he couldn't make it out. There was a tingling in the back of his neck and the muscles in his shoulders were straining with tension. He willed himself to relax.

He smelled something. Truck exhaust, cigarette smoke and urine. He looked at the road and saw the imprint of the truck tires. He turned as he followed the tracks to their vanishing point on the road ahead and far beyond that he saw another glimmer of dawn, but this was in the west and it flickered like a distant movie projector. Becker moved silently back to his companions and gathered them almost into a huddle before speaking.

"There's something ahead," he whispered. "Light. There shouldn't be light."

"Wait? Or go?" Angie said.

"Dawn's coming. We can't wait. We don't want to be out in the open in daylight," Becker said.

"Go back or keep going?" Brown asked.

"I think the only chance of finding out where we are is that way." Becker pointed west. "But it might also be our best chance of getting killed."

"Matt, you're a hell of a salesman," Angie said. "Let's just get going."

"Everybody load up," Becker said. "And be ready to dive for the ditch."

Brown watched as Angie and Becker opened the bolts, put five-round stripper clips into the guides of the open breach and pushed the clips into the magazine. He followed suit and waited for the next step.

"OK, Elsaw. Close the bolt and keep your finger off the trigger. Like this," Angie said. He pushed the bolt forward and the clip slid cleanly from the clip guides of the magazine to the ground. Brown and Becker mimicked him in unison and heard the tinny ring of the clips hitting the road.

"We just leave those?" Brown said.

Becker picked up the three pieces of metal and tossed them into the darkness. "Won't need them, but no sense leaving sign for someone to follow."

"Last of the Mohicans," Angie said. "Elsaw, this is your safety. Remember to turn it before you shoot or you'll have a real hard time hitting anything."

As Brown looked at the loaded weapon with reverence Angie made an instant's eye contact with Becker, a quick turn of his head indicating that he would not be putting his weapon on safety. Becker nodded and turned to take the lead again. "Move to the side of the road and spread out just a little more," he said as he walked away.

The glow on the western horizon grew brighter and Becker made it out as man-made light. Headlights, but stopped in the road, not moving. Shadows flickered in the blackness as figures passed back and forth in front of them. He held up his hand to stop his companions and listened. He heard distant shouts and the sound of revving engines and shifting gears, as if vehicles were executing turns in the confines of the narrow road. He walked back to Angie and Brown.

"The trucks are ahead," he said.

"Praise the Lord," Brown said. Becker shook his head.

"They're stopped on the road and I don't know why," Becker said.

"Stopped with their lights on?" Angie said. "Something ain't right." All the youth had drained from his face and his coal-black eyes shone with the awareness of some lethal presence. Brown looked at him and froze.

"We circle," Becker said.

"Right, left or both?" Angie said.

Becker took out his compass. "Our lines are to the right. If we have to run, we run to the right. We try to stay together."

"And the packs?" Angie asked. Becker knew there was no right answer to this question. Their rucksacks held too much of value but were sure to slow them down.

"I'm for keeping them," he said. Angie nodded, then gave Brown a hard look.

"Elsaw, can you shoot that rifle?" he said.

"I can pull a trigger good as any man, but I can't truly say where the bullet will go. Drilling with broom handles and the like ain't done me much good."

Angie drew his .45, chambered a round and gave it to Brown. "You've got seven shots. Hold it in two hands, like this." Angie cupped his left hand under his right. "It's ready to fire now, safety if off, so keep your finger off the trigger."

Brown moved to sling his rifle, but Angie stopped him. "Not on your shoulder. Too much noise. Carry the pistol in your right hand and the rifle in your left till we get where we're going."

Brown nodded once. He took no offense at Angie's tutelage and bore no shame at his ignorance.

"Let's get off this road. Keep a little distance between us and, for God's sake, move quietly," Becker said.

They watched as Becker moved off the road and about ten feet down a steep shoulder where he crossed a muddy ditch and moved toward cover. They could just make out his silhouette waiting in a crouch as first Brown and then Angie descended the damp slope. When they made it up the other side, Becker was already moving silently through a grove of olive trees parallel to the road.

The shouting grew louder. Becker could now make out both Spanish, English and a third language he couldn't identify but he couldn't discern any actual words. Commands, protests and a single piercing scream. He looked behind him and saw that Brown and Angie were still with him. He suppressed an evanescent image of Brown accidentally discharging the .45 into his back. Forget it, he thought. Angie told him not to touch the trigger and Brown's no fool.

They were close now, perhaps fifty yards from the road, but the view was blocked by the trees. Time to stop walking and start crawling, Becker thought. He motioned his companions to drop to their knees and at that instant the road exploded with the sound of gunfire. They went from their knees to flat on their faces, hugging the earth, sure they had been seen, waiting for the bullets to find them in the trees and rip through their bodies. They heard rifle fire, explosions, the sound of a heavy machine gun and a few shrieking ricochets.

The shooting stopped in less than thirty seconds and all three men realized they had not been the targets. Their ears will be ringing,

Becker thought. Now is the time to move up. He gestured frantically to Angie and Brown who shook dirt off their faces as they pushed themselves to their hands and knees and began to follow Becker's path across the damp ground. Their progress was agonizingly slow. Each man moved by sliding his right hand and rifle forward across the ground and placing it silently before drawing up the right knee and then repeating the process on the left. They tried to move silently, but it seemed an impossible task and each man was sure that he would be the one to give them away.

The road came into view and Becker suddenly recalled another nightmare lit by headlights. One of the troop trucks lay on its side, its underside facing toward them. The other was stopped on the right shoulder of the road, parallel to the first. In front of the wreck, two smaller vehicles were parked, idling with their lights on. One was an open staff car with room for four passengers. The other was a tracked vehicle, something like a Great War tank Becker had seen pictures of, but much smaller. Barely reaching the height of a man's chest, it appeared to have room for only two passengers, but it carried a heavy machine gun, wisps of smoke rising from its barrel. Two soldiers sat in the turret, smoking cigarettes.

The American volunteers lay everywhere; dead on the road, the shoulder, in the ditch and in the back of the overturned truck. Some had sought refuge in a culvert but as a Moorish legionnaire shined his flashlight inside, Becker concluded they had been finished off with Mills bombs or something similar. A few had apparently made it halfway up the far side of the ditch trying to escape. Their arms were outstretched, hands clawing the earth. Another sergeant with trimmed beard, puttees and a turban moved among the bodies, firing an occasional pistol shot to the head, picking up personal items, pocketing some, casting others aside. One pulled a cap from one of the bodies and used it to daintily wipe blood from one of his boots.

"Why is he shooting those dead men?" whispered Brown.

"Just making sure," Angie said. "Or just plain mean."

Four enlisted men were collecting the volunteers' rifles, ammunition and Mills bombs and moving them from the roadside to the back of the far troop truck. One ran his finger along the barrel of a rifle and held it up to show his comrade. He shouted an incomprehensible phrase and both burst into laughter.

Becker tried to get a clear count of the enemy as they moved in and out of the light, hoping not to miss one or count anyone twice. Four enlisted, two NCOs, two tankers. There must have been others, he thought. Probably left after the massacre. Then he saw the faint light of two more cigarettes approaching from outside the range of the headlights. Two figures emerged from the darkness. Spanish officers in peaked caps, boots and riding breeches. They stood next to the staff car and surveyed the scene with obvious distaste. This was a task well below their status. Becker tried to guess their rank but realized he knew next to nothing about enemy uniforms, or any other kind for that matter. He made a mental note to educate himself at the soonest opportunity. Three stars above one man's left tunic pocket. He seemed to be in command. He said something to one of the NCOs and received a salute and a reply of "*Sí, capitán!*", before tossing the butt of his cigarette on the ground and getting into the passenger side of the staff car. The other officer got behind the wheel, started the engine and backed up. The headlights swept in a semicircle as the car turned around, then faded with the sound of the engine as it drove away.

Becker looked at his companions. Brown was biting the inside of his cheek, his eyes shining with unshed tears. Angie looked back at him, alert but showing no expression.

"How many you count?" he said, his voice less than a whisper.

"Down to eight," Becker said.

"Nine," Brown said. "There's a man just come out of the bushes, zipping his pants. He's having himself a smoke on the far side of that wreck."

Becker and Angie looked but the cab of the truck was half-blocked from view and obscured by shadows.

"Elsaw, you sure?" Angie said.

"He's there," Brown said.

"OK, so it's nine," Becker said. "We can't take on nine."

"What are you talking about, 'take on'?" Brown said.

"Elsaw, we need wheels," Angie said. "The sun is gonna come up soon and we'll never get back to our own lines on foot. We need that truck, if it still runs."

Angie waited as Brown tried to take in what he was saying. Becker resisted an urge to join in, sensing that he'd given enough lectures for one night.

"You got any ideas?" Brown said finally.

The three men were speaking with their heads almost touching, trying to stay quiet. The smell of their breath told Becker that they were all queasy with a combination of hunger, fear and anger. A dangerous mix, not conducive to good judgment. He hoped it wouldn't be his mistake that got them all killed.

"Matt?" Angie said. After the night at the airfield, it was Becker's turn to come up with the plan and Angie preferred ambush to attack anyway.

"We can't take nine, so we split them up," Becker said. "Elsaw, you take three Mills bombs and go fifty yards down that road. Keep yourself in the darkness."

"You can bet on that," Brown said.

"Toss one bomb onto the road. That should draw some men and some attention away from the trucks. When you hear footsteps or voices coming, throw another. After a minute, throw the last one and get your ass back here as fast as you can."

"And you boys?" Brown said.

"Angie and I will come at the trucks from this end. When the first bomb goes off and they start to split up, we'll come out of the dark at them from behind. If we can get through them, we'll move toward you. If we can't, well."

"If we can't, you'll be on your own. Stay out of sight and head for our lines," Angie said.

Brown made ready to move out. Becker gave him a fourth Mills bomb.

"Won't you need some of these?" he asked.

"We don't want to be throwing bombs near the truck, and I don't think they'll be much use against that bulldozer they got out there," Angie said.

"True enough, I suppose," Brown said.

"Elsaw, I'm afraid I need to ask for my pistol back."

Brown handed him the weapon with care. "Damn sure you'll make better use of it than I will."

Angie took the .45, checked the chamber and put it in his shoulder holster.

"Elsaw, you got the plan?" Becker said.

"Fifty yards down, throw the bomb. They come, throw another. One minute, last one and run like hell."

Becker moved to shake his hand but Brown simply gave a quick nod to both men and moved away into the darkness.

"He said 'damn'. First time I ever heard him use bad language," Angie said.

Becker was going to comment, but the words that came to mind sounded too much like an epitaph. "You want this side or that side?" he asked.

"You're the sneaky one," Angie said.

"We gotta drop the tank guys first," Becker said.

"That'll be the go signal," Angie said.

"I'm going." Becker paused, feeling some type of farewell was in order but apparently Angie didn't think so. He looked straight ahead, like a sprinter waiting for the gun. Becker gave his shoulder a gentle punch, said "See ya," and crawled off into the trees.

Three minutes later he was crouching on one knee, ten long steps back from the nearest truck. He had considered hiding in the far ditch, but finding himself in total darkness as he crossed the road, decided against it. He didn't want to take the time climbing out or risk slipping in the muck once the action started. Angie had descended from the trees on the opposite side and taken position across from Becker in a seated firing position, one elbow on each knee. As they waited, two soldiers walked to the back of the truck, heavy burdened with armfuls of rifles and slings of ammo packs over each shoulder. Becker held his breath, but soon realized that they were oblivious to his presence. The men exchanged a brief word, then walked at a leisurely stroll between the two trucks, one overturned, the other upright. They lit cigarettes and one sat on a cab step, the other on a front tire of the wrecked truck. Their voices carried the familiar timbre of working men bemoaning the futility of their labors but the language itself was still unfamiliar. Becker felt an instant's hesitation at what he was about to do, but then his eyes caught sight of the heaps of bloodied khaki beyond them and knew their time had come.

The first Mills bomb went off, more of a loud crack than the explosion they had expected. Heads turned but none of the soldiers stirred. The right tanker's face became an exploding shredded blossom as he tumbled backwards off his turret. Becker realized his mind had been elsewhere, cursed himself, raised his rifle and put a round through the chest of the other tanker two seconds later, the light frame of the unfamiliar weapon kicking him viciously in the shoulder. Angie had left his rifle on the ground and was already up, drawing his .45 as he walked between the trucks and put two rounds into each soldier before they could rise. Becker came around the left side of the overturned truck, saw the hidden man shouting and trying to unsling his rifle but his ears were still ringing and he barely heard his own shot as he fired his .45 into the man's chest.

As he stepped over the body, he saw the fourth enlisted man fall to his knees in front of the headlights, his arms raised in supplication. He was unarmed and Angie was holding the .45 on him. Angie looked in Becker's direction for an instant.

"They took off that way," he said, pointing up the road.

"Elsaw," shouted Becker, breaking into a sprint as he heard Angie's .45 go off like a starter's pistol.

"I'll turn the truck around," he heard Angie shout as he passed the tank and hurtled into the darkness. He figured the two NCOs couldn't be more than ten seconds ahead of him but it was even less. As his hearing returned, he heard the slap of boots running on the road ahead. The stride was uneven and he made out the sound of labored breathing as he realized he was coming up fast on one of the sergeants. Ten feet from the target, Becker stopped, raised his pistol and fired at a point directly between the shoulder blades. The man was dead before he could raise his arms to break the fall and his jaw splintered like dry kindling as it hit the road.

"Elsaw! It's Matt!" he shouted, visualizing the third Mills bomb floating through the air toward him like a Hail Mary pass. His chest heaved as he tried to catch his breath.

"I'm here, Mr. Matt," came Brown's voice from the darkness ahead.

"Watch out. There's one more," Becker said.

Becker walked toward the voice until he saw Brown standing over the second NCO, his rifle in his hands. The man lay face up on the road, his nose and mouth smashed and his head caved in from at least two heavy blows.

"Man plum ran into me," Brown said.

"Glad you didn't throw the third bomb," Becker said.

"Didn't have a chance." Brown looked down at the body, then up at Becker. "Beg pardon Mr.-" He took two quick steps toward the roadside before vomiting once onto the shoulder. He waited for a moment with his hands on his knees, spitting and catching his breath before standing and wiping his mouth with a bandana. "Sorry, Mr. Matt. I seen a lot worse, just never done it myself, if you get my meaning."

"Welcome to the club. Done my fair share of getting sick, last few weeks."

"You just saying that for me, but I take it kindly."

"Angie's waiting," Becker said. He could hear the truck engine revving and imagined Angie's impatience.

"And dawn's a-coming," answered Brown.

Good as his word, Angie had already turned one of the trucks when they got back to the scene of the massacre. It was idling as he did his best to disable the engine of its twin. The distributor lay on the ground and he was now using a long-bladed knife taken from one of the dead soldiers to slice through hoses, wiring and cables.

"I doubt this one could run if they got it upright, but I want to be sure," he said.

"What about the tank?" Becker said.

"Did what I could to the engine. Couldn't figure out how to drive it or I would have run it into the ditch," Angie said, stepping down from the front bumper.

All three men looked at each other as they realized the carpet of dead bodies would have to remain as it was.

"Nothing more we can do here," Becker said.

"I found these in the cab," Angie said, pointing to a cardboard box on the ground. "Looks like brigade files."

"Any maps?"

Angie shook his head. "Not a one. Just a pair of field glasses."

Becker imagined his uncle Martin looking over his shoulder, ready to deliver a homily on intelligence. A burning file box on the side of the road wouldn't attract any more attention than what had already happened.

"Let's mount up. You get the glasses, I'll take care of the files," he said.

Becker looked over at Brown as he took a gasoline can from the tank and soaked the files . He was walking slowly among the bodies, whispering, his hands clasped and his head bowed, apparently in prayer.

"Angie. Matches?" Becker asked. Angie patted his pockets, took out a small box and tossed them over. Becker lit one, dropped it into the box and walked toward the truck as it billowed in flame and acrid smoke.

"Elsaw," Angie called softly.

Brown turned, put his helmet back on and walked back to them. "I'm with you, Angelo," he said. "Let's leave these boys in peace."

CHAPTER 17

Darkness melted away as the truck sped east toward an overcast dawn, Angie driving and slowly increasing speed as visibility improved. Becker looked at his two companions, tried to read their haunted, exhausted faces and saw only his own torment. He felt alone, exposed and ashamed. In spite of all the boredom, discomfort and discontent in the past weeks of waiting and training, they had all felt a sense of camaraderie and common purpose. That was gone now. Their brothers lay dead on the road, butchered without firing a shot. Others were somewhere ahead, preparing for battle or already in one. The three of them were somewhere in between, living, breathing and uninjured.

"What do we say?" Brown asked.

No one spoke. Angie focused on the road as he put in the clutch and coasted around a curve in the road. Becker put his head against the side window and looked at nothing, nearly overcome with weariness. For the first time in days, he saw Sandy's face, her image emerging from the kaleidoscopic reflections in the glass. He heard April's voice and imagined her tiny arms around his neck. The warmth of Sandy's kitchen enveloped him as he imagined the safety and humanity of home.

"Matt?" Angie said.

Becker snapped back to the present. "Angie, we've got to stop." Angie coasted to a stop at the side of the road, put on the brake and rested his forearms on the wheel as he looked over at his friend. "If we get stopped by our side, riding alone in this truck, we'll probably be shot."

Angie's deeply sunken eyes cleared instantly. He put the truck in reverse, turned the wheel left to its lock point and using only the side mirrors, quickly backed to the opposite roadside. He then shifted into low, locked the wheel to the right and steered the truck in a tight turn till it was pointing back the way they came. The entire maneuver took less than ten seconds.

"Let's get our gear," Becker said. The three men got out of the cab, walked to the back of the truck and took out packs, weapons and helmets. Angie pulled a small box of tools from under one of the benches and found a screw driver. He looked at Becker and pointed toward the ditch. Becker shrugged.

Two minutes later, they had pushed the truck off the shoulder. It had come to rest nose-down on the cab, the right front wheel twisted under, the front axle snapped and its rear wheels in the air. Angie stepped carefully down the slope of the ditch and used the screwdriver to put a hole in the fuel tank. Gasoline trickled from the puncture into the tiny stream at the bottom of the ditch. Anyone who examined the truck would assume it had either run off the road in the darkness or run out of gas. Either the puncture or the crash would have occurred after the fact as a means of disabling the truck. It would remain a mystery, as would the disappearance of its passengers.

"Angie, were there plates on these trucks?" Becker asked.

"I left them back at the...back there," Angie said.

They set out on foot, keeping to the road for what seemed like an hour. Twice they heard planes pass overhead, either hidden behind clouds or gone before they could distinguish their markings.

They used the field glasses to check the road ahead and the surrounding terrain every few minutes. Becker kept a careful watch on his compass.

"Hold up," Angie said. He was looking through the field glasses at something far ahead of them. "Down." They all dropped to one knee. "I think it's a roadblock. There's a junction up there."

"Let's get off the road," Becker said. The group quickly moved off the road to the left into a small grove of trees.

"Ours or theirs?" Brown asked.

"I'm guessing it's ours, but I don't think it matters, Elsaw. We don't need it," Angie said, refocusing the field glasses.

"How far off?" Becker asked.

Angie considered his answer, scanning the horizon for reference points, twice lowering the glasses to use the unaided eye. "I make it a thousand yards, give or take."

"Do we bypass it or try to talk our way through?" Becker asked.

"Bypass how?" Brown said.

"We're moving almost due east. If we cut cross-country to the northeast, we should hit the north-south road."

"You think this is where our drivers got lost?" Angie asked.

"Must be. It's the first turnoff we've seen," Becker said.

"We all got papers, we all in uniform," Brown said.

"And we're coming from the wrong direction," Angie said.

Both men looked at Becker. "Angie, let me have a look," he said. There was a T-junction with three foot soldiers and wooden sawhorse barriers painted red and white standing across the north-south and east-west road. He saw, or imagined, steam rising from cups they held in their hands as they chewed on pieces of sausage and bread. The sight made Becker nauseous with hunger.

"They're eating breakfast," he said.

"Good," Angie said. "I say we shoot them and take the food."

Brown stared at Angie, aghast. "Angelo, ain't no call to be talking that way after what we seen this night."

Becker watched for Angie's reaction. He had never known him to sit still for a scolding.

"Elsaw," Angie began. "Don't..." He drew a deep breath. "Don't take it personal. I'm just hungry. I've either puked up or shit out everything in me. I need some food."

"Got some goobers if you want 'em," Brown said.

Becker and Angie looked at Brown and each other. "What did you say?" Angie asked, a razor-sharp edge to his voice.

"Goobers. I got all I could before we left last night." He patted the pockets of his field jacket.

"What the hell is a goober?" Angie asked. Brown reached into his pocket and held out his hand.

"Peanuts," Becker said. "I could use some of those." Brown poured a handful of peanuts from his giant palm into Becker's woolen cap, then did the same for Angie. The three of them sat with their legs outstretched, capfuls of peanuts in their laps, peeling and eating as fast as they could. While chewing, Becker watched the junction.

"There's an infantry squad moving north up the hill toward the roadblock," Becker said. Brown and Angie squinted into the distance but couldn't make out the details. "There's a salute. They're moving the barrier. No identity check. They're through." Becker lowered the glasses and rubbed his eyes. "They just walked through. Maybe Elsaw is right."

"Won't we move faster cross country?" Angie asked.

"Yeah, but two things worry me. One, we surprise someone who doesn't see us coming and they shoot too soon."

Angie nodded as if to say 'Yeah, well, there is that.' "Can't wait for number two," he said.

"We walk into a mine field or get caught out in the open by a heavy machine gun," Becker said.

"Sold to the man from Jersey for a handful of goobers," Angie said, in a respectable W.C. Fields imitation. "Matt, you got enough Spanish to talk us through there?"

"I probably don't have enough to get myself-" Angie's eyes darted toward Brown for an instant. Becker checked himself. "-a date, but I think I can sound like some half-assed foreigner who got himself lost without too much trouble." Angie and Becker had found themselves tacitly accommodating Brown's aversion to profanity and foul language. As they walked back to the road, Becker's fatigued mind dwelled on the relative vulgarity of the expressions 'get laid' and 'half-assed', wondering if either of them had crossed the line, or whether there really was a line.

They walked single file toward the junction, their rifles slung on their shoulders, Becker in the lead. They agreed there was chance shooting would start before they ever got there and that single file looked more military and at least gave the second two men a chance to dive for cover. They did their best to look like soldiers in an orderly march, but fatigue, sore muscles and aching joints made them look more like walking wounded.

The walk took a little less than fifteen minutes, but the guards didn't take notice of them until the last five. They were Republican regulars wearing long brown greatcoats and loose-fitting balaclavas which covered the head and neck but sagged enough to leave much of the face exposed. One guarded the east-west barrier with his rifle held waist-high and pointed in their general direction, but the others didn't seem alarmed. Another sat on an upturned bucket, spooning beans into his mouth and onto the front of his coat, the third leaned against the north-south barrier smoking a cigarette with one hand and holding the other in his armpit for warmth.

As they came nearer, they saw that the soldier with the rifle was just a boy in his teens. He clenched his weapon and stared at them with a comical intensity which they returned with looks of earnest good will and propriety.

"*Alto!* Identify yourselves!"

"We are with the Brigades," Becker said.

"From where?"

"America."

"No. I ask you from where are you coming now," said the boy.

"We got separated from our trucks. We got lost in the darkness."

"Separated?"

"We have..." Becker's mind went blank as he struggled to remember the word for diarrhea. He knew he had heard it before but hunger, physical and mental fatigue kept it just out of reach. "We have an infirmity of the stomach."

"Ah, the shits," said the seated man. "All you foreigners get the shits." The two older men smiled but the boy remained deadly serious.

"This is a Moor?" he said.

"A negro from America. American, like us," Becker said.

"Show your identity cards," said the boy. They all took out the brigade identity cards they had been issued and handed them over. The soldier held them up and matched the pictures with the faces.

"Now he pretends he can read," the man leaning on the barricade said.

"*Idiota,*" the seated man said. "Can't you see they are Americans? Look at their manner. Look at their teeth, for God's sake." The man carried himself as if he were the senior member of the group.

"I've seen English, Polish, German, Italian – all manner of foreigners with the Internationals. I've heard of no Americans," the man on the barricade said.

"They've been here since Madrid," the seated man said, through a mouthful of beans.

"You've seen them?"

"No, but many said they had come."

"Your comrades went up that road some time ago, toward Chinchon," the senior man said. "Miguelito, enough. Lower your weapon."

"How much time has passed?" Becker said.

The man shrugged. "We were not yet on duty."

"One can walk?" Becker asked.

"One can always walk. Perhaps a truck will come and you can ride."

"Matt, ask for food," Angie said.

"Pardon, comrade. We are very hungry," Becker said.

"Everyone is hungry," the man on the barricade said.

"There is no food?"

"They brought us food at dawn, but it has been eaten," the senior man said. "One regrets that there is only this." He took a sausage from his knapsack and tossed it to Becker.

"You had a sausage?" the man on the barricade said.

"I was saving it."

"Many thanks, comrade," Becker said. *"Muchas gracias,"* Angie and Brown echoed.

"It is nothing. Miguelito, let them pass." The boy slung his rifle and stood aside as the three Americans swung their legs over the barricade. As Becker came closer he could see an insignia with an upturned chevron on the senior man's uniform.

"Pardon, but you are a sergeant?" he asked.

"This?" The man pointed at the insignia. "This means 'corporal'. How do you come to speak Spanish?"

"It is only some simple Spanish," Becker said. "As you can see, I have few words."

The corporal, who Becker could now see might be old enough to be his father, gave him a kindly look.

"It's of no importance. The shooting starts, no one can hear and everyone has few words."

"I'm sure you are right." There was a strained silence as the six men looked at each other. "Well," Becker said. "One must walk. Thank you for your kindness."

The man on the barricade had stood and moved it back to let them pass. "May you return safely," he said as they walked by him.

"Thank you. And you also."

"For us there is no return," the corporal said. *"España* is our home. Here we will live and die."

"Viva España," Becker said.

"Viva la República," the corporal replied.

Someone had coined the name Lincoln Brigade for the American volunteers but no one knew if it would stick. There were Cuban and Irish contingents attached to the group for lack of a better place to put them and transfers in and out occurred at random intervals, piecemeal or en masse, without any appearance of a master plan. Their general was Russian or German or Austro-Hungarian. The colonel under him was something similar, maybe Yugoslav or Russian or both. There were a few American officers and noncoms , but they came and went so often due to injury, desertion, drunkenness or political infighting that it was hard to keep track of them. Many insisted there were good ones but few agreed on who they were. Some of the frontline volunteers split into factions supporting one or another.

After several days of waiting, they were moved up. At nightfall, a German sergeant led them to a position on high ground ordered them to dig in, but they had nothing to dig with, so they used bayonets and helmets. It was bitterly cold but they knew the enemy was out there somewhere so they worked until the sweat began to soak through their shirts and trousers. By dawn, there was a shallow trench, more of a ditch really, just deep enough to lie down in. To Becker, it looked more like a shallow grave than a safe point from which to stage or repel an attack.

In the growing daylight, they realized that their position was at the top of a small hill, the enemy occupied the high ground to the west, perhaps a thousand yards distant, and that the rising sun gave a perfect view of their position against the skyline. Enemy gunners took notice and artillery rounds began to find the range, first landing several dozen yards beyond them on the far side of the hill, then steadily walking up the rocky ground in giant pounding, rumbling steps toward the trench. Soon they were filling the air with invisible, burning shards of razor-sharp metal.

The machine gunners were quicker to zero in. They had the advantage of tracer rounds and the glowing streams of fire cracked as they broke the sound barrier above the volunteers' heads. Sniper fire was more random, equally deadly, but somehow more merciful, passing through helmets, bone and brains well before the target ever knew he was in danger. Fast service guaranteed. This world to the next, no waiting.

Sometime later in the morning, a few picks and shovels began to appear in the trench but it would have been suicide to use them in the time-honored fashion. Instead, the men did their best to use them lying down, swinging the tools with comical sideways or over-the-head motions, trying to scrape out a few more inches of cover without exposing arms, heads or buttocks to the scythe of enemy fire.

During lulls in the shelling, flights of enemy bombers appeared and dropped bombs but few found their marks and the planes either left of their own accord or were chased off by Republican fighters. Spirits rose momentarily on the very few occasions that one was actually shot down, but the joy was short-lived.

At some point, Becker realized his watch had disappeared in the frantic efforts to deepen the trench but he decided to regard it as a blessing rather than a loss. There was nothing to be gained by reckoning the passage of time. With the sun, moon and stars hidden by the overcast sky, it was only the irregular intervals between explosions or bullet impacts that held any meaning. Each one that passed without death or mutilation meant another unit of existence come, gone and forgotten.

He had lost track of Angie and Brown in the nighttime march to the knoll top and hadn't seen them in days. He didn't know the men next to him and the forced intimacy with his trench companions did little to form friendships, since each secretly wished it would be they who survived and the others killed or wounded. Each feared that it would be the other's movement that would attract the notice of the enemy gunners; each hoped that another's body would intercept an incoming round and spare them and each resented that their comrades might be witness to what they felt was their own cowardice. But of all the conflicting emotions, the worst fear was that they would let their brothers down when the time came.

When the noise was the greatest, the thought came to Becker that some great cosmic pendulum had paused at the top of an arc and was beginning its downward sweep. How many lives had he taken in the past weeks? He would start to count and stop himself. Some lives counted and others didn't. He found that he regretted Jarek and Bozzoli most of all, Jarek because he showed no fear of death, Bozzoli because he must have suffered such fear before he died. Both were deaths that Becker might have averted. But the worst pain came when he thought of Sandy standing at the side of the road clutching her heart, her face streaked with tears. That was his doing. Concussions rocked his body, bullets and shrapnel kicked up dirt near his head and he knew that a debt was due for collection and soon he would have to come across.

Another night came, bringing a break from the snipers but not random artillery rounds or machine guns. Word came down to use the cover of darkness to move to new trenches further west near the San Martin road. An offensive was planned for the next day. When morning came, they waited, but nothing happened. More news, the attack would begin near sunset. Attacking into the sun? Becker thought. Brilliant, but fortunately the steel-wool sky gave up little light. They spent the day checking and rechecking rifles, bayonets and equipment, trying to decide what they should carry and what they should leave behind. How far? Through the olive trees and up the hill, four or five hundred yards. We can do that. Someone said they would get cover from Soviet tanks and the brigade machine gun company but this was hotly disputed. The machine guns were crap, Great War rejects, and no one had been able to get them working. The tanks always came late or not at all. Shut up! Do you want to get us all shot?

Becker heard the tanks coming up the road and decided to risk a quick look. He popped his head up and saw two T-26s turn off the road into an olive grove and begin firing through the light cover toward the enemy positions with their 45-mm guns and heavy machine guns. Seeing small groups climb out of the trenches, others followed hesitantly until there were disorganized clumps of men moving like frightened sheep across the road and into the trees. Some took the time to kneel and fire hastily aimed shots toward the top of the hill, others sought cover behind the olive trees or dove to the ground, jamming their rifle muzzles full of dirt or dropping them entirely.

Becker knew the enemy was good but he didn't think they were likely to hit a sprinting silhouette at this range. Once he cleared the trench he held his rifle at port arms and ran as fast as he could to-ward the far side of the olive grove, dodging trees and leaping over bodies as if he were back on the football field. As he neared the end of the trees he saw a line of tracer fire tracking laterally across the clearing toward him and threw himself six feet through the air to land at the base of the largest tree he could find. An instant later he heard the trunk being chewed to pieces as small branches fell on him and bullets threw up tiny geysers of dirt around his legs.

He rolled over onto his back tried to minimize himself as a target by lying with his back straight, his elbows tucked over his torso and his hands holding his rifle along the center axis of his body. The tracers left for other destinations and then returned at leisurely in-tervals. Am I playing dead? he thought. No, I'm playing invisible.

One of the tanks exploded in a brilliant flash of ignited fuel and high explosive, lighting up the grove like a homecoming bonfire and burning away the shadows that had been the main source of cover. Snipers joined the machine gunners in picking off the stumbling, staggering groups of volunteers who had now resorted to burrow-ing under fallen comrades to escape notice or dodge bullets. The momentum of the attack had been halted by an overwhelming su-periority of enemy fire. By midnight, most of the men had found their way back to cover. Only the dead and dying remained on the field.

The attack had been a farce but had fallen short of utter catas-trophe. No one had a sure count of the dead but it couldn't have been more than a couple dozen, maybe three times that many wounded, out of a total strength of a little under five hundred men. The Brigade was still intact and ready to fight. They didn't question themselves, but they began to wonder if their commanders knew what the hell was going on.

Becker felt he had contributed nothing to either the cause or his own self-worth. The trench was still taking sporadic sniper and ma-chine gun fire at daybreak, and the enemy, mostly Moors like the ones he had seen at the ambush, were walking casually around in their positions with a *sang froid* which he began to take personally.

If they know we're here, crouching in terror at the bottom of this hole isn't going to help much, he thought. Over a period of an hour, he slowly assembled a crude firing position out of rocks and sand-bags, camouflaging it with a fallen tree branch which was shot up enough to provide tiny firing apertures through the leaves while still hiding muzzle flashes from enemy observers. After the half a dozen shots needed for him to adjust the sights and get the feel for the weapon, he began putting deadly accurate rounds through openings in the enemy line every time a turbaned head appeared. Soon, they were moving on their hands and knees, just like the Lincolns.

Word came down that another attack was planned in two or three days, but no one could confirm it. The American noncoms had disappeared and any actual military orders came from British, German or Belgian stand-ins. Still, in spite of the constant grumbling, it was considered risky to openly question or confront anyone of a higher rank, especially the commissars. Rumors of arrests and executions continued to spread and men swore that comrades had been taken out of the line by armed guards and never seen again. Becker still heard word passed about Angie's André Marty carica-ture, the possible identity of the artist and the comical furor it had caused, and tried to interject doubt by commenting that it was probably just a rumor, but he was afraid to overplay it and mostly shook his head or stayed silent when the stories were retold.

Once again they moved to new trenches, these even worse than the last. The irregular, convoluted terrain was a combination of low rolling hills and deep gullies gouged out of the rocky soil and the opposing lines were a tangled confusion of loops and curves. They soon discovered that they were taking fire not only from positions ahead of them but also from higher ground on each side.

"Like hogs in a pen," one volunteer said.

"Fish in a barrel," said another.

"Lambs to the slaughter," said a third, putting an end to the dis-cussion.

They settled into the same routine of trying to deepen and shore up the trenches, scrounge food, steal a few hours of sleep and still keep their heads from getting shot off. The night before the attack, a few dozen new recruits found their way to the front. One to Becker's right stumbled into the trench in a near panic, bent double under the weight of his pack and still wearing the clothes he had worn on the ship.

"Got any food, comrade?" Becker said.

"Maybe a chocolate bar," said the recruit, his head up, his eyes searching the darkness.

"Are you saving it for something?"

"It's in my pack," he answered, waving the muzzle of his rifle past Becker's face as his head darted back and forth. A machine gun opened up and a line of tracers approached the trench twenty yards down.

"Get your head down. Now." The recruit stared in Becker's direction, frozen, until Becker reached a hand up and jerked him off his feet.

"Kid. Comrade. You're not going to see them, but if you keep trying a machine gun is going to open your head up like a melon. Now, you were saying something about a chocolate bar."

The recruit delved into his pack and produced every possible irrelevance, as if he had packed for a weekend in the country. Becker saw three Spanish textbooks, two in hardcover, a week's worth of socks and underwear, a hand-knit beige sweater.

"Give me the alarm clock," Becker said. He smashed it with his rifle butt. "Go on. It has to be in there somewhere," he smiled.

Becker confiscated a small, metal shaving mirror before the chocolate bar made its appearance. It was broken into pieces but the recruit managed to get it open and offer some to him without dropping any into the muck at the bottom of the trench.

"My name's Klein."

"MacCready."

"Why'd you take my mirror?"

"Nothing personal. I don't want you to give away our position." That might have been true, but after the last assault, Becker had decided that looking around corners was a bad idea and had other plans for the mirror. "One more thing. You gotta stop pointing that rifle at people."

"It's not loaded."

"Nobody wants to take your word for it. It's just bad manners."

Becker waited while Klein digested this and began to wonder how old the boy was. "Did they show you how to load it?"

"Down the hill, before we came up."

"Maybe you ought to load it now." The boy put down his chocolate and pulled the rifle onto his lap, the muzzle pointed at Becker's guts. "Are you pointing that weapon at me?" he asked.

"Sorry."

"Did you hear anything about tomorrow?" Becker asked.

"Tomorrow morning. Artillery and air attack, then we go up."

Becker knew what the ground ahead looked like. Another clearing, another olive grove, hardly distinguishable from the last. Then another clearing and a vineyard leading to the high ground defended by a phalanx of heavy machine guns. He tried to imagine what the terrain would look like from the air or on a map, contorted gray meanderings like the spilled entrails of some giant, slaughtered animal. How could anyone direct artillery or drop bombs into a maze like that?

"What are you doing?"

"Digging," Becker said.

"You're digging sideways," said Klein.

"Yup. It keeps me warm."

Klein didn't know how to respond and sensed he had already made a fool of himself. "Do you want some help?"

"Thanks, but there's only one shovel," Becker said. "If you keep your head down and don't draw any fire, that'll help plenty. Trust me."

Becker was using an entrenching tool he had stolen from one of the Franco-Belge units to dig steps into the side of the trench. The ground was hard and rocky enough to support his weight but as he got closer to the bottom of the trench the mud and filth became too soft. He used sand bags shored up by rocks for the bottom step.

When the time came, he wanted to be up and gone before the enemy gunners could draw a bead on him.

Ammunition, tea and bread came up a few hours before dawn. Most men had used little of what ammo they had, which was fortunate because the new supply was an odd mixture of calibers. Becker went through several boxes before finding the 7.62 rounds he needed. The food and tea calmed the growling of empty stomachs but did little for the growing nausea of fear.

Commissars appeared during the night to outline the plan of attack. The air force would lead off with bombing and strafing. Then the artillery would lay down a devastating barrage. Tanks would follow, flattening barbed wire and chopping up enemy positions with their machine guns. The volunteers would advance with the support of a full Spanish brigade, overwhelm what was left of the Fascist resistance and secure the enemy trenches as a huge wave of reinforcements flooded westward.

They told their stories well, but given the events of the previous attack, gravity would have served them better than zeal. Listeners had lost all illusions long before joining this fight. Most were veterans of many marches, protests and rallies. They had heard many promises made, but few kept. They had seen many fists waved in the air but few speakers that actually struck blows for the cause. They listened in silence, hoping for a whisper of truth, but heard only the tinny echo of platitudes and slogans.

Light made a reluctant appearance in the east. No one could call it dawn with so much cloud cover, just a gradual lightening of the damp, misty grayness. Men stretched their necks skywards searching for the promised air support but nothing appeared. Officers and noncoms shouted at each other up and down the line, arguing, demanding, contradicting. Runners scurried back and forth to the command post. Some rifle fire broke out from the Spanish Brigade to the right and the Lincolns tried to give support but were soon forced down by a wave of machine gun fire. More waiting, more cowering in the trenches. More shouting of confused orders. Volunteers watched as two comrades ran onto the road to lay down a signal for the planes. They struggled to spread out an odd pattern of sheets and underclothes but the enemy gunners cut them down in seconds.

Where was Angie? Becker thought. Is he seeing what I'm seeing? Of course he is. I wish I could hear what he's thinking. He'd have some wisecracks to lighten things up. Who is he with? Does he have good people backing up? What's going through his mind? He's cursing the day I got him into this. He's damning me for my pathetic, romantic notions of right and wrong.

Becker allowed himself less than a minute of luxurious self-recrimination before closing the book on it. Angie doesn't do that, he thought. You just worry too much, as usual.

The fog cleared and shells began passing overhead. "Those are ours, right?" said Klein.

Becker was focused on trying to see where they landed without getting his head taken off and didn't answer. He saw explosions to the south. Weren't there other Internationals in those positions? Who was spotting for the artillery?

"MacCready?"

"They're our .75s, but they're still finding the range." He heard more frantic shouting in at least three languages up and down the line, watched more panicked runners sprinting in every direction. The artillery stopped. Hundreds of eyes and ears waited for the gunners to readjust their aim and fire for effect. The longer the guns fired, the longer they lived and the better the chances when they moved up.

The barrage had stopped, hardly a barrage at all really. A silent dread passed through the trenches. Two T-26s advanced from a turnoff a couple hundred yards up and began firing their guns. The Spanish Brigade used the cover to emerge from their cover but few had the chance to move even a few steps. The Lincolns watched horrified as human bodies were shredded by intersecting lines of fire. The tanks shifted into reverse and disappeared.

Now Becker wished he had his watch. It must be mid-morning by now. The enemy machine gunners seemed to be amusing themselves by cutting up the sandbags with steady back-and-forth streams of fire. All that ammo, he thought. Did they really have that much to waste? How many rounds a minute could they fire? Five or six hundred? How many in a belt? Two hundred? Two-fifty? How many guns, how many belts and how many times had they changed the barrels on the guns?

Which brought him to the inevitable question, Where are our guns? He knew the answer. They weren't working or they were under too much fire for the men to stand up and feed a belt into them and even if they did, it would just draw fire from a half dozen enemy guns.

At that moment, he knew how this whole war would end.

Becker heard English accents and looked up to see two British commissars strolling through the lines like they were on a parade ground. They wore grim smiles and muttered encouragement to the Lincolns as they stepped over the tangle of legs, bodies, weapons and discarded equipment. One held a riding crop under his arm, the other tapped an automatic against his thigh.

"Right, Lads. Check your weapons now. Clear the muzzle, clear the breech. Fix bayonets and stand ready."

He's cracked, Becker thought. Not his fault. He wouldn't be the first. Sure as hell won't be the last. Klein stared as if witness to an apparition.

"Sir, we're taking fire. There's a space here if you'd like to take cover," Becker said.

"No time for lolling about, Comrade. Going over the top in just a bit. Ah, there's the whistle."

As the man said, a chorus of whistles had broken out along the line and the Lincolns were straggling out of the trenches in a disorganized swarm. Some men froze with terror and had to be forced out at gunpoint. Others got no more than a glance at the battle before taking rounds through the face, forehead or helmet. Most got over the sandbags and forced their cramped, frozen limbs to carry them forward, searching frantically for the sanctuary of a tree, ditch or shell crater that wasn't already occupied.

Once again, Becker knew speed was his only recourse. He put his back against the far side of the trench and focused on an olive tree fifty yards across the clearing, tracking the tracer fire with his peripheral vision, waiting for a pattern of traverse which would give him an opening. The commissar saw his face and saw only a frozen figure and the vacant stare of daylight madness.

"You there. Up you go, now lad. One foot in front of-"

Becker used his pre-cut steps to clear the trench in less than a second and was halfway across the clearing before the man could finish his sentence. Once again he dove to the base of a tree and waited for the guns to start ripping into it but the firing nearly stopped. Bursts lashed out here and there, but the steady stream of fire had dropped off to a trickle. The ammo, Becker thought. They're running low or reloading. All of them? Not likely.

He watched the Lincolns dragging themselves out of the trenches, tripping on sandbags and their own feet, the raw recruits still carrying overloaded packs and suddenly he knew. The enemy gunners were waiting until they were all in the open.

"Move!" he shouted, his voice breaking. "Move your asses, you're sitting ducks!" A few men looked his way and broke into a trot but it was as if Becker's call was a "Fire at will" order. A giant invisible hand swept across the clearing, speckling the milling crowd of brown uniforms with flashing bursts of crimson. A score of men fell in the first pass, an equal number as the tracers swept back. Another dozen were shot dead and fell back into the trench. The Lincolns' commanding officer raised his arm to wave the men forward and was spun off his feet with a shot through the shoulder. One of the British commissars appeared to lose the lower half of his face.

Becker knew the enemy spotters had all the time in the world and eventually they would decide to finish him off, even if they had to shred his tree down to the stump. It was time to move, but another sprint was out of the question. As the tracers passed his position, he got his knees under him and looked for anyone who might have made it this far. He saw three men moving from tree to

tree about fifty feet to his right and broke into the clearing even
with them as they moved forward at a slow trot. They either forgot
their training or never had any because they stayed too close together. A single sweep of tracers knocked them to the ground in a
writhing, screaming mass. He ran faster. A concussion slammed his
eardrums followed by a gust of burning air and dirt. The ground
rushed up at his face, the barrel of his rifle hit him across the bridge
of his nose as he fell, stunned him and made his eyes water. Deaf-
ened, he hugged the ground and heard only his own voice calling,
"God, God, God!" followed by another cursing him for a fool. God's
not here, you chump, and if he were, what difference would it
make? This isn't Euripides. It's Nietzsche. To punctuate the
thought, a foot stomped on the back of his knee, another into the
middle of his back as a volunteer tried to run over him, then the
moist crack of a bullet passing through bone and brains as the man
fell with one leg on each of Becker's shoulders.

The wind was knocked out of him when he fell, then again when
the man ran over him. He fought to regain his breath without moving too much but succeeded only in choking on his own spit,
inhaling a mouthful of dirt and breaking into violent spasms of
coughing. A line of tracers slapped into the corpse above him. Had
he been seen? He filled his lungs with air and held it, fighting the
urge to cough again. The reflex faded and he slowly released his
breath.

His feet had been knocked from under him, but by what? Was it
a mortar round or a bullet? He was sure there had been an explosion. Was he hit? He tried to take stock of his extremities. Right
foot, right leg – both could move. Left, same, but something was
restricting his movement. Injuries? The only pains were his nose
and where the soldier had stepped on the back of his knee. It was as
if he had been bound at the ankles. He was lying face down, not in
dirt but on some springy mass of vegetation. He turned his head to
the side and managed to look under the leg of his dead companion
past the burning body of a volunteer on fire from incendiary
rounds. The olive grove ended just before a short depression of

open ground followed by the upward slope of a dead vineyard- an impassable obstacle of tangled, twisted vines. Becker tried to clear the fog from his memory. An explosion, a gust of hot air and dirt, legs immobilized, a fall and a blow across his nose.

His feet were tangled in the vines, trapping him in the middle of the kill zone, partially shielded from fire by a corpse and a slight depression in the ground. At least some of the enemy gunners had taken him for dead but that would certainly change if he tried to free himself. What time was it? They had started in mid-morning and there was still too much light to attempt a move, either forward or back. Men were still advancing from the rear, alone or in small groups. Some shouted as they charged, others tried for stealth. All were cut down, some in the olive grove, others in the clearing, still more when they reached the vineyard. Some died silently, others with choking, gurgling screams. Many were cut open by bullets or shrapnel and lay calling out for first aid, their buddies or their mothers until a sniper or machine gunner found them.

Smoke from the burning body was drifting straight over Becker's position, not enough to give cover but strong enough to turn his stomach. He spent the better part of an hour willing the wind to shift and the flames to die down. The agonized screams of the wounded abated but they were replaced by a low, intermittent keening from the near-dead. Many called for water or wept. Some-where behind and to the left there was one game volunteer who was spitting blood and probably had a bullet through his lung but found the breath to direct an eloquent flow of vitriol at the Brigade com-manders who had "hatched this whore-loving, half-assed, cockeyed, corn-holed, cluster-fucking circle-jerk" as well as cursing them with every imaginable venereal affliction and damning their souls to an eternal Inquisition of torments in the afterlife. The commentary drew to a close after about twenty minutes with a final "Damn it all to hell".

Amen and well-spoken Brother, Becker thought.

He fell asleep or lost consciousness, awaking with a dull ache in his side. A Mills bomb was digging into his hip bone. He shifted to the side until it was pressing into his lower abdomen and had a sudden, pressing need to urinate. He tried to open his eyes and found that one was partially caked with blood. The rifle must have opened a cut when he fell. He looked under his dead comrade's leg again and saw only darkness. A gentle but steady rain was falling and the daylight was going fast. Wait, maybe your eyes will adjust, he thought. Five minutes passed but he could only see a faint glow somewhere back beyond the trees. The enemy gunners had either taken a break or run out of targets. He tried to draw one knee up to the side and felt a vine pulling at his ankle. He stopped pulling, rotated the foot and pointed the toe. It came free. He extended the leg and lay it slowly down on the bed of vines, keeping his silhouette as low as possible. He repeated the process with the other leg but it seemed to make things worse. The grip of the vines seemed to tighten. If only he could see what he was doing.

"MacCready," someone called a tone just above a whisper.

"Here," Becker said.

"One more time." The voice was calm, but it dropped to a whisper.

"I'm here."

"I'm close but I still can't make you out. Can you move?" said the voice.

"Only my foot. There's a body on top of me."

"OK, raise your foot," said the voice.

"And get it shot off?" Becker asked.

"The firing has dropped off. It's pretty dark, Matt."

"Lowry?"

"Yeah, it's me."

"OK, I'm lifting my foot." Becker bent his leg at the knee until the sole of his shoe was parallel to the ground.

"Got you. OK, put it down." Becker heard the sound of a body crawling through the vines and saw a black form take shape on his right. "Are you hit?"

"I'm not sure. I don't think so. My left ankle is wrapped up in some vines," Becker said.

"Hold on. I've got a knife." Lowry stayed flat on his belly as he drew a knife from his belt and cut away the vines from Becker's ankle. "OK, you're free. If you can crawl out of the field, you'll be OK. The ones that are left are walking back to the trenches."

"What about you?"

"I'm looking for Michaels," Lowry said.

"Don't know him," Becker said.

"Short, curly hair, glasses, tooth chipped in the front."

"Are you talking about Mekharian from Pittsburgh?"

"That's the guy," Lowry said.

"He crawled over me in the trench yesterday. That's the last time I saw him."

"I saw him head out of the grove maybe two minutes ahead of you."

What was Lowry's first name? He knew it back on the boat, a lifetime ago.

"Walter, listen. I don't think anybody ahead of me made it. Don't get yourself killed for no reason," Becker said.

"It's not for no reason. I promised him. Good luck, Matt." Lowry started to crawl away.

"Wait. What are you going to do if you find him?" Becker said.

"Bring him back."

"Alone?"

Lowry said nothing. Becker couldn't see his face but he could hear him breathing. "What's your best guess about his direction?" Becker asked.

"Up and to the left," Lowry said. Becker had heard nothing from that direction in hours.

"You lead, I'll stay a couple yards behind you," Becker said. "And Walter, if I'm hit, you leave me here and get yourself back. You hear me?"

Around two in the morning they found Michaels. He lay face up with his head downhill, stitched across the middle by a heavy machine gun. Another sweep of tracers had taken his left leg off at the knee. Lowry closed the man's eyes and took his wallet and a small packet of letters from inside his coat. It was about a fifteen-yard crawl to get out of the vineyard, make it to the clearing and run for the trees. Becker took one shoulder strap, Lowry the other as they began a slow, dry-land sidestroke, dragging the body two or three feet at a time before pausing to listen for any sign they had been detected.

Halfway to the clearing, Michaels' torso separated from his lower body at the waist. Steam rose from the open abdomen carrying an odor that made them both wretch. Lowry buried his face in the crook of his arm. Becker unzipped his jacket and pulled it up to cover his mouth and nose. They both crawled a few feet away from the body.

"Walter?"

"I guess we'll be leaving him here then," Lowry said.

"Whatever you say," Becker said.

"You think he'd understand, right?"

"You know him better than me, but I sure would."

When they made it to the olive grove, they saw that men had gradually moved from crawling to their hands and knees and finally to a slump-shouldered, shuffling stagger. Some supported the injured or exhausted, others tried to drag the badly wounded until their strength gave out or the stricken succumbed to shock or loss of blood.

The trenches were soaked, muddy ditches running with tiny rivulets of blood, vomit and ice-cold rainwater. The occupants were half-mad with fear, pain, cold, hunger and outrage. There was no place to sit or lie down without pushing someone else aside so men did their best to stumble through the dead, wounded or exhausted bodies to the rear. Cries could still be heard from the olive grove, some from the vineyard beyond, but no one dared venture out to retrieve them for fear of drawing fire from the enemy machine gunners.

Becker suddenly realized he didn't know how long he had been walking, where he was going or what he would do when he got there. He and Lowry saw a man with a bloodied shoulder crouched against the wall of the trench, shivering with cold as he tried with his one good arm to pull a blanket around his back. They dropped to the ground on either side of him, got the blanket over his shoulders and linked arms behind his back, doing their best to warm him with their body heat. Within minutes, they had dozed off as their heads tipped against each other in a comical three-man huddle.

CHAPTER 18

They held the tiny piece of ground for hours as they were battered by the passing of an irregular file of cursing, weeping or mumbling men. They were stepped on, stepped over and struck across their heads, elbows and knees by rifles, canteens and helmets. Their souls were damned to hell and their pardons begged dozens of times. Finally, one man collapsed and bled to death at the bottom of the trench directly in front of them, providing a stable human flagstone as his body was steadily trodden into the blood-soaked earth.

They were awakened by the smell of greasy hemp sacks of goat meat being passed down the line, followed by flagons of a caustic local brandy which Becker thought redolent of something automotive or industrial. Nonetheless, they grabbed what they could, putting the meat in their laps and drinking the brandy from the small cooking pots of their mess kits.

Becker waved the brandy under their companion's bowed head. "Hey, buddy. This will warm you up. And there's a little food here if you can get it down."

"Matt," Lowry said. "He went a couple hours ago."

Becker nodded and took a sip of brandy himself. "Did you get a name?" he asked.

"There's a brigade ID card, but it's soaked through with blood. I can't read it." Lowry passed over the card and a photo of a fair-haired woman holding an infant in her arms. He turned it over. "Love always, from Donna," it read. Becker put both back in the man's shirt pocket and buttoned the flap.

"Does he have any ammo or water on him? Anything useful?" Becker asked.

"Looks like he dropped everything," Lowry said.

They both stared into space for minutes. They could see a faint brightening in the east and knew that soon whatever remained of the command structure would be sending up orders and they dreaded what those orders might be.

"Who do you think is running this show?" Becker asked.

Lowry just shook his head slowly from side to side. "I saw the Captain go down. I don't know if he's still alive. The second in line refused to take command. At least one of the British commissars is down and I haven't seen our commissar in a couple days. As far as I know, that colonel, what's his name, Copic? He's still back at head-quarters."

"So you know as much as me," Becker said. As the light improved, Becker tried to see through the mist, looking up and down the line to estimate their remaining strength. He saw only a few dozen men that appeared capable of walking, much less mounting a defense. If the enemy counterattacked, the Lincolns would be better off shooting each other now, rather than facing the Moors hand-to-hand in the corpse-strewn trench.

As he looked down the line, he slowly made out a figure walking toward them. The man's shoulders were back and he looked straight ahead as he made his way through the living and dead obstacles in his path. Another goddamn officer, Becker thought. No, not an officer. He's still got his rifle.

The man approached them. "Elsaw," Becker said, his voice a toneless croak.

"Who's that?"

"Down here," Becker waved his hand feebly. Brown dropped to one knee, squinting in the darkness but showing no signs of recognition.

"Comrade?" Brown said.

"Elsaw, it's Walter and Matt, from the boat," Lowry said.

Becker wasn't expecting a hug, but Brown's face went grey and the skin drew tight across his cheekbones. He put his left hand lightly on Becker's arm and reached across to touch Lowry's head and lift the bill of his woolen cap. They all looked at each other for a long time.

"Ain't you a sight," Brown said.

"You want some of this?" Becker said, raising the tin of brandy. Brown started to reach for it but got a sudden whiff of the contents.

"No, thanks. I think that shine might do a body some harm, if you get my meaning."

"Cheers," Becker said, raising the pot.

"You been hit?" Brown asked. Lowry and Becker both shook their heads.

"Who's your friend?" They still had their arms around the dead body. There seemed to be some warmth left in it.

"Don't know. He died during the night. His ID is useless," Becker said. "Elsaw, where you been?"

"I been a runner. Running here and there, up and down those damn hills, carrying messages."

"No field telephone?" Lowry asked.

Brown made a chopping gesture. "Artillery. But most of our positions never had no phones to begin with. And when I got where I was running to, most of the time there was no one to give the messages to anyway." His eyes looked far away, toward the dawn.

"Elsaw, where are the other runners?" Becker asked.

"No more, far as I know."

"Where are you going now?" Lowry asked.

"Don't know. Looking for someone in charge. Someone to report to. But every time I ask who's in charge I get some awful cursing back at me. Men that can walk are leaving the lines for the rear."

"How many men?" Becker asked.

Brown lowered his voice. "I think sooner or later this whole line will be up and gone. Some of these men are gonna make a run for Barcelona. Others are going to make for the border on their own." His voice dropped to a whisper. "Matt, I think some of these boys are looking to do murder."

"Murder who?"

"Anyone in command," Brown said. "They saying that last attack should have never gone ahead, what with no planes in the air, no artillery support and all our machine guns not worth a good goddamn."

Martin's words about competence kept running through Becker's head. He needed to believe in this cause. He wanted to believe he was doing something right. Why did Martin go on? Why had he sacrificed so much? Had Martin been duped? That was too much to accept. Had he knowingly sent Becker off to a pointless slaughter? "If you're going to die, do it for a reason," he had said. That I can believe in, he thought. But what was the reason for that last charge?

"Matt, there's something else," Brown said.

"What else?"

"They looking for you. They looking for Angelo."

"Who's they?"

"First I heard was a Frenchman, come up from Albacete. Said he was from Marty's staff. He was roaring mad about Trotskyite this and Trotskyite that, waving some drawing someone done up on a mimeograph. He was looking for Angelo and he said 'any of his other conspirators'."

"When was this?" Becker asked.

"About two nights after..." Brown looked at Lowry and cut himself short. "After we got here."

"Was he alone?"

"He had two corporals with him. Real hard looking, like they was ready to shoot Angie on the spot."

"Did they find him?"

"Don't think so. Nobody was paying them much mind. In fact, some officer gave that man a dressing down like I never seen in a language I don't know. Then some artillery started falling and everybody went for the shelter. Next I knew, they was nowhere around."

"You said 'first'. There were others?" Becker wanted to ask 'Anyone sound like they were from Jersey?' but resisted the impulse.

"Officers. They come looking for you and Angelo. They knew your names. They had papers," Brown said.

"Up here? On the line?" Becker said.

"No," Brown almost laughed. "Back at the command post. They was real well done up. No mud on their uniforms."

"What kind of officers?"

"Can't rightly say. Not Spanish. Not British or Americans neither, though they spoke English to me."

"Elsaw, what did you make of them?" Becker asked.

Brown was already crouched on one knee. He now crossed his arms on the other and gazed at the horizon. "Two in uniform, but not those riding boots and baggy pants. Brown pants, black jackets, not a lot of fancy ribbons and such. They had those fancy little Russian pistols on their belts. One civilian in Sunday clothes and a long black coat and hat. Matt, they was real military, but not angry. Nothing like that crazy Frenchman. More like you and Angelo was some movie stars and they wanted to lay eyes on you and tell their friends."

"Doubt it," Becker said, absent-mindedly.

"Matt, what were you and Angie doing when you were away? After we left you in Paris?" Lowry asked.

"Mostly running errands, Walter. Nothing mysterious. One of my relatives back home knows somebody else's relatives in the Party," Becker said. Lowry tried to read his eyes, but the pre-dawn shadows kept them hidden. "Elsaw, you talked to these men?"

"They asked me if I knew you," Brown said.

"And you said?"

"I said I knew who you were from the boat and when we was all in Villanueva."

"And?"

"They asked if I knew where you was," Brown said. "I said up on the line, like everybody else, far as I knew, but I didn't know where, which was the God's honest truth."

"And that satisfied them?" Becker asked.

"They just nodded and sat themselves down. They sat at the colonel's table too, which made him none too pleased, I can tell you." Brown smiled at the memory. "The other officers made themselves real busy around these men, mostly trying to be elsewhere."

"When was this?"

Brown passed his hand over his face and rubbed his eyes. "Before lunchtime yesterday. Before the first charge," he said.

"And do you know where Angie is now?" Becker asked, as gently as he could.

"When they blew the whistles, he went over the top like most of them. Three men went down on his right. He hit the dirt and then got up again. I saw him go into them olive trees, moving along at a pretty good pace. Ain't seen him since. Don't know if he made it back."

Brown had warmed to his narrative and some of the color had returned to his face. He now looked remorseful at all the bad news he had brought and exhausted from the telling. But Becker needed more information. He had grown used to the luxury of being told what to do and where to go these past weeks. Now the ground had been cut from under him and he was hoping for something to force his hand.

"Elsaw. You've been up and down this line. What's going to happen here?" he asked.

"Matt, as for the Lincolns, there ain't no more line to speak of. Command is sending in replacements from countries I never heard of. And like I said, the Lincolns that are still alive are mad as a hornet's nest. Once they get some food under their belts, they likely to do anything. And this here bathtub moonshine they pouring ain't gonna help none. No, it certainly ain't." Brown shook his head disdainfully as he watched Becker take a swallow.

"Elsaw, it's a kind of brandy. They call it *coñac*. It won't make you go blind," Lowry said.

"Walter, you take my word. I seen many a good man get the devil in him from the wrong kind of liquor. 'Specially he being pressed and these men here been sorely pressed."

"And if they leave the line?" Becker asked.

"I don't get your meaning," Brown said.

"What are they going to find if they go east?"

"If they looking for blood, the command post is in an old mill and it's pretty well defended. No, that won't come to nothing. If they looking to get away, there's some kind of foreigners patrolling on horseback back towards Morata. They picking up deserters. Some get shot. Some get a trial, then shot. Some get sent to the labor battalions. That much I know. I heard other things I can't rightly credit."

"Tell me, Elsaw," Becker asked.

"Prisons, torture. Making war on our own. Lot a shooting going on got nothing to do with the enemy."

It was no more than confirmation of rumors they had heard for weeks, well before the actual fighting had begun. General Mola had coined the term "fifth column" to describe a clandestine group of subversives in the Republican ranks waiting to support his attack on Madrid, but the term had caught on more among the Republicans than the Fascists. A fractured mosaic of divergent leftist philosophies, the Republican cause was forever at war with itself. Anarchists, Communists, Unionists, Socialists and untold numbers of splinter groups all hated each other as traitors more than they hated the Fascists as enemies. For many, the Fascists were an abstraction, something far away and unseen across no man's land and death from an enemy bullet or artillery round was at least a quick and honorable passing. But the fear of treachery in the ranks or somewhere in the command fed a constant waking nightmare that death would come wearing their own uniform.

"Matt, what do you think we should do?" Lowry asked.

"I can't do anything till I find out what happened to Angie," Becker said. "Elsaw. I need to know where he went over the top."

Brown looked back up the line the way he had come, his head

slowly moving from side to side. "If I try to tell you, you'll never find it. I can show you, but it's a fair amount of crawling to get there."

"Elsaw, I can't ask you to go back there. Just give me a landmark."

"Matt, you know there's no making sense of this countryside here. There's only uphill, downhill and a whole lot of gullies in between. Besides, if you go sticking your head up looking for this or that, one of them Africans yonder going to shoot it right off your shoulders. No, I'll be taking you to the spot. What else I got to be doing? Walter?"

"I don't want to get shot by my own side. If you guys don't mind, I'll stay with you," he answered.

Every joint seemed to creak as they rose from their dead companion, gathered their gear and started a slow trek back toward the front trenches. True to Brown's account, Becker saw clean uniforms and heard the voices of Franco-Belgian volunteers and another language he couldn't identify. He stopped next to a man gnawing on a piece of goat meat and tried English.

"Comrade. What country are you from?" The man raised an eyebrow in response and held up a small sack of more meat in offering. Becker shook his head and smiled before trying French, Spanish and finally German. A light went on in the man's eyes.

"Ah! *Magyar!*," the man responded, tapping an insignia on his left shoulder.

Becker nodded enthusiastically and pointed to himself and his companions. "America," he said.

The man nodded warmly, patted Becker's shoulder with a greasy hand, said something in his own language and concluded with what little Spanish he had picked up.

"Gracias! No pasarán! No pasarán!"

Brown, Lowry and Becker all answered with the same stock platitude of the Republic, "They shall not pass", but it was already sounding false and hackneyed to the Lincolns. They lifted their hands in farewell and continued working their way forward.

"So?" Lowry said.

"Hungarian," Becker said.

"And the Lord did there confound the language of all the earth," Brown said. Unlike your average Communist, Brown had a fondness for quoting scripture, but Becker and Lowry knew there was no keeping up with him in that regard so they stayed silent. "Matt? You think the Lord is punishing us for prideful ways? Sending us all together to fight where there's no understanding each other?"

Becker tried to think of a response, but Brown was pulling ahead of them and he decide to let it lie as he sped up his pace.

They made the last two hundred yards on their hands and knees. The growing light of morning had brought sniper fire and occasional machine gun bursts from the Fascist lines but no sustained effort at counter-attack.

"He went over right here," Brown said.

"You're sure?" Becker said. They were sitting with their backs against the wall of the trench, ten yards past any of the replacements, with several inert bodies littering the area around them.

"There are two rows of olive trees just past a little heap of white rocks. He ran into the grove right there."

Becker got out the mirror he had taken from the recruit before the attack and held it up to get a view of the terrain in front of the trench. He saw the small cairn of rocks, and the rows of trees beyond, just as Brown had described.

"Hey, buddy! Who are you shoving?" said a voice next to Brown. Becker and Lowry looked as Brown recoiled in horror. One of the bodies they had taken for a corpse was in fact a live volunteer wrapped in a poncho.

"Comrade, you OK?" Lowry said.

"Took one in the foot," the corpse said defensively. Quite a few volunteers of various nationalities had self-inflicted wounds to escape the massacre. He had an east coast accent that Becker couldn't immediately place.

"Why weren't you sent to the rear?" Brown asked.

"And how am I gonna get there? Can't walk. The stretcher bearers are all out there, lying dead in the trees."

"Let's take a look, comrade. I know a little first aid," Becker said.

"I'll get by. Look after yourself," the man said, with an edge to his voice.

"Brother, you get gangrene and it's a slow, screaming death and there's not a thing anyone can do. No harm in letting us take a look," Becker said, trying to sound as meek as he could.

The man looked at Brown, Lowry and Becker, all of them waiting for his reply.

"Just don't want to make trouble for anyone else." He sat up, keeping the poncho around his shoulders and extended his left foot. It took him some time to unwrap strips of a torn up t-shirt used as a makeshift bandage. The last layer of cloth was stuck to the dried gore of the wound and the man grunted in pain as he pulled it away. The little toe was gone and the next toe was swelled up to twice its normal size but any other damage was hidden by bruising and scabs.

"Nasty wound," Becker said. "Have you got a sock we can put on it once we clean it up and change the bandage?"

The man reached into a satchel and took a clean sock from an unused pair.

"Where's the boot?" Becker asked.

The man started to reach behind him, but stopped and stared back at Becker, his eyes wide.

"Go ahead," Becker said. "Let's see it."

The man sat in a state of paralysis. His eyes moving from Brown to Lowry and back to Becker, who sighed with fatigue as he drew the .45 from under his jacket.

"Show me the boot," he said softly. "I ain't got all day."

"I don't have it," the man said. "I lost it when I got hit."

Becker eased back the hammer on the .45 until it locked with a sound that shook the man to his core. He reached behind him, grabbed the boot and threw it across the trench. Brown picked it up and showed it to his companions. It was muddy and well-used but there was no bullet hole.

"So the way I see it," Becker said. "You were running through the battle with only one boot on when you got shot in the left toe by some sharpshooter in an airplane. He must have been in an airplane because that wound was made from a weapon fired directly from above. Here, I'll show you how it must have happened."

Becker pushed himself wearily to his feet, took two steps toward the man's head and pressed the .45 into his skull. Brown and Lowry rushed forward to grasp his arms.

"Matt. Dear God don't be doing this," Brown said. "There's no good will come of it. They'll shoot you for sure."

The wounded volunteer seemed to be choking as he struggled for breath but it was only a combination of fear and sobbing that left him gasping, unable to form words. He shook his head and managed to emit a single "No!" before covering his face with his hands and turning his head away.

Becker eased the hammer back down with his thumb and tried to give a reassuring smile to Brown and Lowry, but fatigue and his dirt streaked face made him look half-crazed.

"There's no round in the chamber, Elsaw," he said.

They released his arms, patted his back and urged him to sit down, "rest his bones a spell" as Elsaw put it. After seating himself on a relatively dry sandbag and leaning back against the wall of the trench he realized the .45 was still in his hand.

"Hey, asshole," he said to the wounded volunteer. The man looked up. "Put on the sock, put on the boot, lace it up and get lost."

"I can't walk!" answered the man.

"You got two hands and two knees. That's enough to get you out of my sight. Leave the poncho."

When the man was gone, Becker wrapped himself in the poncho, still warm with body heat. A blessed, soothing weariness started to move through his body and he knew that real sleep was only moments away.

"Jesus Lord, Matt. Remind me never to cross you," Brown said.

"Elsaw, you never crossed anyone in your life. You ain't got it in you."

"I thank you for that, but all the same." Brown seemed to pause in mid-thought and Becker raised his head to look at him.

"Walter, what's eatin' at you brother? You ain't hardly said two words all day," Brown said.

"There's a friend out there in two pieces and I couldn't bring him back," Lowry answered.

"Walter, don't you go takin' that on your own shoulders now. The Lord brings all his children home sooner or later."

CHAPTER 19

Becker dreamed he was flying, but as in all his flying dreams he wasn't quite in control. In this dream he was flying backwards and he couldn't reverse it. His arms wouldn't move to change direction. His feet flailed helplessly. There was no sensation of falling but he was moving faster and faster at a speed he couldn't control. He woke up.

Two men had reached into the trench and lifted him out by both arms. They now pulled him, bearing most of his weight, his feet barely touching the ground as he watched the trench line disappear in the distance. He looked for Brown and Lowry but couldn't see a single face he knew, though many watched his departure with blank, 'there but for the grace of God' expressions.

Words raced through his head but he discarded them as soon as soon as they formed into sentences. "Put me down!" Too pathetic. "Where are you taking me!" Like they're going to change their minds and take me someplace else? "What is the meaning of this?" He actually gave that one some serious thought, just for humor, but he didn't think anyone would get the joke. At least I don't have to walk, he thought.

They came to a stop at a troop truck and Becker was finally turned to face forward. Two Republican privates held rifles on him as the first two men indicated that he should climb into the back. Once inside, they followed him in and tied his hands behind him with a rough hemp rope, then lowered him to the floor of the truck, tied his ankles and finally ran another rope between his ankles and wrists. Hog tied, Becker thought. A pillow case was pulled over his head. It smelled of bad breath and mildew but Becker thought it less ominous than a black bag. One of the men jumped down from the back of the truck and he heard footsteps go around to the cab, the door open and close, the engine turn over and the gearbox clank. The truck began to move.

Becker took inventory of his situation. Two men had taken him, one larger than the other, but his eyes had been too unfocused and it had been too dark to make out their faces. They had been professional but not abusive. Strong enough to lift his entire hundred-eighty-odd pounds without effort. He hadn't been struck or kicked. His hands had been tied but they had made no effort to wrench his arms out of their sockets when they pulled his arms back. He'd been treated much worse by American cops. Strangest of all, he hadn't been frisked. In fact, as he lay on his left side, the .45 was digging painfully into his rib cage. He debated with himself what to do about it. "Hey, guys, you forgot something," just didn't seem right. He hadn't been gagged, but any attempt at speech might result in a kick in the ribs or a blackjack behind the ear. What was the point?

The most mixed blessing was that they had left his rucksack behind. Their job had been to grab him and not take a stray bullet in the process. If they had brought it, he had no doubt they would be relieving him of everything of value he owned. These were pros. They would have found the money he had sewn into the lining of the pack. Worse, they would have found the extra clips and ammo for the .45. Why had they missed the pistol? Because they were pros and they assumed he wasn't. By sheer luck, neither of them had brushed up against the shoulder holster when they took his arms and they figured that as another useless American volunteer, his only weapon would be the rifle which was now lying in the mud at the bottom of the trench.

Becker knew that if Brown got hold of his pack, it would be safe. Lowry? He didn't know, but he knew that it was safer wherever it was than with him.

He smelled a cigarette, but not the odor he had become used to. Not American, French or any of the other odious combinations of floor sweepings he had encountered in the trenches. He was also aware of a completely different type of body odor. Like a mixture of stale sweat and boiled vegetables. The truck also had a leak in the exhaust which was sending a steady draft of fumes through the floorboards. The lack of breathable air combined with the pounding of the truck over rutted and potholed roads brought waves of nausea and dizziness.

His abductors exchanged barely a dozen words during his abduction. Not enough for Becker to determine the language but he knew it wasn't Spanish, French or German. What did that leave? The smart money was on Russian, but there were certainly enough nationalities in this fight that it could be just about anything.

The truck stopped twice, but no one got in or out. The second time he heard artillery rounds dropping, perhaps a mile away. More? No way of knowing. Close enough for concern, too far for real panic. After the barrage stopped he heard the driver call something to his guard and receive a muted grunt for an answer before the truck continued on its journey.

The whole trip took less than forty minutes. How much distance had they covered? With the darkness, frequent stops and detours it could have been a half mile or ten. Becker felt relief as the rope between his ankles and wrists was cut, then the one binding his ankles. The guard pulled him to his feet and held his arm to be sure he was steady, then pulled the pillowcase off his head and walked him to the tailgate. A slap between the shoulder blades told him that he was expected to jump out, but his eyes hadn't focused yet and he couldn't make out where the ground was. He hesitated. A second slap knocked him forward. He tried to keep his knees together and land solidly on both feet but his left leg had gone to sleep during the ride and it folded under him on impact. He rolled with it and came up on both knees, his hands still bound behind him. The larger man let out a brief chuckle, but the other cut him off. Was he being told to shut up or just not damage the merchandise?

Pulled to his feet again, he was led into a single story mud-brick house like the dozens he had seen dotting the flatter parts of the landscape. A farm house? What could anyone possibly farm in this soil? Maybe the former owners made a living from the olives, he thought. At least the roof was intact and they would be out of the cold. He stood in what was probably once the kitchen and waited as the big man went into another room and closed the door. His partner, a lean, graying cadaver with raptor's eyes, stood a casual guard on Becker, who stomped his feet and hugged his torso with his bound arms, trying to warm himself but also hunching his shoulders in an attempt to cover the shape of the automatic which was still hidden under the thick leather of his jacket.

After about five minutes the door to the next room opened and he was waved forward. He found himself in the main room of the house, which might once have been furnished with a sofa and armchairs but now held only three steel frame beds, a desk littered with papers and a table with two chairs. The only other furniture was an upended wooden crate which kept a field telephone off the dampness of the floor.

A man sat on one of the beds. He was dressed in flannel trousers with the suspenders slipped off and hanging at each side and a long sleeved undershirt with three buttons at the neck. He had a two-day growth of beard and slicked back hair but Becker couldn't see his face. He was rubbing his eyes and the bridge of his nose, like a man who had tried for a quick nap and unexpectedly found himself in the abyss of an exhausted stupor. He took one hand from his eyes and made a vague waving gesture toward one of the chairs. Becker pulled the chair out with his foot and sat. The man rose from the bed with some effort, arched his back, stretched his arms above his head and took the chair across the table from him. He looked at Becker with heavy-lidded eyes.

If this was the boss, Becker wanted to take careful stock of the man. He had a high forehead and thick black hair with no hint of gray, which might put his age on the near side of forty. His nose was narrow and straight and the top of his ears lay flat against the side of his head, as if glued there. The most prominent feature of his face were his lips, which Becker thought almost comically large and might have looked better on a woman. But there was nothing comical about the man or how he carried himself. He was around Becker's height, perhaps a little taller, and might once have had an athletic build, but like many others Becker had seen recently, he seemed to have lost weight and his clothes hung loosely on his frame.

"English, yes?" the man said, and coughed, his voice still raspy with sleep.

"American," Becker answered.

"Your language is English," the man said.

"Yes."

"*Et le français?*"

"Yes."

"*Et l'allemand?*"

"What?" Who ratted me out, Becker thought. Who knows I speak German?

"*Und der deutschen Sprache?* I have information which tells me you speak German. Is it not so?"

"My mother speaks German and my father a little. I speak some, but how good it is...," Becker shrugged.

"Then we will continue in German, if you don't mind. For me it is more..."

"Can I have a cigarette?" Becker asked. I need to give him a reason to cut these ropes.

"We have only Russian cigarettes. You are familiar with Russian cigarettes?"

"I'm afraid not."

The man frowned. "I fear they would not be to your liking. Actually, they are not to my liking." His eyebrows suddenly went up.

"We have some tobacco and cigarette papers but I am not proficient...as you can see." He held up his right hand parallel to the ground for Becker's inspection. The last two fingers and at least one bone in his hand had been broken and badly set. "In this weather, the aching. It is most annoying."

"I can make a cigarette, if you have the materials," Becker said.

"Borya!" the man called through the door. The larger of Becker's original escorts answered something unintelligible and opened the door. His host spoke a few words and was brought a small paper bag, which he opened and began searching through. A few more words and the big man produced a butcher's boning knife from under his coat and cut Becker's bonds before turning and walking out the door.

As he rubbed his wrists, Becker found himself looking at a half-full bag of tobacco and a crushed packet of cigarette papers.

"Will it do?" the man asked.

Becker said nothing but did his best to restore the packet to its original shape and started pulling out papers. The third one seemed usable.

"The tobacco is quite dry," Becker said as he began rolling. His father had taught him when he was eight or nine and he had taken a child's pride in being allowed to roll them. He had nothing approaching his father's speed or skill, but he could do a respectable job. He finished one and passed it over to his host, who looked at it with interest as he patted his pockets for matches. He lit it, inhaled deeply and turned his head to blow a huge cloud of smoke toward the ceiling.

"Much better. Very well done." He looked across at Becker and raised an eyebrow. "Please. One for yourself."

Becker unzipped his jacket, took out the .45, racked the slide and pointed it across the table at the man. He was silent for a moment as he searched his mind for an appropriate phrasing in German, finally deciding that English would do.

"Exactly who the fuck are you?"

The slightest flicker of alarm had passed over the man's face when he saw the gun. If Becker hadn't been watching closely, he might have missed it. But the man never lost his composure and now looked back with an expression Becker couldn't define. Perhaps the face of a person who hears a strange noise coming from somewhere in his car and doesn't know if it's cause for worry.

"You won't have a cigarette?" the man said in German. Becker almost smiled, but tried to keep his face cold.

"In fact, I rarely smoke," Becker answered, also in German. "Sometimes I enjoy a cigarette, but for some reason, I never acquired the habit. But if you would be so kind as to answer my question."

"I suppose that for our purposes, you would call me Alex."

"And a surname?" Becker asked.

"At present I am using Korsky. It is easy enough for our Spanish comrades. And what shall I call you?"

"Matthew."

Neither man spoke for perhaps a full minute.

"A pleasure," Korsky said.

"Likewise," Becker said. "And you represent?"

"The Party."

Becker responded by looking at the ceiling and let out a deep sigh.

"You Americans are so cynical," Korsky said. "Very well. I work for the Soviet government. We are here to help in the struggle against-"

"So you are NKVD?" Becker asked. Korsky paused before answering.

"Yes, I am an NKVD officer." He nodded toward the pistol. "Do you intend to shoot me?"

"More importantly, do you intend to shoot me?" Becker asked.

"It would have been a terrible waste of fuel when a single bullet would have done the job," Korsky said.

"I am unconvinced. For now, let us say that if either of those men opens the door again, there will be a great deal of noise."

"Why?"

"I object to the manner in which I was brought here."

"It is the procedure," Korsky said.

"Nonetheless," Becker said, suddenly not knowing where he wanted to take the conversation. "Can't you people afford real handcuffs?"

Korsky actually showed embarrassment. "Our last pair was being worn by a prisoner who...didn't return."

"The nerve of some people," Becker said. "So why did you bring me here?"

"Some letters found their way to us with some difficulty. One of them described work you did for the Cause in Paris. You and a companion." He turned in his chair and took a piece of handwritten letter paper from the clutter on the desk behind him. "A Mr. Vincent?"

"Angelo," Becker said.

"Just so," Korsky said.

"And?"

"It is felt you would be more useful in other endeavors."

"Such as?"

"Such as the duties you carried out in Paris," Korsky said.

"We recovered money which had been stolen from the Cause. More money has gone missing?" Becker said.

"You also dealt with the traitor responsible and dispatched two Gestapo."

"What is Gestapo?" Becker had not heard the word before.

"*Geheime Staatspolizei*." The Secret State Police.

"I came here to be a soldier, to fight the Fascists. I'm not a policeman, secret or otherwise. The fact is that I have never cared much for police of any kind."

"And if you should happen to shoot me and the two men outside tonight, how long do you think you will live, Matthew?" Korsky asked, with the look of someone who now had the upper hand.

"Well, Alex," Becker said, emphasizing the use of the man's first name. "It's doubtful that I would have survived tomorrow had I stayed in the trenches. If I shoot you and those two, it will be with the knowledge that you wished me harm. If I am killed in the process, I am still no worse off than I was two hours ago. I have lost any illusions that I will survive this war. You have given me the opportunity to die fighting."

As Becker spoke, Korsky's face had gone from grim acknowledgement and an unconscious nodding to mild amusement and a wry smile.

"We wish you no harm, Mr. Mac – I am sorry, I cannot pronounce your surname."

"It's not important. I take no offense at 'Matthew'."

"We believed that you and your companion would be of use to the Cause, as you said, as soldiers. But not simple cannon fodder to be slaughtered like beasts in the trenches. We need men who can go to the other side of the lines and engage in guerilla warfare."

Becker felt a sudden interest, but immediately reproached himself. Does this appeal to the romantic in you? he thought. What an idiot. This is a pitch, and you're supposed to buy it. So you're going to be The Scarlet Pimpernel? Wake up. After what you've seen in the past month?

"And if I'm captured, I'll be stood up against a wall and shot," Becker said.

"Matthew, my friend. If you're captured out there, you will also most likely be shot, without the benefit of a wall to stand against. Of course the *shvarzers* may simply cut your throat."

Did he just speak Yiddish to me? Becker thought. Is this guy a *landsman*? He tried to remember if *shvarzer* was real German or Yiddish, finally deciding it was both. But there was something in the man's tone or pronunciation. What does he know about me? He thought back to the woman who had taken Mendy away after giving him the Sabbath greeting. Is this the beginning of real paranoia?

"My belongings. My rucksack was left behind when your men took me," Becker said.

"Perhaps it can be found. May I?" he gestured toward the door. Becker nodded and held the .45 below the table. Korsky called once more for "Borya!" who put his head in the door. Korsky spoke to him rapidly in Russian. The man's face registered disbelief as he looked at his watch and asked one question which Becker assumed must be "You mean, now?" to which Korsky patiently nodded. Borya closed, the door, muttering.

"That is his name?" Becker asked.

"Borya? Yes. Well, Boris actually, but it is a common nickname. The other is Gunter," Korsky said.

"Gunter? It sounds German," Becker said.

"Please, do not even suggest," Korsky said, shaking his head. "No, he is Russian. One hundred percent."

Becker started to look at his wrist but then remembered he had lost his watch. He tried to guess the time and realized he had no idea. Looking around the room, he saw an alarm clock ticking away on the floor beside the bed but its face was turned away. He gestured toward it.

"What time is it?" he asked. Korsky turned in his chair and picked up the clock.

"Twenty-five minutes past one in the morning," Korsky answered.

"And Borya will return to the trenches at his hour?"

"Safer to do so now, don't you think? Really, we are not so far from the front."

The room was silent, but sounds intruded from outside. Distant vehicles, large and small, shifting gears as they labored up and down steep hills. Voices shouting commands, perhaps directing traffic. A single volley of gunfire. A firing squad? Inside the room only the ticking of the clock and the occasional creak of their chairs disturbed the quiet. Becker tried to make sense of what was happening, but it was as if he were watching the whole scene from the cheapest seats in the house and couldn't hear the dialogue or make out the actors' faces. There were too many possible moves and lurking dangers to consider and he worried that whatever he did, there would be some disastrous consequence which he would be powerless to undo. He replayed the events of the past hour in his mind, looking for some tactical advantage.

"You have news of Mr. Vincent?" Becker asked.

"As I said, we had hoped to make him part of this enterprise," Korsky said.

"You 'had hoped'?"

"He survived the slaughter at Jarama, but when my men went to retrieve him they discovered he had been arrested by members of a security detail working for André Marty. Or perhaps by one of Marty's underlings," Korsky said.

"Arrested for what?"

"Trotskyite subversion. It is one of Marty's favorite, ah, there is an English word I am especially fond of. Is it 'bugbear'?"

"I think 'bugaboo' is the current expression," Becker said.

"Oh, no. Really?" Korsky seemed unconvinced. " 'Bug-"

"Bugaboo. What about Vincent?"

"The details are hard to credit. There was some unflattering caricature of Marty circulated at Villanueva which eventually made its way to Albacete. Some fools actually created a stencil and were able to print numerous copies with a mimeograph. Two men have already been shot for subversion, but no one has been identified as the actual artist. The search goes on, an unforgiveable waste of manpower. Vincent was among those arrested. They will no doubt try to obtain a confession of sorts before he is shot."

"And if he is innocent?" Becker asked.

"Do you believe him to be innocent?"

"Of subversion? You're unlikely to find a better soldier among the Lincolns, or anywhere else." The answer sounded flimsy, even to Becker, and he cursed himself for playing the hand badly.

"So he drew the picture?" Korsky said, a faint smile on his face.

Becker said nothing.

"I saw it," Korsky said. "It's really quite good. Quite amusing." He shook his head slowly as he admired the even burning of his cigarette, as if nostalgic for the days when amusement was a permissible luxury.

"So you will permit him to be shot? If you have the authority to abduct me from the trenches, you must have the authority to intervene," Becker said. He knew his voice had an edge of desperate anger and he tried to rein it in, but he felt his heart pounding in his chest and knew he was very near to a lethal loss of control. Did

Korsky know it? Becker knew that this man must have seen scores of desperate men in his time and was probably reading him like the funny pages.

"If it were in the interests of the struggle to secure his release, perhaps something could be done," Korsky said.

Neither man spoke for some minutes. Becker's head slowly cleared and the situation came into focus.

"Party platitudes aside, it must have been 'in the interests of the struggle' or you wouldn't have gone looking for him in the first place," Becker said, calmly now.

Korsky nodded, content that Becker saw things clearly. "He would be of use?"

"He speaks Italian. His Spanish is improving. More importantly, he is an expert marksman and an efficient killer, when the situation calls for it."

"Are you?"

"Not for me to say. But you have your own sources of information."

Korsky stubbed out his cigarette. "Enough chat. I love chess. I loathe badminton. You are needed for behind the lines operations. Do you agree?"

"I agree. As you say, I would be of more use."

"And can you speak for Vincent? He will join us in this business?"

"We have always been a team. Since childhood. Without him, the operation in Paris would have been impossible," Becker said.

"Then I will use the field telephone and you will not shoot me. Yes?"

Becker hesitated, his thought processes cramping up with language fatigue. A positive verb and a negative verb. Yes, I will shoot you? Yes, you will use the phone? No, I won't shoot you and you won't use the phone?

"I will not shoot," he answered.

Korsky walked to the phone, put the receiver to his ear and cranked the handle. He did it twice more.

"The line is cut. Again." Korsky uttered some Russian oath under his breath, walked to the door and pulled it open. He shouted something into the other room. An irritated, drowsy voice answered something barely audible. A brief exchange of information and Korsky slammed the door.

"There is a school some distance from here where Brigade prisoners are held before being taken back to Albacete," Korsky said. "With luck, we can find him there."

"A school?"

"Schools have many rooms. With some work they can be used as cells."

"He'll be taken to Albacete for trial?" Becker asked.

"Matthew, my dear fellow. I doubt they will waste the gasoline. I expect he will be shot when there is enough light. That is, if they have not shot him already."

"So?"

"When Borya returns with the truck, we will make our way to the facility, if there is enough fuel. Once there, I'm confident we can obtain his release."

An hour later they were bouncing down a back road which might have been paved at some time in the distant past but was now only a black sash of ruts and potholes stretching ahead into the darkness. The windscreen was greasy with a long accumulation of cigarette smoke and the air of the cab was dense and fetid with the stench of damp wool, body odor and bad breath. Becker was twisted sideways to make room for Korsky and Borya, who was driving. Gunter was in the back.

"Poor Gunter. He must be freezing back there," Korsky said.

"At least he can breathe," Becker said.

Borya grunted something in Russian. "He says he can imagine Gunter snoring like a pig," Korsky said.

"They don't get along?"

"They are cousins," Korsky said, as if that explained it.

The truck moved up a slight grade which was actually the shoulder of a paved, two-lane road. Borya downshifted to make the climb and turned east, immediately shifting up with a sigh of satisfaction as the ride smoothed out and the truck gained speed. After a few minutes on the paved road, Becker saw the tiniest glint of a smile from his yellowed front teeth turn to a sudden snarl as he swung the wheel. The truck swerved to the right, throwing up gravel from the shoulder, its left side rising off the road as the strident shriek of clashing sheet metal and the sound of a heartfelt Russian curse rang in their ears. I wish I knew what that one meant, Becker thought, as the truck came to rest. It sounded like a Russian translation of "Touchdown!"

A truck like the mirror image of their own had appeared out of the darkness, taking its half of the road out of the very center. Both drivers had turned at the last instant, but the collision was unavoidable. Through a combination of skill, reflexes and sheer Providence, Borya had managed to save them from a head-on crash and keep their truck from being forced into the ditch or rolling over. He sat now with his forearms resting on the wheel, a wide-eyed look of jubilant madness on his face as Korsky patted his upper arm, praising him in words Becker couldn't understand but tones one might use for a big winner at the roulette table.

The driver's side door had been jammed by the impact but Borya hit it once with his massive shoulder. It creaked open and he jumped out. Korsky followed him.

"I must see to this," he said. Becker nodded and followed them, afraid of missing something.

Two Republican enlisted men were at the wreck of the other truck. One was bent over with his hands on his knees and obviously the driver. The other was scaling the side of the vehicle like a mountain climber, trying to gather and piece together shredded strips of canvas that had been torn loose from the frame. Becker heard Borya's voice speaking Spanish, strangely calm considering his mood a few moments before.

"Quién es el conductor?" he said. Even with the heavy Russian accent Becker could make out *Who is the driver?*

Hearing the accent, the driver answered by standing up and assuming a military bearing, certain that he must have the upper hand in any dealings with a foreigner. He was tall in comparison to many of the soldiers Becker had seen, certainly taller than anyone present.

"Yo soy-"

Borya struck the man across the left side of the head with his open hand. The man stepped once to his right with the force of the blow, trying to keep his balance, but before he could reach his hand up to touch the side of his face, he fell unconscious onto the pavement. Borya grabbed the man's collar with one hand and pulled him onto the shoulder of the road. Is he going to roll him into the ditch? Becker thought. No, only moving him to a place of safety. Violent and solicitous, just as he was with me. Dragging me out of a trench, hog-tying me and gently laying me on the floor of the truck.

"Necesitamos gasolina," he said to the other soldier. *"Somos NKVD."*

"Sí señor," the soldier answered with a salute. *"Tenemos gasolina."*

"His Spanish is quite limited," Korsky said. "But his powers of persuasion are remarkable."

"And lucky," Becker said.

"Ah, yes. Quite resourceful. Somehow I knew he would find fuel."

"I was thinking about the accident."

"Oh, that." Korsky looked grim, as if it shouldn't have been mentioned. Perhaps he is superstitious, Becker thought. Or it is some Russian thing, like speak of the Devil.

"Fortunam citius reperias quam retineas," Korsky said.

Becker had no response. His mind reeled from yet another language thrust at him. He replayed the phrase in his mind, hoping he had understood it but Korsky was already walking over to speak with Borya and Gunter, who had come down from the back of the truck with two empty jerry cans. Finally it came to him.

Easier to meet fortune than to keep it.

The Republican soldier had wrestled a large drum of gasoline to the back of his truck, but it was too full and heavy to consider taking it further. There was a small hand pump and a hose, but it would be necessary to bring the two vehicles closer. Borya jumped into the cab of their truck, started the engine, and deftly maneuvered the vehicle until it was alongside the other. The soldier hurried to begin the fueling operation, waving away any offers of assistance with an occasional glance toward his still unconscious compatriot on the side of the road. Becker stuffed both hands into his jacket for warmth and discovered the tobacco and rolling papers. Might as well make myself useful, he thought. He sat cross-legged on the side of the road and began rolling cigarettes. Korsky saw what he was doing and approached.

"Superanda omnis fortuna ferendo est," Becker said, as he handed the first cigarette to Korsky. *We master fortune by accepting it.*

Korsky raised an eyebrow and nodded his thanks as he took the cigarette.

"Not so cynical for once," he said. "Caesar?"

"Vergil. And yours?" Becker asked.

"In all honesty, I must admit that I cannot remember. A former colleague told me many years ago but the name did not stay with me. Still, I feel it often applies. Although in this case, Borya tells me that he intended to hit the other truck."

"Intended?"

"We needed fuel and there was no other way to be sure it would stop."

"True enough." Becker nodded but wasn't sure he believed the story.

"You are an educated man?" Korsky asked.

"I can roll cigarettes," he said, handing a second one to Korsky. "I can also shoe horses."

"Do you play chess?"

"I know how the pieces move, but I know nothing of strategy. Or even tactics."

"We must play sometime," Korsky said, taking two cigarettes in his hand. "I will give these to Gunter and Borya. I pray that one of them has matches."

It was hard to believe that Borya was finding his way in the darkness but he drove with calm determination and no hint of uncertainty. They went up and down hills, passed other vehicles and negotiated winding, switchback curves without the use of brakes, only coasting or downshifting on the rare occasions that he yielded to the need for caution. He shifted gears and finessed the clutch like an artist, producing a ride free of the usual back-and-forth lurch of a troop truck, only a gentle side-to-side motion which made the eyelids grow heavy. Becker drifted off as surreal dream images of the last days and hours filled his mind.

"We're here," Korsky said, with a nudge from his elbow.

Becker tried to force himself awake but nothing would come into focus. He found the door handle and stumbled into the night, the sudden blast of icy, damp air wakening his body but leaving his mind half-conscious. At first he saw only the darkness of the road and realized that the truck had been parked facing back the way they came. Looking behind him, he saw the school at the top of a small rise, perhaps twenty-five meters away. It was a long, single story building of scarred concrete and many broken windows. A troop truck and a staff car were parked in front. Two soldiers sat on the ground on either side of the front door, sleeping with their rifles on their laps. They had awakened as the truck approached, but when they saw only civilians, neither had bothered to stand up. I guess this isn't maximum security, Becker thought.

Borya and Gunter listened and gave an occasional nod as Korsky talked to them in Russian at the back of the truck. Gunter produced a Tokarev from his greatcoat pocket and checked the chamber, but Borya showed no weapon. Becker knew he had the boning knife somewhere on him and Korsky's greatcoat had something heavy in the pocket which had to be a large pistol. He finished his conference and came over to Becker.

"You have the Colt?" he asked. Becker answered by patting the front of his jacket. "Of course. Please do not display your weapon unless it is necessary. Your function is to identify Vincent and help us to retrieve him. We do not wish a major disturbance."

"Understood," Becker lied, wondering how this was going to be played.

Korsky walked ahead of the other two Russians with Becker at the rear as they approached the building. The guards got grudgingly to their feet. The younger of the two held his rifle at port arms but the other rested his against the wall as he stretched.

"Where is the commandant?" Korsky asked in Spanish, his voice barely audible.

"Not here," the older man said.

"Where is he?"

"Home. Sleeping."

"Who is in command?" Korsky asked.

The older man cocked a thumb toward the inside of the building. The door had long ago been torn from its hinges. "The sergeant."

"Take us to him," Korsky said.

"And who the hell are you?" the older man said. The younger soldier had been watching the exchange nervously, but now he smiled.

Korsky slowly took out a black billfold and opened it for the man to see.

"If you can read, you can see that we are NKVD. I will speak with the sergeant now." Korsky's voice had a tone of weary patience, but Becker thought that the faint echo of *or I will have you shot* hung sweetly in the air all the same.

"*Sí Capitán!* Immediately! Please follow me! This way!" The man's sudden groveling was painful to witness as he rushed inside to turn the responsibility over to someone even less fortunate.

"And I happen to be a colonel," Korsky said.

"Oh, your pardon excellency!" Becker heard the man squeal from down the hallway.

As the man neared the end of the hallway, the Republican sergeant stepped out of an office doorway. The soldier spoke to him with frantic gestures, but the sergeant appeared to remain master of his emotions.

"Gentlemen," the sergeant said. "How may I be of service?" He did not salute.

Korsky looked over the man's shoulder into the office, but saw there was only a single chair behind a desk lit by an kerosene lantern.

"You are holding a prisoner from the 17th Battalion?" Korsky asked.

"There are four prisoners from the 17th," the sergeant said.

"I will see their files," Korsky said.

"I regret, *Señor-*"

"Colonel."

"I regret, Colonel, that many files of the 17th have been lost," the sergeant said.

"You are holding soldiers of the Comintern here, in this shithole, without paperwork?"

"They are Trotskyite subversives, Colonel. They are to be executed in a few hours. When the commandant returns."

"Are you telling me they allow you morons to actually fire your weapons?" Korsky said

Korsky's Spanish was slow, but very precise and Becker had no trouble following it. In another time and place he would have enjoyed seeing anyone who threatened Angie get dressed down, but he found himself in a baffling daze of alternating allegiances. One instant, he was rooting for Korsky. The next, he was sympathizing with the sergeant, a mid-level flunky caught in a situation he couldn't control.

"Colonel, it is I who perform the duty," the sergeant said, taking umbrage.

A single bullet to the back of the head, Becker thought. That tears it. Shoot this motherless bastard and let's get on with it.

Korsky produced a pair of black leather gloves and took some time putting them on and adjusting the fit as he digested the sergeant's last comment with evident distaste.

"You will take us to the prisoners now," he said.

"As you wish, Colonel," the sergeant said. He walked to the desk in the office, took a ring of keys from the top drawer and picked up the lantern before returning to the hallway.

"I will first relieve you of your side arm," Korsky said, holding out his gloved right hand.

"Colonel, I protest," the sergeant said.

Korsky said nothing, but left his hand out. The sergeant looked at the faces of the other three men and realized there was no appeal. He unsnapped his holster, took out a long barreled automatic and placed it on Korsky's upturned palm. Korsky handed it to Becker.

"Take this," he said in English. "But whatever you see in the next few minutes, I order you control your emotions." Becker looked at the pistol. It was a Spanish make, one he did not recognize.

Korsky extended his hand in a sweeping motion to indicate that the sergeant should lead the way. The man stood briefly to attention and headed down the corridor, trying to maintain what was left of his dignity. The others followed.

They stopped in front of a solid oak door which had been fitted with a hasp and secured by a heavy padlock. The sergeant raised a lantern with his left hand and held the key ring at arm's length with his right, trying to focus his eyes as he fumbled through the keys one by one. The Russians looked on stone-faced. Finally, Becker reached over Gunter's shoulder and took the lantern, allowing the sergeant to use both hands.

"Gracias, Señor," the sergeant said.

"It's *Capitán*," Becker said.

"Oh, your pardon."

Becker thought he heard a grunt from Borya at his last comment, but the man had found the key, opened the lock and pushed the door open with his shoulder.

The air that escaped the room was thick with the stench of human filth. Becker's nose wrinkled involuntarily but the Russians appeared to take no notice, or to have expected it. He saw nothing at first, but as he held up the lantern and moved around the room, he made out a mound of bodies lying in the corner to the right of the door. It consisted of four men, huddled together for warmth, using a tattered window curtain for a blanket. Becker stood still, remembering Korsky's admonition, but the Russian looked at him and gave a slight forward nod toward the prisoners. Becker set the lantern on the floor, knelt next to the bodies and pulled back the makeshift blanket.

The four men were locked together, spoon fashion, their faces buried in the collars of their greatcoats. He knew he would recognize Angie's leather jacket, but he didn't see it so he started at the man nearest the wall and pulled down the edge of the collar to see the face. The eyes were swollen shut, the cheek smashed and the eyebrows cut in several places but the man was breathing through the dried blood around his nose and mouth. The next man seemed to be in better shape. His eyes opened when the light shone on them and he managed a clear "Go fook yourself, comrade," when his face was exposed. When he came to the third man, Becker recognized Angie's hair, greasy, matted and grey with dust though it was. He felt for a pulse.

"Angie," he said. His face was turned into the armpit of the greatcoat in an attempt to profit from the heat of his own breath. Becker pushed gently back on his shoulder until his face was visible. Like the first man, he had taken a fearsome beating but his scalp had also been split open above the temple and had bled heavily, leaving a delta of blood from his earlobe to his jawline and on into the collar of his shirt. Becker couldn't make out if he was breathing. He lifted one swollen eyelid.

"Hey, Mac, you wanna get that fuckin' light out of my eyes, or what?" Angie said.

"Angie, it's Matt," Becker said.

Angie's eyes stayed closed. He didn't move.

"Angie, it's Matt. You gotta wake up."

"Matt who?" Angie said.

"Matt Becker. Cut the bullshit and wake up."

"Never heard of him," Angie said.

"I'm gonna get you out of here."

"Sure," Angie said. He drifted off again.

The first man had come around and was fully conscious. "They gave it to him pretty hard," he said.

"Who did?" Becker asked.

"This bastard and the fookers he's got with him," the man said, indicating the sergeant with a motion of his head.

"Who are you and these others?" Becker asked.

"I'm Doyle. This is Lynch and the other one is – I forget his name. Everyone just calls him Billy."

"Irish?"

"That's right."

"How did Angie end up with you?" Becker asked.

"He came tumbling into our trench in the middle of the night, dragging one of our lads from the olive grove. We took him in," Doyle said.

"Why are you in here?"

"Some of Marty's goons came looking for him a day or two later. We managed to pull the wool over and send 'em off, but somebody down the line fingered him and they were back, and in none too fine a temper. They tried to take him. We told 'em to fook off. But they had the guns, and our guns had no bullets."

"You had no ammo?"

"The sent up crates of seven millimeter, but our rifles wouldn't take it. So we got into a brawl and ended up here."

"They're gonna shoot the lot of you if we don't get you up and out of here," Becker said.

"You can do that?" Doyle asked. "Lynch me boy, wake up. We're getting out." He started shaking his companion's shoulder.

Gunter had appeared at Becker's side with a canteen of water and some gauze. He had checked the man in front and was now wiping the blood from the side of Angie's head. He held the lantern raised Angie's eyelids one by one before saying something over his shoulder in Russian to Korsky.

"Gunter says the boy is dead," Korsky said in German. "Perhaps you should tell the others. He also says your friend has many injuries. His condition is grave. There may be a concussion. Also internal injuries."

"Doyle. Your friend. Billy? I'm sorry, but he didn't make it," Becker said.

"Dead?" Doyle said. Becker nodded once. "Poor bugger. I half expected it. His head got rattled by a mortar round and he hasn't been the same since."

"What did they do to Angie?" Becker asked.

"Same as the rest of us. But they really got the boot in and I think they laid his head open with a rifle butt. He's been in and out since last night."

Becker decided this was all taking too long. He got both feet under him, reached his arms under Angie's armpits and started to lift him to his feet. But Gunter put a hand on his arm to stop him and spoke to Korsky.

"Gently, Matthew. Gunter says he must be moved with care," Korsky said.

Minutes later Borya and Becker were carrying Angie outside using the makeshift blanket as a stretcher.

"Hey. Where're we going?" Angie said, his speech slurred and raspy.

When they reached the truck, Becker found that the tailgate was still up and latched on each side. He supported his share of Angie's weight with one hand, managed to get one latch open and was working to unjam the other when Gunter appeared at his side, said something in Russian, and opened it easily. He jumped up into the back and helped slide Angie's body onto the floor of the truck before wrapping it snugly in the blanket. Becker took a moment to stretch his shoulders and back and wondered where his strength had gone. Not enough food and rest, he concluded.

He smelled something burning and looked back toward the building. Korsky was standing a few steps away, smoking a cigarette. The deeply unnerved sergeant was speaking to his turned back, too fast for Becker to understand. Korsky approached and held out a pack of cigarettes.

"I took these from one of the privates. Please," he said.

Becker thought it rude to refuse. He took one from the pack and allowed Korsky to light it for him, shielding the wooden match from the elements with cupped hands. He inhaled shallowly and allowed a single choking cough to escape his clenched teeth. He felt his face go red as he fought back a second.

"Vile, are they not?" Korsky said.

"I'm hardly a connoisseur," Becker said. "What now?"

"The other men. English?"

"Irish."

"Ah, that explains it. I find the dialect incomprehensible," Korsky said. "They are not our concern."

"What would you have me do?" Becker asked.

"Do as you see fit," Korsky said. His tone was emphatic, but there was something unspoken. Becker sense he was being tested and Korsky suddenly reminded him of his uncle Martin.

"As I see fit," Becker said.

"Just so," Korsky answered.

Becker worked his way warily through the cigarette, taking little satisfaction but enjoying its warmth.

"You leave this to me?" Becker asked.

"As you see fit," Korsky repeated.

"Security is important."

Korsky paused for a moment, as if resisting the need to speak clearly. "Essential."

Borya joined them, ignoring the protestations of the increasingly indignant sergeant. He showed them a handful of rifle cartridges. Korsky picked one up and nodded in approval.

"Matthew," Korsky said. "We will wait here. If you would be so kind as to deal with this man. Also, the privates appear to be carrying the seven millimeter Spanish Mauser. They are fine weapons and may prove useful. But it will be dawn soon." He ended the discussion by climbing into the cab of the truck.

"Colonel! I must-" the sergeant shouted.

"You may speak to the captain," Korsky said from the cab as he rested his right arm on the edge of the window. Borya got in behind the wheel. Becker was alone with the sergeant.

Becker tried to summon all the Spanish at his command, rapidly conjugating verbs, sorting through vocabulary, composing sentence fragments, rephrasing, finally deciding that he would settle for a simple present tense and hoping the sergeant would attribute his reticence to an imperious nature.

"You have the property of the prisoners?" Becker said.

"What?" the sergeant said. Did I use the wrong word? Becker thought. Is he questioning me or did he just not understand me?

"Possessions. The possessions of the prisoners," repeated Becker.

"*Sí Capitán,*" the sergeant said.

"Show me now," Becker said.

The man could read nothing in the pale, drawn face of the foreigner. He looked toward the truck but Korsky's face was a silhouette and the other windows were opaque in the darkness. "This way, *por favor,*" he said.

Both Spanish privates stood at attention now, port arms with what Becker assumed were empty rifles. He ignored them in defiance. The sergeant ignored them in embarrassment. The two Irishmen were standing near the office door as they entered the building, watching Becker and the sergeant approaching, trying to understand what was happening.

The sergeant went into the office ahead of Becker and pointed at a waist-high mound of garments, bags, belts and assorted other belongings, both personal and military. Too much for Becker to sort through. He spoke through the door to the Irishmen.

"You gents want to get back some of your kit?" he said.

They had brushed past him almost before the words were out of his mouth and began tossing items in the air and on the floor as they extracted wallets, belts, sweaters, socks, a small notebook and other items Becker was sure didn't belong to them.

"This is Billy's," Doyle said, holding up the notebook, which was stuffed full of papers and bound with a strip of cloth tied in a bow. "There's letters to 'is mum in here. Best we see that she gets 'em."

Becker nodded. "Got everything?" he said as they fastened the buckles on their packs.

"And a bit more," Lynch said, to no one in particular.

"Wait by the front door, but don't try to get past the guards," Becker said.

"What are you gonna do, mate?" Doyle said.

"Business," Becker said. "Hurry it up. It's gonna be dawn soon."

"Right," Doyle said. He nodded once to Lynch and both men were out of the room in an instant.

Becker turned to the sergeant. He remembered something Korsky had done and took out his leather gloves, putting them on slowly for dramatic effect.

"The rest," he said.

"What?" the sergeant said.

"The possessions of the American. A leather coat, like mine. A rucksack." Becker looked at his watch. "You have sixty seconds."

The sergeant paused, the color draining from his face. Becker knew the man had no way of knowing whether his next actions would prove his salvation or damnation.

"Forty-five seconds," Becker said. Should he take out the Colt? Not yet.

"A moment," the sergeant said. "They are in the armoire. For safety." He walked to the back of the office and quickly produced the jacket and rucksack, placing them on the desk.

"And the contents?" Becker said.

"All there, *Capitán.*"

"Show me."

The sergeant unfastened the buckles on the rucksack, pulled back the flap and took out Angie's .45 and the extra clips. Becker walked forward to get a closer look, using the opportunity to put his hands on the bag and check the lining for the cash hidden there. He felt the rectangular shapes and wondered, How did they miss this? He replaced the .45 and closed the bag.

"Where are the keys for the two vehicles outside?" Becker asked.

"In them," the sergeant said.

"You have no files. But there must be some written record of the prisoners you keep here."

"Of course, *Capitán.* All is proper," the sergeant said.

"Show me," Becker said.

The sergeant opened a large, rectangular ledger and laid it on the desk. Becker looked, but could make little sense of the script. He pointed at the open page.

"Which are the names of...," he searched his mind for the proper phrasing. "Of these prisoners?" he asked finally, gesturing toward the outside.

"No names," the sergeant said. "You see? 'Four foreign subversives. Trotskyites.' The entries to the right indicate 'transferred', 'deceased' or 'executed'."

And how many have you executed, you bureaucratic piece of dog shit? Becker thought. Not now. Stay in control.

"Understood. One is deceased. For these other men you will enter 'transferred'," Becker said.

"*Sí, Capitán.* And the Capitan's surname, *por favor?*"

"Smith," Becker said.

"Ah, yes. I know the spelling of this name," the sergeant said. "And the Colonel's surname?"

Again Becker felt the clock was against him, but he was alone and knew that he must keep the situation from disintegrating. A Russian surname?

"Jankowski," Becker said. "NKVD."

"Very good," the sergeant said. He finished writing. The mundane task had restored some of his confidence.

"Thank you, Sergeant," Becker said. Call your men. I will speak to them and to you before leaving."

"*Sí, Capitán.* Immediately."

Three minutes later, the two Irishmen watched Becker come out of the office with the two Spanish Mausers. He closed the door gently and walked over to them.

"Can you drive?" he asked.

"Well enough," Doyle said. "Are you all right?"

"I'm with Angelo and the others," Becker said, pointing toward the truck.

"No, I mean, in there. We heard-"

"You heard what?" Becker said.

"We heard nothing, mate," Lynch said with a glance at Doyle.

"Right. All's well here," Doyle said. "What happens now?"

"You gotta get out of here. Fast," Becker said. "You're probably better off in the truck than the staff car. He said the keys are in it. There's no record of you being here. You've got your Brigade ID?"

Both men nodded.

"Take this," Becker said, handing the sergeant's automatic to Doyle. "You could probably return to the front if you wanted. Or make a break for the border. But I can't say much for your chances. For now, just get as far away from here as you can."

"We'll give it a go," Lynch said. "You give Angie our best when he comes around."

"Done," Becker said. "Thanks for looking after him."

Doyle and Lynch shook hands with Becker, grasping his arm, their eyes moist. But Becker's face looked like a death mask in the false dawn. He turned and walked toward the truck.

"Wait, Brother," Lynch said. Becker turned. "It's Billy."

"What about him?" Becker asked.

"Can you take him in your truck?"

Right, Becker thought. They can't take time to bury him and God knows what will happen if they leave his body here.

"Get him."

Becker knew that if the two Irishmen were to carry the body to the truck, Korsky might send them back, so he had them drape Billy's body over his right shoulder. The boy couldn't have weighed one-fifty. He held the Mausers in the crook of his left arm and started toward the truck.

"Should we take another run at the office?" Doyle said.

"Don't be a bloody idiot. You heard him. We've gotta leg it, and in no small hurry," Lynch said. "And I don't wanna see what's in that office anyway."

CHAPTER 20

When the truck reached the farmhouse, Becker got out, walked to the back and dropped the tailgate. Gunter stood and threw back the flap. Korsky and Borya appeared from opposite sides and listened as Gunter spoke. Becker waited for the translation, but he knew what was coming.

"I regret to say that Mr. Vincent has died," Korsky said. His tone was even.

Becker nodded once, took a deep breath and climbed up into the truck. Gunter had pulled the blanket over Angie's face. Becker pulled it back and put his hand on Angie's forehead, as if checking to see if he had a fever. The eyes were closed but the mouth was partially open in a silent "oh". He thought of trying to close it but knew that the Russians were watching him.

"See you soon, Ange," he said, pulling the blanket back to cover the face. He stood up, arched his aching back once, walked to the edge of the truck bed and jumped to the ground.

"His worst injuries were not visible," Korsky said.

"Right," Becker said.

"It is often so."

Is he offering up sympathy? Becker thought. He didn't know how to respond.

"Is there a shovel I could use? A pick would help also," he said.

Korsky was shaking his head. "The ground is too hard. There are many rocks. Also, it is frozen in places. You could dig for hours and still not have a proper grave. We have tried and it is not suitable."

"What is suitable?" Becker asked

"There is a shell crater over that way," Korsky gestured toward the side of the house. "We will sacrifice one jerry can of fuel donated by the Republic to cremate Mr. Vincent and his comrade there."

"We're going to start a fire? Here?" Coming from the front, where even a single match could cost the lives of an entire squad, Becker was unable to conceal his astonishment.

Korsky was calm. "It is the only way. And in the daylight there is no danger. We are far enough from the front and fires are not such a strange sight on a battlefield."

Becker nodded. "I've become overly cautious of open flame."

"I understand, but you will see. Ours will not be the only fire."

Minutes later they stood at the edge of the shell crater, looking down at the bundled corpses. Becker reached to unscrew the cap of the jerry can, but paused when he heard a voice.

"Do you wish to say something?" Korsky asked.

"About?"

"The dead."

Becker paused, but decided he didn't want to show emotion in front of the Russians. "Angelo would want something with humor. At the moment, nothing comes to mind," he said

"Sometimes, silence does just as well."

"There is something," Becker said, half to himself.

Becker stepped sideways down into the crater with the jerry can. The bodies were face up. Becker turned them so they were lying back to front, spoon fashion, as he had first found them in the cell. He then emptied the contents of the can over the bodies. When he emerged from the crater, Korsky was holding a rolled piece of newspaper, which he lit with a match. He extended it toward Becker.

"Would you care to...?"

"You do it," Becker said, turning and walking back toward the farmhouse. He heard a muffled gust of air as the gasoline ignited.

Becker judged that it must be well past dawn but the windows were shuttered against the cold and no light penetrated from the outside. He sat at the same battered wooden table, shivering occasionally. He couldn't seem to get warm. Korsky came in from the front room holding two small plates of beans with steam rising from them. He placed one in front of Becker and the other at his end of the table. He then made another trip and returned with four inches of sausage and a wedge of black bread for each of them.

"I find the diet of beans to be nearly unbearable, but if one warms them on the stove they are easier to get down," Korsky said.

"You said 'letters'," Becker said.

"I beg your pardon?"

"Before we left for the schoolhouse. You said you had received 'letters' regarding me and Angelo. I took it to mean more you had received more than one."

"Ah, yes," Korsky said, as if he had just remembered. "It appears there is news from home." He turned his chair, sat at the desk and began searching through the disordered mound of papers. After a moment, he turned his chair back to face the table, held up a buff office paper envelope and pushed it slowly across the table.

"Please take your time. I will not disturb your reading." Korsky's voice held no trace of irony. His face showed no emotion. Becker picked up the unsealed envelopes and saw a single word scrawled across the front in Cyrillic script. "I regret that the original envelope was destroyed in the censoring process," Korsky said.

The envelope contained two separate folded sheaves, one of plain, lined notebook paper and the other of smaller, beige letter paper. Becker held one in each hand and looked from one to the other quizzically.

"Which do you think I should read first?" he asked. Korsky leaned forward and squinted across the table.

"That one would probably be best," he said, pointing toward Becker's left hand. Becker unfolded the notebook paper and immediately recognized Martin's jagged, angular Continental script, with so many hard edges that it might have been pressed into clay with a stylus. He wrote in French.

Mathieu,

I hope this letter finds you and that you are still alive, though I have no high hopes on either account.

J-B and Anneliese are both dead, but perhaps there is some mercy in it. He was in much distress at the end - days and weeks of some fearsome mental agony. Apparently, his wife saved up a large amount of sleeping or pain medicine over a long period and gave it to him with his food. She then took the same herself and lay on the bed beside him. The end came peacefully. The suffering is finished. They were found the next day by the older daughter who has now taken the younger into her care. They are both well, considering.

Two bodies were found in Pennsylvania. After some time, they were identified as members of an organization in Philadelphia. They were known to have a grievance over the death of an associate and they blamed certain parties in Brooklyn for his demise, unaware or unconcerned that the associate's death had been sanctioned by a governing alliance. Their quest for revenge was considered to be an unforgiveable breach of propriety and if they had not died in the forest, they no doubt would have been dealt with in short order.

The man they assaulted is recovering. His injuries, though severe, did not endanger his life. His associates (and his family) feel that some debt is owed to those that rescued him. I am not sure that this is a positive development, but the fact remains. As for the two gentlemen in the city, no one knows the reason for what happened, but many questions are being asked. I am staying alert to any developments.

I visited the farm in the country, as promised, but found only a letter nailed to the door, which I enclose. I made inquiries and learned that the residents had moved away. Some people said they had gone north, but it was impossible to learn more.

Please tell our friend that his mother his well, though she misses him very much. We speak at least once a week and if there is anything she needs, she can call on me.

With affection,

M.

Becker read through the letter twice, looking for hidden meanings but realized that Martin was not one to speak in riddles. He had recounted no more or less than necessary and had given away no information that couldn't have been easily found elsewhere.

"I am going to indulge in alcohol," Korsky said. "Will you join me?"

"What is there?" Becker asked.

"Only vodka, I'm afraid."

"Then I'll have what you're having," Becker said.

Korsky nodded, walked to a wooden crate on the floor and took out a bottle and two coffee mugs. He placed one in front of Becker and filled it halfway, then did the same for himself. Raising the mug, he exclaimed something in Russian. Becker stared blankly. Was it a warning? Korsky's face softened.

"Forgive me, I meant to say '*Prost!*'"

"*Prost!*" responded Becker. Korsky drained his mug in a gulp. Becker took a small sip. It had a sour, oily, caustic bite and he looked at what remained in the mug with bewilderment. What did it taste like? There was nothing in his experience to compare it to.

"Better to swallow it all at once, my friend, sincerely," Korsky said. Not to be outdone, Becker took the rest in one shot. It burned fiercely going down, but seemed oddly appropriate to the time and place. "Perhaps it is not to your liking."

"On the contrary," Becker said. "It's exquisite."

"Ah, you make the humor again, and at such a time," Korsky said, suddenly cutting off the thought. "Have another?"

"Thank you," Becker said, holding out his mug.

"Please, continue with your reading," Korsky said. "Forgive my interruption."

"Your pardon." Becker unfolded the letter paper and began reading.

Dear Matt,

Wherever you are, I know that you are in danger and for that reason I ask you to forgive me for writing this letter.

As you must know by now, I have taken April and moved away. It is better that I don't tell you where, because in my heart I know that we can never see each other again.

Matt Darling, when you told me what had happened that night, I only half believed what you were saying. Really, I didn't know what to believe. But when I read in the papers about the police finding the bodies of those men, I knew it must have been true. It terrified me and made me realize that I've been a fool all this time.

You were always very good to me and to April, but I know now that we were never meant to be together and that I could never truly understand a man like you. You are a good person, but there is something dark and frightening in you that I will never be able to touch. Men like you and Angie and your uncle Martin – you live in a different world than other people. It's a world that I am afraid to be a part of – afraid for me and my daughter.

I think I know where you are and I hear terrible things about the fighting there. Maybe you are already dead. I hope not. I hope that somehow you can get through the war safely and have a normal life someday.

Please don't hate me for this. I loved you – I still love you – and I know you loved me. But please put me in the past. It's over now. It must be.

I think you understand.

Love always,

Sandra

Becker could hear Korsky's breathing above the background noise outside. "You sound like you might have a cold," he said.

"I beg your pardon?" Korsky said.

"A cold," he repeated. "You sound a bit hoarse."

"The climate. Too much smoking, I suppose. The vodka. All bad for the health," Korsky said. "I doubt any of us will live long enough to die of it."

Live long? Jesus, I hope not, Becker thought. But he knew that disease was the unsung reaper in war, and he wondered how many of the slightly wounded had died from exposure in the past few nights. His thoughts went suddenly to the unknown comrade who had shared the last of his body heat with him and Lowry.

"Is there somewhere I can dispose of these?" Becker asked, holding up the letters.

"Dispose of?"

"Burn."

"You don't want to keep them?" Korsky asked.

"Hardly secure, don't you think?" Becker said, his own voice growing quite rough.

"As you say," Korsky answered, nodding and taking a box of matches from the table. "I believe we have a suitable..." He went to the side of the desk and picked up what appeared to be a large can that might have once held beans or cooking oil but was now serving as a waste paper basket. "Perhaps we should step outside. The smoke, you know."

Becker instinctively checked the .45 to be sure there was a round in the chamber, returned it to the shoulder holster and zipped up his jacket. They walked through the adjoining room, past Borya and Gunter who were also drinking at their own table, and went outside. Both men held out their palms to see if it were raining, but neither could tell if it were real rain or just the usual, ice-cold mist. Korsky put the can on the ground and took out the matches. Becker took one page of Sandy's letter and held it so that Korsky could get a flame under it. As it caught, he turned it gently to make sure it would not go out before placing it in the can and, one by one, fed the remaining papers into the fire. As he dropped in the last page of Martin's letter, the oddly ritualistic nature of the task suddenly struck him.

"So much ceremony for a small amount of garbage," he said.

"Forgive me, comrade, but words are not garbage. Certainly not the words of our loved ones," Korsky said. "One never knows when they will fall silent."

Becker could only nod. No words came to him. He squatted on his haunches, watching the pages writhe, curl and blacken into dust, making out fragments of sentences in the light of their own pyre before they were consumed. *"terrible...fact remains...many questions...forgive me...a fool all this time...a man like you...".*

There was still a slight burning in his throat from the vodka, but apart from that sensation there was only a vast emptiness inside him. He saw a flickering image of his mother spoon-feeding medicine to his father and another of Sandy clutching her heart as tears streamed down her face. April waving as her tiny form disappeared in the distance. All finished, he thought. No good in remembering it.

He heard a familiar metallic sound and looked up. The Russian had stepped back a safe distance and was pointing a small black automatic at his head. Becker took a deep breath and let it out slowly in a weary sigh. For a moment he considered asking "Where the hell did that come from?" but decided it sounded nonsensical.

"Do it," Becker said.

"I beg your pardon?" Korsky said.

"Shoot. It is necessary."

"Why is it necessary?"

"It is not secure to leave me alive." Becker paused. "And I have no desire to wait for a bullet in the back of my head."

"You're distraught," Korsky said. "But there are certain things I wish to make clear."

Becker tried to shrug, but realized it was a waste of effort. His face went blank as he stared into the darkness. Another speech from a commissar.

"It is not appropriate for me to be held at gunpoint by my subordinates," Korsky said.

"I am your subordinate?"

"If you choose to be."

Becker said nothing. He was suddenly weary of the sound of the German language, which kept reminding him of his mother, and tired of inane attempts at banter. Is this why humans have the power of speech, he thought? It's all a waste of breath.

"Herr Becker," Korsky continued. "I am not a political operative. I am judged purely on results: supplies diverted or destroyed, enemy officers eliminated, communications disrupted. You are here to pursue those ends. If I felt you were a danger to our mission, I could have killed you back at the school."

It made sense, but Becker wasn't sure he trusted his own judgment. In any event, if Korsky planned to kill him, he would already be dead.

"Where do we go from here?" he asked.

"For the next twenty-four hours, I think we shall rest. Eat, drink, rest some more," Korsky said.

"And then?"

"I think that after tonight we will all be in need of a thorough delousing. After that, we must spend some time on your training. Not long. A few weeks perhaps."

"What kind of training?"

"Gunter will teach you some basic sabotage. Borya has some skills he can impart. I'm sure you can imagine. And I understand you have some talent with a rifle. We believe you can be of some use in the area between Cordoba and Seville," Korsky explained.

"In what capacity?"

"For now, let us just say that Gunter has a passion for trains," Korsky said.

"Riding them?"

"Oh no, my dear comrade," Korsky laughed. "Derailing them."

Korsky continued to hold the automatic but he was no longer pointing it directly at Becker.

"This is most wearisome," he said.

"Your point is taken," Becker said. "I regret holding you at gunpoint. I shall refrain in the future."

Korsky appeared to be composing an answer when they heard footsteps and turned to see Borya's silhouette filling the doorway. He said something in an irritated grunt.

"Borya wishes to know why we are standing in the cold when we could be inside by the stove drinking vodka," Korsky said, putting the pistol into his coat pocket.

"If there's going to be shooting, better to do it out here than to make a mess inside," Becker said.

"I consider that to be settled," said the Russian, with finality. "Really, comrade. You must have hope. We will teach you what is necessary to survive."

Becker said nothing. Looking out at the horizon, he saw that there were indeed several fires burning. The nearest was less than a kilometer away. He couldn't bring himself to look toward the shell crater, though occasionally the early morning breeze would carry the smoke in their direction.

"You do wish to survive, do you not?" Korsky asked.

"I would be content with a single, brief moment of understanding before my time is up."

Korsky put both hands in his pockets and took a single long, deep breath before letting it out slowly and nodding.

"So, Matthew. You seek some meaning in all that has happened?"

Becker realized he had said too much.

"I'll settle for a balancing of accounts," he said.

"Then come inside, drink vodka, eat and rest."

"I'll be along in a few minutes," Becker said.

"Don't stay out here too long," Korsky said. "You'll catch your death." The Russian turned and walked back into the house, closing but not latching the door. Becker sat on the ground and stuffed his hands into his pockets. He felt the bag of tobacco in one and the papers in the other. He took out the papers and fumbled with the packet until he found a usable sheet. Taking out the tobacco, he realized there wasn't enough for another cigarette. He crumpled the bag together with the paper and threw them into the can, but the fire had gone out long before.